The Bone Garden

Kate Ellis

Thomas Dunne Books
St. Martin's Minotaur ⋘ New York

THOMAS DUNNE BOOKS.
An imprint of St. Martin's Press.

www.minotaurbooks.com

ISBN 0-312-30037-9

First published in Great Britain by Judy Piatkus (Publishers) Ltd

First U.S. Edition: July 2003

10 9 8 7 6 5 4 3 2 1

With many thanks to Ingrid Wood for all her help with the West Indies connection.

Also thanks to Olly for sharing his cricketing expertise, and to Tom for creating www.kateellis.co.uk

The Bone Garden

Near Bordeaux, France

The man stared at the shape lying beneath the faded cover on the ancient iron bed and took another sip of wine. Château des Arbres, last year's vintage: full bodied with a hint of oak, just as a claret should be. It tasted good. The fact that he had been party to its creation – that he had tended the vines and had picked the plump grapes with his own hands – gave him a glow of satisfaction. He rolled the wine around his mouth and swallowed. This year's vintage would be even better, he thought. But this time he wouldn't be there for the grape picking. He would be gone well before the hectic days of the harvest.

He drained the dusty glass and listened to the sounds of the night: the low hum of the château's generator in the outhouse across the courtyard, the insistent noise of the crickets and the occasional screech of a hunting owl. Then he stood, walked to the bed and looked down at the prone figure for a full minute before summoning the courage to touch the face. He brushed the back of his rough, calloused hand against the cheek and found it to be as cool and lifeless as marble, despite the warmth of the evening.

He looked around the sparsely furnished room with its whitewashed stone walls and its ill-made second-hand furniture. The outhouse roughly converted into workers' accommodation by the owners of the château had been his home for the past two years and he had some good times there: he recalled the lazy summer evenings of wine and lovemaking and the drunken bonhomie of the grape harvest. But now he was leaving the château for good. He picked up the hold-all that contained all his worldly possessions and checked

1

that he had everything he needed before stepping outside into the cobbled courtyard, shutting the flaking wooden door carefully behind him. The inexhaustible crickets still chirruped in the warm, lavender-scented air, but otherwise all was silent – just as he had hoped it would be.

A door creaked open near by: probably one of the other workers emerging from his room to head for the primitive lavatory in the corner of the courtyard. The man pressed himself against the stone wall, hardly daring to breathe. But the velvet darkness of the night shielded him and he watched, statue still, as the man he recognised as Jacques staggered across the cobbles, too preoccupied with his bladder to look about him.

He relaxed as Jacques disappeared round the corner. Then he picked up his hold-all and scurried towards the great poplar-lined drive that led away from the château, thinking of the lifeless figure on the bed and hoping desperately that it wouldn't be discovered until the morning.

Devon, England – A Year Later

The lost gardens of Earlsacre had been stripped of the weeds and briars that had choked them and hidden their form. The work had begun two months before, and over the long midsummer weeks rude mechanical diggers and buzzing strimmers had intruded into the gardens' secret places and laid bare the walls and the gatehouse that had guarded them from the eyes of the world for so many years.

Jacintha Hervey, poet in residence to the Earlsacre Project – as it was called in official circles – sat on the crumbling terrace over-looking the gardens, pen poised, perched on the canvas stool that she had brought especially for the occasion, and watched the workers below, hoping for inspiration.

A line about the awakening of Sleeping Beauty in her impene-trable castle flitted through Jacintha's head but, other than that, she could think of nothing to write. She chewed the end of her cheap ballpoint and stared down into what remained of the walled garden, now a mess of holes and trenches as the archaeological team went about their work.

She watched as the crouching, soil-caked young diggers worked in their rectangular trenches, sometimes chatting, sometimes silent and lost in their task. Surely their earnest activity would inspire a poem of some kind, even a few lines about the young uncovering the old. But still no words came. Jacintha reached for her Thermos flask. It was time for an inspirational coffee . . . laced with something stronger to get the creative juices flowing.

As she sipped the reviving liquid she sensed that the calm, absorbed atmosphere in the garden had altered. The change was subtle at first – urgent whispered words, a flurry of activity here and there. Then the archaeologists who had been working in other parts of the gardens downed tools and converged on the walled garden, crowding around the centre. One of them produced a tiny mobile phone from an inside pocket and began to talk into it urgently. Something was happening. Something had been found. Jacintha stood up and strained to hear, but she was too far away to catch any telltale words.

A young man was running towards her. He was about to rush past, but she put out a hand to stop him and gave him her sweetest smile.

'Jake.' Her eyes met his. 'What's going on? Have they found something exciting?'

Jake glanced towards the ruined house, torn between duty and potential pleasure. He eyed Jacintha's ample curves appreciatively and chose pleasure. 'They've uncovered a human hand in the middle of the walled garden, buried underneath that stone plinth we lifted this morning.' Their eyes met again and Jake made no effort to move. 'I'm going to tell Martin. We weren't expecting to find human remains on this dig so we'll have to inform the authorities – he won't be best pleased. We can't afford a hold-up.' Jake stood still, his eyes on Jacintha's breasts, clearly visible beneath the thin cheesecloth of her white top.

'Hadn't you better go and tell him, then?' Jacintha said with a sly smile. 'And if you're free at six o'clock tonight why don't you join me in the King's Head. You look as if you could do with a drink.'

'Why not?' He gave her a knowing smile. She was at least twenty years his senior, but what did things like that matter nowadays?

Jake turned and ran towards the house, and Jacintha watched the back view of his tight faded jeans appreciatively. Then she strolled down the steps towards the walled garden. The crowd had dispersed, leaving a solitary archaeology student squatting on the brown earth, staring at the ground.

Jacintha approached slowly. 'What's everyone so excited about?'

The young man looked up at her. 'Looks like we've found human remains – it'll be another hold-up we can't afford.'

Jacintha looked down at the ground. The bones stood out stark against the darkness of the soil. A skeletal hand protruded from the earth, the bony fingers scratching, grasping, as though trying to escape.

'It looks as if he's trying to get out, doesn't it? Clawing his way to the surface – just like he's been buried alive.'

Jacintha turned away and shuddered. Then she took her notebook from her bag and began to scribble. Inspiration had come at last.

Chapter 1

*Good gardens at Earlsacre but not as the mode now is. Walled
garden with shell grotto and fine parterres and a curious sundial
at its centre. I liked not this garden, the place being somewhat
cold. The other gardens fine with shady walks and arbours,
fruitful trees and odiferous herbs. The house is also fine in its
way but the furnishings are not of the latest. The hospitality of
Sir Richard Lantrist is somewhat rough, as one might expect of
one who has never known good society.*
    *From Jacob Finsbury's Account of His Travels around the
                                    Houses of England, 1703*

Brain Willerby, partner in the firm of Blake, Willerby and Johns,
Solicitors, sat staring at the file on his desk, his heart pounding and
his mouth dry.

He put his hand up to his balding head as though trying to run his
fingers through some imaginary luxuriant mane. What was the best
course of action? What was the right thing to do? Should he involve
the authorities? Or was he overreacting? Perhaps there was some
perfectly simple explanation. There must be. The alternative was
unthinkable.

Willerby stared down at the file again. He needed proof, solid
proof one way or the other. He stood up, walked over to the window
and looked down on Tradmouth's bustling High Street. It was one of
the advantages – or disadvantages – of having an office on the first
floor above the Morbay and District Building Society that distraction
was always there on tap in idle moments.

He spotted a young woman in the crowd. She was dark and slender
and wore a tight Lycra top which displayed her assets to best

advantage. His eyes followed her down the street longingly until she disappeared into a shoe shop. He swallowed hard. Then he noticed two policemen in shirtsleeves ambling through the crowd and an idea came to him. If he could speak to someone unofficially, off the record . . . someone who would guide him as to the best course of action.

There was that detective sergeant he'd met at the police station when he had been called there to represent one of his less salubrious clients. Brian had noticed him particularly; a young black man, a rare representative of the ethnic minorities in the local force. And it wasn't only the colour of his skin which had marked him out as different from his colleagues: he had been well spoken, obviously well educated; an unassuming young man with a sympathetic manner. Brian wrinkled his brow in an effort to remember the sergeant's name. Patterson? No. Peterson. Wesley Peterson.

He picked up the phone and dialled the number of Tradmouth police station.

'How can people be so gullible?' Detective Constable Rachel Tracey said to nobody in particular.

Wesley Peterson looked up from his paperwork. 'What do you mean?'

'A report's come in from Morbay. An old man told a tourist he'd lost his wallet and claimed he couldn't get home to some faraway place. The tourist lent him fifty quid which the man said he'd return by first-class post as soon as he got home. This was ten days ago and the tourist hasn't seen hide nor hair of the money since.'

Wesley shrugged. 'The man might have lost the address.'

Rachel smiled as if she thought Wesley was being particularly naïve. 'It sounds like a clever scam to me . . . playing on people's better natures.'

'Any similar incidents been reported?'

'Not yet. Give it time.'

At that point DC Steve Carstairs walked into the office and, ignoring Wesley, sat down and tried to look as though he was working.

Rachel walked over to Wesley's desk and leaned over his shoulder. He could smell her perfume, feel the warmth of her breath on the back of his neck. 'Now there's someone who keeps his better nature well hidden,' she whispered.

Wesley smiled and looked over at Steve, who rewarded him with

6

a blank stare. But there were some things it was best to ignore, and Steve Carstairs was one of them.

The telephone on Wesley's desk began to ring. He picked up the receiver and recited his name.

The voice on the other end of the line sounded nervous. 'Sergeant Peterson. I don't know if you remember me but we have met at the station. My name's Brian Willerby of Blake, Willerby and Johns, Solicitors.'

'Hello, Mr Willerby. What can I do for you?' Wesley racked his brains, wondering which of the constabulary's not-so-valued customers the solicitor was ringing to discuss.

'I'd like your advice,' Willerby began.

'About one of your clients?' His furtive tone had aroused Wesley's curiosity.

'Er, no. Actually it's a personal matter. You see, I'm in rather a quandary about . . . In fact I'm very worried and I really need to . . .'

Wesley heard a door open in the background and a muffled voice. Then Willerby's voice again. 'I'm sorry, Sergeant. Something's just come up. We'll have to talk another time. Goodbye,' the man concluded with businesslike confidence. Willerby obviously hadn't wanted whoever had entered his office to overhear their conversation.

Rachel looked across at him. 'Everything all right, Wesley?' she asked quietly.

'I don't know.' He shrugged and returned to sorting through a pile of witness statements. It was probably nothing.

But he found he couldn't concentrate on the paperwork and after a while he stood up and marched over to the inspector's glass-fronted office. After a token knock he let himself in.

Detective Inspector Gerry Heffernan sat at his desk, his sleeves rolled up to reveal a fine pair of nautical tattoos, relics of his days in the merchant navy. He looked up at Wesley, grinned and scratched his head. 'Hi, Wes. What can I do you for? Everything all right out there, is it? No armed robberies? Serial killings?'

Wesley smiled at his boss. 'Looks like we've hit a quiet time. All the local villains must be on holiday.'

'So all's quiet on the mean streets of Tradmouth.' Gerry Heffernan sat back and his standard-issue inspector's chair creaked dangerously under his weight. 'Let's make the most of it, eh, 'cause I can't see it lasting for long.'

'It's giving everyone a chance to catch up on their paperwork.'

Wesley paused for a moment. 'But it could just be the calm before the storm.'

'You know what you are, Wes? A born pessimist.'

Wesley grinned. 'Actually, I wanted to ask you something.'

'Fire away.'

'Do you know a solicitor called Brian Willerby?'

'I've met him a few times. Not a barrel of laughs,' Heffernan said dismissively. There were some who didn't appreciate the inspector's sense of humour: Willerby was probably one of them.

'He rang me just now and said he wanted to discuss a personal matter; something he was very worried about. Then he was interrupted by someone and he put the phone down. He sounded . . .' Wesley searched for the word. 'Furtive.'

'I didn't know you knew old Willerby.'

'I don't. That's the point. I've only met him a couple of times and then only in the company of the villain he was representing. I've no idea why he picked on me. I just wondered what you knew about him.'

'Nothing much. He's been a partner in Blake, Willerby and Johns ever since I can remember. Him and his wife come to divisional dos from time to time.' Heffernan thought for a moment. 'That's all, really. He's just your average solicitor; turns up at the station when a villain asks for his services. "Keeps himself to himself", as the neighbours always say in a murder inquiry. I'd file him under B for boring.'

'Wonder what was worrying him.'

'No doubt you'll find out eventually.'

Wesley left Heffernan's office, shutting the door quietly behind him. He looked around the main CID office. There was a subdued holiday atmosphere and his colleagues seemed more relaxed than usual, enjoying the brief ebb in the normally relentless tide of criminal activity.

But as Wesley sat down at his desk he felt a nagging unease. He remembered Brian Willerby's nervous voice and his instincts told him that something was wrong. And he kept wondering why Willerby had chosen to confide in him, a comparative stranger. But no doubt, as Gerry Heffernan had said, he would find out eventually.

Neil Watson ran his fingers through his long brown hair and looked around the newly modernised room in what had once been an old stable block. He noted the freshly painted walls, the brand-new office furniture and the stainless-steel sink in the corner – perfect for washing the finds – and smiled with approval.

'Not bad,' he said to Jake Weston, who had been given the task of showing him round the Earlsacre Hall dig. 'All the latest computer equipment as well, I see. Most digs I've been on we've been lucky to get a glorified garden shed. Nice. How far behind schedule are you?'

'The grand opening is in five weeks and all the archaeological work has to be completed well before then so that the gardening experts can move in and recreate the old gardens. The problem is that we've been short staffed and reliant on inexperienced volunteers. We were well behind before this skeleton was found and now things are even worse.'

'Skeleton?'

'Yeah. It – or rather she – was buried in the middle of the walled garden underneath a stone plinth. The coroner accepted my verdict that it was probably a few hundred years old and said we could carry on with the work, but it still slowed us down for a day or so. I suggested we call in more professional help so the director agreed that I could see if anyone was available from the County Archaeological Unit. An American foundation has put a lot of cash into the project.'

'So we've arrived like the US cavalry . . . just in time to save the day,' said Neil with satisfaction. 'It's worked out well, as a matter of fact. We're just finishing off a dig at Stoke Beeching: Anglo-Saxon farmstead with an en suite Viking burial, no less. Two of my colleagues are tying things up there and they'll be along here tomorrow.'

Jake looked relieved that his workload was about to be shared. 'I'll take you to meet Martin Samuels,' he said, making for the door.

'Who's he?'

'The trust director.'

'What's he like?'

'Enthusiastic,' said Jake simply. 'This whole project was his idea. He raised the money to buy the place from the last owner, set up a trust, even got lottery cash for turning it into an arts centre when it's all restored. It's very much his baby.'

Neil followed Jake out of the stone building and they began to walk towards the house, passing through what remained of an ancient gatehouse that led into a large walled garden. The walls had been rebuilt or repointed very recently: the mortar between the rough stones looked fresh. A new-looking doorway set into the wall to their left stood open to reveal another garden where figures in hard hats were working industriously with spades and wheelbarrows.

Neil stopped and looked around. The walled garden had been partially excavated, and he recognised the decorative cobbled paths running around its edge as late sixteenth century in style. A network of gravel pathways had been exposed, weaving between rectangles of rutted earth which, in happier days, would have been decorative parterres full of fragrant beauty.

Neil noticed that a large stone plinth was carefully propped against one of the garden walls. The holes at its centre suggested that something had been secured there in days gone by; probably a sundial or some other focal point at the garden's heart that had been the last word in horticultural fashion in some bygone century.

'You should have seen this place when we first started work,' said Jake. 'The whole area had been grassed over in the nineteenth century so you wouldn't have known this lot was underneath. The entire garden had gone to rack and ruin – self-set trees, weeds, brambles, the lot – and we had to clear it all before we could assess it, but when we saw the geophysics results we knew we had found something pretty spectacular in historical garden terms. You could see the layout clearly on the print-out; typical Renaissance walled garden.'

'Tell me about this skeleton that was found,' said Neil.

'Just there, slap bang in the middle of the garden.' Jake pointed to the plinth. 'That great lump of stone was over it. It had probably held a sundial and it didn't look as if it had been moved for years, if not centuries.' He turned to Neil, his blue eyes twinkling like those of one about to tell a particularly terrifying ghost story. 'And the curious thing is that the skeleton looked as if it was clawing its way out. A pathologist had a look at it and said that the poor woman had probably been buried alive then had that great slab plonked on top of her. What a way to go, eh?'

'Which pathologist was this?' Neil asked, trying to sound casual.

'I think his name was Bowman. Nice chap. Very chatty. You wouldn't think someone'd be so cheerful in that line of work.'

'I know him. He's helped me out a few times when human remains have turned up unexpectedly.'

'Well, let's hope we don't need his services again.'

'Too right,' said Neil with some feeling.

They had arrived at the house. In its day it had been a desirable country mansion; not large, but probably home to generations of comfortably off Devon gentry. But now it was a shell. The outer walls stood solid, stripped of the ivy that had covered them and the rendering that had hidden the sturdy stone construction. The ivy had been replaced by scaffolding and the roof was a skeletal framework of new timbers.

'Martin's restoring it,' said Jake as Neil studied the building. 'It's being done up and turned into an arts centre.'

'Interested in the arts, is he?'

'Oh, yes. We've even got a poet in residence who floats round the place watching us dig and writing bad poems about it. She's quite a lady is Jacintha,' Jake said with a significant grin. Neil suspected there was a story there somewhere. 'You'll enjoy it here, Neil. Never a dull moment.'

'So how did this Martin Samuels come to buy the place?'

'He's always had a passion for old gardens. The owners of this house had abandoned the place for something more modern years ago and put tenants in. Martin visited it back in the 1980s, saw what was left of the gardens and got quite excited. When the tenants moved out in 1986 the place went to pieces and the house was badly damaged in a fire. Eventually Martin set up a trust and raised the money to buy the estate from the family who owned it. He's very single-minded – a man with a mission.'

'How did he manage to raise the money?'

'Donations from locals, various heritage charities, the lottery – and an American foundation has been extremely generous. Funding's not a problem at the moment but time is. That's why we're glad to see you here,' Jake added as they passed under an archway and walked up a wide flight of stone steps leading on to a high raised terrace in front of the hall. From here Neil had a good view down into the walled garden below.

'I've not done much garden archaeology,' he said modestly. 'It should be an interesting experience. How long have you been working for the trust?'

Before Jake had a chance to reply a man emerged from the once impressive main doorway of Earlsacre Hall. He was probably in his early sixties, tall, with steel-grey hair which peeped out from beneath the hard hat he was wearing. There was something in his upright bearing which suggested that he might once have been a military man.

'Martin, this is Neil Watson from the County Archaeological Unit. He's come to give us a hand. Two of his colleagues will be arriving tomorrow.'

Martin Samuels' eyes lit up and he shook Neil's hand heartily. 'Splendid. You've arrived in the nick of time. Jake's been our only archaeological expert, along with a couple of postgraduate archaeology students, and they've had to organise a horde of volunteers with little or no experience of a dig, so things have fallen behind. Perhaps you and your colleagues could tackle the area around the gatehouse that leads to the walled garden – there's also the area near the centre of the wall on the east side of the garden where there's evidence from old paintings that there was a grotto or summerhouse of some kind built against the wall. Our volunteers have cleared the vegetation for you so . . .'

'That sounds fine. I'll have a look at the geophysics results right away to get an idea of what's down there,' said Neil. Martin Samuels' passion for the project was infectious.

Neil turned to go. The secrets of the gatehouse and the grotto awaited him and he would lose no time in getting started.

'I hope you're not superstitious, Neil,' said Martin unexpectedly. Neil turned round, curious. 'A few people who've worked here have been put off by some strange stories attached to this place. The walled garden has a reputation with the locals for being haunted, apparently.'

Neil shrugged. 'Doesn't bother me. I don't believe in that sort of rubbish.'

'It never used to bother me either,' said Martin with a secretive smile. 'Until I came here. And then we discovered that skeleton that had been buried alive . . .' He didn't finish the sentence.

Neil made no comment. He considered himself immune to ghost stories. And he had work to do.

He and Jake took their leave of Martin Samuels with no further mention of the supernatural. They had begun to walk back to the walled garden in amicable silence when they saw a plump, dark-haired girl running towards them.

When she spotted them she stopped and bent double, trying to catch her breath, her eyes wild with panic. Eventually, when she had regained her composure, she stood up and looked Jake in the eye. 'Andy said to find you. There's another one.'

12

'Another what?'

'Another skeleton . . . buried underneath the first one.' She bent down again, still gasping for breath.

'I suppose we should really let the police and the coroner know again,' sighed Jake, resigned to another delay.

Neil extracted a small mobile phone from the pocket of his tattered jeans. 'I'll do it. I've got a mate who's a detective sergeant at Tradmouth. He did archaeology with me at uni. He knows the score,' he told Jake reassuringly.

'It was a couple of constables from Neston who came last time. They trampled all over the bloody site like a herd of elephants. So if your mate's available . . .'

As they strolled towards the walled garden, now filling up with the ghoulish and the curious, Neil dialled Wesley's number and waited for him to answer.

Craig Kettering, having lost most of last week's wages in one of Morbay's seafront amusement arcades, was financially embarrassed and in need of some ready cash.

Caravans were the easiest. No decent locks, no burglar alarms, always a window open. People got careless when they were on holiday. Craig wandered through the Bloxham View Caravan Park at three o'clock in the afternoon, trying to look casual, as if he had every right to be there. Three o'clock was a good time. Everyone was out at the beach or sampling the attractions of Morbay.

Craig strolled from caravan to caravan trying the doors. At first he had no success. But half an hour later he struck lucky. On one of the smaller caravans kept for rent in the top field the handle turned sweetly and the door swung open without a sound. The floral curtains at the windows were shut. Craig hoped this didn't mean it was empty and unlet.

He knew he had to be careful. There was always a chance that someone might be inside. There was no need to go into the bedroom at the end – just grab any money and valuables from the living area, then leg it. He eased himself carefully up on to the single metal step. The interior was dark: the curtains must have been thicker than they looked.

Something was wrong. Craig could sense it. He could hear the steady, low-pitched buzz of flies. Then the smell hit him and his hand shot up to his nose.

As his eyes adjusted to the dim light he could just make out a shape lying on the floor next to the upholstered seat opposite the door. A human shape giving no sign of movement, no sound. There was just the relentless hum of the flies. With his breath held, Craig squatted down and touched the shape. But he withdrew his hand sharply when the tips of his fingers came into contact with ice-cold, waxy flesh. The thing was dead – naked from the waist up and dead.

He saw the eyes, vacant and staring, and felt he ought to cover them; to find a towel or something to hide them so that they couldn't watch him reproachfully as he intruded into the private world of the dead. But there was nothing to hand so he just looked away. He could smell blood: the smell of meat just on the turn. And when an angry fly buzzed at his face, he leaped to his feet again.

Craig backed away. His eyes half registered some cash on top of a cupboard but his heart was pounding and nausea rose in his chest as his nostrils were filled with the stench of decay. He had to get out of that metal box, that swollen coffin. He opened the door again and slammed it behind him, inhaling the fresh air and looking around to make sure that nobody was about, that nobody had seen him leaving the caravan.

After spitting on the ground to expel the taste of death from his mouth, he began to run down the sloping fields towards his parked van. And as he drove back to his bed-sit in Morbay, exceeding the speed limit by a good fifteen miles per hour, he couldn't stop his hands from shaking on the hard, cold steering wheel.

Chapter 2

I took me to the inn in the village of Earlsacre (the conversation with Sir Richard being somewhat strained) and found the ale there to be of most excellent quality. At the inn – which was named the King's Head – I was afforded the best seat by the fire and the landlord's best pie which, like the ale, was fine enough for the most particular palate in London. At the inn I heard many tales, some doubtless true, some fanciful, as is the way in such establishments. Sir Richard, I discovered, did in 1685 join the Duke of Monmouth in his fight for the Crown – as did many men of the West Country – and was transported to the West Indies to be sold as a slave (as were eight hundred of his fellow rebels) for his dissenting ways. He had found his way home but four years since to claim the estate of his late father. Perhaps Sir Richard's suffering in his years of enslavement accounts for his taciturn ways. I heard other tales regarding Earlsacre Hall of a more sinister nature which I shall set down in due course.

From Jacob Finsbury's Account of His Travels around the
Houses of England, 1703

'Nice, this, Wes. A day out in the country. We should have brought a picnic.' Gerry Heffernan sat back in the passenger seat with a beatific smile on his chubby face as Wesley steered the car carefully through the narrow, high-hedged lanes. 'What did you say it was? A skeleton?'

'There was one found a few days ago. Neston dealt with it. Now another one's turned up.'

'Well, if Neston dealt with the first . . .'

'It was Neil who rang me. Colin Bowman had a look at the other skeleton and reckoned it was old. This one that's just turned up was buried underneath it apparently.'

'Which makes it even older. So we're just going along for appearances' sake, are we? There's no suggestion of foul play?'

'Not recent foul play, at any rate. But Neil said the first skeleton they found had been buried alive.'

Heffernan shuddered. 'Nasty. So more bodies might turn up in this garden place. Looks like we might have our serial killer after all.'

'The bodies were buried underneath an early eighteenth-century plinth which probably hadn't been moved for years, so there's not much chance of getting the culprit bang to rights now,' said Wesley with a grin. 'But I suppose we can think of it as an intellectual exercise.'

Heffernan grunted. 'I tried intellectual exercise once and I pulled a muscle. I leave that sort of thing to you graduates. Hey, did that Brian Willerby ever ring you back?'

'No,' said Wesley, mildly surprised by the sudden change of subject. 'Whatever was worrying him couldn't have been that important.'

'Probably fussing about some client of his. He's a bit of an old woman is Brian Willerby,' the inspector said dismissively. 'How's your Pam, by the way? I've not seen you two in the Tradmouth Arms for a couple of weeks.'

'She's been busy getting ready for the beginning of term. Her maternity leave's come to an end and she starts teaching again next week. So what with that and her mother . . .'

'Having mother-in-law trouble, are you, Wes?' asked Heffernan with relish. 'I know a few good jokes about mothers-in-law.'

'I'm sure you do, sir, but Della isn't exactly that sort of mother-in-law . . . quite the opposite in fact. I suppose you could say it's a reversal of roles. She's like a giddy teenager while Pam's the sensible, disapproving parent. Della's always been a bit . . . but since Pam's father died . . .'

'Stop.'

Wesley slammed on the brakes automatically. 'What is it?'

'That gateway. It says Earlsacre Hall. We're there.'

Wesley backed the car up and swung it round into the driveway. The drive itself had been resurfaced in the not-too-distant past. Saplings had been planted along its length and mature trees had suffered the attentions of tree surgeons. Beyond the trees to his right

Wesley could see what looked like a cricket pitch with a neat white wooden pavilion. It looked slightly out of place, untouched by the work that was going on around it.

As he continued up the narrow drive Wesley sensed an air of expectation, of preparation, about the place. He drove on slowly until he saw the house in front of him, swathed in scaffolding with workmen crawling like insects over its ancient walls. Then he parked his car near what seemed to be a stable block. There was an ancient yellow Mini parked at the end of the row which wore its rust spots with pride. He recognised it as Neil's. The two men left the car and picked their way over the uneven cobbled ground.

'Neil did warn me it was still a building site,' said Wesley. 'They're restoring the garden. And they're turning the house into an arts centre.'

'Very nice,' commented Heffernan. 'So what's your mate Neil doing here? I wouldn't have had him down as a gardener. I can see him cultivating illegal weeds but little else.'

'They usually call in archaeologists when they're restoring ancient gardens. They can turn up all sorts of lost features and give a good idea of the layout from hundreds of years ago. Take formal Renaissance gardens, for instance . . .'

'I'd rather not. Where's this skeleton, then?'

Ahead of them was what appeared to be an ancient stone gate-house, flanked on either side by high walls constructed of a slightly different stone. It was hard to tell its age; it could have been anything from a sixteenth-century status symbol to a Victorian folly. Wesley and Heffernan looked at each other and, as if by unspoken agreement, headed for the archway. As they passed through it, Wesley looked down at the ground.

'Those cobbles are very well preserved. Probably sixteenth- or seventeenth-century.'

'Look like a load of old cobbles to me,' the inspector muttered under his breath. 'Where's this body, then?'

It wasn't long before his question was answered. They spotted a group of people in the middle of the garden, staring down at the ground. Neil was among them. And in the centre of the group, holding court, was Dr Colin Bowman, who spotted the two detectives and waved them over cheerily.

'Gerry, Wesley. So glad you could come,' he said, as though he were hosting a party. 'Interesting one this. A skeleton was found here a couple of days ago; a young woman who had obviously been buried alive . . . nasty case. Now our friends here have turned up another complete skeleton buried a couple of feet beneath the first. A man this time, as far as I can tell. There seems to be a bad head wound which is the likely cause of death; probably the proverbial blunt instrument. So it looks as if we could have two murders on our hands. That's the bad news. The good news for you two is that, according to our experts here, the plinth they were buried under dates from the late seventeenth or early eighteenth century, so the burials might well be several hundred years old.' Bowman stood back, looking pleased with himself, and peeled off his rubber gloves. 'Naturally, I'll have to get the bones back to the mortuary and conduct a thorough examination. But from the evidence it really does look like an old burial.'

'Good,' said Gerry Heffernan. 'We can all go home and have a cup of tea, then.'

But Wesley stood his ground. 'I think we owe it to these two people to find out who they were, at least. What do we know about the history of this place?'

Gerry Heffernan rolled his eyes to heaven. 'Why make work for yourself, Wes? If the burial's that old it's not our problem.'

'I can tell you who lived here at the end of the seventeenth century,' said a deep, authoritative voice. Wesley swung round to face the speaker, a tall man with steel-grey hair and a military bearing. 'You're Neil's policeman friend, I presume. I'm Martin Samuels, Director of the Earlsacre Trust.' He held out his hand and Wesley shook it firmly. 'Neil tells me that you're an archaeology graduate yourself.'

'That's right.'

Gerry Heffernan, standing behind him, muttered something incomprehensible.

'And this is Detective Inspector Heffernan.' Wesley decided that his boss was angling for an introduction.

'Delighted to meet you, Inspector. The constabulary are doing us proud this time. We only got a couple of constables on the last occasion.'

'Well, if there's a serial killer on the loose . . .' Heffernan was unable to resist a spot of stirring.

'Dr Bowman's as certain as he can be that the skeletons are old,' said Wesley quickly, seeing a look of alarm cross Martin Samuels' face.

'Well, I suppose we'll have to be grateful for small mercies. I was going to tell you something of the history of the place, wasn't I, Sergeant?'

Wesley nodded. Neil and his gaggle of fellow archaeologists had fallen silent and were listening intently.

Samuels took a deep breath, which made Wesley suspect he was about to embark on a long story. 'The house was built by a Robert Lantrist at the end of the sixteenth century. Probably a yeoman farmer who'd done well in the reign of Elizabeth: one of the new middle classes. He was a wealthy man and, in the manner of wealthy men, liked to show off to his neighbours, so he built a substantial house in the latest fashion and created a series of gardens to match his status. The walled garden here probably began life as a knot garden but was revamped in the seventeenth century to keep up with the latest trends. Fashion, alas, is nothing new. The fortunes of the Lantrists fluctuated, however – at one point at the end of the seventeenth century they were said to be close to bankruptcy – but they eventually recovered and the estate was passed from father to son in the usual way until the family died out in the eighteenth century and a distant cousin inherited the estate. The line died out again in the 1940s and the place was inherited by a distant relative in Australia who never came here and let it to tenants. Then the house was used by the US Army for a while in the war, and in 1946 it was bought by the Wilton family, who lived here until the sixties. Then a family called Cramer bought it, but they ran out of money and sold it to its last owners, the Pitaways. They only lived here a few years, then they moved into a modern bungalow in Dukesbridge and let in out to tenants. Eventually the place deteriorated and was abandoned, and it was Charles Pitaway, their son, who sold it to the trust. Actually he's moved back into the area and has been taking quite an interest in the project. Nice chap. He's set up a garden design consultancy, so he's been doing quite a bit of work for us.'

'So if the plinth has been there since the early eighteenth century, the skeletons probably date from the time of the Lantrists?' said Wesley. He always like to be sure of his facts.

'It certainly looks like it. Bit of a mystery, eh?'

There was nothing more to be done at Earlsacre Hall. Gerry Heffernan strode on ahead to the car, anxious to get his hands on a warming cup of tea, and Wesley followed, looking around, taking in his surroundings. He put his hands in his pockets. The summer was drawing to an end and there was a chill in the air.

'Anything the matter, Wes?' the inspector asked as they climbed into the car. 'You've gone very quiet.'

'I was just thinking that it was a coincidence.'

'What was?'

'The name Lantrist. It's unusual. I've never heard it anywhere else before. It's my mother's maiden name.'

'Well, it's a very small world,' Gerry Heffernan pronounced philosophically as they drove out of the gates of Earlsacre Hall and on to the winding lane.

Craig Kettering stared at the fruit machine, then at the solitary coin in his hand.

Perhaps he had been too hasty when he had fled from the caravan. He was sure he had spotted some cash on top of the cupboard by the door. Maybe he should have stayed and searched the place, taken what he could. Somehow the hours that had passed since his grim discovery had lessened the horror. There in the gaudy safety of the amusement arcade, with its cheery flashing lights to lure in the unwary punter, the stench of death and the staring dead eyes seemed a world away. Perhaps he should go back and take a look – after all, the man was dead, so he could hardly complain.

He put the coin into the slot and punched the button. No luck. Why was it always the same? Farther down the arcade he heard the solid clunking of a machine paying out. He looked over at the expressionless recipient of this good fortune – a man around his own age with a shaved head and a silver stud through his top lip – and felt a pang of envy.

But sometimes you make your own luck. Maybe he would go back.

Craig walked the fifty yards to where his rusty white van was parked in a hotel carpark (for residents only) and drove out to the Bloxham View Caravan Park. A dead man couldn't hurt him.

Gerry Heffernan pushed open the door to Tradmouth police station, letting it bang dramatically behind him, and made his entry into the foyer with his usual panache. 'Hi, Bob,' he called to the large sergeant on the desk. 'How are things? All quiet?'

Bob Naseby drew himself up to his full height and stroked the beard he was cultivating. 'It was till you came in, Gerry.' He grinned. 'Not much happening at all. Still, it gives us a chance to catch up on the old paperwork, doesn't it, and I don't expect it'll last for long – never does. Is Wesley not with you?'

'He's just parking the car. Why?'

'Oh, I just wanted a word with him,' said Bob, sounding cagey.

At that point Wesley appeared, shutting the door gently behind him. Bob Naseby's eyes lit up. This was it. The final challenge. Ever since Wesley had told him in casual conversation that his great-uncle had played cricket for the West Indies. Bob – trusting in the hereditary principle – had longed to recruit him for the divisional team. In recent weeks he had sensed that Wesley's resolve was weakening so, like any predator, he prepared himself for the kill.

'Wesley,' he began with an appealing smile, 'it's the next-to-last match of the season on Saturday. We're a man short. It'll only be in the afternoon from one till five: limited overs. I wouldn't ask but we're really desperate.'

'I don't know, Bob. I haven't played since school.'

'That doesn't matter. We just need an extra body. Please?'

Wesley looked round at Gerry Heffernan for support but soon found it was no use relying on his boss for back-up. 'Go on, Wes. The old sound of leather on willow, eh? Nothing like it. I'll come and watch,' Heffernan offered generously.

Wesley sensed a trap. But perhaps it was as well to bow to the inevitable.

'And if you find I'm no good I won't be asked again?'

A smirk of triumph spread over Bob Naseby's face. 'Sounds fair to me. We're meeting at a place called Earlsacre at half twelve. It's a little place between Neston and Dukesbridge.'

'He knows where it is, Bob,' said Heffernan. 'We've just come from there. Couple of old skeletons have been dug up.'

'Not buried on the wicket, I hope?' Bob looked genuinely worried.

'Don't worry, they were nowhere near the cricket ground. That's settled, then, Bob. Saturday it is.'

Bob nodded, a grin of triumph on his face.

'That was rather rash of you, Wes, agreeing to play in Bob's team,' said Heffernan as they climbed the stairs to the CID office.

'Bob's been going on at me to join the cricket team ever since I arrived in Tradmouth. When he sees I'm no good he'll let the matter drop. I'm looking upon Saturday as an investment.'

21

Gerry Heffernan gave a hearty laugh. 'I should have known there'd be method in your madness. I hope it's worth the risk.'

They walked into the office. Wesley saw that Rachel was perched on his desk speaking on the telephone. She looked up as he came in and smiled shyly. 'Wesley, it's a Mr Willerby for you,' she said in a stage whisper, covering the mouthpiece.

Wesley took the receiver. 'Hello, Mr Willerby. How can I help you?'

'Sergeant Peterson, I'd like us to meet if that's convenient. I have something of a rather sensitive nature that I wish to discuss with you. I don't want to talk about it over the telephone.'

'Why don't you come into the station tomorrow?' said Wesley, trying to hide his impatience.

'I'll be away in London all day tomorrow. Could we meet tomorrow evening?'

'Sorry – family commitments,' said Wesley, remembering that Pam's mother was joining them for dinner.

'Would late on Saturday be convenient?'

Wesley hesitated, mildly irritated that this man seemed to think he could trespass on his weekend leisure. 'Er . . . I'm not free on Saturday. Playing cricket actually. But afterwards . . .'

'Is that at Earlsacre, by any chance?' Willerby's voice suddenly became animated, even mildly excited.

'As a matter of fact, yes.'

'Splendid. I'm playing there too. I turn out for the Earlsacre team occasionally. Perhaps we can meet at the match and discuss the matter during the tea interval, say . . . or after the game.'

'Very well, Mr Willerby. I'll see you on Saturday.' The line went dead. Willerby had rung off without the courtesy of a goodbye.

'Well, what was all that about? What did Willerby want?' asked Gerry Heffernan, who had been standing by the desk blatantly listening in to the conversation.

'I've still no idea. But it turns out he's playing cricket for the opposing team on Saturday so we're going to meet and discuss it then. Why can't the man just say what's bothering him . . . or come into the station some time if he wants a confidential chat? All this cloak-and-dagger stuff is beginning to get on my nerves.'

'Looks like he's taken a shine to you, Wes,' the inspector said mischievously before disappearing into his office.

Wesley sat down in his chair and sighed. Why did Willerby have to pick on him?

Craig knew he'd have to take care. One or two families were starting to drift back to the caravan park after their day's outing. But it was still quiet up on the top field. If he was careful he wouldn't be seen.

He parked in the big carpark near the entrance again. He didn't want to risk his van in the field which was muddy from last night's rain – he needed it tonight for his pizza deliveries . . . and he might need to make a quick getaway.

He walked quickly up to the field, head down, hands in pockets, trying to look as though he wasn't there. He had no difficulty finding the caravan again. Its image was etched on his mind. He took a deep breath before opening the door again and braced himself for the sight of the half-naked body, the smell, the flies.

He let himself in with unaccustomed agility and shut the door gently behind him. No one had seen him, he was sure of that. He tried not to look at the body but he could see it out of the corner of his eye. And he could hear the flies, louder now.

Craig concentrated his mind on the money lying on top of the cupboard near the door. It was still there waiting for him, almost as though he had been meant to find it. He snatched it up and stuffed it in the pocket of his denim jacket.

Then, covering his mouth with his left hand, he opened the caravan door silently and emerged into the fresh air. Then he felt a wave of nausea rising in his stomach. He rushed round to the back of the caravan and vomited into the hedgerow.

It was 5.30 when Wesley Peterson let himself into his modern detached house perched on the hill overlooking the ancient port of Tradmouth. Pam heard his key turn in the lock and hurried out of the living room to greet him.

Wesley caught her around the waist and kissed her, glad to see her, glad to be back in his own home. 'You look pleased about something. What is it?' he said, kissing the tip of her nose.

'You're home on time for once,' she said firmly, squirming from his grasp and making for the kitchen. 'If I'd known you were going to be here so early I'd have made you do the cooking. I've had a bloody awful day.'

'What's the matter? Is it Michael? Is he all right?' All sorts of

23

possibilities ran through his mind: sickness; accident; the onset of meningitis; all the ills that could befall a precious six-month-old body.

'Michael's fine.'

Wesley relaxed. Whatever it was couldn't be that bad if Michael was all right.

'It's my mother,' Pam continued. 'She called round today. She's only gone and picked up a man in a supermarket.'

All sorts of inappropriate pictures began to flash through Wesley's mind: Della, his mother-in-law, wheeling a trolley down the supermarket aisles with a man sitting obediently inside; a checkout girl searching for a bar code on some inaccessible part of the man's anatomy. He began to laugh.

'It's not funny, Wesley.' Pam nudged him, trying hard not to laugh herself. 'I never know what she's going to get up to next. There was that mature student of hers last year – the one who turned out to be married; a small fact she hadn't bothered to tell me. And she admits that she doesn't know anything about this new man. He could be an axe murderer for all she knows.'

Wesley put an arm around his wife. 'There aren't that many axe murderers about, in spite of what the tabloids say. What's this man's name? Bluebeard?'

'It's James Delmann.'

'Well, as far as I know he's not on our wanted list.' He tried to look serious. 'You should be pleased your mum's getting out and about. It's three years since your dad died. She needs a social life.'

'I know. And I'd be pleased that she'd met someone if she wasn't so . . . so silly. She's just like a giddy teenager; worse than I ever was. And that's not all. You know she's coming round for dinner tomorrow night?'

Wesley nodded, wary.

'Well, she only wants to bring this Jamie with her.'

'Then we'll be able to judge for ourselves. Stop worrying. Della's old enough to look after herself.'

Pam didn't answer. Wesley was probably right: she found it hard to admit it, but he usually was. She was overreacting.

Wesley knew he couldn't put it off any longer. It was time to drop his bombshell. 'I'm playing cricket on Saturday afternoon,' he said, trying to sound casual.

Pam looked at him as though he'd just told her he'd volunteered for a NASA mission to Mars. 'Cricket? Why?'

'Our desk sergeant's been after me to play for the team ever since I arrived, so I thought that if I showed him how bad I was he'd leave me in peace. Besides, they're short of players and he sounded pretty desperate. The match is at a place called Earlsacre; it's between Neston and Dukesbridge.'

'And am I invited to this great sporting occasion? I hope I'm not expected to make the sandwiches,' Pam said with token feminist disgust.

'Bob told me there's been some trouble about the teas. Apparently the wives and girlfriends refuse to make them any more.'

'Quite right too.' She looked him in the eye. 'This cricket's not going to become a regular thing, is it?'

'Not much chance of that.'

'In that case, Michael and I might come along to watch if the weather's decent,' she said with a gracious inclination of her head.

Then Wesley remembered his appointment with Brian Willerby. Pam's presence would give him a good excuse for a quick getaway if the solicitor was fussing over some trivial matter. 'Yeah, good idea,' he said with what he hoped sounded like enthusiasm.

'It'll make a change from planning lessons and the fresh air will do Michael good,' Pam said. 'And as you say, it's a once-in-a-lifetime experience.'

'Too right it is.'

Pam turned and made for the kitchen just as Michael began to cry. But the crying stopped as soon as Wesley picked his son up out of the playpen. The proud father was rewarded with a wide, gummy grin. As he entertained the baby he suddenly realised that there was something he hadn't yet mentioned to Pam; the fact that Neil Watson was working up at Earlsacre. Wesley sat there shaking a rattle and defending his best silk tie against tiny grabbing hands while he pondered the best way to break the news.

Jacintha Hervey walked towards the cricket pavilion at eight o'clock precisely. Jake had given her the key and told her to wait for him.

Martin Samuels and some of the team were meeting up at the house to discuss the progress of the work. The meeting had been due to finish at ten to eight. She had already seen Charles Pitaway driving away in his red sports car, heading home to his new apartment in Dukesbridge. She thought of Charles and smiled. She had made subtle approaches but so far he hadn't responded: perhaps he was gay, she thought . . . which would be a terrible loss to the female sex; or perhaps he just needed time and a little more persuasion. It never crossed her mind that not all men found her irresistible. But in the meantime she had Jake, an energetic young man who would do nicely for the time being.

Jacintha looked round furtively as she opened the pavilion door, but there was nobody about. Nobody had any reason to come to the small cricket ground on the edge of the estate. It wasn't the most salubrious of trysting places but at least it was private. They would be quite safe.

She swung her canvas handbag over her shoulder, picked up the bulky carrier bag she had brought with her, and stepped inside the wooden pavilion, shutting the door carefully behind her. Unlike some pavilions, which housed carpeted bars and comfortable chairs, Earlsacre Cricket Club made little concession to modern sporting comforts with its splintery benches, rusty lockers and worn linoleum floor. The place had been converted from an army hut, left behind by the Americans when they had used Earlsacre as a base during the war, and its atmosphere was still decidedly utilitarian.

A pair of ornate and battered garden statues stood incongruously in the corner, but otherwise the room was bare and austere, smelling faintly of sweat and linseed oil. Jacintha breathed in deeply. The smell was masculine, sexy. She wrestled a stained double duvet out of the carrier bag, laid it carefully on the hard floor, and looked at her watch. He had said eight o'clock. He was late.

At seven minutes past eight Jacintha heard a noise, a scrabbling at the door. She stiffened and held her breath as she watched it open slowly. The hinges creaked like in some horror-film. She could see a shape in the doorway against the fading light.

'Jake? Is that you?' she asked breathlessly, staring at the door.

Jake stepped forward. He reached out for her and pulled her towards him. 'Who else were you expecting?' he asked softly. They kissed passionately, his tongue exploring her mouth and his hands her body.

She began to unbutton his shirt. 'How did the meeting go?'

'Fine.'

Her busy hands fell to her side. 'Tell me about it,' she said.

Jake stepped back, a little relieved. 'Okay. They've roped in some more archaeologists to give me a hand, so there's a good chance that the work will be completed on schedule. Charles Pitaway's working on the garden plans. They're good.'

'I wonder if Charles ever feels sad about losing Earlsacre. If it had been mine it would have broken my heart to sell it.'

Jake looked mildly embarrassed by the passionate sincerity in Jacintha's voice. 'I don't think it bothers him. He was telling me that his parents moved out and let the place when he was five. And the trust paid him a good price for it. I mean, would you swap a brand-new apartment overlooking Dukesbridge harbour for this old ruin?'

He put his hand out to stroke Jacintha's long, auburn hair, but she turned away, and picked up the capacious canvas bag that she had discarded on the floor in the first moments of passion. She began to search through it. 'I want to show you something,' she said earnestly. 'I've been working on it today.'

Jake Weston sighed. It would be another of Jacintha's poems. If the duvet that lay stretched out so invitingly on the floor of the cricket pavilion was to be used that night, he would have to try to feign interest.

Jacintha drew a sheet of creased paper from the bag. 'It's only a draft. It's probably best if I read it to you. It's called "Earlsacre Awakened".' She cleared her throat and began, squinting to see the words in the dim light that seeped through the large, mesh-protected windows.

The centuries pass: a house and garden lost in weeds and time.
Built by Lantrists in the first Elizabeth's mighty reign.
Laid out with trees, parterres, walls and strange grottoes.
Its beauty flourished then withered to earth like leaves of fall,
And was lost to Lantrists when the first George reigned.
Then others; Wiltons, Cramers, Pitaways . . .

Jake nodded encouragingly, anxious to get it over with. 'Go on.'

Came to know its secrets and its mournful ghosts.
Till Earlsacre fell asleep beneath its eiderdown of briars,
Awakened only at millennium's dawn.
But what secrets lie within?
What ghosts still walk in Lantrists' lost land?

She looked at Jake like a puppy eager for approval. 'Well? What do you think?'

'Marvellous,' he said quickly. 'Very good.' He knelt down on the duvet and held out his hand.

Jacintha hesitated for a moment, then fell to her knees beside him. They kissed once, then again. Then, as the fevered scramble to remove clothing was reaching its inevitable conclusion, Jacintha let out a muffled cry.

Jake rolled his eyes. 'What is it? What's the matter?'

'A face . . . at the window. Someone was watching us.'

Jake zipped up his jeans. 'I'll go and have a look,' he said with a weary sigh.

He opened the door slowly. The resultant creak would have alerted all but the deafest of peeping Toms. 'There's nobody there,' he called to Jacintha. 'You must have imagined it.'

'But I didn't. There was someone there.'

'Probably the resident ghost,' he said with a laugh, unzipping his jeans. 'Now where were we?'

Five minutes later Jake and Jacintha were far too preoccupied to hear the retreating footsteps outside treading softly on the cricket pavilion's rickety wooden veranda.

Craig Kettering had lain awake all night. At first he had blamed the heat, the unbearable stuffiness, as he stared at the cracked ceiling of his shabby bed-sit on the top floor of a crumbling Edwardian house in Morbay. He had wriggled and rolled from side to side in a search for comfort, but had only succeeded in pulling the sheets out to expose the stained mattress until they lay crumpled in a wrinkled mess. He pushed back the top sheet and lay there naked.

The corpse in the caravan had been naked from the waist up. Craig couldn't get the image out of his head, and when he finally drifted into an exhausted half-sleep he dreamed that the body, surrounded by a halo of buzzing flies, had risen from the caravan floor and was walking towards him, pointing accusingly. He woke, sweating, and sat up, still wrapped in the grubby, clinging sheets. He should never have gone back for that money.

The glowing red numbers on the dusty radio alarm clock told him that it was eight o'clock. Too early. He had been out delivering pizzas until two o'clock the night before, and he usually slept in until ten at the earliest. But that was before he had discovered the corpse in the caravan.

He should never have gone back, he kept telling himself. It had been a mistake. But then he thought of the cash – sixty-five pounds in all; enough to pay off a few debts and keep him in burgers and lager until Mr Bonnetti gave him his wages for the pizza deliveries. Perhaps it had been worth it after all.

He lay down again in the crumpled bedding and closed his eyes tight against the light that streamed in through the thin curtains. He must have drifted off to sleep because the next time he glanced at the clock it was 10.15. The night had left him exhausted; his mouth was dry and his brain fuzzy from lack of sleep. He rose from the single divan bed and stumbled over to the sink, where he picked up a chipped cup from the draining board and poured himself some water.

He knew what he should do. He should call the police. But in Craig's circle of mates, casual acquaintances and dealers in illegal substances, nobody made contact with the police: if they were unlucky the police would eventually contact them.

But there was no need for the police to know his name. All he had to do was to report it anonymously. Craig looked in the cracked mirror above the sink and gave himself a smug smile.

He would ring from the phone box at the end of the street. Problem solved.

Chapter 3

I am not of a fanciful disposition but I did detect a strange atmosphere around the house at Earlsacre which I at first did attribute to an unseasonable chill in the air and the manner in which the breeze blew around the walled garden.

Yet I seem not alone in my misgivings. In that most excellent of establishments, the King's Head, I hear strange tales of footsteps and sounds in the night when there is no person present. It is said that one of the maidservants disappeared from the face of the earth, that another died of fright there and a third lost her wits at the horrors she witnessed and was confined to the attic. It is said that the gardener there dabbles in witchcraft and evil deeds. But I possess no evidence of these events and as a rational man I do not believe what I do not experience with my own eyes and ears.

Yet there is a strange chill about the place.

From Jacob Finsbury's Account of his Travels Around the
Houses of England, 1703

At 8.30 on Friday morning Wesley Peterson felt that he was at last getting the better of his paperwork. A lull in criminal activity had been just what was needed to get the backlog clear. Then Colin Bowman had rung to say that he'd completed his examination of the Earlsacre bones.

'Is our journey really necessary?' asked Gerry Heffernan as Wesley pushed open the swing-doors that led to the mortuary.

'Got to go through the motions, sir. If human remains have been found we have to get official confirmation that it's not up to us to investigate the deaths,' replied Wesley officially but with a very unofficial smile on his face.

'I might have known you'd be over the moon about looking at a couple of old skeletons, what with you having spent three years learning how to dig things up at the taxpayers' expense.'

Wesley ignored his boss's last comment. He had learned from experience to take Gerry's jibes with a hefty pinch of salt. 'Colin called me and, as things seem to be quiet at the station at the moment with our local villains working to rule, I thought we should check with him that these skeletons are really as old as everyone seems to think they are. If Colin's discovered that they've got a mouthful of modern fillings we need to know.'

Gerry Heffernan had been in CID long enough to recognise an excuse when he heard one. Wesley was intrigued by the gruesome discoveries at Earlsacre and was itching to find out more about them. And Gerry Heffernan had to admit that he was a little curious about them himself.

They found Colin Bowman in his office. He was sipping tea from a bone-china cup while studying a pathology report. He looked genuinely delighted to see the two police officers lurking in his doorway. 'Gerry, Wesley. Come in.' He stood up and headed straight for the large china teapot that stood on a table in the corner of the room. When Wesley and Heffernan were safely seated, each furnished with a cup of the finest Darjeeling, and after the social niceties had been observed, Wesley was able to broach the subject of bones.

'Both skeletons certainly seem fairly old,' began the pathologist. 'But of course I can't say exactly how old unless . . .'

'You do further tests and that takes months,' Wesley interrupted. 'We know, Colin. We're not asking for miracles. I'm just curious to know what you've found out so far.'

Colin Bowman took a deep breath and stood up. 'Well, if you've finished your tea, I'll take you to meet the objects of our curiosity.'

He led them down the corridor and into a bright, white room. In its centre were two trolleys, each covered with a crisp white sheet which lay in snowy peaks over the irregular shapes beneath. Colin whipped back the sheets to reveal two complete skeletons. 'There you are, gentlemen. Our mystery guests from Earlsacre gardens.'

'What can you tell us about them?' asked Wesley.

'I know it's considered politically incorrect but I'm going to say ladies first and start with the female here,' said Colin mischievously. 'From the position the archaeologists found her in, she had almost

31

certainly been buried alive.' He pointed to the grinning skull, which was surprisingly small, almost as delicate as a child's. 'Dark stains on the facial bones indicate rupture of blood vessels suggesting that asphyxia was the likely cause of death, which all fits in.' The pathologist shook his head in disbelief. 'Nasty business, very nasty.'

Wesley said nothing but nodded in agreement.

'So you reckon someone just dumped her in a hole and buried her alive, then?' asked Gerry Heffernan, who was leaning against the wall with his arms folded. 'You wouldn't think it'd be that easy to bury someone alive.'

'Who knows, Gerry? Whoever killed her might have knocked her out or drugged her, then she regained consciousness in the grave and tried to claw her way out. Only by that time there was a dirty great stone plinth on top of her. As I said . . . very nasty.'

'How old was she?' asked Wesley, staring down at the small, frail-looking bones.

'She was in her late teens, I'd say. She was around five foot tall; never given birth; a few bad teeth and no sign of modern dental work; no obvious indicators of disease. That's about all I can tell you. Poor girl,' he added with sincerity.

Wesley stood in silence for a while, trying not to visualise the horror of this young girl's death. Being unimaginative, he thought, would have its advantages.

'What about the other one?' he asked quietly.

Colin Bowman turned to the other trolley. 'Ah, yes. Now as far as I can tell he was well and truly dead when he went into the ground. Probable cause of death was a fractured skull. The proverbial blunt instrument. He was found a couple of feet below the young woman, so we can assume that he was buried first and then for some reason the grave was opened up and the unfortunate girl was placed on top of the first body while she was still alive, then the plinth was put on top of them both. All very macabre, don't you agree?'

'You can say that again.' Gerry Heffernan scratched his head.

'So what can you tell us about the man?' asked Wesley.

'About five foot ten; average build; mature adult . . . probably in his thirties or forties; moderately good teeth and again no sign of modern dental work; healed fractures on three of the ribs and the left tibia but no obvious indications of disease. I think our friend here had been in the wars at some stage in his life.'

'Wars?'

'Just a figure of speech. He could have been in some sort of accident . . . or been beaten up outside his local tavern. Or, indeed, he might have been in some battle or other and received the injuries then. Who can say? All I can tell you is that these healed injuries probably occurred some years before his death. He almost certainly died from that head injury . . . blunt instrument wielded by person or persons unknown.'

'So what have we got?' said Wesley, trying not to look at the female skeleton. 'A man in his thirties or forties, injured many years before in some accident, brawl or battle, is killed with a blunt instrument then buried in the middle of the walled garden at Earlsacre. Then a girl in her late teens is somehow buried alive on top of the first body and a stone plinth is placed over them both, probably some time in the early eighteenth century.'

'I think that just about sums it up. Interesting. I think we can safely say these deaths are too old to be of any concern to you profession-ally, Wesley, but if you or Neil find out who these bones belonged to or how they ended up in the middle of that garden, you will let me know, won't you?'

'Of course I will, Colin.' Wesley glanced over at his boss, who was showing characteristic signs of impatience. And Wesley himself wanted to get out of the room, to escape the thought of suffocating death. 'Thanks.'

Heffernan shuffled his feet, anxious to be away. 'Yeah, thanks, Colin. Nice cuppa you serve here, but let's hope we won't be back too soon, eh? I certainly don't want to see another murder around these parts for a very long time.'

'Here's hoping your wish is granted, Gerry,' said the pathologist with feeling as the two police officers left the stark white room.

'I think we can be certain about a couple of things,' began Wesley as he pushed open the big double doors that led out of the mortuary. 'They must have been connected with Earlsacre Hall and I reckon they were both killed by the same person. Do you agree?'

'They could be victims of Jack the Ripper himself, but so long as they're a few hundred years old I don't care. It's not our problem.' Heffernan began to stride out, a man who knew where he was heading.

'Aren't you just a little bit interested?' said Wesley, catching up.

'All I'm interested in is getting to the Fisherman's Arms for one of Maisie's hotpots. Coming?'

Wesley answered in the affirmative. He was hungry. Then he heard the urgent ring of his mobile phone and after a brief conversation he looked at the inspector apologetically. 'Sorry, but there's just been an anonymous phone call to the station saying there's a dead body at a caravan site near Bloxham. I've told Rachel to get some uniforms up there searching right away.'

Wesley expected a few colourful naval oaths from the inspector but, to his surprise, the older man's eyes lit up with the excitement of the chase. 'Right, Wes. We'd better get over there now. We'll grab a butty on the way.'

It was a fine day for the back end of the season. Curious holidaymakers had forsaken their planned mornings on the beach to watch the shirtsleeved police officers as they knocked on the door of each caravan in turn.

The informant hadn't been specific. He had made a bald and mumbled statement to the effect that there was a dead body in a caravan at the Bloxham View Caravan Park; when asked for further details he had hung up. But at least he had had the decency to name the caravan park. If the police had been really unlucky they might have found themselves searching every holiday park near Bloxham – and there were a good many of them, some small, some vast, with seemingly endless rows of shiny metal caravans stretching over the headland.

By the time Wesley Peterson and Gerry Heffernan arrived, all the caravans in the main field at Bloxham View had been searched. While the small team of uniformed officers knocked on caravan doors, Rachel Tracey was standing at the gate leading to the far field with a clipboard, looking cool, blonde and efficient. She glanced up as Wesley approached and gave him what she considered to be a businesslike smile.

'So what's going on? Found anything yet?'

'Nothing. We've caught a couple in a rather compromising situation and provided a lot of entertainment for the holidaymakers, but apart from that there's no sign of a dead body. Everyone in the main field is very much alive and kicking. Nothing suspicious at all so far.'

'So what exactly was said in this mysterious phone call? Was it a man or a woman?'

'A man. He said there was a dead body in a caravan at Bloxham

View Caravan Park and we should get someone round there. Then he hung up. He didn't give his name, obviously.'

Gerry Heffernan had been chatting to a couple of the uniformed constables, but now he lumbered up to Wesley and Rachel, grinning enthusiastically. 'Right, you two, we're starting on the top field now. The owner says it's usually quieter up there – fewer families with kids. And half the caravans are empty. Well, come on, what are we waiting for?'

Wesley and Rachel exchanged a glance, then followed their boss through the wooden gate into the next field. Rachel, a farmer's daughter, could see immediately that the drainage in the top field was inadequate. The cars driving up to the caravans had left muddy ruts, which were still damp even though it hadn't rained for two days. Two rows of static caravans stood at the far side of the field, but for the touring variety this was the overspill field, used only at the height of the season. Now, at the start of September, many of the statics were obviously empty, with curtains drawn across windows and an air of neglect.

As they picked their way through the sticky furrows they heard a string of colourful four-letter words behind them. Heffernan swung round. 'Steve. Glad you could join us. What time do you call this?' He looked at his watch ostentatiously.

Steve Carstairs was standing there studying his feet, one of which was encased in an unpleasant brown substance. 'These bloody trainers cost a fortune, sir.'

Gerry Heffernan folded his arms and rolled his eyes to heaven. 'When I first joined CID my inspector told me that I should never wear anything I wouldn't mind a drunk throwing up on. Get your foot out of that mud and start knocking on these caravan doors like the rest of us. Where have you been anyway? We already solved three murders and half a dozen armed robberies before you had your ruddy cornflakes.'

'Didn't feel well this morning, sir.'

'None of us do after a night out clubbing it in Morbay. Now get your finger out and do some work. If you'd rather be directing traffic in Tradmouth High Street, that can be arranged.'

Steve shot the inspector a resentful look, extracted his foot from the glutinous mud, and limped away towards the row of static caravans lined up against the far hedgerow.

Wesley found himself teamed up with Rachel. He walked beside

35

her, breathing in the fresh sea air and her musky perfume. The view from the top field was indeed spectacular. The site was perched on the headland overlooking the fishing port of Bloxham, which stood between the town of Tradmouth and the sprawling seaside resort of Morbay. Bloxham was stretched out far below them, its tiny pale houses tumbling down to the vast glittering sea. Large vessels crawled across the distant horizon while smaller boats scurried like insects across the calm waters of the English Channel.

'Lovely view,' he commented.

Rachel looked at him and smiled shyly. 'If you start at the end of this row, I'll do the next one. I don't think we're going to find many people at home.'

'Mmm. There seem to be a lot of closed curtains.'

'So either no one's in or there's hanky-panky going on inside,' said a loud Liverpudlian voice behind them. The inspector was back. 'I've done plenty of house-to-house inquiries in my time but never a caravan-to-caravan.'

Wesley didn't reply. He knocked on the door of the first caravan in the row while Rachel gave her attention to the one next door. Gerry Heffernan stood behind him expectantly, but after a while Wesley turned to him and shook his head. Nobody home.

'Well, try the door.'

Wesley hesitated, then attempted to turn the handle. The door was locked. Then the inspector disappeared round the back, moving quickly for a big man. A minute later he returned, disappointed. 'I've looked in all the windows . . . nothing. Come on.'

He bypassed the next caravan, where Rachel was talking to a young red-haired woman, and carried on down the row. But there was nothing even remotely suspicious. The caravans were either empty or occupied by ordinary citizens going about their lawful holiday business. Not a corpse in sight.

Just as Wesley was starting to suspect that the telephone call had been someone's idea of a joke, he heard Steve Carstairs shouting. Without a word Wesley and Heffernan began to run over to the far row of caravans.

Rachel caught up with them. 'Was that Steve shouting?'

'Sounded like it.'

'Probably stepped in some more mud and ruined his other trainer,' mumbled Heffernan uncharitably.

But when they reached the far row of static caravans they found

Steve sitting on the step leading up to the door of the fourth van with his head in his hands. Wesley began to sprint towards him, leaving the other two behind.

When he reached the caravan, Steve Carstairs looked up at him, the usual wariness gone. 'In there,' he muttered. 'Been dead a few days, I reckon.'

Wesley stepped past him and opened the caravan's flimsy door, taking a deep breath and dreading the sight that would greet him inside. At first he saw nothing. The curtains were drawn and it took his eyes a few seconds to adjust to the dim light. But he could hear the low-pitched buzzing of flies. And he could smell death.

'So he wasn't having us on,' said Gerry Heffernan softly as he entered the caravan. Wesley stared for a few moments at the body which lay like a marble statue on the floor. Then he averted his eyes. He would never become hardened to the sight of violent death.

Heffernan turned to Rachel, who had just come in behind them. 'Get the others down here will you, Rach, and get the scene secured. And radio for SOCO.'

'Is it suspicious, then, sir?' asked Rachel, craning to look at the body. The carpet and the brown upholstered bench seat near by were splattered liberally with crusted blood.

'Unless he was a contortionist who could stab himself in the back, I'd say it looks very suspicious. Give Colin Bowman a ring and all, will you.'

Rachel left the caravan quickly, relieved to be out of the place. Gerry Heffernan stood beside Wesley, staring down at the body. 'Now how did this poor bugger come to end up stabbed to death in a place like this?' he said, scratching his head.

Wesley had been wondering the same thing himself. 'Your guess is as good as mine,' he replied softly, before walking out into the sweet, fresh air.

It had started. Bloxham View Caravan Park (family-run with shop and modern toilet and shower facilities) was now awash with police officers. The curious were kept well back behind the blue-and-white tape than cordoned off the crime scene, and Scenes of Crime Officers, clinical in their white overalls, came and went up and down the caravan's clanging metal step, absorbed in their grim tasks.

With true British reserve, the people in the nearby caravans had studiously ignored the young man in static caravan number sixty-three. And the young man had gone about his business quietly, had no antisocial habits, and had attracted little attention. He had kept himself to himself and had therefore gone unnoticed.

Steve Carstairs had recovered from his shocking discovery with what seemed like indecent haste, and was soon out knocking on caravan doors with the rest of the CID team. Wesley was about to join them when Gerry Heffernan called him back.

'I think you and me should have a word with the owner of the site. It's a Mr Fielding. He lives in that ugly bungalow down by reception.'

Wesley had noticed the bungalow, a concrete box designed in the 1960s on an architect's off-day.

'He might have a name for us,' said Wesley hopefully as they walked through the fields of caravans towards the site entrance. Gerry Heffernan didn't reply but marched purposefully onwards.

They found Mr Fielding in the site shop, talking animatedly to a young girl who wore an expression of habitual boredom. Fielding was in his late thirties and almost bald apart from a few wisps of reddish hair at the back. He looked worried, anticipating cancelled holidays, demands for refunds and a heavy dint in the reputation of the caravan site that was his sole source of income. He hurried the two officers out of the shop and through the front door of the bungalow: he didn't wish to be seen consorting with the forces of law and order.

'This is awful,' he said as he invited them to sit down on a large, shabby sofa. His accent was northern. Heffernan pinpointed it to around forty miles from his native Liverpool, somewhere in the Manchester area. 'Are they sure it's murder? I mean, yesterday afternoon one of our visitors told me that they'd seen a lad going round trying caravan doors, but I can't believe . . .' He shook his head, trying to convince himself that it was all some horrible mistake.

'This lad who was trying doors . . . did you report it to the police?'

'Yeah. A constable came up from Bloxham but said that as there had been no damage done and nothing had been reported missing there wasn't much that could be done. He just told me to keep an eye on things. You don't think it's got anything to do with . . .'

'Someone made an anonymous call to say that there was a body in one of the caravans. If there was an opportunist thief trying doors it's possible that he discovered the body and decided to report it to us,' said Wesley.

Fielding looked at Wesley with thinly disguised curiosity, then nodded.

At that moment the door opened and a woman walked into the living room. She was thin, almost skeletal, with short fair hair. She looked young but the fine lines on her face betrayed her age. She stared at the two policemen, her eyes lingering on Wesley, then turned to her husband.

'What's going on, Barry? What are all these police doing here?'

'Er . . . this is my wife, Dilys. These are policemen, love. There's been a body found in one of the statics in the top field.'

Dilys Fielding looked worried. 'What was it? A heart attack? It wasn't an accident, was it?' she added anxiously, mentally going through the liability clauses on the site's insurance policies. 'We make sure everything's checked thoroughly, you know. The electrics and the gas flues. We always do everything by the book. You can't take any risks these days.'

'I'm afraid it looks like murder, Mrs Fielding,' said Wesley gently.

Dilys Fielding's hand fluttered up to her mouth. 'Oh, Lord. That's awful. What happened?' she asked with what seemed like genuine shock.

'A young man's been found dead in caravan sixty-three, love,' said Heffernan bluntly. 'What can you tell us about him?'

Dilys glanced at her husband. 'I'll need to look it up on the computer.'

Gerry Heffernan nodded to Wesley, who followed Dilys into the room next door, which was furnished as an office.

'This must be a shock to you, Mrs Fielding,' he said. 'But anything you can tell us about the dead man will be very useful.'

She gave Wesley a weak smile, grateful that at least one of the local police force was behaving sympathetically. She booted up the computer and summoned up the details of caravan sixty-three from the files.

'He just turned up on Monday and paid for a week in one of the statics we let out. He hadn't booked in advance or anything. We normally do Saturday to Saturday, but out of season we can't be that fussy. He didn't have a car either, so I've no record of any registration number.'

'How did he get here, then?'

'I asked him that when he arrived. He said he'd taken a bus to Bloxham and walked.'

'Did he tell you anything about himself? Where he came from?'

'No. He mentioned that he'd taken the bus from Plymouth. He didn't have a lot of luggage, only a rucksack. That's all, really.' She thought for a moment. 'He seemed a pleasant sort of bloke. Very well spoken . . . quite posh, really. He was young – in his twenties, I'd say. We don't usually let our caravans to young single men but he was on his own and he didn't look the type who'd get legless on a few pints of strong lager and come back here to cause trouble . . . not like some. As I said, he seemed nice. He wasn't smart, just dressed in jeans and a T-shirt. And he wasn't really the chatty type. He didn't say much.'

'Did he give his name and address?'

'He said he was in the middle of moving flats so there wasn't much point in giving an address. And his name was Jones . . . John Jones.'

'And he didn't say where he lived?'

'No. He never said where he came from and I never asked.'

Wesley nodded and was rewarded with another weak smile. The next question was one that he hardly liked to ask, but it was necessary.

'Would you or your husband be willing to have a look at the body; just to confirm it's the same man who rented the caravan?'

Dilys Fielding wrinkled her nose in distaste. 'I'll let Barry do that. I'd probably throw up.'

'That's all right, Mrs Fielding. We'll ask your husband. Are you sure this John Jones didn't say where he lived?'

'No. Definitely not. Mind you, come to think of it, he was a bit cagey. But nice . . . he seemed nice. Very polite.'

'What about payment? Cheque? Credit card?' said Wesley hopefully.

'Sorry, no. He paid in cash.' She swung round on her swivel chair and gave Wesley a shy smile. 'You're not from round these parts, then?'

'I transferred here from London about a year ago. My wife's from round here and . . .'

Dilys Fielding looked slightly disappointed at the mention of a wife. 'Do you like it here?'

'Yes.'

She sat forward as though she were about to share a confidence. 'I'd love to get out of this place and move to somewhere with a bit more life.'

'Why don't you?'

'Because my husband loves it here. He used to live in Manchester and couldn't wait to get out into the country. You always want what you don't have, I suppose,' she added philosophically.

'You could be right,' said Wesley. He sensed that the woman wanted to talk so he stood still, waiting, hoping that he could steer the conversation back to the dead man.

'You must be mad leaving London,' she said with a flirtatious smile. 'I'd love to be in the middle of everything.'

Wesley shook his head. 'It's not all it's cracked up to be, you know. Dr Johnson said that when a man is tired of London he is tired of life, but I can't say I agree with him.'

She looked Wesley in the eye. 'You should try clearing up after a load of holidaymakers in this place. Anywhere looks good if the only excitement you get is cleaning communal loos all day and taking a trip to the wholesalers in Plymouth to stock up the site shop.' There was bitterness in her voice. Dilys Fielding was a woman who was not content with her lot.

'Well, you've got some excitement now, I'm afraid.'

Dilys looked at him with half-closed eyes. 'Does this mean you're going to be around here a lot?' she asked hopefully.

'It's possible.'

'You'll have to tell me all about London, then.' Her voice was mildly suggestive. 'Perhaps when you're not doing whatever it is you do, I could take you to the Trawlerman's Arms down in Bloxham. They serve good crab sandwiches. Locally caught . . . the crab, I mean, not the sandwiches.' She smiled at him coquettishly.

Wesley, sensing he was being selected to provide a little excitement in this particular bored lady's life, decided that rapid retreat was the best course of action.

'Wes,' a voice called loudly from the neighbouring room. 'Have you finished in there or what?' Gerry Heffernan sounded impatient.

'Thank you, Mrs Fielding.'

'Oh, Dilys, please.'

'I really must get on.'

'Sergeant,' she called as Wesley was about to leave the room. 'I've just remembered something.'

Wesley took a deep breath and turned round. 'What is it?'

'John Jones. He came into the site shop a couple of days ago when I was serving. I remember because he bought a bottle of wine . . . only the cheap stuff, mind. He asked me about a place. Had I heard of

41

it; was it open to the public yet? It was a place that's been in all the local papers and even some of the nationals. Those lost gardens . . . oh, what are they called?'

'Earlsacre?' suggested Wesley tentatively.

'That's right. Earlsacre. He asked about Earlsacre.'

Chapter 4

*In 1685 the eighteen-year-old Richard Lantrist, younger son of
Sir John Lantrist of Earlsacre Hall, joined Charles II's
illegitimate son, the Duke of Monmouth, in his attempt to seize
the throne of England from King James II. Lantrist, like many
men of the West Country, was a fervent supporter of the
Protestant faith and feared than the King's Catholic inclinations
might lead the country back to Rome. Lantrist fought bravely at
the Battle of Sedgemoor in which many Devonshire men were
killed. He was captured and, although he escaped the gruesome
death sentence for treason so frequently and enthusiastically
handed down by the dreaded Judge Jeffreys, he was one of
almost a hundred and fifty men from Devon who were sent as
slaves to the West Indies. Fourteen years later Richard Lantrist
managed to return to Earlsacre, where he found that his father
and elder brother had died and that the estate was now his. He
married the daughter of a neighbouring landowner and lived an
uneventful life thereafter.*

> *From The Manor Houses of South Devon and Their Families*

SOCO had finished. The body of John Jones had been examined by
Colin Bowman, identified by Barry Fielding, and then whisked away
in a discreet black mortuary van.

'Right then, Wes,' said Gerry Heffernan as he stepped into the
caravan, scratching his tousled hair. 'Let's have a shufti at his things,
shall we? See what we can find out about Mr Jones . . . if that was
really his name.'

Wesley looked around. There was nothing he could see in the
caravan's living area that he would have described as personal. Most

things looked as if they belonged to the caravan: a portable TV, a radio, glasses, oatmeal-coloured crockery. Apart from a tin of beans and a loaf of bread, there was nothing that John Jones could have called his own.

They walked through to the bedroom, just large enough to squeeze in a double bed between the flimsy walls. Wesley glanced into the tiny bathroom on the way. There was nothing there apart from a toothbrush, toothpaste and a bar of pale green soap. Jones travelled light.

The bedroom told the same tale. A pair of denim jeans, a plain black T-shirt and a checked shirt – all common makes – were the only clothes hanging in the tiny wardrobe. Three pairs of socks and two pairs of grey underpants were stuffed in the bottom of an ageing rucksack. An electric razor lying on the bed and another pair of washed-out underpants beneath the duvet were the only other relics of the dead man.

'Is this all his stuff? Didn't have much, did he? Have all the cupboards been searched?'

'Yes, sir. There's nothing else here that seems to belong to him.'

Heffernan went over to the bedside drawer and opened it. 'No money, no credit cards, no identification of any kind. What do you make of it, Wes?'

Wesley thought for a moment. 'It's just an impression, but it's almost as if this man was trying to conceal his identity . . . or his killer was.'

'Any clues in his clothes?'

Wesley shook his head. 'Not that I can see. They're all common brands, available anywhere.' In spite of the fact that he was wearing plastic gloves, Wesley tentatively picked up the discarded underpants between his thumb and forefinger to look for a telltale label. 'Marks and Spencer,' he sighed. 'Seen better days – probably a few years old. I think our best hope is to look in all the nooks and crannies . . . somewhere he might have hidden his valuables, somewhere the killer wouldn't think to look, especially if he or she was in a hurry.'

Wesley stared at the bed, trying to think the dead man's thoughts. Caravans weren't the most secure of places – perhaps Jones had hidden his money and credit cards in some inaccessible crevice that hadn't yet been searched.

He flicked back the duvet, a thin type with a plain pale pink cover, Bloxham View provided bedding for their guests. When he and Pam had first holidayed in France they had stayed in a caravan, and they had hidden their passports and money underneath the mattress. It was a tactic probably well known to an experienced thief, but somehow it had given the young couple a sense of security, however unfounded. He recalled that holiday now, with its heady mix of red wine and new love, as he knelt down by the bed. A warm thought in a sad place.

He lifted the edge of the mattress and ran his hand underneath. His searching fingers made contact with paper. At first he thought he had discovered where the dead man had kept his cash. But as he drew the paper out, he realised it was far too thin to be money . . . and too large.

Gerry Heffernan watched impatiently as Wesley pulled the sheet of paper from its hiding place. 'Well, Wes, what is it? What have you found?'

Wesley placed it on the bed and unfolded it, smoothing it carefully. It was a page torn from a newspaper; one of the more middlebrow national tabloids. The page bore the date 15 August, just over two weeks ago. Wesley studied it, noting each story in turn. It was home news: a brutal murder in the Cotswolds; a keeper mauled to death at a zoo in the Midlands; a big rise in house prices in the southeast. But in the top right corner of the page was a black-and-white photograph of three men and a beautiful young woman with long dark hair. They were standing in front of some scaffolding, all smiling dutifully for the camera. The caption beneath read 'Members of the restoration team at the lost gardens of Earlsacre in South Devon pictured in front of the proposed new arts centre'. Wesley recognised two of the men: the trust Director, Martin Samuels, and Jake Weston the archaeologist. But the other man and the young woman were unfamiliar.

He began to read the short article aloud to Gerry Heffernan. 'Work on the important lost gardens of Earlsacre in South Devon continues as the team of experts and archaeologists hurry to beat their deadline ready for the official opening of the gardens in October. "An autumn opening and the completion of the main archaeological work give us the opportunity to prepare the gardens for a spectacular display next spring." Trust Director Martin Samuels (pictured above left) told our reporter that Earlsacre is a fascinating example of a rare Renaissance garden and many garden features still remain from the seventeenth century . . .'

'Like skeletons,' mumbled Heffernan. 'Carry on.'

Wesley took a deep breath and continued reading. 'Including an ornamental walled garden with a sixteenth-century gatehouse. Project historian Claire O'Farrell (pictured above right) said that there were still many exciting discoveries to be made about Earlsacre Hall's past. The work has been generously supported by the Simeon Foundation of the USA as well as by local people and the Department of Heritage. Martin Samuels and his team have additional reason for celebration as it has recently been confirmed that money from the National Lottery will go towards the restoration of Earlsacre Hall to create an arts centre.' Wesley looked up. 'That's all, sir. Just a standard article.'

'Maybe he kept it for something else on the page. What about this murder in the Cotswolds? Could he have been connected with that? Or maybe he planned to visit the zoo? Or wanted to buy a house in the south-east?'

Wesley pushed the sheet of newspaper towards the inspector. 'If you look carefully you'll see he's marked the article about Earlsacre ... see those pencil crosses? And Mrs Fielding said he asked her about Earlsacre. It seems he was taking quite an interest in the place.'

'But why, Wes? And why keep this tatty bit of newspaper under his mattress like something valuable?'

'Perhaps when we find out who he was we'll know the answer.'

Neil Watson rested on his spade. There was a chill in the air but digging was hot work. But he knew that it wouldn't be long now before they reached something interesting; the foundations of the structure that had stood against the east wall of Earlsacre's walled garden. But first the topsoil had to be removed from the marked-off trench and, as he suspected the remains lay close to the surface, Neil had rejected the idea of using a mechanical digger, which might damage any delicate finds. The geophysics results had been promising: the print-outs from the machines that measured the electrical resistance of the soil, giving a computer picture of what lay beneath, had shown the outline of a small square building, possibly a summerhouse or grotto built by some Lantrist of old to impress his neighbours. Hopefully they would soon find out.

He looked across at his colleague, Jane, a classy blonde in tattered jeans and a white shirt tied at the waist, and smiled. He had worked with Jane for over a year now. They knew each other's ways. But he harboured no romantic hopes: Jane's boyfriend, Matt, was working away over by the gatehouse.

'There's stone here. I think it could be the base of the wall,' said Jane, matter-of-factly. 'And look at all these seashells – loads of them.' She put down her spade, took a trowel from her tray, knelt down and began to scrape away at the earth.

Neil began to dig again, taking off the topsoil, expanding the trench to the limits he had marked out, until he too felt the hard resistance of stone against the spade. 'It's nearer the surface than we thought,' he said. 'Jake says there's a mention in the old records of a shell grotto. This could be it.'

Jane smiled and carried on, scraping away with her trowel until a small section of stone wall was clearly discernible, surrounded by a carpet of tumbled shells. Neil too scraped away to reveal his portion of wall. Things were going well. He was just contemplating asking Jake if he could spare any of the volunteers to help with the digging when he heard a scuffling at the side of the trench.

'Hi. Are you Neil Watson?'

Neil looked up to see where the female voice with the slight Irish accent was coming from. Then, feeling at a disadvantage, he scrambled to his feet, not taking his eyes off the pretty young woman with long black hair and sapphire-blue eyes who stood at the edge of his trench, smiling.

'Sorry if I startled you. I'm Claire O'Farrell, the project historian. I thought we might be able to help each other out.' Her smile widened, revealing a set of perfect white teeth.

Neil, uncharacteristically flustered, wiped his soil-stained hand on his T-shirt and held it out to Claire. 'Er . . . this is Jane. She's with the County Archaeological Unit too, and there's Matt; he's working on the gatehouse trench.' Jane raised a hand and smiled at the newcomer.

'You lot have arrived just in time,' said Claire. 'The deadlines the trust set were a bit ambitious for Jake to cope with, if you ask me.' She paused, still smiling. 'I hear that one of the policemen who came about our skeletons is a friend of yours.'

'Yeah . . . Wes Peterson. We were at uni together.'

'So how come he joined the police? Did he drop out or something?'

Neil shook his head. 'On the contrary. Our Wes got a first. I thought he'd go on to do postgraduate work but he surprised us all and joined the forces of oppression. Don't ask me why. Mind you, he was always addicted to those Sherlock Holmes books. And they do say that inside every archaeologist there's a detective struggling to get out, don't they? And his granddad was some sort of high-up detective in Trinidad, so that might have had something to do with it. He's okay is Wes . . . useful man to have around.'

Claire smiled coyly. 'So you're a bit of a detective yourself, then?'

'I've had my moments,' Neil said modestly, studying his feet.

There was an awkward pause, then Claire broke the silence. 'Have you seen where I work yet?'

'Can't say I have.'

'I've some maps and prints that you might be interested in. They show the gardens at different stages in their history. You'll probably find them useful. And there are documents too. I haven't had time to go through them all yet but some of them date back to the late sixteenth century.'

'Where did you find them?'

'A family called Wilton bought the place in 1946. It had been used as a base for US troops during the war, and when they moved in there were loads of wooden huts down by what's now the cricket pitch. In fact I think the pavilion there is the last remaining one. Anyway, the Wiltons took a great interest in the place and did it up. They also acquired lots of papers connected with the estate. They sold it in 1965 but somehow they kept the papers. Which is great for me because the family has been very helpful and allowed me free access to them. There's loads . . . all fascinating stuff.'

Their eyes met. 'Great,' muttered Neil, lost for words.

'I've just been looking at an old painting of the garden that someone's brought in to me. It shows a shell grotto quite clearly . . . like a stone summerhouse covered in thousands of seashells. As you seem to be digging on that spot, would it help you to see what it looked like in all its glory?' She inclined her head to one side, a smile playing around her lips.

'Yeah. Great,' said Neil, aware that he was repeating himself.

'Come on, then. I'll show you where I work.'

Claire turned and began to walk in the direction of the stable block. Neil followed, gazing at her glossy black hair, which tumbled down her back.

A few minutes later they were leaning over an eighteenth-century oil painting laid flat on the long trestle table in Claire's office, their shoulders touching. Neil found it difficult to concentrate on the painted scene before him: his senses were distracted by the faint herbal smell of Claire's shampoo, by the stray strand of hair that touched his cheek, by her very presence. At that moment Neil Watson's mind was straying from the subject of history.

But he forced himself to look down at the picture. Earlsacre Hall stood proudly in the centre of the canvas surrounded by a patchwork of gardens, one seemingly leading into another. But it was the garden directly in front of the hall, the walled garden, which drew Neil's attention. The gatehouse stood out, large and prominent. The original building was quite substantial, with a room on either side of the central arch; the present gatehouse was a shadow of its former self. Standing against the east wall adjoining the water garden was something that looked like a square stone-built summerhouse. The shell grotto – at least he now knew what he was excavating. His eyes travelled upwards to the centre of the walled garden. There, among the elaborate parterres and paths, stood what looked like a sundial, a skeleton globe set on a stone pillar. Below it was what looked like a large plinth.

'What date is this painting?' asked Neil.

'It's there in the corner: 1745.'

Neil could feel his face redden as he mentally kicked himself. Why hadn't he noticed the date? It was there, clear enough, by the artist's signature.

'So we know our skeletons must have died before then,' he said, trying to redeem himself. 'There's the plinth. Look.'

'Couldn't it have been moved?' Claire thought for a second. 'No, I don't suppose it could. It was exactly on that spot and it took a dozen men to lift it. I think you're right. If we can find the date that plinth was put there then we've probably found the date of the burial. You'll have heard that one of them was buried alive, I suppose?'

'Yeah. Nasty.'

Claire looked at him challengingly. 'How much do you know about the history of this place, then?'

'I was hoping you'd tell me,' said Neil eagerly. This was his chance.

Claire took two tattered paperback books off a makeshift shelf supported by bricks and handed them to him. 'Here you are. *The Manor Houses of South Devon and Their Families* and *Jacob Finsbury's Account of His Travels around the Houses of England.*

The first just gives you the plain facts and the second was written at the beginning of the eighteenth century by an old gossip who travelled from house to house freeloading off the local gentry. There's quite a large section on Earlsacre. He seemed to be quite taken with the place . . . or taken with Lady Lantrist, reading between the lines,' she added mischievously. 'He also mentions strange goings-on, which is rather pertinent in the light of what's been found in the walled garden. Take them home and read them. Enjoy.'

Neil clutched the volumes to his chest. 'Thanks.'

'I've got loads of old documents to go through. If I find anything exciting, I'll let you know. I've a feeling that somewhere among this lot there must be something that'll tell us who those skeletons belonged to and how they ended up where they did.' She gave him a shy smile which he returned.

Neil backed out of the room, still clutching the books, not taking his eyes off Claire. 'Thanks,' he muttered. 'Er . . . see you later.'

He walked back to the gatehouse, hardly aware of his surroundings, still holding the books close against his body. He would read them tonight . . . and absorb every precious word.

The investigation into the death of John Jones had begun. Everyone on the caravan site was being interviewed but so far nobody had admitted to seeing anything suspicious. The computer was consulted as ancient Greeks once consulted their oracle. The description of the dead man was circulated to other forces in an attempt to discover whether he matched any missing persons on their books. The post-mortem was booked for first thing in the morning.

Wesley watched as his boss paced up and down his office like a caged rhinoceros. In some brave new scientific world some time in the next century, forensic reports, fingerprint matches and feedback from inquiries might be instantaneous. But things didn't move that fast in Tradmouth CID . . . and Gerry Heffernan might have his share of virtues, but patience wasn't one of them.

At half past six Heffernan came to the conclusion that there was nothing more to be done that night and they should all go home and get some rest in preparation for a busy weekend. Steve slunk off to the gents, anticipating a night out on the tiles of Morbay, and Rachel made a quiet exit. Wesley guessed that she was indulging in more heart-searching about her turbulent love life. But that, he told himself firmly, was none of his business.

50

'I suppose this means my debut on the cricket field is cancelled,' he said as Gerry Heffernan perched his large backside on the edge of his desk with an ominous creak.

'On the contrary, Wes. I think we should take every opportunity to lurk around Earlsacre and indulge in a spot of espionage. You're playing the local village team, right?'

Wesley nodded.

'Well, talk to them; mention the case. See if you get any sort of reaction. Why was this John Jones so interested in Earlsacre? There must have been a reason.'

'Perhaps he was just into old gardens. Some people are.'

'No, Wes. There's a connection there – I can feel it in my water. And don't worry about this cricket match: I'll be there on the boundary cheering you on.'

'Great,' said Wesley. That was all he needed.

'And don't forget you've got that date with Brian Willerby.'

'How could I forget?'

'Now don't be like that, Wesley. We've got to keep in with our legal friends.' Heffernan grinned wickedly. 'But rather you than me, eh? I don't know what his cricket playing's like, but the man could bore for England.'

He chuckled as he lumbered back into his office and reached for the shapeless jacket that hung on the coatstand in the corner. 'I'm off now, Wes,' he called out cheerfully. 'Choir practice tonight. Getting ready for harvest festival.'

'Already?'

'Unlike our forensic department, our choirmaster doesn't believe in hanging about. If there's no word from forensic by lunch-time tomorrow, chase them up, will you, Wes. And why don't you knock off and get home for a square meal and a bit of marital bliss while you've still got the chance,' he concluded ominously.

Wesley opened his mouth to speak, to tell his boss that there wasn't much chance of marital bliss that evening as Della was descending on them with lover boy in tow. But Heffernan had already breezed out of the office, singing a snatch from Haydn's *Creation* in a rich baritone voice.

Detective Constable Steve Carstairs had stayed behind at Tradmouth police station on the pretext of finishing off some reports. But his true motives were carnal. There was one of the civilian staff, a young typist in the CID office, he'd been planning to make a move on for several weeks. Her name was Jackie and she had shoulder-length red hair. She lived in Morbay, not far from his own flat . . . and he had heard through the station grapevine that her car was currently in for repair. As his mother had always said, you've got to make the most of your opportunities.

He strolled over to her desk and perched on the edge. 'I hear your car's out of action. You live near me, don't you? If you've finished for the day, how about I give you a lift home?'

Jackie looked up with a simpering smile. He was good-looking, she thought. A bit on the macho side, but then he was a copper. And she didn't like the way that stuck-up Rachel Tracey treated him, like he was some kind of idiot. Jackie had been annoyed when her gearbox had given up the ghost. But every cloud has a silver lining, so they said. 'Thanks,' she said breathlessly. 'That'd be great. Saves me waiting around for the bus.'

Jackie's delight increased when she saw the gleaming red Escort XR3i that awaited her in the station carpark. She climbed into the passenger seat, pulling down her short skirt with last-minute modesty. Steve took the wheel confidently, drove, too fast, out of the gates, and pointed the car towards the main road out of town.

They were passing the memorial park when an old man almost stumbled in front of the car. Steve let out a string of foul expletives and earned himself a dirty look from his companion.

'Stop,' she said with determination.

Steve put his foot on the brake pedal, causing the car behind to sound its horn. 'What is it?'

'That old man. I want to see if he's all right.'

Steve swore again under his breath but parked the car. He could see the old man in his rear-view mirror. He was leaning against the park railings looking decidedly ill. Steve leaned on the wheel impatiently. He'd let Jackie do the good Samaritan bit if she wanted: he was having nothing to do with it.

'Well, come on. Aren't you getting out?' she asked shrilly.

Steve got out of the car slowly and followed Jackie to where the elderly man was standing. He was dressed in respectable tweeds. His silver hair was neatly cut. This was no tramp. Perhaps Jackie had a point after all. But even if she did, Steve wanted to get going.

'That's very kind of you, my dear. Most kind. I'm afraid I just had a little dizzy turn. Nothing to worry about. It's probably because I haven't eaten. I lost my wallet, you see. No money. And my credit cards are gone as well. It's very foolish. I don't know whether it's been stolen or whether I've just left it somewhere.' He was well spoken and, as far as Jackie could judge, genuinely distressed.

'You reported it to the police?'

'Yes, but the officer I spoke to wasn't very optimistic.' The man put a hand to his head and closed his eyes. 'Oh dear. I'm sorry to be such a nuisance. All my money was in the wallet, you see, and I've arranged to travel back up to my home in Manchester tonight. The train tickets were in the wallet too. And the banks are shut now. My daughter's meeting me at the station. I really don't know what to do.'

Jackie opened her handbag and took out her purse. 'I can give you ten pounds. I'm sorry, but that's all I've got. That'll get you something to eat.'

The elderly man looked embarrassed. 'Oh, I couldn't possibly.'

'No, take it. I insist.' She pressed the note into his hand.

'That's really most kind of you. Have you any paper to write down your address? I'll repay the money as soon as I get home. I'll let you have my address too. How about that?'

'It's really not necessary.'

'No, I insist. Although it might be a while before I get this mess sorted out and get back home. I've nowhere to stay, you see, and . . .'

Jackie turned to Steve, who'd been standing with his hands in his pockets, paying no particular attention to her charitable act. All he wanted to do was to get back to Morbay and test the waters where Jackie was concerned. He glanced at his watch and hoped she wouldn't take much longer.

'Steve? How much money have you got on you?'

He looked at her apprehensively. Did she mean what he thought she meant? 'About eighty quid. Why?'

She turned to the elderly man, who was busy scribbling his name and address on the back of Jackie's slimline diary. 'Would eighty pounds be enough to buy you a train ticket?'

'Oh, I couldn't possibly . . .'

'Of course you could. Your daughter's meeting you, isn't she? She'll be expecting you. You can send us the money as soon as you get back.' She turned to Steve with an outstretched hand. 'Come on, Steve, hand it over. This gentleman's need is greater than yours and it's only for a couple of days.'

Steve was about to tell the man to get lost. But then he looked at Jackie's expectant face. If he failed this test, he'd stand no chance. But if he impressed her with his generosity, he was on a definite promise. Slowly, trying his best to hide his reluctance, he opened his wallet and handed over four crisp twenty-pound notes.

The man seemed overwhelmed. There were embryonic tears of gratitude in his eyes. 'Thank you. Oh, that's so kind. I never expected . . . I'll repay it as soon as I can, of course.' He looked Steve in the eye. 'May I have your address, young man? I promise I'll send you the money as soon as I get home. Would a cheque be all right?'

Steve nodded, lost for words.

'Thank you,' said the old man gushingly, stuffing the notes in his trouser pocket. 'God bless you for your kindness. I'll repay you as soon as I get back to Manchester, I promise . . . and I'll let you have my address, of course. If I get home tonight I can put cheques in the post tomorrow. You should get them at the beginning of next week.' He grabbed Steve's hand and shook it heartily. 'Thank you,' he said for the last time before walking unsteadily off in the direction of the bus stop.

'Hang on,' called Jackie. 'Are you catching the train from Morbay? We can give you a lift if you like.'

The man hesitated. 'I really couldn't impose on you any more . . .'

'It's no trouble. Get into the car.'

Steve was silent as they drove to Morbay. The man and Jackie chatted pleasantly. It was only when she announced that Steve was a detective constable that the conversation flagged a little. They dropped him off at the railway station, his thanks and his promises to repay the money still ringing in their ears.

'It's nice to be able to help someone, isn't it?' said Jackie sentimentally when they were alone.

'Mmm,' replied Steve, unconvinced. 'Fancy coming to my place? It's Friday night. We can get a takeaway and have a drink . . . maybe go on to a club. What do you say?'

'Sorry, Steve, but I've arranged to meet my boyfriend later. But thanks for the offer,' she added as they drew up at her flat.

'Shit,' said Steve under his breath as he watched Jackie open her front door, promising himself that that would be the last time he would do anyone a good turn.

*

Gerry Heffernan took a leisurely stroll home to his small, white-washed cottage at the end of the cobbled quayside four minutes' walk from the police station.

A few holidaymakers straggled along the cobbles; middle-aged and elderly couples, not the families with young children who had swarmed there in the height of the tourist season, catching large crabs in small buckets at high tide. The late-season visitors were content to sit quietly on the wooden benches provided and admire the picturesque view across the wide River Trad. Unlike the noisy crabbing kids, these late, contemplative tourists caused Heffernan no disturbance.

The sun hung low in the sky, its rays catching on the sails of the yachts making stately progress up the river. Gerry Heffernan stood there for a while and breathed in the salty air. He gazed across the water to where his beloved yacht, the *Rosie May*, bobbed on the water, and felt a wave of proprietorial pride. He would take her out over the weekend and sail round the headland. For Heffernan, sailing banished any number of cobwebs and helped him to think. He breathed the salty air, taking slow, deep breaths. If it wasn't for the fact that September was the fourth anniversary of his wife, Kathy's, death, summer's back end would be his favourite time of year.

He took his key from his pocket and opened his front door. As he stepped inside the house the silence was almost tangible. Until last week his son, Sam, had been there, home from university in Liverpool. But now he had gone back up to his father's native city to catch up with some work for his veterinary course and to search for somewhere to live next term. Heffernan missed him; he missed the company and the life the young man had brought to the place. He sat down at the baby grand piano in the middle of the living room and began to pick out the melody of a Chopin nocturne, one of Kathy's favourites.

But just as he felt the first stinging discomfort in his eyes that heralded the imminent arrival of an unwelcome tear, the telephone rang. He rushed to answer it, to have contact with another human being.

The voice on the other end of the line made Gerry Heffernan smile again. 'You're back,' he said, trying to suppress his delight. 'How was the States? Do you fancy coming to a cricket match tomorrow?'

The answer was affirmative. Susan Green, widow of the parish of Stokeworthy, was back from visiting her sister in Boston and had agreed to accompany Gerry Heffernan to Earlsacre to witness Wesley's debut on the cricket field.

He had first met Susan several months earlier, when her next-door neighbour had been murdered, and since then they had shared the occasional visit to a country pub or restaurant. He had just been getting to know her when she had disappeared off to her native USA. Perhaps they would see more of each other now that she was back. But, whatever the future held, Susan's call had raised his spirits. After he had put the phone down, he was surprised to find he was singing to himself as he trotted into the kitchen to make himself something to eat.

In his single, merchant navy days – before Kathy had lured him ashore to join the police force in Tradmouth – Heffernan had become a useful cook. But it was no fun cooking for one, so he prepared and ate a humble supper of beans on toast before heading down the narrow, restaurant-lined streets of Tradmouth towards the medieval church of St Margaret.

He slowed down as he neared the church, and began to sing to himself softly, trying to remember the bass part of Haydn's 'The Heavens Are Telling'. By the time he reached the church porch he thought he had got it spot on.

Pam Peterson was feeling harassed. There was a lasagne in the oven. Nothing fancy: she didn't want to set a precedent. Her mother and Jamie would have to take them as they found them. After all, Della had invited herself, so what could she expect. All these justifications whirled round in Pam's head as she peeped into the oven at the lasagne which looked sadly inadequate for four healthy adults.

The doorbell rang – two sharp rings which made Pam drop her oven gloves.

'I'll go,' Wesley called from the hallway. His voice sounded tired, unenthusiastic. He had just embarked on a murder investigation and Pam knew that that meant long disruptive hours and a husband whose mind was elsewhere. She just hoped her mother wouldn't overstay her already shaky welcome.

Wesley opened the door suspecting that his welcoming smile had turned into more of a snarl as he watched Della flounce in wearing a pair of gigantic silver earrings and a skirt that was just a little too short for her years. Following her was a tall, distinguished-looking man. He was dressed in a smart suit with a buttoned-up shirt and no tie, and his steel-grey hair was swept back in a neat ponytail.

Pam came through into the hall and stood with her arm linked through Wesley's, waiting expectantly for an introduction.

'This is Jamie,' Della gushed. 'Jamie, this is my lovely daughter, Pamela, and this is her husband, Wesley.' She winked shamelessly at her son-in-law, who feared they were in for a long night.

Wesley led the way into the living room with a fixed smile on his face, wondering if things could get worse. As Pam hurried back into the bowels of the kitchen, he poured four glasses of the wine Jamie had brought. He stole a surreptitious look at the label. It was good stuff: better than the supermarket special offers he and Pam downed after a hard day's work.

'So, Wesley,' Jamie began. He smiled, a charming smile that didn't spread to his eyes. Wesley tried to guess what he was thinking, but couldn't. 'I hear you're a policeman . . . CID.' He had a smooth, deep voice; easy to listen to; persuasive.

'That's right,' Wesley answered, studying Jamie's face for signs of discomfort. But there were none, not even the uneasiness many law-abiding citizens experience in the presence of a police officer.

'Much crime around here?' asked Jamie.

'There's crime everywhere. And crime in rural areas is on the increase, I'm sorry to say.'

Jamie smiled again. 'One of the more undesirable aspects of this modern age, I suppose.'

'I expect the criminally inclined, like the poor, have always been with us,' answered Wesley, wondering how he could change the subject. He didn't relish the prospect of an evening spent discussing the constabulary's crime figures. 'Are you from round here?' he asked.

'I moved down from Leeds a year ago. I fancied a change of scenery and this really is a lovely part of the world.' Jamie rearranged his legs, looking completely relaxed on the sofa beside Della, who had placed her hand on his arm proprietorially. He smiled at her – the type of smile one gives a pet or a small child.

'Why don't you tell Wesley about your work, darling?'

'I'm sure he wouldn't be interested,' Jamie said quickly.

'Don't be so modest. He's ever so clever, Wesley. He's advised me to take all my money out of the scrappy old savings account where it was earning practically nothing and invest it in these shares. I don't know anything about it, of course. Jamie's the expert.'

'What shares are these, Jamie?' asked Wesley, trying to sound casual.

The smile appeared again as Jamie shuffled his feet awkwardly, avoiding Wesley's eyes.

But before he could answer they were interrupted by Pam calling from the kitchen with the vital news that the dinner was on the table getting cold. Wesley detected an edge of panic in her voice. He picked up Pam's glass of wine along with his own to take through to the dining room, and Jamie and Della followed him, arm in arm. Wesley caught Pam's eye and smiled reassuringly as they sat down, noting that she had used the small plates for the lasagne and thinking that he would have to fill up on the cheese and biscuits later.

It was almost ten o'clock when Gerry Heffernan stepped out of the porch of St Margaret's church into the chilly night. As his mind was on the music, he almost missed seeing the man who was scurrying along the pavement opposite. In fact if Brian Willerby had looked less guilty he might well not have noticed him at all. But the solicitor was treading softly, looking from left to right furtively like a striped-jerseyed burglar in a silent film. Heffernan slipped back into the shadows of the church porch and watched.

Willerby seemed to hesitate before knocking on the glossy black front door of the pink-washed terraced house directly opposite the church. There was no answer and after half a minute he knocked again, glancing round anxiously.

At last the front door opened slightly, then wider to admit the solicitor, who slipped swiftly inside. Gerry Heffernan, his curiosity aroused, strained to see who had answered the door. But it was no use. Whoever it was had stood well back so as not to be seen by any passer-by.

Heffernan once more stepped out of the porch of St Margaret's church. The melody of 'The Heavens Are Telling' had completely gone from his mind, which was now turning over what he had seen, rejecting one fantastic speculation after another. Brian Willerby had looked like a very worried man, and Heffernan wondered what he was so anxious to discuss with Wesley. The possibilities occupied his mind that night until he finally fell into a deep, dreamless sleep.

'Good morning, gentlemen. Lovely morning.' Colin Bowman stood at the entrance to the post-mortem room, grinning genially in his

green gown and plastic apron. 'You're in for the matinée performance, I take it. You're just in time for curtain up. Come and take your
places in the stalls, if you please.'

Wesley Peterson and Gerry Heffernan exchanged looks. It was
8.45 in the morning. Far too early for this sort of thing. Wesley
wondered, not for the first time, how Colin Bowman managed to stay
so cheerful. It must be something to do with not having living
patients burdening him with their troubles and ills. Wesley had never
known his own parents and sister – all doctors who dealt with the
living – to be so jovial early in the morning.

He himself felt a little the worse for wear. Della and Jamie had
stayed till midnight the previous evening, overstaying their welcome
by a good hour. Since Michael's birth, sleep had become a precious
commodity and, once ten o'clock had passed, he had struggled to
hide his irritation at the fact that Della could be so inconsiderate. That
morning he had left Pam and the baby asleep. Now he was trying
hard to keep his own eyes open.

A few minutes later Colin was studying the body of the mystery
man. Naked there on the table, he looked thinner than he had done in
the caravan and, now that they could see his features clearly in the
strong light, much younger, more vulnerable.

As Colin recorded his observations into a suspended microphone
before making the first incision into the pale flesh, Wesley stared at
the body, willing it to give up its secrets. In a moment, when the
cutting began, he would look away as he always did. He had had no
inclination to follow the rest of the family into a medical career; he
hadn't the stomach for it.

But Gerry Heffernan had no such qualms. He chatted away
cheerfully as the pathologist went about his gruesome tasks. 'So what
do you reckon, Colin?' he asked as Bowman began to stitch up the
body.

'Well, I can't give you a definitive answer without the usual tests,
Gerry, but my preliminary findings are that he's a well-nourished
male in his mid-twenties, five feet eleven inches tall, no visible scars
or tattoos, and healthy until someone stuck a knife in his back. He
was killed with something that's probably like your common-or-
garden chef's knife about a foot long, and he was stabbed twice.
There was no sign of sexual activity prior to death and the assailant
was right-handed and would have ended up with blood-spattered
clothing.'

'Was much force used? Could a woman have done it?' asked Heffernan.

'I'd say a woman could have done it, yes,' said Bowman, staring down at the body. 'He had been dead approximately forty-eight hours when he was found, which means he died, say, Tuesday night or early Wednesday morning. I can't say for certain. I'm afraid that's all I can give you so far.'

He paused, staring at the body. 'There is one thing that might be relevant. There seem to be some threads caught in the wounds; I'll send them off for analysis. It's my guess that he was wearing something when he was stabbed, a T-shirt say. The killer must have removed it after death. Interesting?'

Wesley nodded. 'Might be.'

Heffernan shuffled his feet, as keen as Wesley to be out of the post-mortem room. 'Thanks, Colin. Let us have the other test results as soon as you can, won't you.'

'Have I ever let you down, Gerry? When I've cleaned myself up, do you fancy a coffee?'

There was nothing the two policemen would have liked better, but there was work to be done. When they had said their farewells they walked back to the police station in amicable silence, each preoccupied with his own thoughts about the young man lying in the mortuary.

When they reached Heffernan's office they found a pile of crisp new reports on his desk. The inspector picked them up with the glee of a child opening a Christmas parcel. 'Here they are, Wes. Just what we've been waiting for.' He plonked himself down in his swivel chair, which gave an ominous groan. Wesley sat himself down in the office's other chair and awaited the verdict.

'No matches with the dead man's fingerprints, which means he's not been one of our loyal customers. The pattern of the bloodstains confirms what Colin said. He was stabbed from behind, probably when he was standing by that bench seat next to where he was found. He might have been reaching up to get something from the cupboards above. And someone had gone round and done a good job of wiping the place of fingerprints around the living area and the caravan door. The rest of the caravan hadn't been cleaned up so we can assume that the murderer only got as far as the living area.'

'Or the killer wore gloves to search the rest of the caravan. As we didn't find anything to identify the victim I think it's likely that the place must have been searched thoroughly. Which means he – or she – had come prepared. It was all planned.'

Heffernan nodded. Wesley's theory made sense. 'Anyway, another set of fingerprints was found in the living area.' He grinned, as though he were about to reveal some tantalising secret. 'And guess who they belong to.'

'I give up, sir. Who do they belong to?' said Wesley obligingly.

'Only Craig Kettering. A lad who's been a loyal customer of ours ever since his first appearance at the youth court. Burglary and petty theft are his specialities. There's a rumour going round the canteen that he's been seen delivering pizzas. Useful cover for a burglar, eh? Gives a whole new meaning to the word takeaway.'

'So he might have been trying his luck at the caravan park and stumbled on the body,' said Wesley, catching on quickly. 'Do you think it was him who reported it?'

'It fits. Knowing Craig as I do, I can see that he'd prefer to remain anonymous when dealing with the local constabulary. Let's go and have a word with him, eh.' He looked at his watch. 'He'll still be asleep. We'll give him an alarm call in half an hour, shall we?'

'Whatever you say. Is there anything else in that forensic report?' Wesley stifled an unexpected yawn.

Heffernan shook his head. 'Nothing of any importance.'

'We know Craig Kettering was at the scene but you seem to have ruled him out for the actual murder?'

'I've known Craig since his first caution. Murder's hardly his style. Go and look him up on the computer and tell me if you agree. I think he just found the body while he was on his rounds, as it were.'

Wesley returned to his desk and called up Craig Kettering's details on his screen. Gerry Heffernan was right. Craig was a petty thief with no history of violence. Even when he was once cornered by an irate shopkeeper, he had waited patiently in a storeroom for the police to arrive and had come quietly. He was a model villain: stabbing a stranger in the back, as the inspector had said, just wasn't his style at all.

As he stared at the computer screen, Wesley remembered something. He had promised himself that he would check Jamie's name, just to make sure that Della wasn't consorting with anybody undesirable like a mass murderer, an armed robber . . . or a fraudster. All through the previous evening he had had a nagging feeling that something wasn't quite right about the man, but he hadn't been able to pinpoint exactly what. But knowing Della, he thought, a colour-fully criminal past might prove attractive in a man: might give her added kudos in the sociology department, where she taught. There was no accounting for the way his mother-in-law's mind worked. He tapped out the name James Delmann and waited.

But there was no match for the name. James Delmann had led a tediously virtuous life – either that or Delmann wasn't his real name. He had claimed to come from Leeds. He wondered whether he should get on to the Leeds police and see if they knew of anyone answering Jamie's description defrauding unsuspecting widows in their area. But then he rebuked himself. He had found James Delmann too smooth by half – but perhaps he was just prejudiced against the silkily confident. Or maybe his work in the police force was making him too suspicious. He would report back to Pam that all was well and that her mother wasn't in immediate danger of rape, murder or robbery.

'Got a minute, Sarge?'

Wesley looked up to see Steve Carstairs standing there, shifting awkwardly from foot to foot.

'Yes, Steve. What is it?' He pressed a key and wiped James Delmann's name from the computer screen.

'I've been through all the statements from the people staying in the caravans near the dead man's,' Steve said, avoiding Wesley's eyes. 'Nobody saw nothing. But a woman in a caravan in the next row thought she heard raised voices late on Tuesday night . . . around one in the morning, she said.' He put a pile of papers on the desk.

'Thanks. It might be worth having a word with her to see if she can tell us anything else. When's she due to leave the site?'

Steve looked at him blankly.

'When does her holiday finish? When's she going home?' Wesley did his best to hide his impatience.

'I think she said Monday,' Steve mumbled, his hands in the pockets of his expensive leather jacket.

'Well, why don't you get over there now and see if you can have another word with her. Find out exactly what she heard.' Steve turned to go. 'Take Paul Johnson with you. Okay?' PC Johnson was a sensible, if spotty, young constable on secondment to CID. Wesley could rely on him to provide a steadying influence.

As Steve left the office, jangling the keys to his precious Escort XR3i ostentatiously, Rachel came over and perched herself on

Wesley's desk. 'How's it going?' she whispered, leaning towards him. 'Steve doesn't get any easier, does he? I've heard rumours that he wants to apply to join the Met.'

'That's all the Met needs,' said Wesley. 'As if they don't have enough problems. I shouldn't have thought he'd want to leave his home comforts. Am I right in thinking he has a flat in Morbay and his mum comes in and does all his cleaning and washing?'

'That's right. No wonder he thinks women are there for his convenience. How did the post-mortem go?'

'How do post-mortems ever go? Unpleasant. The victim was stabbed twice in the back and it's possible the murderer went through the place taking anything that would identify the victim and wiping away any incriminating fingerprints. It seems he or she was efficient.'

'So we've drawn a blank?'

'It's early days but the boss and I are going to have a chat with Craig Kettering. His fingerprints were found at the scene and the boss has a theory that he's the one who found the body and made the anonymous phone call. We'll see if he's right.'

'What do you think?'

'I don't know. But I suspect there might be some connection with a place called Earlsacre. He asked the woman who owned the caravan park about it and we found a newspaper cutting about it under his mattress. It's an historic garden that's being restored. Neil's working on it.'

'Is he indeed?' said Rachel significantly. She had met Neil, had seen how Wesley's old friend could reawaken his interest in archaeological mysteries at the siren drop of a trowel. She didn't see the appeal in dead dusty ruins herself, but Wesley seemed to find them fascinating, so she tried to take a polite interest. 'What do they need an archaeologist in a garden for?' she asked, puzzled.

'They're excavating the seventeenth-century garden that's buried under the present one. They've discovered lots of things – paths, buildings, flower-beds . . . couple of skeletons.' He grinned.

'So I suppose you'll be seizing every opportunity to get down there.'

'Not at all. If I go to Earlsacre it'll be strictly in the line of duty,' Wesley said convincingly. 'Apart from this afternoon, of course.'

'What's happening this afternoon?'

'Bob Naseby's cricket match: the Divisional XI versus Earlsacre Village XI. He's persuaded me to play, but when he sees how bad I am he won't ask me again,' he said with fragile confidence.

'Oh, Wesley, I'm surprised at you, I really am. You realise your weekends won't be your own now?'

Wesley looked at her, unable to work out whether she was joking or not.

'So you're not coming down to cheer us on, then?'

Her lips tightened. 'I lost a boyfriend to the cricket field once. Every spare moment he spent there. If it wasn't interminable matches it was practising in something called "the nets". Just watch it, that's all. Cricket's an addiction like any other.'

'I'll remember.' Their eyes met and Rachel began to smile. 'How are things at the farm?' Wesley asked. 'How's Dave?'

The smile disappeared. 'Okay.' She changed the subject, probably deliberately, Wesley thought, and waved a piece of paper she was holding in front of his nose. 'I was coming to show you this. There have been another two reports of an old man borrowing money from tourists which they never see again . . . one in Morbay and one in Bloxham. Same description and same MO. I think he's almost certainly obtaining money by deception.'

'That's all we need.'

Gerry Heffernan lumbered out of his office. 'Right, Wes. Let's go and give Craig Kettering his wake-up call, shall we?'

Rachel touched Wesley's hand gently. 'See you later.'

'See you later,' mumbled Wesley as he watched Rachel Tracey walk back to her desk.

Still half asleep and dressed in a not-so-fetching ensemble of grubby off-white T-shirt and faded boxer shorts, Craig Kettering opened the peeling front door of the large Edwardian terraced house wide to let the two officers in. He greeted Gerry Heffernan with a grunt and looked Wesley up and down with curiosity before leading the way up the uncarpeted stairs to his small bed-sit on the top floor. In the days when Morbay was the last word in seaside respectability the building would have housed a comfortably-off bourgeois family complete with loyal servants and distinguished paterfamilias. But now, along with the seaside resort, it had come down in the world and was divided into six non-too-salubrious bed-sits. The cream gloss paint on the banisters, once crisp and clean, had been chipped away over the years to reveal the dark wood beneath. The floors of the hallway and landings were covered in ancient linoleum, the pattern of which was too worn or dirty to make out.

Craig's bed-sit wasn't much better than the rest of the house. A cheap, badly fitted cord carpet covered the floor and a small kitchen area in one corner was half hidden by a greasy curtain of uncertain design. There was no bathroom: presumably he had to share.

Gerry Heffernan sat down on the grey-sheeted unmade bed which reminded Wesley of an unsavoury exhibit in an avant-garde art exhibition – only this one was for real.

'We just called to say thanks,' began Heffernan cheerfully.

Craig stood there with his mouth open. He was an unprepossessing youth with lank, mousey hair and a bad complexion. Wesley caught a whiff of body odour and found himself wondering whether he'd fancy eating a pizza handled by anybody so cavalier with his personal hygiene.

'What do you mean?' Craig asked nervously after a few moments.

'For the tip-off. The body you discovered in the caravan. We found it all right. Got it to the mortuary, did all the tests. Did you know it was murder?'

Craig's face froze in a mask of horror. 'Murder?' he squeaked.

'Yeah. He was stabbed. Didn't you see?'

'I just saw there was a lot of blood . . . and he had no clothes on his top half. I sort of touched him, like. He was cold so I knew he was dead. Look, it's got nothing to do with me. I never done nothing,' Craig pleaded, willing them to believe him.

'So what were you doing there, Craig? Charity work? Bringing hot soup to the poor . . . or hot pizzas?'

'Yeah.' Craig seized on the suggestion as a way out. 'That's right. I were delivering a pizza. Got the wrong caravan.'

'We can check, Craig,' said Heffernan quietly. 'Try again.'

'Okay, Mr Heffernan, I'll come clean. I were out looking for stuff. But I never found nothing.' He looked at Wesley as if pleading for back-up. 'Honest. On my mother's life I never took nothing. And I didn't break and enter. That caravan door was open . . . unlocked. I just opened the door and went inside and then I saw . . . well, you know what I saw. Look, I never done nothing.'

'Okay, Craig. But you know we'll have to question you down at the station, don't you?'

Craig nodded, resigned to his fate. Although the person who finds a body is often the first suspect, somehow Wesley couldn't see the rather pathetic youth standing before him as a vicious killer, even though he sensed that there was something he was trying to hide. But sometimes appearances could be deceptive.

Chapter 5

I find Sir Richard's wife to be a handsome woman and amiable and so much younger in years than her husband.

One evening when her husband seemed to be in an ill humour she walked with me to the walled garden after we had taken supper. As I admired the fine sundial in the middle of that fair garden, she seemed most agitated and I asked her what was the matter. Then she told me of the things that she had heard in the house: most strange noises and apparitions. But the walled garden she said was the most fearsome. She had felt such terror there that she was loath to go there alone even in the hours of daylight. Naturally I took it upon myself to comfort the lady in the shell grotto to which she was not averse. I hear she is now with child.

From Jacob Finsbury's Account of His Travels around the Houses of England, 1703

Steve Carstairs considered that he was doing PC Paul Johnson a favour giving him a ride in his pride and joy. He parked the red XR3i in front of the caravan site's reception. There was no way he was risking his suspension on those muddy fields.

They walked up to the top field in silence as Steve made no effort to speak and Paul could think of nothing to say. Paul had been wary ever since Steve had sneered at his passion for off-duty athletics, saying that he couldn't see the point of spending time on the running track: bedroom athletics were more Steve's style, or so he claimed. And of course there were the remarks he'd heard Steve make about Wesley, a man Paul had a lot of time for. Consequently, Paul kept his thoughts to himself when Steve was around.

Paul looked down at his clipboard. 'It's caravan forty-eight. A Mrs Wheeler.'

'Go on, then.' Steve trailed behind as Paul marched up to caravan forty-eight and rapped on the door.

A buxom woman answered. She was wearing very brief shorts and a T-shirt which pronounced that she was 'ready, willing and able'. From the look of her, Paul had no doubt that the claim was true. 'Mrs Wheeler?' he asked, flashing his warrant card.

'Hello, love,' she said with a seductive twinkle in her eye. 'It must be me lucky day. It's not often I have two young men knocking on me door.' Her accent was pure Lancashire. 'Come on in. I'll put t'kettle on.'

'Thank you, madam. A cup of tea would be nice.'

Steve followed Paul up the caravan steps and they both sat down on the upholstered bench seat opposite the door. The two men looked around. The caravan was identical to the dead man's except this one was cluttered where the dead man's had been bare. Children's toys, clothes and beach equipment occupied every surface. A drying-rack filled with generously sized women's underwear stood in front of the unlit gas fire.

'The kids are out playing,' announced Mrs Wheeler as she returned from the narrow kitchen area with two steaming drinks in oatmeal-coloured cups. She put them down in front of the two police officers. Paul thanked her and Steve gave a slight grunt.

'We only decided to come down here at the last minute,' she began. 'We've not been able to afford a holiday since their dad upped and left a couple of years back, but me mam said I needed a break so she paid for a week here, Monday to Monday 'cause it were cheaper, like. And it were our last chance 'cause they're back at school on Wednesday. Me mam and dad came to this site a couple of years back and they said it were nice and peaceful. So I didn't expect a murder on me doorstep.'

'No. I hope it hasn't spoiled your holiday too much, Mrs Wheeler,' said Paul Johnson sympathetically.

Steve shot him a withering look. 'Right, then, love. About these voices you heard. What were they saying?'

Mrs Wheeler looked taken aback. Perhaps, she thought, this was how the police operated, just like interrogations on the telly: nice cop and nasty cop. 'Well, they weren't shouting but their voices were raised – angry, like. But I couldn't rightly make it out . . .'

'Just do your best, Mrs Wheeler,' said Paul, striving to maintain good relations with the public. 'Now can you tell me when this was exactly?'

'It were on Tuesday night . . . around one in the morning, I think, though I can't be certain 'cause I've not got no clock in the bedroom here. Anyroad, I heard these voices. Two men. I went over to the window which looks out to the side but I couldn't see nowt so I thought the men might have been out round the back, like. Anyroad, after a while it all went quiet. Then I never heard no more.'

Steve finished his tea and put the cup back on its saucer with a loud clink. 'So you couldn't make out what was said? Think about it, will you? It's important.'

'If you could, Mrs Wheeler, it'd be a great help,' said Paul apologetically, glancing at Steve.

'I could just make out the odd word. I think I heard something like "You're not getting away with it" then the other one said something . . . a name . . . Duke something?'

'Dukesbridge?' asked Paul, leaning forward. 'That's a town near here.'

Mrs Wheeler shook her bottle-blonde head. 'No, it weren't Duke but something like that.'

'Earlsacre?' suggested Steve.

'Yeah. That sounds like it. He said "I'm going to Earlsacre" or "I should go to Earlsacre" . . . something like that. It wasn't long after that it all went quiet.'

After Mrs Wheeler had made a formal statement and they were walking away from the caravan, Steve turned to Paul in triumph. 'See, it's no use pussyfooting around – you've got to be firm if you want to jog their memories.'

Paul Johnson smiled to himself. 'Very clever of you to think of Earlsacre.'

'Well, I've had more experience in CID than you,' Steve replied with mock modesty.

'Did nobody else hear anything?'

'Nah. Half the caravans in the top field are empty, the rest are full of wrinklies who had had their Horlicks and were well away by the early hours. Looks like our Mrs Wheeler's the only witness.' His mouth spread in a lecherous grin. 'See that T-shirt? Ready, willing and able? I bet she'd be up for it, eh?'

Paul Johnson didn't reply.

'Eh, mister,' called a youthful Lancashire voice. Paul looked round to see a thin, freckle-faced boy, about ten years old, running towards them from the direction of the site shop. 'You coppers?' he asked confidently as he reached them.

'That's right, kid. What do you want?' asked Steve, vaguely menacing. He had no time for kids: to him they were just another minority group who had got above themselves.

'Is something the matter?' Paul Johnson bent his six-foot frame down to the lad's level. 'Have you got something to tell us?' he asked encouragingly, trying to redress the balance.

'Aye, mister. It were me what saw the murderer,' the boy said to Paul with relish, having decided wisely to ignore Steve.

'You wouldn't be Master Wheeler by any chance?' The boy nodded. 'We've just been talking to your mum. What did you see exactly?'

'I couldn't sleep so I looked out of the window. I saw a man coming out of the murder caravan. Clear as I see you now. It's only at the back of ours, you know. And where I sleep the window looks out on it.'

'Why didn't you tell anyone this before?'

The boy shrugged. 'No one asked. And when I told me mam she didn't believe me. She said I were making it up, but I weren't.'

'Did you hear any voices?'

The boy shook his head. 'Nah. I didn't hear nowt.'

'Can you give us a description of the man you saw?' asked Paul eagerly, still squatting at the child's level.

'Like in all them detective programmes?'

'Just like that, yes.'

'Oh, aye. I remember what he looked like. I can help you make one of them photofits like on *Crimewatch*.'

Paul Johnson unfolded his body to his full height. 'Come on, then, Master Wheeler. I can't keep on calling you that: what's your first name?'

'Billy.'

'I'm Paul. Come on then, Billy. Let's go and have another word with your mum. See if you can help us with our inquiries.'

Paul Johnson and Billy Wheeler began to stroll back towards the top field with a reluctant and frowning Steve Carstairs bringing up the rear.

*

Wesley hovered on the threshold of Gerry Heffernan's office. 'I feel bad about going off to play a game of cricket in the middle of a murder inquiry.'

'I've told you once, Wes. We need someone to keep an eye on what's going on up at Earlsacre,' Heffernan replied with a knowing grin.

'Well, if that's the case I can ask Neil to keep an eye on things.'

'Yes, but he won't know what to look for.'

Wesley smiled. 'Let's face it, neither do I.'

'Aye, but you'll know it when you see it. Have you heard the latest from Steve and Paul? Their little trip to the caravan park has turned up a couple of witnesses: a woman who heard raised voices on the night of the murder and her ten-year-old son. The kid was awake and looking out of the window when he shouldn't have been, luckily for us. He claims he saw a man leaving the dead man's caravan late on Tuesday night. They're bringing him and his mum down to the station to try and get a photofit made. The mum heard two men talking in raised voices and she says she heard one of them say the name Earlsacre. Which means now there's even more reason for you to get down there and see what you can find out. Now have you got everything?'

'A friend of Bob's from Traffic has lent me some kit and Bob's lending me one of his own bats.'

'Good. I'll be along later to cheer you on.'

'Must you?' said Wesley quickly. This was all he needed.

Heffernan blushed visibly. 'I'm, er, meeting someone there.'

The inspector was hiding something. And there was something in his manner, a sort of suppressed excitement, which suggested that he was looking forward to that afternoon. Wesley wondered why.

'I'll see you later, then.'

'Don't forget your meeting with Brian Willerby, will you? Did I tell you I saw him last night when I was on my way home from choir practice? Lurking around, he was, like a burglar in one of them silent films – all he needed was a mask and a bag with "swag" written on it. He crept into one of them houses opposite St Margaret's like he was on some top-secret mission. I don't know what on earth he was up to but maybe you'll find out today. Maybe that's what he wants to talk to you about.'

'Maybe.' Wesley hesitated, suddenly reluctant to leave.

'Good luck, Wes. Off you go and knock 'em for six. Nothing like

71

the sound of leather on willow, eh?' Heffernan chuckled as Wesley walked slowly out of the CID office.

Wesley was relieved that, now the tourist season was drawing to its close, the roads were no longer cluttered by battalions of slow-moving sightseers. As he turned into the driveway of Earlsacre Hall he looked at the clock on the dashboard. Twelve-fifteen. He was early. Perhaps he would be able to have a quick word with Brian Willerby before the match – get it over and done with.

He drove on past the cricket ground where half a dozen cars were already parked on the grass verge and stopped when he reached the stable block. It shouldn't be hard to find Neil . . . unless he was taking a liquid lunch down at the King's Head.

But Neil had resisted the lure of the local. Wesley found him alone, digging earnestly in the now visible foundations of the building that had once stood against the east wall of the ancient garden, completely lost in his task.

'Coming to watch the cricket match?'

Neil looked up from the trench, startled. 'Bloody hell, Wes, don't creep up on people like that. You gave me the fright of my life . . . or maybe it's this place making me jumpy.' He looked down at the object he'd just dug from the ground – half of a large scallop shell. 'I'll try and pop down to the match but I can't be away from here long. We're working to a tight deadline. They want the place excavated as quickly as possible so that they can start restoring and planting the gardens in time for the opening. Jane and Matt have just gone down to the King's Head for a sandwich. They're bringing me one back.'

'So you've not found any more skeletons?'

'No, thank God. Just a load of seashells, some seventeenth-century pottery, and a couple of late-eighteenth-century glass bottle seals bearing the name George Lantrist – bit of a status symbol having your own bottle seals, I should think. And Jake found a piece of beautiful sixteenth-century tile in a drainage gully over by the gate-house.' He looked up at Wesley coyly. 'And I've found the most amazing woman; she's a historian here. I think I'm in love, Wes.'

Wesley was lost for words. He had come across policemen in his time who were 'married to the job' and he had always put Neil in the same category. This lack of concentration on things archaeological wasn't like Neil at all. 'What's her name?' he asked, fascinated.

'Claire O'Farrell.' Neil said the name lovingly, as though the very sound of it held a special magic.

'I think I've seen her photo. We found a press cutting about Earlsacre at the scene of that murder at the caravan park. She was in it.'

But Neil wasn't listening. 'I thought I might ask her out for a drink tonight. And she's lent me some books,' he said, starry-eyed. Wesley had never seen him like this before. The change was dramatic.

'Well, I suppose that's a good start. But don't let things drift like you usually do. Be more positive.' Wesley felt duty bound, as a married man, to offer his friend a little advice. He himself had once benefited from Neil's vague and casual courting rituals: when he had first met Pam she had been going out with Neil, and it had hardly been difficult to lure her away. He could easily imagine his friend watching helplessly while Claire was swept off her feet by someone with more drive.

Neil shrugged. It was hard to break the habits of a lifetime.

'Why don't you bring her down to watch the cricket match?' Wesley suggested helpfully.

'Might do.' Neil suddenly frowned, worried. 'Did you say you found her picture at the scene of that murder? You don't think she's got anything to do with . . .'

Wesley was swift to reassure him. 'It was just a cutting from a newspaper; a piece about restoring the gardens. She just happened to be in it, that's all.'

Neil looked relieved.

'I'm going to get changed for the match,' said Wesley firmly, trying to practise what he preached. 'I might see you later, eh?'

'Yeah,' said Neil, with a faraway look in his eyes. 'See you later.'

Wesley returned to his car and drove down the pitted driveway to the cricket field, keeping a lookout for Brian Willerby and hoping against hope that he wasn't about to let Bob Naseby and the Divisional XI down.

Billy Wheeler turned out to be a star witness. He built up a photofit picture of the man he had seen emerging from the dead man's caravan with the self-assurance of a true professional. There was no hesitation, no doubt. When the picture was finished, Billy nodded before turning to his mother and younger sister, who were sitting behind him. 'That's him,' he said. 'That's the murderer,' he added with bloodthirsty relish.

'Are you sure, Billy? Would you like some more time?' said Rachel Tracey gently. Gerry Heffernan had asked her and Paul Johnson to take charge, knowing Rachel to be good with children and old ladies. 'Is there anything you want to change? Think hard, now.'

'That's him. I don't want to change nowt. That's what he looked like. Do I get my sweets now?' He looked expectantly at Paul Johnson, who began to delve in his pocket.

'What's this, Paul? Bribing a witness?'

Paul blushed as he handed over a Mars bar. 'I think the lad's deserved it, Rachel. He's done very well,' he said defensively.

Rachel grinned to reassure him that she was only joking. 'Yes, you're right. Do you mind waiting while I show this to the inspector?' she said to Mrs Wheeler as she picked up the finished picture. 'I shan't be a tick.'

She dashed into Heffernan's office and laid the picture on the desk before him. Heffernan looked at it with his mouth open. 'Is he sure?'

'Oh, yes. He's very confident. No hesitation. He went straight for it.'

'I think I'd better have a word with the lad.'

'Why, sir? Is something wrong?'

'I'll tell you in a minute.'

Heffernan lumbered out into the main CID office where young Billy had been holding court and drew up a chair beside Mrs Wheeler. 'You've done very well here, Billy. Great. But are you absolutely positive this was the man?'

Billy Wheeler looked at the inspector as if he were a Smartie short of a packet. ' 'Course I am. Why does everyone keep saying am I sure? 'Course I'm sure.'

'Right you are, Billy. Thanks. Rachel, can I have a word?'

She followed the inspector back into his office. 'What is it, sir?'

'This face . . . I know it. I know who it is.'

'Really, sir. Who?'

'It's a solicitor called Brian Willerby . . . or his twin brother.'

Rachel stared at the picture again. 'Yes. I thought it looked familiar. I've seen him once or twice around the station.'

'I know where he'll be this afternoon . . . the cricket match at Earlsacre. And he said he wanted to have a word with Wesley.'

'To confess?' she suggested tentatively.

'How should I know? I'm meeting someone there later anyway, but I'll get down there now. You stay here and hold the fort with Paul and Steve, eh?'

'Right, sir.'

As they stepped back into the main office, a high-pitched voice with a distinctive Lancashire accent was making its demands. 'I want another Mars bar before I go and one of them big packets of Smarties. And I want a lift back in a police car . . . fastest you've got. And I want sirens . . . and lights.'

'That lad'll go far,' mumbled Gerry Heffernan as he disappeared out of the office.

Wesley Peterson, clad in pristine white, tucked the bat under his arm and stepped through the pavilion doors out into the sunshine. A polite ripple of applause rose up from the onlookers dotted about the edge of the field as Wesley passed PC Napier from Neston, who had just been given out lbw. Napier smiled and nodded. 'Just watch that bowler . . . he's a sneaky bugger,' he advised under his breath as they passed.

Wesley thanked him, trying to conceal his sudden attack of nerves. He was relieved that his team had elected to bat first. At least his ordeal would soon be over.

He took his place at the crease and looked around. He could see Pam sitting on a deckchair a few yards from the boundary, the baby on her knee. She was sitting quite still, as if holding her breath. Gerry Heffernan sat beside her, grinning widely and giving a thumbs-up sign. This was the last thing Wesley needed . . . an audience.

He searched the field for Brian Willerby. Because the solicitor had turned up late, Wesley hadn't had an opportunity to talk to him. But he spotted him now, standing out on the boundary. There was, however, something much more urgent that required Wesley's attention – a bowler six foot two inches tall, who doubled as a rugby forward in the winter months, was pounding towards him like a charging elephant.

The ball shot from the bowler's hand. Wesley's grip tightened on the bat as he tried to recall the advice his cricketing great-uncle had given him as a child on holiday in Trinidad. Keep your eye on the ball, keep the bat straight. As his eyes followed the swiftly moving red sphere, he imagined himself back on that warm, palm-fringed beach and executed a perfect forward defensive stroke which scored no runs but made Wesley feel rather pleased with himself.

The bowler ran up again, his bovine face set in determination. This time Wesley relaxed and swung at the ball, which soared through the air and landed just beyond the boundary. The white-coated umpire raised both hands to signal a six. Wesley looked round and saw that Pam and Gerry Heffernan were applauding enthusiastically.

Wesley's next stroke produced a couple of runs and a look of frustration from the large bowler. It was at this point that he realised that he was beginning to enjoy himself. After a couple more unproductive defensive strokes came what Wesley considered to be his very best shot: a heart-warming crack of leather on willow which sent the ball sailing up into the air for another certain six.

But a cheer had gone up from the opposing team and Wesley saw that a tall, dark-haired fielder stationed on the edge of the boundary near the trees on the far side of the pitch had flung himself energetically on to the ground to catch the ball. One glance at the umpire's face confirmed it, and Wesley tucked the bat beneath his arm once more and began to remove his gloves as he walked back to the pavilion. Eight wasn't a bad score, considering.

When he reached the pavilion he was greeted by Bob Naseby, who slapped him heartily on the back. 'Well done, Wesley. Bad luck about that catch; if someone hadn't been on their toes I reckon you could have made fifty at least. So what was all that about you being no good at cricket? Hiding your light under a bushel, that's what you've been doing,' he said good-humouredly, taking off his floppy cricket hat and placing it squarely on the head of a garden statue – a haughty nymph standing incongruously to the side of a row of shabby metal lockers.

To Wesley's genuine surprise he hadn't disgraced himself and, contrary to his expectations, he had actually enjoyed the experience.

He took off his pads and sneaked round the edge of the pitch to join his wife and his boss, feeling that inner glow of satisfaction of every hero returning in triumph. Pam planted a kiss on his cheek and he gave her a hug. 'You were great,' she said. 'You looked really confident out there.'

'I didn't feel it,' he said modestly. He sat down by Pam and held his hand out to Michael, who was sitting in his pushchair. The baby grabbed his finger and started exploring it with his mouth.

'No escape now, eh, Wes?' chuckled Heffernan. 'Next season Bob'll have you playing every Saturday and . . .'

'Not if I can help it,' said Pam with quiet determination.

'Perhaps occasionally,' said Wesley with a finality that declared the subject to be closed. He turned to Heffernan. 'There's Brian Willerby fielding over the far side by the boundary near that bloke who caught me out. I didn't have a chance to speak to him before the match because he turned up late.'

Heffernan leaned towards his sergeant conspiratorially. 'You haven't heard.'

'Heard what?'

'I want a word with Willerby myself. A little lad staying in a caravan near to John Jones' – if that's his real name – was looking out of the window in the middle of the night, and guess what?'

'What?' said Wesley impatiently.

'He only drew up a photofit picture of a man he saw leaving the dead man's caravan. And you'll never guess who it looked like.'

'Who?'

'Brian Willerby. I suggest we collar him as soon as they stop for tea or whatever it is they do. Normally I'd be round at his house for a spot of questioning but if we can do it more tactfully . . .' He turned to Pam. 'Sorry, love, but there's no rest for the wicked. I'll let you have him back as soon as possible. Promise.'

Pam nodded with resignation and adjusted the sunshade on Michael's pushchair. 'I'm used to it,' she said in a martyred voice, giving Wesley a reproachful smile.

'Hi, Gerry. Long time no see,' said a female voice with a hint of an American accent.

Gerry Heffernan sprang to his feet and swung round. Standing there behind the deckchairs, smiling patiently, was a tall woman in her fifties with short, jet-black hair. Her pleasant face, unadorned by make-up, was dotted with freckles, and she wore a long floaty dress of a vaguely ethnic design.

'Susan,' gasped Heffernan. He glanced at Wesley and Pam before leaning forward to kiss the newcomer awkwardly on the cheek. Social kissing was as alien to Gerry Heffernan as the fertility customs of some exotic lost tribe from deepest Borneo, but somehow it seemed appropriate at that moment.

The woman smiled shyly. 'I told you I'd make it.'

'You know Wesley, don't you? And Pam?'

'Sure. How are you?' She leaned forward and touched Michael's hand. 'And this must be Michael. Hey, you sure are cute,' she said as the baby gave her a welcoming gummy grin. 'Say, is anyone going to tell me the rules of cricket? I've lived in this country for years now and I've never been able to figure them out.'

'I think they call them laws, not rules.' Pam smiled. 'That's how seriously they take it. And I've never been able to grasp the intricacies myself, so you're not alone.'

'You've just missed Wesley batting. Brilliant he was,' Heffernan boomed, causing the spectators near by to turn round and stare.

But before the inspector could embark on a blow-by-blow account of his sergeant's sporting triumphs, a fresh ripple of applause broke out and all the white-clad figures scattered over the cricket pitch began to drift untidily off the field, mostly in the direction of the pavilion.

'Tea,' said Wesley. 'I'd better get back.' He looked at Heffernan meaningfully. 'I'll see what Willerby wanted to talk to me about, then I'll bring him over to have a word with you. Okay?'

'Yeah, Wes. Keep it casual, eh? We don't want to put the wind up him just yet.'

Wesley hurried back to the pavilion, looking for familiar faces in the crowd. He noticed Martin Samuels, the trust director, disappearing in the direction of the hall. Neil and the object of his newly discovered affections were nowhere to be seen. But he didn't have time to look for his friend now. He had to find Brian Willerby . . . fast.

But there was no sign of him. He walked into the pavilion and accepted a welcome cup of tea from Bob Naseby's Thermos flask. Bob explained sadly that the wives and girlfriends of the home team had, in a fit of feminist fervour, refused to provide refreshments . . . so it was every man for himself when they played at Earlsacre.

There was no sign of Willerby inside the pavilion either. Wesley took his tea outside on to the veranda and scanned the faces scattered about the field. He could see Pam in the distance, and he felt a stab of guilt for abandoning her. But police work had no respect for family outings. He looked round the field again, more carefully this time, but his quarry was nowhere to be seen.

Wesley felt a tap on his shoulder. 'Fine six you hit. Lucky I caught you.' He swung round. Standing there, smiling breathlessly, was a young man in cricket whites with the dark, even features of a

Hollywood matinée idol. He put his hand out to Wesley. 'Charles Pitaway. It was me who took the catch, I'm afraid.'

Wesley shook the man's hand firmly. 'I know. I recognised you. Fine catch.' Then Wesley realised where he had seen Pitaway before: he had been the unnamed third man in the newspaper photograph found beneath John Jones' mattress. His was a hard face to forget.

'I hear you're a friend of one of our archaeologists up at the hall . . . Neil Watson?' said Charles with casual charm.

'That's right. Are you working there yourself?'

'Yes. I've been helping out with the designs for the restored gardens. I've got my own garden design business and I was doing some very routine work on the showhouse gardens for a new estate just outside Dukesbridge when Martin asked me to come up with something for Earlsacre. As you can imagine, I was delighted to take him up on his offer. My family used to own the hall. I sold it to the trust.'

'It must be strange for you seeing all this work going on,' said Wesley, his eyes still scanning the veranda and the field for any sight of Willerby.

'Not really,' Charles replied. 'I was five when we moved out, so it doesn't hold many memories. I've come back to live around here, so I've been taking quite an interest in the plans for the place. Fascinating stuff the archaeologists are finding; especially those skeletons.' He paused and looked over Wesley's shoulder. 'I'm sorry, but I'll have to dash. I can see Jacintha, our resident poet, looming on the horizon. I expect Neil will tell you all about her. Don't look round. Will you do me a favour? If she asks, say that you don't know where I am.' Charles looked round furtively, preparing to disappear.

'Before you go, have you seen Brian Willerby anywhere around?' asked Wesley quickly before Charles had a chance to vanish.

'Not since we stopped for tea. Sorry. He turned up late for the match and the captain was more than a little annoyed. Perhaps he's keeping a low profile.' Charles Pitaway looked around again, then raised a hand in farewell and hurried away, pushing through the throng of white-clad men. Wesley noted that he was holding his right leg and limping slightly: Charles Pitaway was paying the price for his catch.

He turned to see a woman in her forties, draped in floaty Indian fabrics, barging her way through the crowd. She was making for

79

Charles like a homing missile, her long auburn hair flowing behind her. But Wesley didn't have time to find out whether she met her target: he had to find someone who knew where Willerby was.

He began to wander round the edge of the field, stopping for a word with his wife and his boss.

'Any sign of him yet, Wes?' shouted Heffernan, his deckchair close to Susan Green's.

'No. He turned up late for the match and everyone I ask says that they haven't seen him since we went in for tea.'

'Keep looking. His team are batting next, aren't they? He can't have gone far. Probably just nipped home to polish his bat or whatever it is they do.'

Wesley looked at his watch and gave Pam a quick smile. 'I'd better get back to the pavilion . . . see if Willerby's turned up.'

'Off you go, then,' said Pam, resigned. 'Bowl them all out quickly, will you, so we can all get home.'

Wesley returned to the fray. After a brief and uneventful spell of bowling he spent most of the innings fielding near the boundary. He watched as batsman after batsman came in, waiting in vain for the familiar face of Brian Willerby.

After a while he began to sense that something was wrong. The odd look, the furtive whispers shared by batsmen between overs. But it wasn't until the match was completed that Wesley discovered the truth. Brian Willerby, the man chosen to bat third for the Earlsacre team, hadn't been seen since the start of the tea interval. The captain of the Earlsacre team had rung Willerby's home and been told by his wife that she hadn't seen him since he had left for the cricket match . . . half an hour before it was due to begin: he hadn't wanted to be late.

It seemed that Brian Willerby had disappeared into thin air.

Chapter 6

I informed Sir Richard that I would take my leave of him the next day. He made no effort to persuade me to stay. As it was my last evening in his company, I grasped the opportunity to satisfy my curiosity concerning strange stories I had heard in that most admirable of hostelries, the King's Head.

He talked for a while about his estate and how he had rebuilt the gardens when he found them quite overgrown on his return from the West Indies. The good wine fuelling my impudence, I then inquired as to the whereabouts of a certain Jinny Cartwright, a young woman of the village who had come to Earlsacre as a maidservant and who had disappeared two years before in the summer months. Her disappearance was still much spoken of in the village and her family's distress has occupied my thoughts. Sir Richard was silent at first. Then he spoke up, saying that the cook told him Jinny had run off with a soldier. He would discuss the matter no further, saying he did not concern himself with the doings of servant girls. When I asked if the tales of strange hauntings in the walled garden were false, he threw his glass into the fire and left the room without a word. Sir Richard Lantrist is indeed a troubled man. Before retiring I visited my lady in her bedchamber to bid her farewell. See how the Earlsacre wine banishes all caution and prudence.

I had words with the cook before I left the house the following morning. The good woman did swear she knew nothing of Jinny Cartwright and any soldier.

> *From Jacob Finsbury's Account of His Travels around the*
> *Houses of England, 1703*

81

'I think we've pussyfooted around long enough,' Heffernan announced. 'Willerby wanted to see you so why don't you get round to his house after you've changed, eh? He only lives down the road in Earlsacre village. It's time he was asked a few pertinent questions.'

'I've tried ringing his house, and the captain of his team's been trying too. He's not there. And we've no evidence he's done anything, sir. It's hardly a crime to leave a cricket match half way through.'

'But what about young Billy Wheeler's photofit?'

'So the man looked something like Willerby. We've absolutely no other evidence that he even knew the dead man.'

'Instinct, Wes. I can feel it in my water that all this is linked. It has to be. Don't forget I saw him going into that house near the church and I know a man with something to hide when I see one. When you're changed you can go round and have a word with his missus . . . see what you can find out.'

Wesley nodded, unconvinced. There were times when Detective Inspector Heffernan tended to get carried away . . . and this was probably one of them.

'You'd better get back to Pam and Mrs Green,' Wesley suggested. 'They'll be wondering where we are. And Pam's looking forward to having a takeaway from the Chinese tonight.'

'That's a good idea. If we get the Willerby business out of the way quickly why don't Susan and I join you?' He grinned.

Wesley's heart sank. He and Pam were looking forward to a quiet night in after their experience with Della and Jamie the night before. 'Yes, er, if you're sure Mrs Green won't mind.' He noticed that Pam was deep in conversation with Susan Green. The two women seemed to be getting on well: perhaps he would have to bow to the inevitable.

Wesley strolled back to the pavilion. The warmth of the early September day meant that there were still a lot of people sitting around the cricket pitch enjoying the sun. He looked for Neil but he was nowhere to be seen: the Earlsacre staff with their looming dead-lines were probably still at work.

Wesley had hoped to make a quick getaway from the match and he felt a sudden wave of irritation towards Brian Willerby. Why did the man have to mess him around; intrude on his precious free time? Why had he seemed so anxious to speak to him that afternoon and then disappeared without any explanation? He had never actually spoken to Willerby alone face to face: he had only seen him at the police station, talked to him briefly on the telephone, and seen him as a distant, white-clad figure at the other end of the cricket pitch. But he was already starting to dislike the man.

Les Cumbernold, the opening batsman of Earlsacre's narrowly defeated cricket team, pulled the stumps out of the ground and tucked them under his arm. Then he remembered the ball lost at the end of the seventh over of the visiting team's innings when their captain had whacked it over the boundary. He had distinctly seen it hurtling towards the trees that edged the pitch on the eastern side. There was no harm in having a quick look. The red ball might not be difficult to find against the green undergrowth at the edge of the woodland; and cricket balls didn't come cheap.

Les, a heavy man with an impressive beer gut, lumbered towards the trees and made for the spot where he had seen the ball disappear. He stepped into the deep green shade of the trees, using one of the wooden stumps to poke about in the undergrowth. The ball had to be there somewhere.

Then he heard a sound; a giggle, then a moan, then another small cry of pleasure. He walked farther into the trees, stepping softly, stopping suddenly each time a twig snapped beneath his feet. All thoughts of the lost cricket ball fled from his mind as he approached the clearing. He slowed down: he knew that was where they would be.

They were in front of him, lying in the dead centre of the clearing on a carpet of soft bark chippings, dramatically lit by dappled shards of sunlight which had seeped through the tall trees. They had kept their clothes on in spite of the day's warmth and the young man lay on top, moving rhythmically. Les hid his large frame behind the thick trunk of an ancient oak tree and watched. He saw the woman's face, the greedy pleasure she took from her young partner as she ran her grasping fingers through his dark, curly hair.

Les knew her: she called herself a poet. He remembered her name: Jacintha. And he had seen the man around Earlsacre Hall. Les smiled to himself. She was a bit of a girl was that Jacintha.

With a gasp of delight it was finished. Les knew they would soon be sitting up and making themselves decent: it was time for him to make a rapid exit.

He took a few steps backwards, careful to keep out of sight behind the trees. He stepped to the side, where a particularly thick tree trunk

83

seemed to offer ample protection, then turned and began to pick his way over brittle twigs back towards the open ground. In his excitement he had forgotten all about the cricket ball, but now his eyes focused once more on the ground in a token effort to locate it.

He wasn't aware of making a noise when he saw Brian Willerby lying in the undergrowth staring up at him with dead, unseeing eyes. But he heard a woman's voice coming from the direction of the clearing. 'Jake, what was that? Did you hear something?'

'Yeah.' This time the voice was male. 'I'm going to take a look. You stay there, Jacintha.'

'Not bloody likely. I'm coming with you,' she said with determination.

Les Cumbernold took one last look at Brian Willerby's startled face and began to run towards the daylight. He was just emerging back on to the cricket field when he heard Jacintha's scream.

'So who's the bloke who found him?' asked Gerry Heffernan as Colin Bowman knelt by Brian Willerby's body, examining a thermometer.

'A member of the Earlsacre team,' said Wesley. 'Name of Les Cumbernold. And not only is he a fellow team member, it also turns out that he's Brian Willerby's next-door neighbour.'

'So who was that woman who kept screaming? Had she been in the woods with this Cumbernold character for a bit of naughties?'

'Er, no, sir. It seems she was in the woods for a bit of naughties, as you so elegantly put it, with someone else entirely. A Jake Weston, one of the trust's archaeologists.'

Gerry Heffernan grinned wickedly. 'You mean one of Neil's mates has been up to a bit of how's your father with . . .'

'With a lady called Jacintha Hervey. She's poet in residence here.'

'Poet in residence, eh?' mused Heffernan, staring down at the body. 'Pity you never got a chance to find out what this poor bugger wanted to talk to you about.'

'Yes,' agreed Wesley quietly.

The inspector turned to Colin Bowman. 'Well, Doc. Any ideas?'

'There's some bruising; marks on the temple. But I won't be able to say anything for definite until I've had a better look. PM first thing tomorrow suit you?'

'I suppose so. You don't think he died of a heart attack, then?'

Bowman shrugged. 'It's always possible.' He looked at Wesley.

'You were playing, weren't you, Wesley? Do you know if he received a blow on the head from a cricket ball during the match?'

'Not that I know of. But it's not impossible. The players who were fielding with him should be able to tell us.'

'Mmm,' said the pathologist, deep in thought, staring down at the body.

'Could someone have taken a swing at him with a cricket bat? Lethal things them bats in the wrong hands,' said Heffernan.

Bowman smiled. 'Sorry, Gerry. It's definitely not a bat. Wrong pattern of bruising altogether.'

'So it could be natural or accidental, from a fall?' Wesley liked to know what he was dealing with.

'What about time of death?' asked Heffernan.

'I'd say he's probably been dead a couple of hours.'

'That fits with him dying during the tea interval,' said Wesley.

The pathologist smiled. 'Well, hopefully all will be revealed tomorrow. Goodbye, gentlemen. Must be off. I've got a dinner tonight . . . mustn't be late.'

They watched as the pathologist marched jauntily off towards his car, contemplating the coming event in his lively social life. The discreet gatherers of the dead came in Bowman's wake with their shiny trolley, scooped up the mortal remains of Brian Willerby and transported them to the waiting mortuary van. Wesley and Heffernan were left staring at the space where the body had lain, searching for inspiration as the white-overalled Scenes of Crime Officers worked industriously around them.

Wesley broke the silence. 'I suppose we'd better start asking some questions. Handy it's the police team that were playing. I told them to take the names and addresses of everyone who was at the match. Willerby's team are waiting in the pavilion. I said we'd want a word with them.'

'We'd better get on with it, then. See if anyone can throw any light on what became of Willerby after the first half.'

'Innings, sir. Half is in football.' Wesley hesitated. 'I suppose I'd better tell Pam the bad news . . . if she hasn't already heard.'

Heffernan rolled his eyes heavenward. 'Susan! I'd completely forgotten about her. What am I going to do?' He looked at Wesley helplessly.

'She was talking to Pam when I last saw her. I'll go out there and appease them both, shall I?'

'Yeah. You're much better at that sort of thing than I am. You'd better tell them it could take some time. Best of luck. I'll meet you in the pavilion in ten minutes.'

Wesley noted a grin of relief on his boss's face as he walked away to face the women in their lives. Pam was used to police work disrupting her best-laid plans; but she still didn't like it, especially now that, with Michael, their time together was precious. Susan Green's tolerance had yet to be tested.

The Earlsacre cricket team sat uncomfortably on narrow benches in their dusty pavilion awaiting the attentions of the local constabulary. They were a mixed bunch: locals and newcomers; farmworkers and hi-tech commuters; schoolboys and the early retired. Most wore an expression of puzzled innocence. None had known Brian Willerby well, or so they claimed, but all uttered pious regrets at his passing.

Not that they were much help. Brian Willerby hadn't been a very noticeable man, and at the end of the first innings they had either wandered back to the pavilion in ones and twos or scattered to talk to friends who were watching the match. Only one person admitted to having seen Willerby approach the trees: that was a lad from the sixth form of the local comprehensive who was on the lookout for a girl he fancied who'd promised to meet him at the match. The boy had noticed Willerby go into the trees alone but had assumed he was looking for the lost ball and had taken no notice. He hadn't been aware of anyone following him, which wasn't surprising if he had other things on his mind. Willerby wasn't seen again. After the first innings he had simply disappeared.

And another thing puzzled Wesley. If Willerby had set out for the cricket match half an hour before it was due to begin, why had he been so late? His house was in the village, ten minutes' walk away at the most. What had he been doing during those missing twenty minutes?

When Wesley had finished questioning the local doctor, who was last in the queue, he looked round and saw Gerry Heffernan scratching his curly head impatiently. 'Can I have a word, Sergeant?' he said, making for the door.

Wesley followed him outside on to the creaking wooden veranda.

'What do you reckon, Wes?' Heffernan began as soon as they were out of earshot. 'I've drawn a blank. Any likely candidates among the lot you questioned?'

'Aren't we jumping the gun a bit, sir? We don't even know it's murder yet.' Wesley stood for a moment staring out on to the small, tree-lined cricket pitch. After a while he spoke. 'One thing struck me as strange. Nobody seems to have had any opinion about Brian Willerby one way or the other. He appears to have been a classic case of "keeps himself to himself". He never mixed much with the other people in the village, never frequented the King's Head, never attended the village church or any social events. The only socially minded thing he ever did was turn out for the cricket team when they were short of players, and apparently it was one of the other partners in his firm who put his name forward . . . he didn't even volunteer himself.'

Heffernan nodded sagely. 'That figures.'

'I found out one interesting fact, though. The man who found the body, Les Cumbernold, lives next door to Brian Willerby, and apparently they didn't get on.'

Heffernan's eyes lit up with the excitement of the chase. 'Tell me more.'

'Well, one of the other players, the landlord of the King's Head in fact, told PC Wallace that Willerby was going to sue Cumbernold about some trees that were blocking out his light. It seems they weren't on very good terms at all.'

'Worth bearing in mind. Anything else? What about our two young lovers in the woods?'

Wesley grinned. 'I don't know whether you'd class Jacintha Hervey as young. She's forty if she's a day, but word has it that she has a taste for younger men. I picked up quite a bit of gossip about her on my travels.'

'Come on, Wes, tell all.' Heffernan rubbed his hands together in anticipation.

Wesley tried to conceal a smile. It wasn't the first time he'd noticed his boss's ears prick up at the promise of scandalous gossip.

'Well, according to Neil, Jacintha has been making a play for Jake for quite a while. And popular rumour has it that she's also been pursuing Charles Pitaway, who's working on the garden designs, although I don't think she's had any luck there as yet.' He turned round and looked through the pavilion window. 'That's Pitaway over there . . . tall, dark hair. In fact he was the third man in that cutting from the dead man's caravan, remember? He was trying to avoid

Jacintha's attentions when I was talking to him during the tea interval.'

Heffernan peered through the window. 'So we've got a love triangle, have we? Jacintha, Jake and Charles. You don't reckon Brian Willerby was making it a square, do you?'

Wesley smirked and shook his head. 'I shouldn't think so. From what I saw, Charles was definitely the one being pursued . . . no jealousy there. And anyway I can't imagine that Willerby would be her type. I think Jacintha's what they call a free spirit, if you know what I mean.'

'I know what you mean all right, Wes. I've come across plenty of them, especially when I was at sea. I had a free spirit in every port.'

'Really, sir?' said Wesley, mildly surprised. This was an aspect of his boss's past he had never heard about before.

'Happy days, Wes, happy days.' Heffernan sighed, then changed the subject quickly. 'So what did our not-so-young lovers have to say for themselves?'

'Well, they were, er, at it in the clearing in the woodland at the side of the pitch, about thirty yards from where the body was found. They claim they didn't hear or see anything suspicious until they heard a noise and went to investigate. They saw Les Cumbernold running off towards the cricket field and then they stumbled on the body. They each confirm the other's version of events.'

'And what about Cumbernold?'

'He's sticking to his story about going in there to look for a lost cricket ball and coming across Jake and Jacintha. He watched for a while, he said. Then, when they were adjusting their clothing, he decided to make a swift exit, and that's when he saw the body. He must have uttered some sort of cry of surprise, which Jake and Jacintha heard, then he said he ran off for help.'

'Is it common to look for lost cricket balls after a match?'

'I should think so. They're not cheap.'

'Have you come across anyone who saw Willerby being hit by a cricket ball during the match?'

'No. They were quite positive about that. He almost took a catch, apparently, and dropped it, but there's no way the ball hit him on the head.'

A sudden flash of panic crossed the inspector's face. 'Susan and Pam: I'd forgotten all about them. What did Susan say? Was she annoyed?'

'Resigned is more the word. I think Pam invited her back to our house for a Chinese.'

Heffernan looked relieved. 'I feel a bit bad about it, you see, Wes. I've not seen her for a month or so while she's been in the States, and I go and invite her to a cricket match and a meal afterwards then this happens. Brian Willerby always was an awkward bugger,' he added, looking at his watch. 'I suppose we ought to pay our respects to the grieving widow. Tell you what, Wes, I'll go back to your house and cheer up the ladies and you get Rachel over to visit Mrs Willerby – she's wonderful with grieving relatives and it shouldn't take long. Find out what you can about Willerby and see if she knows what he wanted to talk to you about. You'll be back in no time and we'll save you some fried rice.'

'Great,' said Wesley, unconvinced. Why did he feel that he'd just drawn the short straw?

Neil Watson walked slowly towards the stable block, Claire O'Farrell by his side.

'What did you tell the police?' Claire asked anxiously, looking Neil in the eye.

'Nothing much. Why?'

'What did they ask you?'

'Just where I was during the tea interval; did I know that dead man; that sort of thing. I tried to see Wes but they said he was busy. I don't think we should worry too much; he was found well away from the dig so it won't hold up the work.'

Claire had fallen silent. She looked strained, worried. Her bright blue eyes had lost their sparkle.

'What's the matter?' asked Neil. 'He was only some guy from the village. They didn't even say his death was suspicious: it could have been an accident or a heart attack for all we know. Don't let it worry you.' He paused. 'You didn't know him, did you?'

Claire didn't answer. Instead she gave him a distant smile. 'If you can spare a minute I'll show you those maps I was talking about. There are some old accounts books too that are rather interesting.'

Neil glanced through the wide archway of the gatehouse into the walled garden. He knew Matt and Jane would be working there. Jake, he had heard on the dig's efficient grapevine, was still recovering from his little adventure with the voracious Jacintha.

The original layout of the garden was now clearly visible – a patchwork of raised flower-beds separated by gravel pathways. Neil's eyes were drawn to the middle of the garden; to the deeply excavated rectangle of earth where the central stone plinth had stood for centuries, concealing the grizzly secrets that lay beneath.

'I should really get back and give the others a hand,' he said, his conscience nagging him, torn between duty and Claire's presence.

'Wouldn't you like to see an account of the materials used to build the shell grotto?' Claire asked, almost as if she knew Neil's weaknesses. 'The household accounts from 1701 when Richard Lantrist tarted up the gardens? Can I tempt you?' she added coquettishly.

The combination of Claire and a contemporary account of the creation of Earlsacre gardens was irresistible. He walked closely by her side as they proceeded towards her office in the stables. 'You could tempt me to do anything,' he whispered softly in her ear. Then he fell silent feeling that perhaps he'd overstepped the mark. Commitment wasn't his style; he would have to remember that.

A few minutes later Neil and Claire were sitting close together, bent over an old map of the Earlsacre estate. It was dated 1710 and showed the gardens clearly: the walled garden with its parterres, paths and sundial on the central plinth, the shell grotto clearly visible against the east wall, and the gatehouse in all its glory. Then the water garden next to it with its pools and fountains, now being lovingly restored. The humbler kitchen garden clung sulkily to the house, a place of usefulness rather than beauty. To see it all there in front of him, drawn when it was new and fresh, gave Neil a vivid picture of what he was bringing back into the world ... except for the skeletons: there was no clue to their identity on the map.

'Have a look at this.' Claire pushed what looked like an ancient notebook into his hands. 'It's the garden accounts. The work and materials Richard Lantrist ordered and what he paid for them.'

Neil took it from her and began to flick through it. He knew what he was looking for. And it wasn't long before he found it. Richard Lantrist had ordered a slab of Beer stone to form the centrepiece of his fine walled garden at Earlsacre, and had commissioned a fashion-able sundial to set on top of it. The date on which the stone slab was set into place by a team of estate workers was 4 July 1701: the men had been paid an extra penny each for their trouble. Neil shuddered. A penny to bury a young woman alive. But at least they now had a definite date for one of the probable murders.

'What is it, Neil? You seem miles away.' Claire's voice brought him back to the present.

He took his mobile phone from his pocket. 'I've got to ring my mate, Wesley. I want to tell him about . . .'

'No, don't do that,' said Claire sharply. Then more calmly, 'Can't it wait? I thought we could go out for a drink tonight when you've finished.' She tilted her head and looked at him appealingly.

Neil put the phone back in his pocket. Wesley would probably be busy anyway. He reached across and touched Claire's hair and soon they were kissing, lost in oblivion.

It was six o'clock when Rachel Tracey answered the telephone which stood on the dresser in the cluttered living room at Little Barton Farm. She had left Tradmouth police station at four and driven home, looking forward to a free evening before starting work again the next day. The investigation into the death of the man at the Bloxham View Caravan Park meant overtime – lots of it. However, she was quite unprepared for this latest interruption to her precious leisure time, but the fact that it was Wesley's voice on the other end of the line made the imposition a little easier to take.

She broke the news to her boyfriend, Dave, that their planned trip to the cinema in Morbay would have to wait, and drove out to Earlsacre. Dave was a man of few words at the best of times, and he accepted his disappointment without comment before settling himself down to watch an action movie on the television with Rachel's youngest brother.

Wesley met Rachel at the gates to Earlsacre Hall as arranged. She climbed out of her car, her short skirt revealing a great deal of shapely leg, which Wesley tried his best not to notice.

'So what's this about a suspicious death at the cricket match? Someone died of boredom?' she asked with controlled venom as she strolled up to him. Then she smiled and her voice softened. 'How did it go? Did you do okay?'

Wesley shrugged modestly. 'Scored eight runs and my bowling was nothing to write home about. In fact we were having a good afternoon until one of the opposing team went missing. Then he was found dead after the match and it put a bit of a dampener on things.'

'Is it murder?'

'We won't know until Colin Bowman does the post-mortem. It could be an accident. But there's one thing you should know.'

'What?' she asked, curious. She knew Wesley well enough to realise that he had something on his mind; something more than the sudden death of an anonymous cricketer.

'The dead man was Brian Willerby, that solicitor; the one who said he wanted a confidential word with me.'

'Which he never got.'

'Quite right.' He hesitated. 'I just wondered whether it was important . . . whether someone might have killed him to stop him talking to me.'

She laughed but saw that he looked worried. 'That sounds like something out of a spy novel – I think you're being a bit fanciful there, Wesley.' She touched his arm reassuringly. 'Willerby had a reputation in the station for being a bit of a fussy old woman, you know. He probably only wanted to discuss some routine case. And who'd know he was going to talk to you anyway?'

Wesley nodded. Rachel was probably right.

'Have you heard about the photofit?'

'Yes.' Wesley thought for a moment. 'It's a bit of a coincidence, isn't it – that young lad saying he saw a man who looked like Willerby coming out of the dead man's caravan. There must be some connection.'

'You can feel it in your water?' Rachel said mockingly in a poor Liverpool accent. 'You've been spending too much time with Gerry Heffernan.'

'Talking of Gerry, he wants us to go and see Willerby's widow – break the news and see what she has to say.'

'Great,' said Rachel, raising her eyes heavenward. 'Just what I need on a Saturday night. And what's the great man himself doing?'

Wesley smiled. 'Last I heard Detective Inspector Heffernan was making exhaustive inquiries into a Chinese takeaway at my house with Pam and a certain Mrs Susan Green.'

Rachel grinned. 'When the going gets tough, the tough tuck in, eh? Where is this grieving widow?'

'I've got her address. It's in the village just down this lane.'

'And she doesn't know she's a widow yet?'

'I'm not sure. I shouldn't think so. Apparently the Willerbys didn't mix much with the other people in the village – kept themselves to themselves.'

'Don't they always? Lead on, then. Let's get this over with.'

Wesley heard a car engine, faint at first, then louder as the vehicle coming down the drive of Earlsacre Hall drew level with the gates. It was a Toyota, a sporty red model, new. Wesley and Rachel stepped back on to the grass verge to let it pass, but the driver stopped, wound the window down and leaned out.

'Well, hello again,' Charles Pitaway said with a smile that showed off a row of even teeth. He looked appreciatively at Rachel. 'Can I give you two a lift anywhere?'

'No thanks. We're only going as far as the village.'

Charles nodded and looked at Rachel expectantly. 'Aren't you going to introduce us, Wesley?'

Wesley looked round at Rachel. 'This is DC Rachel Tracey.' Rachel smiled shyly at the man in the car. 'We're just on our way to see Brian Willerby's widow, so we'd better . . .'

'Of course,' said Charles quickly. 'In that case I mustn't keep you. Nice to see you again, Wesley . . . and, er, Rachel. Goodbye.'

Wesley noticed Charles' and Rachel's eyes meet briefly. Then Charles flicked on his indicator and drove off smoothly with a friendly wave of the hand.

'He's nice,' said Rachel as casually as she could manage.

'Yes. He seems a pleasant sort of bloke. He used to own Earlsacre Hall. He sold it to the trust just after he inherited it.'

'Oh,' was Rachel's only comment.

They walked on in silence towards the small village of Earlsacre, which lay just fifty yards down the road. Brian Willerby's house wasn't difficult to find. It was a double-fronted, Georgian building; a giant doll's-house set back from the main village street behind a regimentally neat garden. In contrast, next door to it stood a modern bungalow with a large double garage. Separating the two houses was a row of trees; leylandii – tall and getting taller.

'Must be a lot of money in soliciting,' commented Rachel as they walked up the garden path towards Willerby's well-proportioned house. But as they approached the front door her expression became serious. There was no place for the flippant humour used between colleagues to lighten grim tasks when they were about to confront bereaved relatives. Wesley stood a little way behind Rachel as she rang the doorbell. It was a part of the job that he hated.

The door was answered by a scrawny woman, probably in her fifties. Her long mousey hair was held back by two tortoiseshell slides. She looked at them with suspicion, especially Wesley. 'Can I help you?' she asked defensively.

93

They showed their warrant cards and introduced themselves with appropriate solemnity. Rachel knew that it would be up to her to break the news – and she dreaded it. 'May we come in, Mrs Willerby?' she asked gently. 'I'm afraid we have some rather bad news for you.'

'If it's about Brian I know already,' she said, matter-of-fact.

'I'm very sorry, Mrs Willerby, I know this must be a distressing time for you, but if we can just come in and have a word. We won't stay long,' said Wesley tactfully.

As Mrs Willerby stood aside to let them in, a tall figure emerged from a back room. Martin Samuels stopped dead when he saw Wesley, obviously unprepared for the encounter. Then he rearranged his features into an expression of solemn concern.

'Sergeant Peterson. I suppose you've come about Brian. Terrible business . . . terrible.' He shook his head as though trying to come to terms with the tragedy. But his eyes betrayed him: there was no real grief there; Martin Samuels was going through the motions. 'I suppose it was natural causes? It must have been. One's always hearing of unfit middle-aged men collapsing after taking part in some sporting activity. Terrible. Such a shock.'

'Did you know Mr Willerby well?' Wesley asked as casually as he could. Martin Samuels, Director of the Earlsacre Trust, was the last person he had expected to find comforting Willerby's newly widowed wife.

'Er, yes.' He looked at Mrs Willerby and rested a protective hand on her shoulder. 'Martha here is my sister. Brian Willerby was my brother-in-law. I came over as soon as I heard he'd been found dead. I thought Martha should know as soon as possible.'

'Of course.' Wesley exchanged a glance with Rachel, who was standing quietly by his side. She looked relieved that the burden of breaking the tragic news had been lifted from her shoulders. 'We're very sorry to intrude.'

Martha Willerby, who had seemed to be in a daze, stepped away from her brother's protective hand and suddenly became alert, as if she'd just remembered her manners. 'Please come into the drawing room. Would you like a cup of tea?'

'Thank you, Mrs Willerby. That would be lovely. I'll give you a hand,' said Rachel, giving Wesley a sideways look which said 'I'll get her talking while you find out what he knows'.

Moments later Wesley and Samuels were sitting facing each other beside a fine marble fireplace. A vase of blood-red flowers stood on the hearth. It was an elegant room, the décor and furnishing pale and tasteful. There were obviously no sticky-fingered children here, and Wesley found himself wondering whether there ever had been.

'Were you close to your brother-in-law?' he began quietly.

'No. Brian was a very private person. He wasn't an easy man to get close to. Our dealings were mainly of a professional nature. I used his services when I bought my house in Morbay and he did some of the legal work for the Earlsacre Trust. Not all of it, of course: dealing with the Simeon Foundation in the USA and the various national bodies in this country needed lawyers with a little more clout than a solicitor in a small Devon town can provide, so I use a big firm in London.'

'What kind of a man was he?'

Martin Samuels looked up sharply. 'That's a strange thing to be asking, Sergeant. He did die of natural causes didn't he? That's what they were saying at the cricket club. Heart attack, wasn't it?'

'We won't know that until after the post-mortem, I'm afraid.'

'I heard someone say he'd been hit on the head by a cricket ball. Could that be true, do you think?' Martin Samuels was beginning to sound concerned.

'All sorts of rumours start flying around in a situation like this. I really couldn't say yet. We'll have to wait and see.' He decided to repeat his question. 'What was Brian Willerby like?'

The answer when it came was brutal. 'He was a nonentity, Sergeant. Wouldn't say boo to a sparrow, never mind a goose. No drive, you see.' He paused and glanced at the door leading to the kitchen. 'Martha used to work as his secretary. I'm afraid my sister was an ugly duckling who grew up to be an ugly duck. Neither was she over-endowed with the work ethic. She wanted to get married and she was flattered when one of the partners in the firm made her an offer . . . probably the best she was likely to get. Mind you, I suppose they suited each other: two nonentities together. Good job they had no children.'

Wesley fell silent, rendered temporarily speechless by Samuels' blunt cruelty. He awaited more revelations but they didn't come.

'Neil Watson tells me you got a first in archaeology. Is that true?'

'Er, yes,' said Wesley modestly, wondering how he could steer the conversation back to Brian Willerby. He decided on the direct approach. 'Brian Willerby rang me on Thursday. He said he wanted to speak to me confidentially. Have you any idea what that could have been about?'

Martin Samuels looked genuinely puzzled. 'No. Why should I?'

'He said he would speak to me at the cricket match but he died before he had the chance. Did he seem to be worried about anything?'

'No. I'm sorry, Sergeant, I can't help you.'

'He set out for the match half an hour before it was due to begin but arrived late. Did you see him at all before the match?'

Samuels shook his head. 'Can't say I did. No.'

'Do you know where your brother-in-law was on Tuesday night?'

Samuels looked mildly surprised. 'I really have no idea.'

'And where were you that evening?' Wesley asked formally.

'I was at home on Tuesday evening with Glenda, my partner. We had people round for dinner. You can check if you like.' He handed Wesley a business card. On it was an address on the upmarket side of Morbay and three numbers; phone, fax and e-mail. 'I can't help you, I'm afraid,' he said with finality. The subject was closed.

As Wesley and Rachel left the house they began to compare notes.

'Mrs Willerby said she had no idea why her husband wanted to see you but she's definitely hiding something,' said Rachel as they walked back up the steep lane towards the car.

'Same with Samuels. He became very candid at one point . . . and was hardly flattering about his sister. I had the impression he looked upon the Willerbys with something approaching contempt, almost as if he thought they were beneath him; the country cousins.'

'But Martha said he used Brian Willerby for his legal work.'

'Only the simple, routine jobs. He said he had a big London firm to deal with the more exciting stuff.'

'According to Martha her brother made his fortune in the City,' said Rachel. 'Ended up a millionaire. But he'd always had an interest in old gardens. He'd worked as a National Trust volunteer once when he was a student, and historic gardens became a sort of obsession with him. When his first marriage broke up he took early retirement, and he discovered the Earlsacre estate's existence when he visited Martha. From then on he threw himself into the project of restoring it. He's not an expert himself but he acts as a sort of Mr Fixit, getting experts together and sorting out funding.'

'It sounds as if you found out more than I did,' Wesley said with admiration. Rachel had a valuable knack of getting people to talk. And her talents obviously hadn't been wasted on Martha Willerby.

'Did you ask her where her husband was on Tuesday night when young Billy Wheeler saw the man coming out of that caravan?'

'Of course. She said he was out. In fact she said he's been out every night this week. He claimed he was with clients, but she was a bit vague about it all. She said she didn't know anything about his work.'

'Well, that's a lie for a start. Her brother said she used to be his secretary.'

Rachel raised her eyebrows but didn't answer. They had reached her car. She unlocked it and climbed in. 'I'll see you tomorrow, then, after the post-mortem.'

'Yes.'

She looked at him for a few seconds. 'Fancy coming for a drink? We could have something to eat in a pub or . . .'

'I'd better get back. Gerry promised to save me some food. Sorry.'

She drove off and Wesley walked slowly back up the drive of Earlsacre Hall towards the stable block where he'd left his car. He passed the cricket pitch, now deserted, and noticed a swathe of blue-and-white police tape decorating the trees at the far side, keeping the public away from the scene of Brian Willerby's death. He marched on towards the hall, poking its head above the surrounding trees, shrouded in its armour of scaffolding.

He contemplated looking for Neil, but the place seemed deserted. The people who were working on Earlsacre had probably packed up for the day. Besides, he knew he should get back home and appease Pam. And he was hungry.

As he drove off towards Tradmouth he kept thinking of Brian Willerby. Why did he have the feeling that there had been something in the dull solicitor's life that his wife and brother-in-law wanted to conceal?

Chapter 7

1 July 1701
Memorandum – to plant six apple trees at the west side of ye
kitchen garden.
 Memorandum – to cause ye grass in the water garden to be
mown.
4 July 1701
 Memorandum – the large plinth of Beer stone purchased by
Sir Richard for the walled garden to be set in the middle of the
same garden. (Note – Sir Richard did cause the men to rise early
and did order the stone to be set in place just after dawn. Nine
men paid 1d each.)

From the garden accounts of Earlsacre Hall

Thanks to modern technology, in the shape of a microwave oven, Wesley enjoyed his Chinese meal piping hot. It had been a pleasant evening – the subject of Brian Willerby's death had been mentioned only once, when Wesley gave his boss a brief report of his dealings with the grieving widow and her brother.

Both he and Pam had taken a liking to Susan Green, although they were perplexed as to what she and Gerry Heffernan had in common – apart from a liking for the Beatles. The incongruous couple had left around eleven, with Heffernan giving inappropriately jolly reminders that Brian Willerby's post-mortem was booked for nine o'clock the next morning. Wesley and Pam went upstairs in amicable silence, too exhausted for talk, and fell into bed.

But Wesley's mind was too active for instant oblivion. When he looked at the glowing red numbers on the radio alarm clock he saw that it was ten past midnight. He could hear Pam breathing softly beside him – the sound was soothing and hypnotic. Just as he was beginning to drift towards sleep, the noise of the telephone startled him awake.

Pam moaned, 'Who the hell's that?' as Wesley picked up the receiver. It was bound to be police work.

'Okay, love, I've got it. You go back to sleep.'

A giggle on the other end of the line told him the call was nothing to do with law and order. 'Hi, Wesley. Is my lovely daughter there?'

He held the phone to his wife's ear and whispered, 'It's your mother. I think she's drunk,' he added disapprovingly.

'Hi, Pamela, are you there?'

Pam grunted in the affirmative. 'Do you know what time it is, Mother? We were asleep.'

'Nonsense. You don't want to be asleep and miss all the fun. The night's young. Jamie and I were thinking of getting a taxi and coming over.'

'Now?' Pam spluttered in disbelief.

'Why ever not? The night's young,' she repeated. 'We'll bring a bottle or two.' Yet another giggle and a man's voice whispering in the background.

'No. Wesley's got to work tomorrow. Now can you let us get some sleep . . .'

'But Pamela, darling . . .'

'No, Mother. Positively not. Goodnight.' Pam put the receiver down firmly. 'I don't know what's got into her, Wes, I really don't.'

As Wesley turned over and closed his eyes, a cry went up from the adjoining room. The telephone had woken the baby.

'I'll see to him,' said Pam in martyred tones as she stumbled towards the door.

Wesley no longer felt like sleeping. He lay awake, listening to Pam moving around in the next room and feeling vaguely guilty that he wasn't doing his fatherly bit. But soon he found his thoughts turning to work; to the death of Brian Willerby and the corpse in the caravan. Was there a link? Something obvious he was missing? As his brain became more and more alert, he had the feeling it was going to be a long night.

The next morning Wesley rose bleary-eyed, leaving Pam asleep. He crept out of the house, closing the front door quietly behind him, and walked down the steep streets, silent on this Sunday morning apart from the raucous cries of seagulls overhead. He headed towards the hospital. One of the good things about living in a small town like Tradmouth was that he could walk into the centre, and he took advantage of this to wake himself up with some bracing sea air.

He loved the walk, and the view over the rooftops to the glistening river with its busy boats and the white toy houses of Queenswear dotted along the far bank. It was at times like this that he remembered why he had been so keen to leave the crowded bustle of London behind.

He met Gerry Heffernan in Colin Bowman's office, where he was treated to fresh coffee and croissants; an unaccustomed treat, especially when he hadn't had time to grab any breakfast at home. He just hoped he'd manage to keep them down during the post-mortem.

Colin was silent during his gruesome investigations. When he'd finished he turned to the two police officers. 'I'm rather puzzled by this one, gentlemen. He's a healthy specimen apart from a fractured skull caused by a blow – or series of blows – to the head. But what really puzzles me is what made these marks. Here, have a look.'

The three men bent over the corpse's head. The marks on the dead flesh seemed clearer now than they had the day before.

'Is that stitching? Could it be a cricket ball?' suggested Wesley.

Bowman looked at him and nodded approvingly. 'That's exactly what I was thinking. You can see the impression of the stitching on the seam quite clearly,' he said. 'I suspect that we were meant to think that he was hit on the head by a stray ball, but it must have taken a few blows to finish him off. The marks are all around the same place, but it's quite clear he was hit a number of times: about half a dozen at a guess.' He thought for a moment. 'I suppose someone could have held a ball and hit him, but it wouldn't have been easy: the fingers would have got in the way and it would be difficult to get enough momentum. From the force used I'd say the ball had been bowled at his head at some speed . . . and accuracy.'

'So we're looking for a demon bowler?' said Heffernan. 'Well, that lets the current England team out, eh?'

'The bowling at yesterday's match was pretty ropy,' said Wesley. 'Let's face it,' added Heffernan, 'I can't see that there's anybody in the Earlsacre team with the skill to commit murder by bowling a cricket ball accurately at someone's head several times.'

'A bat would be the usual weapon of choice for the enthusiastic cricketer, I would have thought, gentlemen,' said the pathologist. 'So you're looking for a murderous cricketer with a formidable talent for bowling. Any ideas?'

Heffernan shook his head. 'So it's definitely murder? No chance of it being an accident?' The inspector always liked to get his facts straight.

'As I said, we were meant to assume death was accidental, but I'm afraid all the evidence points to the fact that it was murder. But as to how it was done . . .' Colin Bowman gave a frown. 'That's a puzzle . . . a complete puzzle.'

Neil Watson lay beside Claire O'Farrell in the bedroom of her tiny rented cottage and allowed himself a satisfied smile. He pushed the duvet back and ran a gentle finger along the contours of her naked waist. She stirred and opened her eyes.

'What time is it?' she asked, her voice thick with sleep.

'Just after ten.'

'Neil . . . we're late. The others said they'd be there at half nine.' She sat up, clutching the bedclothes to her bosom in a gesture of modesty.

Neil grabbed at the sheets and pulled her towards him. 'It's Sunday. They won't miss us for half an hour.'

'Martin's called a progress meeting for ten-thirty.'

'Shit, I'd forgotten.'

'Get dressed.' She looked at the alarm clock on the bedside table. 'We're going to be late anyway. Give Jake a ring on his mobile and tell him, will you?'

'Tell him what?' Neil grinned.

'That we're going to be late.' She threw a pillow at him. He ducked and it knocked the alarm clock on to the floor. 'You're an idiot, Neil. Has anyone ever told you?'

He grabbed her again playfully and pushed her back on the bed. She kissed his nose. 'Phone Jake,' she whispered in his ear. 'Now.'

He pulled a pale blue sheet off the bed, wrapped it around himself and staggered down the steep, narrow stairs into the living room, a small, low room furnished in a twee cottagey style which he suspected would hardly be Claire's own choice.

A flowery address book lay by the telephone, probably a present from one of the elderly female relatives back in Ireland that Claire had mentioned last night when they had exchanged life stories, each fascinated by the other's most trivial details. He thought he could remember Jake's phone number but he couldn't be sure: Claire was bound to have it written down.

He picked up the address book and flicked through the pages, noting male names and hating himself for experiencing this symptom of possessiveness. He had always believed in giving girlfriends their own space, that no one person could ever own another. But his first night with Claire had changed that . . . and the unfamiliar feeling disturbed him.

He reached the end of the book. W for Jake Weston. The number was there, written in Claire's neat hand. As he held the book open and lifted the receiver, ready to dial, his eyes scanned the rest of the page. Jake's was the last name listed. He scanned upward. A Dr Williams; a Josie Wood; a Charlotte Wyvern – names that meant nothing to him. But at th top of   something had been scribbled out violently with a pencil. Neil, his curiosity getting the better of him, held the page to the light and could just make out the name ben h the pen scrawl: Brian Willerby. And he could see two a   es – one i. Earlsacre and what loo   d like a business address i Tradmou   couldn't see the handwriting clearly but it seemed to be spidei   i. contrast to Claire's, which was small and neat. He flicked through the book and found that no other addresses had been scribbled out in thi   ple who had moved house merely had a neat line through th   dress.

Claire must have k   Willerby well at one time for both his addresses to be in her b   and, as his name preceded the others, she must have known him for a while. But what had caused her to obliterate his name like that?

He put the address book carefully back where he had found it and dialled Jake's number, trying to put all thoughts of Brian Willerby's death from his mind.

'Of course, it doesn't necessarily have to be one of the cricket team. It might have been a spectator. Anybody who was around Earlsacre yesterday afternoon in fact,' said Wesley as they walked down the police station steps towards the carpark.

Gerry Heffernan nodded silently. 'Might even be a woman. They play cricket at a lot of posh girls' schools. I knew a woman who played cricket once.'

'Really, sir?' Wesley tried to imagine his boss in the clutches of a well-bred lady cricketer, and failed. 'How did your meeting with the Chief Super go?'

Gerry Heffernan sighed. 'You know Stan Jenkins is on his hols, don't you?'

Wesley nodded.

'Well, what you don't know is that Stan's handed in his resignation . . . retiring on health grounds.' Heffernan winked significantly. 'So thanks to Inspector Jenkins' choice of this week to go and play with his bucket and spade, and his decision to jump ship as soon as he gets back, yours truly is in charge of both our murder investigations. But the good news is that we can use Stan's team, so we've got extra manpower – we're setting up an incident room in the stables at Earlsacre Hall. The phone lines and computers are going in as we speak. And the even better news is that I'm now Acting DCI and you – congratulations – Acting Inspector Peterson.' He grinned widely as he watched Wesley's face.

Wesley was lost for words. He had thought that Gerry Heffernan's promises of promotion had been wishful thinking; the products of an over-optimistic nature. 'That's, er, great,' he managed to stutter, feeling a warm glow of satisfaction as he anticipated Pam's reaction to the news, and that of his parents – particularly his parents.

He recalled their disappointment when he hadn't followed them into the medical profession, when he had chosen archaeology out of pure intellectual fascination rather than any thought for status and security. People from ethnic minorities, his parents had always warned, have to try just that little bit harder, and sadly, Wesley thought, they were probably right. But now his abilities had been recognised and he would be one of the youngest inspectors in the force. Surely even his father, so fiercely ambitious for his children, would be proud of that.

'I told the Chief Super that if you were going to do the job you should have the rank to go with it. And when Stan actually retires . . .'

'Thanks,' said Wesley. He could find no other words to say so he kept it simple. The two men climbed into Wesley's car and drove out to Earlsacre in amicable silence.

At eleven o'clock Heffernan looked at the clock on the dashboard and sighed. 'I've had to miss church, Wes.'

Wesley tried to look sympathetic. He knew his boss hated to let the choir down, but it couldn't be helped that morning.

'We'll have to get this cleared up by the end of the month. It's harvest festival. You coming?'

Wesley nodded. 'Probably. The stuff you keep singing around the office sounds pretty good. And Pam seems quite keen to go. She mentioned it the other day.' He smiled to himself. 'When we got married we had all these warnings about how difficult a mixed-race marriage can be. But one of the biggest cultural differences was that my family were never away from church on Sundays while Pam's mother had never allowed her near one.' He raised his eyes to heaven at the mention of Della. 'Did I mention that my mother-in-law rang us after midnight last night? She sounded as if she'd had too much to drink. She was threatening to come round with her latest boyfriend.'

Heffernan chuckled. 'I'll have to rewrite my book of mother-in-law jokes. And did she arrive?'

'Thankfully, no. She just woke Michael and he screamed half the night. I could have done with a lie-in this morning.'

'Not much chance of that when we've got a murder inquiry on, more's the pity.'

Wesley swept the car round into the drive of Earlsacre Hall and drove slowly past the now deserted cricket field. The carpark was packed, mostly with police vehicles, but he managed to find a space next to Neil's distinctive Mini. The two men got out and strolled towards the stable block.

The incident room was almost operational. The phone lines were in and the computers were being tested by earnest young men. The stable block had already been modernised with white-painted walls and carpet-tiled floors in preparation for the day when it would become an education centre for the hall and gardens. So all the police had to find now was a source of tea, the liquid that oiled the wheels of any investigation.

Rachel greeted them. She was already installed at a desk sorting through statements.

'Could you get us a cup of tea, Rach? I'm spitting feathers here,' said Heffernan boldly as he marched towards his chosen desk.

Rachel didn't answer. Wesley smiled at her sympathetically: he knew her opinions on female officers being asked to provide refreshments. 'Found anything interesting in the statements yet?' he asked her, trying to make up for the boss's faux pas.

'Not really. A couple of witnesses saw Willerby disappearing into the trees on his own when the rest of the team were going in for tea.

But nobody saw anyone following him.' She paused and pulled a statement from the file. 'And there's this. One of the cricketers who arrived early – sixth-former at the local comp – said he thought he saw Brian Willerby near the stable block before the match talking to a woman. But he wasn't taking much notice so he couldn't be certain.'

'Is there a description of the woman?'

'The boy was some way away and she had her back to him. He could see that she had long hair but little else.'

Wesley thought for a moment. 'You can get into those woods from the direction of the house, of course. Perhaps the murderer wasn't at the cricket match at all. Perhaps he or she was up at the house and arranged to meet Willerby in the woods.'

'He wouldn't have known what time the tea interval would start, surely.'

'Unless he – or she – was waiting for him.'

'Which broadens the field a bit.' Rachel sighed. 'There were a lot of comings and goings. Most of the people working on the Earlsacre project were watching the cricket match at some time or other, if only for a few minutes, which makes things more difficult.' She stood up. 'I'd better organise tea for the boss. Trish,' she called to a young WPC working in the corner of the room. 'Can you get the inspector a cup of tea, please?'

'Make that two,' said Wesley, admiring Rachel's style.

She relayed the message to Trish and sat down again with a satisfied smile. 'I'm developing the art of delegation,' she explained in a whisper.

'Still after the Chief Constable's job?'

'Just watch me.' She looked at Wesley inquiringly. 'I hear congratulations are in order, Acting Inspector Peterson.'

'Word gets round.'

'Tradmouth police station's grapevine beats all your e-mail and instant communications,' Rachel said with a grin. 'I don't suppose you need an acting sergeant?'

'Stan Jenkins' sergeant is coming to give us a hand. He's good, apparently . . . been on lots of courses.' He detected a look of resentment on Rachel's face. 'But I'll try and put in a word for you if I get the chance, okay?'

'Thanks, er . . . I suppose I should call you sir now, shouldn't I?' She turned away. He couldn't see the expression on her face.

He wished there were something he could do to further her promotion – she deserved it if anybody did. But he was only too aware that he was a relative newcomer, that he had to tread carefully himself. Maybe he would try to have a word with Gerry Heffernan when the time was right.

He strolled over to Heffernan's desk, which was set apart from the others at the end of the room.

The newly appointed chief inspector, seemingly sinking beneath a mountain of files and papers, looked up eagerly, like a drowning man anticipating imminent rescue. 'Wes, come and sit down. Is that tea on its way?'

'I think so.' At that moment Trish appeared bearing steaming cups. Wesley looked at his boss, deep in paperwork, and concluded that now wasn't really the time to broach the subject of Rachel's promotion. 'Any thoughts on where we should start?'

'Right, Wes, let's go over what we've got and see if it makes any sense.' Heffernan looked down at a dog-eared piece of paper. 'First of all I think the two murders are linked. Do you agree?'

'Yes. I think the cutting about Earlsacre and the fact that Billy Wheeler saw a man who resembled Willerby coming out of the first victim's caravan gives us every reason to conclude that there's a link. Any clue to the identity of the man in the caravan yet?'

'Not a thing. His fingerprints aren't on file so he has no criminal record. There's a report of a missing man from Chipping Campden in the Cotswolds who might fit the description. We're still waiting to hear from quite a few other forces, so something else might turn up.'

'So who's this missing man from the Cotswolds?'

'The local police there faxed through a photograph. Tell me what you think.' He handed Wesley a fuzzy black-and-white photograph of a dark-haired young man. 'His name's Michael Patrick Thoresby. He's a postgraduate student at Warwick University – been missing a fortnight now.'

Wesley studied the photograph. 'It looks like his passport photo. It's a lousy picture . . . could be anyone.'

'But could it be our man?'

'It's possible, I suppose. Has he any links with this area?'

'According to his parents he'd been on holiday around here a few times when he was a kid, but nothing apart from that.'

'So he's a possible. I'll get Paul Johnson to ask his local force for a few more details.'

106

Heffernan looked down again at his grubby sheet of paper. 'No sign of the knife used in the first murder. It's probably been washed and been shoved away in someone's cutlery drawer by now. No forensic to speak of. And the ground was dry at the time of the murder: it didn't rain till late on Wednesday, so it's no use looking for footprints in the mud. SOCOs found some vomit in the hedgerow behind the caravan but Craig Kettering's admitted it was his.'

'What about Craig Kettering? He found the body.'

'I get the feeling that there's something Craig's not telling us. I reckon there's a distinct possibility that he nicked something from that caravan; money, I should think, 'cause Craig's always been a bit wary of credit cards. He's like me . . . not one for modern technology. Not that I think our friendly neighbourhood pizza deliverer would really have anything to do with brutal murder.'

'So do we pay him another visit?' Wesley's voice was unenthusiastic as he anticipated another trip to Craig's unsavoury flat.

'All in good time, Wes. I don't think he'll be going very far. We'll pop over when we've had our tea.' He chuckled wickedly.

'So you don't see Craig as the killer?'

Heffernan shook his head. 'I don't think murder's his style. Have a shufti at this, will you, Wes. Forensic report on the John Jones murder.'

He handed him a sheet of typed paper which had already been stamped with Chief Inspector Heffernan's customary tea stain from the overflowing cup on his desk. Wesley read it quickly. ' "The threads found in the wound almost definitely came from a white cotton T-shirt." Not much help to us, is it?'

'Not really, but that's the best there is, I'm afraid.'

Wesley sat down, taking his jacket off and making himself comfortable. 'We've got to remember that whoever killed him must have thought it was important, otherwise he wouldn't have bothered taking the T-shirt off the body, would he. Let's say it had something printed on it . . . like the name of a pub or an organisation.'

'That's a possibility. I reckon that if we knew who the dead man was, it might tell us who killed him.'

That fact had already occurred to Wesley. 'So it's possible the killer is a relative of some kind? Or a close friend . . . business associate? Certainly someone with a connection to the victim.'

'Mmm. What if John Jones had some kind of hold over Brian Willerby? Maybe he's a relative. Grasping brother? Embarrassing long-lost illegitimate son? We'd better ask Mrs Willerby if there are any skeletons in the family closet.'

'And what about Willerby's murder? Was it revenge for the first? Or were the two victims in cahoots with each other and both were killed to stop them revealing something? Perhaps that's why Willerby was so anxious to talk to me – he had something he wanted to tell me.'

'Anything's possible at this stage. But my bet's on the first option. I think Willerby killed the man in the caravan then someone else killed him. Of course, there's always a chance that the two deaths aren't linked – that it's just coincidence after all. Perhaps young Billy was mistaken.'

'There's one way to find out. We can show him a photograph of Willerby among some others from our rogues' gallery that look similar and see what he says. If he insists unprompted that Willerby's the man he saw coming out of the caravan on the night of the first murder, I think we'll have to take his word for it. I'll ask Rachel to go and work her charms with Billy.'

'Tell her to pay a call at the sweet shop first . . . I've never known a witness so susceptible to sweeteners as Billy Wheeler.' He looked down at his piece of paper again and sighed. 'Any thoughts on our second murder?'

'There's a witness, a young lad playing for the Earlsacre team who claims he saw Willerby talking to a long-haired woman near the stable block before the match. But he was too far away to see who it was.'

'And too far away to see if it was Willerby or another of the cricketers?'

'Perhaps.'

'Long-haired women. Who have we got?'

'Jacintha Hervey?' said Wesley with a smile. 'She seems to pop up everywhere. And Martha Willerby, of course: the wife always has to be a prime suspect. And there must have been a few women with long hair watching the match.'

'See if anyone else saw Willerby before the match . . . with or without this mysterious woman in tow.'

'Right you are, sir. I'll put someone on to that right away.'

'What about Martha Willerby and that brother of hers, Martin Samuels? Anyone checked his alibi for last Tuesday? . . . or hers?'

'Yes. She said she was at home on her own and a Ms Glenda

Torrington backs up Samuels' story – he lives with her at a very swish address on the upmarket side of Morbay. However, when PC Wallace questioned the guests they were supposed to be having dinner with, they said that Samuels slipped out at half eleven . . . said he'd left some important papers at Earlsacre and he needed them for a meeting the next morning in London. The guests left at half past midnight and Samuels hadn't returned.'

'Interesting, Wes. Very interesting. Where was Samuels when Willerby died?'

'He watched the match for a while then went back to his office here in the stable block to do some work just before the tea interval, so he says. No witnesses.'

'So he could be our man.'

'He could be.' Wesley stretched out his legs. 'I've heard that Les Cumbernold, the man who found Willerby's body, was going to be sued by him over those trees that were cutting out Willerby's light. We only have Cumbernold's word that he went into those woods and got distracted by Jake and Jacintha's . . . er . . . performance. He might have killed Willerby during the tea interval and gone back to check that he'd left no evidence.'

'What do we know about Cumbernold?' asked Heffernan, scratching his head.

'Apparently he's a bit of a rough diamond – a builder who used to live in the middle of Plymouth and moved out into the country. He's not very well liked in Earlsacre village, by all accounts. But that doesn't stop him turning out for the cricket team. He's a pretty good batsman, so I suppose they're glad to have him.'

'Put him down on our little list, then, Wes. Anyone else?'

'Not that I'm aware of. I've a feeling that this case is going to be like turning over a stone in a garden . . . all sorts of vile things are going to come crawling out into the daylight once we start digging.'

Heffernan looked up at him and grinned. 'That's very poetic of you, Wes. I've not seen your mate Neil yet. What's he up to? Lurking in the undergrowth?'

Wesley leaned forward confidentially. 'I think he's been struck by Cupid's dart. A young lady called Claire who works as an historian here. He was with her briefly at the cricket match.'

'So he was. Very attractive girl – I don't know what she'd see in your mate, but there's no accounting for taste. Does this mean you won't be running off every five minutes to dig things up?'

'I would like to find out more about those skeletons.'

Gerry Heffernan raised his eyes heavenward. 'Come on. Let's send Rachel over to Bloxham to help line the pockets of Billy Wheeler's dentist, and after we've visited Craig Kettering we'll go and see what Mr Les Cumbernold has to say for himself.'

As they left the stable block, Wesley glanced longingly at the closed door to the archaeologists' office. He wanted to know about the skeletons in the walled garden, about the young girl who had been buried alive, choked by the earth beneath the great stone slab. Somehow he felt that someone owed it to her to discover who had been responsible for her fate. But, he told himself, he had enough on his plate for the foreseeable future. Perhaps it was for the best that Neil's attentions were otherwise engaged.

Gerry Heffernan had been right about Craig Kettering. After a little friendly persuasion he admitted to taking some cash from the caravan: it had been lying invitingly on the cupboard by the door, he said, and it was a temptation that he had found impossible to resist. But he denied taking anything else and he swore he'd seen no wallet or credit cards. He had stolen nothing but the cash. With the body lying there and the flies buzzing about, he hadn't felt inclined to stick around long enough to search the place.

Heffernan believed him. So did Wesley. The killer had gone to the trouble of taking a T-shirt off the dead man's body but had left sixty-five pounds in cash just lying there in full view. Concealment of the dead man's identity had been the killer's priority: the money hadn't mattered.

They left Craig alone in his dreary bed-sit and drove back to Earlsacre. As planned, they made straight for Les Cumbernold's flashy new bungalow.

Pam Peterson was an avid fan of home improvement programmes, even though she and Wesley rarely had the time or energy to put their suggestions into practice. So with this wealth of theoretical knowledge behind him, Wesley realised that Les's lounge would have given any interior designer nightmares. The richly patterned red carpet clashed with the gold brocade sofas and the elaborately swagged drapes at the huge picture windows.

The bungalow was large, reeking of money rather than good taste. Mrs Cumbernold, a middle-aged bottle-blonde with the leathery skin of one who had spent too much of her spare time lying on sunbeds, brought the two police officers tea with a polite smile then disappeared, leaving her husband to it.

Les Cumbernold waited until his wife had left the room before he turned to Gerry Heffernan, an expression of open candour on his face. He was a big man with sparse brown hair and an impressive beer gut. An expensive gold watch graced his left wrist below a tattooed skull.

'I'll make no secret of it,' he began, sitting himself down on the edge of a huge armchair. 'I didn't like Willerby and he didn't like me and the wife couldn't stand that stuck-up cow of a wife of his either. We made the effort when we first moved in – three years ago it was. We went over and introduced ourselves and invited them round for drinks but they made it quite clear that they wanted nothing to do with the likes of us. Snobs . . . thought they was too good for us. Never even spoke to us if they met us in the street. We sent 'em a Christmas card the first year we were here. Never got one back.'

He sank back in the armchair. The Willerbys' social rejection had clearly rankled.

'I believe you have been involved in a dispute with Mr Willerby about some trees,' said Wesley.

Cumbernold looked at him with mild hostility. 'The leylandii. I planted 'em on the boundary between the houses and let 'em grow so I couldn't see his bloody house. I didn't want to be reminded of that stuck-up shit every time I set foot outside my own door.' He leaned forward. 'And the wife said he used to watch her, you know . . . when she was sunbathing. Gave her the creeps he did.'

'So he asked you to remove the trees?' prompted Wesley.

'They're on my land so I'm not moving them. He threatened me with legal action. I told him to . . .'

'Quite, sir,' interrupted Wesley. 'It must have been awkward for you at the cricket match, you and Mr Willerby playing on the same team. Did your ill feeling spill on to the cricket field at all?'

'Well, I tried not to let it. One of our other players works – er, worked – with Willerby, and he asks . . . asked him to play some-times 'cause it's hard getting enough men for the team.' He looked Wesley up and down, his initial hostility seeming to fade. 'You weren't bad. Nice six. Pity about the catch but that young Charles Pitaway's turning out to be one of our best players. His family used to own the hall, you know, but he's a good bloke – not a snob like some I could name. Do you play regularly for the police team, then?'

'Not regularly, no,' answered Wesley. 'Can you tell us where you were during the tea interval?'

'I've told the police that already.'

'Indulge us,' said Gerry Heffernan, leaning forward. 'We're very forgetful; have to be reminded.'

Les Cumbernold rearranged his large frame in the armchair before recounting his movements. He had arrived ten minutes before the match and just as it was due to begin he saw Brian Willerby arrive from the direction of the hall: he had looked as though he'd been hurrying ... sort of hot and bothered. Wesley and Heffernan exchanged looks. If Willerby had come from the direction of the hall then this fitted with him talking to the unknown woman.

Les continued his narrative. During the tea interval he'd wandered off to find his wife among the spectators. He hadn't seen Brian Willerby going into the woods. He had been aware that a ball, a new one, had been lost among the trees after one of the police team hit a spectacular six, and he had made a mental note to look for it after the match. Cricket balls weren't cheap. The rest of the story was familiar, but was now peppered with pleas of injured innocence.

When they took their leave, Cumbernold saw them out on to the gravel drive shaded by the row of towering leylandii trees growing to their left. He was walking with them to the gate when his attention was distracted. The pristine white door to the bungalow's large double garage was standing half open. Cumbernold rushed over and shut it quickly, returning to the gate with a nervous smile to see his visitors off the premises.

'Did you see that, Wes?' Heffernan asked when they were standing outside Brian Willerby's elegant Georgian house, well out of earshot. 'There's something in that garage he doesn't want us to see. Wonder what it is.'

Wesley smiled. 'Your guess is as good as mine.'

His mobile phone began to ring and he pulled it from his pocket. After a brief conversation he turned to Heffernan. 'That was Rachel. She said Billy Wheeler's definitely identified Willerby as the man he saw on Tuesday night. And he now says he thinks he saw him at midnight because he remembers he looked at his watch.'

Heffernan mulled this over. 'Now correct me if I'm wrong, Wes, but didn't Mrs Wheeler say she heard voices around one o'clock, but she didn't have a clock in there so she couldn't be sure of the time?'

'That's right. She heard raised voices, but Billy claims he didn't hear anything. Which means that Jones might have received two visits that night and Billy might have gone to sleep by the time the second person arrived. There was Brian Willerby and then someone else, someone he argued with.'

Heffernan turned and stared at the house for a few seconds. 'Has anybody looked through Willerby's things?'

'Not yet.'

'Well, there's no time like the present. Get on that phone of yours and tell Trish Walton and Steve to come over and give us a hand, will you.'

'Isn't there the small question of a search warrant?' Wesley had known his boss to stretch the rules a little from time to time, but it made him uncomfortable. Not doing things by the book could lead to trouble.

'All we're doing is looking through the dead man's things for any clue to his murderer. The grieving widow can hardly argue with that, now, can she?' A smile of angelic innocence spread over Gerry Heffernan's chubby face. He began to walk up Willerby's garden path, but Wesley hung back. 'Come on, Wes, what are you waiting for?'

Wesley punched out the number of the incident room on his phone and followed the chief inspector up the garden path, praying that there'd be no repercussions.

Martha Willerby was alone in the house and seemed almost to welcome the company. To Wesley's relief she invited them in and told them they could search wherever they chose . . . if it would help them to find Brian's killer.

Trish and Steve arrived ten minutes later and joined in the search. Wesley found himself wishing Rachel had been available. She had an intelligence, an intuition, that Steve lacked – his mind was usually on lower things – and Trish, recently seconded to CID, was promising but inexperienced. Wesley asked them to make a search of the bedrooms, paying particular attention to the dead man's clothes and shoes. Were there any bloodstains? Any incriminating notes in pockets? Was there any sign of anything that might have belonged to John Jones?

Wesley and Heffernan climbed the elegant staircase to the first floor and turned their attentions to Willerby's study. It had once been a small bedroom but had subsequently been furnished with oak bookshelves and a grand antique desk. If the dead man had had any secrets committed to paper, this is where they would be.

But they were to be disappointed. Willerby's study contained the paper detritus of everyday domestic life: bills for gas, electricity, phone and water; council tax demands; unexciting credit card purchases. Then there were the share certificates, insurance policies, bank statements, passports, birth and marriage certificates. All the paperwork the average law-abiding citizen manages to accumulate over a lifetime. The fact that there was hardly anything that related to his work indicated that he had kept his home and working life separate.

There was a door in the corner of the room, probably leading to a walk-in cupboard or an adjoining bedroom. Wesley tried it; it was locked.

He turned and saw that Heffernan was watching him. 'This door probably leads into the next bedroom. But I suppose we should check.'

'I don't like locked doors. They're usually hiding something. Is there a key?' Gerry Heffernan moved quickly to the desk and began to search the drawers. But the search was in vain.

Then Wesley had an idea. He went through into the master bedroom where Trish and Steve were searching through the dead man's clothes and asked them if they'd come across a key. They had indeed – Trish handed him an impressive key that she'd found in the inside pocket of Willerby's jacket.

Heffernan had been right: there was something hidden behind the locked door. And it was likely to be something important if its owner kept the key in his inside pocket. Wesley returned to the study and tried the key in the lock. It turned smoothly and the door opened without a sound. He took a deep breath and stepped through into the darkness.

There was silence for a few seconds until Heffernan, unable to bear the suspense, called out. 'What's in there? What have you found?'

'Come and have a look.'

Gerry Heffernan stepped into the room. It had been pitch dark at first in spite of the brightness of the late summer day. But now Wesley had found the light switch and the tiny room, not much bigger than a large cupboard, was bathed in an eerie red light.

'It's a darkroom. Nobody's mentioned to us that Brian Willerby was keen on photography,' said Wesley, puzzled.

'Perhaps it belonged to a previous owner,' Heffernan suggested.

'Willerby kept the key in his jacket pocket. And it's been used recently. Look at those chemicals in the trays. They're not old. And it's clean – spotless. Willerby used it. But why keep it locked?'

'If he developed photographs here, where are they?'

Wesley shrugged. 'I think we'd better have a word with Mrs Willerby, don't you?'

Martha Willerby was adamant. She knew nothing of her late husband's photographic activity. She hardly ever went into his study, only to clean it once a week, and knew nothing of the darkroom. She knew the powder room, as she called it, existed, but she'd never had cause to go inside. It had been used by eighteenth-century gentlemen to powder their wigs, she added as an afterthought. As far as she was aware, photography had never been one of her husband's hobbies: in fact Brian Willerby had never been much of a man for hobbies at all, apart from the odd game of cricket when the village team were short of players. That was it. She sat on the edge of her seat, her hands neatly folded on her lap and her lips pressed stubbornly together. Wesley knew that they would get no more information out of her that day.

But he also suspected that she was being somewhat economical with the truth. The Willerbys' house was larger than most, but surely any woman these days would be aware of what was going on in her own home? Pam certainly would be; and his mother, even though she pursued a demanding career as a GP. The image of the master of the house keeping the key to a locked room to which his wife was not admitted seemed like something from a Victorian Gothic novel: it hardly fitted with what Wesley knew of normal domestic life at the dawn of the third millennium. But there was something a little old-fashioned, a little fey, about Martha Willerby. Perhaps she was telling the truth after all. Who knew what went on in other people's marriages?

Steve and Trish had found nothing of interest; no letters, no bloodstained clothing. Gerry Heffernan found it hard to conceal his disappointment, and the four of them left the house somewhat subdued. The hoped-for breakthrough had not yet come.

Heffernan's stomach told him it was lunch-time. The King's Head looked a good bet, he told Wesley. There was a blackboard propped up outside which promised traditional Sunday lunches at reasonable prices. It was an offer they couldn't refuse.

When they arrived at the pub, they chose to enter via the door marked 'Lounge' and bagged the only vacant table. Things were looking up at last.

'What did you think of our rough diamond, Les Cumbernold?' asked Heffernan twenty minutes later, his mouth full of Yorkshire pudding.

'Well, he didn't like Willerby. But I don't know that I see him as a murderer: if he did resort to violence, I'd expect a good old-fashioned punch-up would be more his style.'

'I tend to agree with you, Wes.' Heffernan took a mouthful of roast potato and chewed for a while, deep in thought.

'Pity we didn't find anything at Willerby's house to link him with the caravan murder. Mind you, if there had been a weapon or any bloodstained clothing there, he'd had plenty of time to get rid of it. Has anyone spoken to the man Willerby worked with, the one who recommended him for the cricket team?'

'Yes. He's a partner in the firm but he claims he never mixed with Willerby socially, even though he lives in the next village. He wasn't playing yesterday and he has a cast-iron alibi. He's away for the weekend but we managed to get in touch with him. He's spending the weekend with his daughter and son-in-law up in Somerset. The son-in-law's a vicar and he confirms his story.'

'Sounds like we can cross him off our list, then,' said Wesley, eating somewhat more slowly than the boss. 'But I think we should arrange to have Willerby's office in Tradmouth searched. He might have decided to keep anything incriminating well away from home. We'll see to that tomorrow morning.'

'I've been thinking about this John Jones, if that was his real name,' said Heffernan, his knife poised to attack a particularly succulent slice of roast beef. 'What did the murderer do with this white T-shirt he was wearing?'

'When Billy Wheeler saw Willerby coming out of the dead man's caravan, was he carrying anything?'

'We asked him that but he said he didn't think so. Of course, there was nothing to stop Willerby going back later to get rid of the evidence, I suppose.'

'And then there's the darkroom in Willerby's house with no sign of any photographs. It's strange, isn't it. The T-shirt and the photographs: things you'd expect to have been there which weren't,' Wesley mused, pushing a sprout around his plate.

'Come on, Wes, eat up. There's apple pie for pudding,' said Gerry Heffernan, patting his substantial stomach.

Wesley sighed. If only everything in life was as predictable as his boss's appetite.

Half an hour later they strolled back up the long driveway to the Earlsacre Hall stable block. Even on a Sunday work was continuing on the hall and gardens. Men in hard hats were walking confidently around the scaffolding that clung to the hall's ancient stone walls.

Wesley felt pleasantly full after his large meal, more substantial than his usual Sunday fare of spaghetti bolognaise. He knew that he should be checking through statements to see if there were any promising new lines of inquiry to be pursued, but instead he found himself thinking of Neil. Considering they were now working from the same building, they had seen very little of each other. But perhaps that was down to Neil's new love interest.

But no sooner did this thought flit through his mind than the man himself appeared around the corner, carrying a couple of old books.

'Wes. I wondered how long it would be before you turned up. You can't move for police around here, and it used to be such a nice place.'

'How's it going?'

'Okay,' Neil replied with a secretive smile. 'Fine.'

'I was wondering if you'd found out any more about those skeletons yet.'

'As a matter of fact I have,' Neil said tantalisingly. 'Claire's found loads of stuff about the estate – books, letters, maps, accounts books, all sorts. One of the books was some kind of record of all the work that was done in the garden. I think we can safely say I've found out who our murderer was – of the girl who was buried alive at least.' He allowed himself a self-satisfied grin. It wasn't often he was able to beat Wesley in the detection stakes.

'Congratulations,' said Wesley. 'Feel like giving us a hand next door?'

'No way I'm ever joining the forces of oppression.' Neil grinned. 'Don't you want to know who the murderer was, then? Don't tell me I've gone to all this trouble for nothing.'

'Come on, then. Who was it?'

'The lord of the manor. Richard Lantrist. You know the girl was buried under that stone slab? Well, Richard Lantrist gave the order for the slab to be put in place first thing in the morning on 4 July 1701. He ordered the men to get up early and paid them a penny each to do the job quickly. What was the rush if he didn't want to cover up his crimes . . . literally?'

'And the other skeleton? The man buried underneath?'

'That'll be one he killed earlier. I reckon I've cracked it – open-and-shut case. I've found the murderer and the actual date of the murder. That's better than your lot usually do.' He paused, and his expression became serious. 'How are you doing with this murder at the cricket match? Any clues?'

'We're pursuing inquiries,' said Wesley with a non-committal smile. 'How's Claire?'

Neil shuffled his feet. 'Fine. Why?'

Wesley had expected gushing enthusiasm, but somehow Neil sounded wary. 'Pam's been asking when she's going to meet her.'

'Er, you'll probably see her around here some time.'

'Everything's all right, isn't it?' For someone who was swearing undying love not twenty-four hours before, Neil was being very cagey.

'Yeah. Everything's fine,' he answered. Lying had never been one of Neil's talents and Wesley knew that something was wrong. 'Er, this Brian Willerby, the bloke who got killed . . . what was he like? I mean, what did he do and all that?'

'As far as we know he was a respectable provincial solicitor but . . .' Wesley stopped, not wishing to give too much away. 'Why do you ask?'

'Nothing. No reason.' Neil turned to go. 'Might see you later, then.'

Wesley watched him walk into his office. He had been his usual ebullient self until the subject of the murder came up. Neil was worried about something, perhaps something to do with Brian Willerby. He had no connection with the dead man but something was wrong. And Wesley resolved to find out what it was.

In the few grey minutes between dusk and dark, the figure crept across the cricket pavilion's wooden veranda and peeped through the windows which were protected from flying balls by rusty wire mesh.

118

Last time there had been people. Young Jake Weston and that poet woman, the one who had been in the woods. But tonight the pavilion was still and deserted.

The key turned sweetly in the lock and the figure pushed the door open and stepped inside. Now was the time.

Chapter 8

I have taken my leave of Sir Richard, gladly I may add. Yet I was heartily sorry to leave her ladyship, who did beg me to remain. I vowed to return . . . yet I doubt I shall visit Earlsacre again.

I paid my last call to the King's Head, where I inquired further of the maidservant Jinny Cartwright. Such tales I heard. Jinny, it seems, was a bright, inquisitive girl. Some said Sir Richard satisfied his lust upon her and did kill her to ensure her silence. Others said she fled the attentions of the gardener there and did drown in the water garden. Not one mentioned a soldier.

I left the village of Earlsacre with a heavy heart, certain that the girl had come to a bad end.

From Jacob Finsbury's Account of His Travels around the Houses of England, 1703

Monday morning brought rain – or drizzle to be more precise. It fell in gossamer sheets over the hilly landscape, turning the greens and golds of the September fields to shades of grey.

But in spite of the disagreeable weather Wesley was glad to get out of the house. Pam was returning to work on Wednesday after the long months of her maternity leave, and she was starting to panic about her workload and the logistics of leaving Michael with his childminder each morning. When she began rushing back and forth with piles of paperwork, and searching through files straight after breakfast, he thought it best to leave her to it.

When he arrived at Earlsacre he found Gerry Heffernan sifting through mountains of statements and reports. He looked up as Wesley entered the room. 'Just the man I wanted to see,' he shouted, making all the officers working at their respective desks look up.

'There's been an incident. Martin Samuels came over first thing and told me that the cricket pavilion was broken into last night. A couple of garden statues were nicked. They're worth a bit, apparently. He was storing them in there 'cause he thought they'd be safe with all the construction work going on. Just shows how wrong you can be.'

'I noticed those statues when I was getting changed for the cricket match. I thought they looked a bit out of place. How did the thieves get in?'

'Broke a window . . . or at least that was what we were meant to think. Only the window was broken from the inside to make it look like a break-in. Which means that whoever did it might have had a key.'

Wesley stood there for a few moments, weighing up the implications of Heffernan's news. 'Do you think it's got anything to do with our murders?' he asked.

'The statues were worth a couple of thousand each, Samuels reckons. Worth killing for?'

'People have been killed for less,' said Wesley.

Heffernan sighed. 'I suppose we'd better get over to Tradmouth, see if Brian Willerby was hiding anything in that office of his – stashes of cocaine inside the photocopier, dismembered corpses in the filing cabinet, that sort of thing.' He took a swig from his cup and began to push the files around his desk in a token display of industry. His hands came to rest on the blurred photograph faxed through from the police up in Chipping Campden. He held it up and squinted at it. 'Do you reckon that could be our John Jones, Wes? The more I look at it the more I think that it doesn't half look like him.'

'We could always get someone down to try and identify the body,' Wesley suggested tentatively.

'That might not be a bad idea. In the meantime we'll ask the police up there to send us a better picture and a few more details.' Heffernan thought for a few seconds, then took a newspaper cutting swathed in a plastic folder out of his drawer. 'It mentions a murder in the Cotswolds on this page that we found under the mattress, you know. A woman was murdered in Moreton-in-Marsh. That's near Chipping Campden, isn't it?'

'Yes. Nice part of the world. I suppose there could be a connection: I'll ask the police there to send us some details.'

Heffernan pushed another piece of paper at Wesley. 'This arrived from Colin Bowman first thing. He's been examining Brian Willerby's head wound again and trying some experiments. He definitely thinks it's caused by a cricket ball but he can't get enough force just striking an object with a ball in his hand to cause that severity of fracture. The ball clearly had more momentum, as if it had been bowled at speed. Which brings us back to the ultra-accurate demon fast bowler theory which, let's face it, doesn't really hold water as far as the Earlsacre team are concerned. Don't forget, I saw them in action.'

Wesley sat back and played idly with a paper-clip. 'So we've got two murders: one unfathomable and one impossible. Not forgetting a theft which may or may not be connected.'

'That's just about it, Wes. Where do we go from here?'

Before Wesley could answer, Steve Carstairs strutted across the office to Heffernan's desk. 'Report's just come in, sir. There's been a break-in at Blake, Willerby and Johns, the solicitors. Nothing much taken, but I thought you ought to know.'

'Thanks, Steve. We'll get over there,' said Wesley, retrieving his jacket from the back of his chair. Steve answered with a resentful grunt. He had been somewhat subdued since the news of Wesley's promotion had come through.

'All go, isn't it? It never rains but it buckets it down,' Heffernan mumbled under his breath.

'Do you think it's a coincidence?' asked Gerry Heffernan as they stood outside the glass door than led to the offices of Blake, Willerby and Johns. The ground floor of the building was occupied by the Morbay and District Building Society, garishly decorated with bright posters to lure in the unwilling investor.

'Believing in coincidence is like believing in Father Christmas: nice idea but . . .'

'My thoughts exactly, Wes. After you.'

Wesley pushed open the etched glass door that bore the name of the firm in bold letters, and the two men climbed the grey-carpeted stairs leading up to the office. They were greeted by a young receptionist who introduced herself as Imogen. She had dyed scarlet hair, a ring through her nose and a calm, otherworldly manner.

'Mrs Potter discovered the break-in when she arrived first thing this morning. They'd got in through the loo window. I suppose it's quite vulnerable really, being next to the fire escape at the back. They went in all the offices but they only made a mess in Mr Willerby's. I've made sure nobody's touched anything, don't worry. The fingerprint people are in there now.' Imogen smiled, suddenly more professional. 'What have we done to deserve a couple of inspectors? When my flat was broken into I only got a constable. But I suppose with poor Mr Willerby . . .'

Wesley nodded. In spite of first impressions, he sensed that there was no pulling any wool over this young woman's eyes. 'I wonder if there's somewhere we could have a word in private?' he said, glancing at Gerry Heffernan, who still had his eyes fixed on Imogen's scarlet hair. Heffernan nodded his approval.

'Of course,' answered Imogen. 'We can use Mr Johns' office. He's been away at his daughter's for the weekend and he's not back until this afternoon.' She led them into a functional office, and Wesley found himself wondering what Willerby's domain was like. After the fingerprint officers had finished their work, he would find out.

'The senior partner, Mr Blake, is away as well,' Imogen said chattily as she arranged herself on a grey upholstered chair. 'He's on holiday in the Caribbean for three weeks, lucky sod. He's going to get a hell of a shock when he gets back next Monday,' she added with relish.

'What was Brian Willerby like to work for?' Wesley asked when Imogen was settled comfortably. Having decided to let Wesley do the talking, Gerry Heffernan sat back and listened intently.

'Do you want the authorised version or the truth?' answered Imogen bluntly.

Wesley smiled. 'I think the second option is going to be of more use to us, don't you?'

'It's just this taboo about speaking ill of the dead: it gets deep-rooted; makes it hard to say what you really think.'

Wesley nodded. He knew exactly what she meant. The dead weren't there to defend themselves: the dead don't answer back. 'Well, do your best. Take your time.' He sensed that Imogen wasn't a young woman to be rushed.

'He gave me the creeps,' she blurted out after a few seconds of silence. 'It was just the way he looked at me, like he was imagining me with no clothes on. Sometimes, when I went into his office to take dictation, he would . . . well, I could tell he was getting, you know . . . excited. Sometimes he'd even have his hands in his pockets and . . .'

'You mean he was, er . . . playing with himself?' asked Gerry Heffernan, incredulously.

Imogen swallowed nervously and nodded. 'Yes. I mean, I thought he was. His voice would go all . . .'

'And you never said anything, never complained?'

'I mentioned it to Muriel Potter – she's the senior secretary but she's nearing retirement – and she said she'd never had any trouble with him. Not that I'm surprised. She said I was just imagining things, and perhaps I was. I mean, he never actually did or said anything. There was never any question of harassment or anything like that. It was just looks – what was going on in his head.'

'But surely if he was . . .' Wesley began in disbelief.

'I can't even be certain that he was. He might have just put his hands in his pockets: it might have just looked that way. I would have made a right fool of myself if he'd turned out to be quite innocent, wouldn't I? And maybe he was: maybe it was just my filthy mind imagining things. As I said, he never actually said or did anything. It was just a gut feeling I had.'

'Would you describe yourself as imaginative?' asked Heffernan with what sounded like genuine interest.

Imogen squirmed in her seat. 'Yes,' she said shyly. 'I suppose I would. I'm actually in the middle of writing my first novel.'

'Romance, is it?'

'Horror, actually.'

'Plenty of sex and violence?' asked Heffernan cheekily.

Imogen reddened. 'Well, er . . . quite a bit, I suppose. But all essential to the plot, of course,' she added righteously.

Heffernan and Wesley exchanged looks. 'Of course.'

When Imogen returned to her duties, they asked her to send in Muriel Potter next. It would be valuable to have another assessment of Brian Willerby's character.

'What do you think, Wes?' Heffernan asked as soon as they were alone.

Wesley shrugged. 'Who knows? Perhaps Willerby had an itch in an embarrassing place and needed to scratch it. And one thing's for certain: our Imogen has admitted to possessing a rather vivid imagination. A sexually obsessed satyr of a boss would fit in rather well with her Gothic view of the world, I should say. And, let's face it, she freely admits that he never actually did or even suggested anything untoward. It's pure supposition.'

124

'I'm inclined to agree with you, Wes. Mind you, if Muriel Potter comes up with the same story, we'll have to sit up and take notice.'

But Muriel Potter was a different animal altogether. She didn't seem to have an imaginative bone in her body. To her Brian Willerby had always been the perfect gentleman. With an unexpected splutter of candour, she stated that Willerby had seemed to her to be a sexually repressed, rather pathetic little man; hardly the voracious lecher of Imogen's imaginings. She dismissed the younger woman's opinions with a patronising smile. 'Imogen's a nice girl and she's good at her job but she does have a vivid imagination,' she said. 'She likes to dramatise everything. She's writing a book, you know, so I shouldn't take too much notice of anything she says.'

At that point a chubby young fingerprint officer poked his head discreetly round the office door and announced that he'd finished.

Heffernan stood up. 'Mrs Potter, would you be good enough to have a look in Mr Willerby's office and tell us if there's anything missing?'

Muriel Potter, the good citizen, trotted enthusiastically towards Willerby's office and opened the door. It was a mess, the chaos enhanced by a liberal dusting of fingerprint powder. 'Oh dear,' was Mrs Potter's only comment as she picked her way over the files scattered on the floor.

She began to gather them up, placing them back in their cabinet in alphabetical order. She was a woman who knew her way around a filing system as London cabbies know their way around the streets of their city. The two policemen watched her work with some admiration.

'Can you tell if anything's missing yet?' asked Wesley, suspecting that it would be early days.

'Oh yes,' the secretary said confidently, stuffing files back into the grey metal cabinet. 'There's no sign of the Earlsacre file. All the others seem to be here but that one's missing.'

'You seem very sure,' said Heffernan.

'Oh, I am, Chief Inspector. All this mess looks much worse than it is. Look, they've not even tried to open the safe.' She pointed to a small safe in the corner which squatted on the floor, smug and apparently untouched.

'Perhaps the safe was too much for 'em if it's just kids seeing what they can find,' said Heffernan dismissively. 'What's in it?'

'A few cheques usually; clients' monies.'

'What about his desk?' asked Wesley. 'Is anything missing from the drawers?'

She walked slowly over to the large oak desk and looked down at the open drawers. On the floor beneath the desk lay a petty-cash box, discarded and gaping open.

'Only the petty cash by the look of it.' She knelt down. 'May I?' She looked up at Wesley inquiringly. He nodded and she picked up the box to examine it. 'All the money's gone. There was about fifty pounds.'

'Was it locked?'

'Not usually. I'm afraid we're rather lax about security. Of course, that'll have to change after this.'

'So all that's missing is the money and the Earlsacre file. Could he have taken the file home for some reason?'

'That's always possible. You'll have to ask his wife about that.'

'Thank you, Mrs Potter. You've been a great help. By the way, what exactly was in the Earlsacre file?'

'Nothing very exciting. Mr Willerby's involvement with the Earlsacre estate was mostly on the conveyancing side, routine stuff. I'm afraid most of the more interesting work to do with the trust Mr Samuels set up was handled by a larger firm, in London.'

'So there weren't likely to be any sensitive or confidential documents in the missing file?' Wesley wanted to make sure of his facts.

Mrs Potter shook her curly, grey head. 'Nothing like that, not that I can recall. I'm sorry.'

'That's okay, Mrs Potter. Thanks for your help.' Wesley gave the secretary a friendly smile. He suspected that she would be a useful ally, a reliable informant on the inside of Blake, Willerby and Johns.

There was nobody left to interview. Blake was sunning himself in the Caribbean, oblivious to the chaos awaiting him on his return – and furnished with a perfect alibi. Johns would return later in the day from a long weekend spent with a clergyman – another impeccable alibi. Gerry Heffernan shambled down the stairs and pushed open the glass door which led on to the street.

Wesley's mobile phone began to ring. 'You should get that phone of yours to play one of them tunes, Wes. Music while you work,' was Heffernan's only comment as he waited expectantly to hear the outcome of the brief conversation.

'That was Rachel,' said Wesley as he returned the phone to his pocket. 'She says the woman who owns the caravan park, Dilys Fielding, wants a word. She asked for me.'

'Oh aye, Wes. How come they never ask for me? You want to watch that one, Wes. I saw how she was looking at you.'

'How is Mrs Green, by the way?' asked Wesley mischievously. 'When are you seeing her again?'

His boss's cheeks reddened. 'Oh, er, it depends on how soon we can get this case cleared up. We're just good friends, you know.'

'I believe you. But will the station gossip machine?' He looked at his watch. 'I'd better get going. I'm meeting Rachel at Bloxham View.'

He left Gerry Heffernan wandering down the High Street towards Tradmouth police station and took the chugging car ferry over the River Trad to Queenswear: Bloxham was a short drive away through hilly green countryside. Rachel Tracey, true to her promise, was waiting in her car by the entrance to the caravan park.

'Mrs Fielding asked for you personally,' she said as she climbed out of the driver's seat. 'You must have made quite an impression.'

'Don't you start. I've had enough of that from the boss. So what exactly did Mrs Fielding say? Why does she want to see me?'

'She just said she wanted to talk to you and that her husband's out all day.' She grinned meaningfully. 'I hope she's not too disappointed when she sees me.'

'Think I need a chaperone, do you?'

'Perhaps.' She began to march towards the Fieldings' bungalow.

He caught up with her and they walked side by side up to the bungalow's ugly front door, a plain sheet of hardboard painted a bilious green.

Rachel's instincts had been right. Dilys Fielding answered the door and she greeted Wesley with a coquettish smile. But as soon as she spotted Rachel standing beside him, the smile disappeared. She stood aside to let them in and led them into the living room. Sitting on the edge of the sofa was the girl they had seen serving in the site shop: her plain, pasty features were arranged into an expression of studied boredom and her mousey hair was scraped back into a limp ponytail.

'You've something to tell us, Mrs Fielding?' asked Wesley.

Dilys glanced awkwardly at Rachel. 'It's Kimberley here. She overheard the dead man talking on the phone. There's a pay-phone in the shop,' she added by way of explanation.

Kimberley looked at Wesley, her boredom replaced by uncertainty.

'What did he say, Kimberley?' he asked. 'Try and remember. It might be important.' He leaned forward, waiting expectantly for the reply.

'The policeman who saw me told me to say if I remembered anything.' She hesitated. 'I didn't think about it at first but then I remembered. I'm sure it was on the Monday at around six. He just came in here to use the phone – loads of people do. Anyway, he's talking all sort of quiet, like, and I didn't get to hear much, but I think he said something like "I need to talk to you" . . . all sort of serious, like. Then he said something like "Could you come here?" and he gave directions. I can't remember anything else. Someone came in and I had to serve them.'

Wesley nodded. The girl was probably in the habit of eavesdropping on people's calls, he thought. Anything to relieve the tedium of her days.

'That's great, Kimberley,' said Rachel encouragingly. 'Is there anything else?'

Kimberley shook her head.

'Can you remember what he was wearing?' asked Wesley. It was worth a try.

Kimberley thought for a few moments. 'He had a white T-shirt . . . with writing on.'

Wesley felt his heart beating faster. 'What was the writing, Kimberley? What did it say?'

'How should I know what it said? It were in foreign.'

Wesley took a deep breath. 'What kind of foreign? Please think carefully.'

'I don't know. It were like one of them shields or a coat of arms with a name underneath. I don't know what it said. I wasn't taking much notice.'

'Well, if you remember any more, please let us know.' He handed Kimberley his card, which she regarded with suspicion.

Dilys Fielding looked at Rachel with some hostility, then she leaned forward and whispered in Wesley's ear. 'You've not forgotten I promised to take you to sample those crab sandwiches at the Trawlerman's Arms, have you?'

Kimberley stifled a giggle.

'Another time perhaps,' he said awkwardly. 'We'd better go.

Thank you, and if either of you remember anything else be sure to let us know. We can see ourselves out.'

Dilys watched them go, her disappointment as clear as a beacon on a hillside. Wesley suspected he'd had a narrow escape.

'What did you make of Kimberley's phone call?' asked Rachel as they walked away.

Wesley thought for a moment. 'He says he needs to talk to whoever it was and asks them to come to the caravan park. But Kimberley herself admits that she didn't hear it clearly. He could have been ringing a long-lost auntie for all we know.'

'Or his murderer?'

'Possibly. What did you make of the T-shirt with the coat of arms and foreign writing on?'

'It would help if we knew what kind of foreign.'

'Mmm. It could be anything. Could even be Latin if it's underneath a coat of arms,' Wesley said, frustrated by Kimberley's lack of observational skills.

'What did you think of Dilys?' asked Rachel.

'Not a happy lady, I suspect.'

'It's a good job I came with you or she would have eaten you alive,' said Rachel with an uncharacteristic giggle.

Wesley thought it best not to comment and carried on strolling up the fields full of caravans towards the top field, where John Jones' life had been brought to an abrupt end. Somebody had felt strongly enough about Jones to kill him, and destroy any clues to his identity . . . whatever that identity was. But why?

The mud in the field had dried up a little. Wesley picked his way over the ruts. He noticed that the Wheeler family were packing a rusting Japanese car up to the roof with the detritus of a completed holiday. Suitcases wrapped in black bin-bags were perched perilously on a roof rack, and the open boot was devouring sandy beach equipment and dirty towels. Mrs Wheeler spotted Wesley and waved cheerfully. He waved back, looking for young Billy, but he was nowhere in sight.

Wesley halted in front of the dead man's caravan, now cordoned off with blue-and-white police tape. He ducked under the tape, Rachel following silently behind, and opened the caravan door. He stood there, staring at the floor where the body had lain. Rusty brown splashes of dried blood were still visible on the sides of the bench seats, the drawn curtains and the light brown carpeted floor. He shuddered a little and walked on through the narrow kitchen area with its fake oak cupboards and the tiny shower room and toilet partitioned off to one side, then he entered the bedroom, stripped and bare. 'What a place to die,' he said under his breath.

'I've seen worse places,' said Rachel.

He turned. He had almost forgotten she was there. 'I mean, it's all so impersonal, so empty.'

'Well, presumably all his things have been taken away,' Rachel answered pragmatically.

'The murderer must have had a fair bit of blood on his clothes. And he must have taken the dead man's T-shirt off. What did he do with it?'

'Put it in a bin? Throw it into the sea?' Rachel suggested.

'It's possible. But he'd still be covered in blood. He must have had to clean himself up somewhere. And how easy is it to get rid of clothes unless you burn them? Also, he must have come here by car.'

'There are so many cars coming and going from this site that . . .'

'I noticed the Wheelers are packing up to go. Let's have a last word with young Billy.'

'I've no sweets on me,' said Rachel.

'We'll have to send some on to him if he comes up with the goods. Come on.'

He left the caravan quickly, glad to be out of the place.

'Mrs Wheeler,' he called as he approached the rusty, laden vehicle which, with luck, would get the Wheelers back up the motorway system to their Lancashire home. 'Can I have a quick word with your Billy if he's about?'

' 'Course you can, love. Billy!' she shrieked at foghorn volume.

Billy appeared at the caravan door and, anticipating sweet rewards, gave Wesley a wide grin. 'How do? Did you want a word?'

Wesley went up to him and spoke confidentially, man to man. 'I've been thinking about cars, Billy. I'm sure someone must have asked you this already, but did you see a car around on the night of the murder? I know you saw the man and you've given us a brilliant description, but did you see car near by?'

He held his breath, waiting hopefully. He had read Billy's statement several times and had noticed no mention of any sort of vehicle. Perhaps there wasn't one. Or perhaps the killer had parked it in the bottom field where Craig Kettering had parked his van. There were so many cars there that an extra one would go unnoticed. But

130

somehow he couldn't envisage Brian Willerby walking up the steep fields from the reception carpark. And it hadn't rained heavily until Wednesday night, so mud wouldn't have been a problem. He would have parked close to the caravan if at all possible. It was a long shot, but Wesley felt he had to ask.

'Oh aye, there was a car,' answered Billy matter-of-factly. 'A Vauxhall Vectra ... dark coloured ... newish. It was parked right next to the dead man's caravan. But I didn't see anyone get into it. Then I heard me mam and had to pretend I was asleep in case she came in.'

'Why didn't you tell us this before?'

'Nobody asked me. Do you reckon it belonged to the murderer, then, this car?' he asked with bloodthirsty relish.

'Are you sure it was a Vectra?'

'Oh aye,' said Billy confidently. 'I know all the makes, me. And the models. Test me if you like,' he challenged.

'I'll take your word for it. I don't suppose you saw the registration number?'

'Nah. It were parked in the shadows. There's no way I could have made out the number.' He held out his hand expectantly. 'That'll be three Mars bars.'

Wesley delved in his pocket and extracted two pound coins. 'That should cover it. Keep the change.'

'Thanks,' said Billy appreciatively, pocketing the cash. 'That'll do nicely.'

'I think we'd better contact the Lancashire force and tell them there's a reliable informant on their patch who'll work for a steady supply of sweets,' said Rachel as they strolled down the fields back to the car.

'Don't knock it,' said Wesley. 'Guess what kind of car Brian Willerby drove?'

'What?'

'Would you believe a dark blue Vectra?'

Wesley Peterson drove back to Earlsacre via Tradmouth, feeling rather pleased with himself.

Chapter 9

14 June 1685
My son, I beg you to persuade your brother, Richard, not to join
with the rebels. I myself fought for parliament against this
present King's father and I long for a return to the liberties of
our faith we enjoyed under the good rule of our late Lord
Protector, Master Cromwell. But I fear this King James will
tolerate no rebellion and I fear for Richard's life should he join
the Duke of Monmouth in Taunton as he is resolved to do. I have
heard talk that the King will deal most cruelly with all who
oppose him.
*   While I am away in London I charge you to look to your*
younger brother and keep him from foolishness. And I beg you,
my son, not to give entry to my creditors. I am in sore debt but
pray that my fortunes will recover soon.
*   Your loving father, John Lantrist*

Gerry Heffernan rubbed his hands together with glee when Wesley
broke the news. 'Let's get down there and pay our respects to the
grieving widow . . . and get Forensic to give his car a good going over
while we're at it. If he used it to get away from the murder scene
there's bound to be traces of blood and gore about. And the dead
man's T-shirt; what did he do with it?'

'All the bins in and near the caravan site have been searched and
nothing's been found. Rachel thinks it might have been thrown in the
sea or burned.'

'Anything's possible. Ask the coastguards to keep their eyes open
for any clothing washed up anywhere in the vicinity, will you?' He

charged out of the doorway of the incident room. 'Tell Rach to come with us and all.'

Wesley passed on the message and Rachel followed without a word. The three walked down the drive of Earlsacre Hall towards the village. Heffernan had decreed that a short car journey was unnecessary, unecological and would give advance warning of their arrival. He also expressed a desire to get more exercise, and Wesley wondered if he could detect Mrs Green's influence somewhere in the background.

They arrived chez Willerby five minutes later feeling fitter. And their journey on foot past the home of Les Cumbernold had allowed them a glimpse through his half-open garage door into the shadowy space beyond. It seemed to be filled with mysterious shapes that held a promise of being more interesting than the usual assortment of junk stored in the average British garage. Wesley found the strange, half-seen objects intriguing, but they were there to concentrate on Brian Willerby – his life, death, and the fact that he was possibly a murderer. His dark blue Vectra stood tantalisingly in the front drive, its inscrutable tinted windows guarding whatever secrets it held.

Martha Willerby answered the door, her plain face devoid of make-up. She looked tired as she stood aside to let them in.

'We're sorry to bother you again, Mrs Willerby,' said Rachel gently, sensing that she was there to dispense the sympathy – and probably the tea as well. 'But we have to ask you a few more questions. We'll try not to keep you very long.'

Gerry Heffernan began. 'We went to your husband's office earlier on this morning. I suppose you know that there's been a break-in there?'

Martha looked up with shocked, reddened eyes. 'No,' she gasped. 'No, I didn't. That's awful.'

'Some petty cash was taken,' said Wesley, 'and Mrs Potter, the secretary, says that one of the files is missing – a file concerning his dealings with the Earlsacre estate. I don't suppose it's in the house? He might have brought it home for some reason.'

'He sometimes brings . . . brought files home to work on. I'll see if it's in his study.'

She stood up and Heffernan gave Rachel an almost imperceptible nod, instructing her to follow the widow upstairs.

While they were gone Gerry Heffernan took the opportunity to look around the room. Wesley went over to the window and stared out into the expansive back garden. 'I wonder if he burned any garden rubbish this week,' he said thoughtfully. 'Good way of getting rid of the evidence.'

'We'll ask. And we can ask the neighbour and all ... get an unbiased version.'

'I'd hardly call Les Cumbernold unbiased.'

But before Heffernan could answer Rachel returned with Martha.

'I'm afraid there's no sign of that file you mentioned.' She sat down, omitting to offer the customary tea. 'I'm sorry.'

'Would you like me to make a cup of tea?' Rachel asked, making up for her hostess's shortcomings.

'Thank you.' Martha watched the other woman disappear into her kitchen without further comment.

'There are a couple more things we wanted to ask you,' began Wesley when Rachel returned with refreshment. 'You said that your husband was out last Tuesday. What time did he get home?'

'I can't remember ... er, late I think. After midnight.'

'And how did he seem when he got home? Were his clothes soiled at all? Was he carrying anything?' He thought the question 'Was your husband covered in blood?' might be a little tactless at this stage.

'I didn't see him. I'd already gone to bed. We don't share a bedroom,' she added coyly.

'What happened to the clothes he was wearing that night?' asked Rachel, ever practical. 'Did you see them in the morning?'

'I really can't remember. Brian was a tidy man; he always put his dirty laundry straight into the linen basket in the bathroom.'

'When you did your washing did you notice any bloodstains on anything?' Gerry Heffernan, not one to believe in beating around any bushes, said bluntly.

Martha Willerby stared at him, shocked. 'I don't think so. He did have a nosebleed and he got some blood on his shirt collar and his handkerchief, but I think that was later in the week; Thursday probably. Why? Why do you want to know?' She took a sip of tea, just for something to do with her fidgeting hands.

Wesley removed a photograph of John Jones from his top pocket. It had been taken after his death but Jones had been tastefully arranged for the camera to look his best. 'I wonder if you'd have a look at this photograph for me,' he said, passing it to Martha. 'Have you seen this man before?'

She stared at the picture for a few seconds. 'Is he . . . is he dead? It looks as though he's dead.'

'I'm afraid we didn't find any photographs of him taken when he was alive. Do you recognise him?'

She handed the picture back and shook her head vehemently. 'No. I've never seen him before.'

Something in her manner told Wesley that he shouldn't give up just yet. 'Please, Mrs Willerby, have another look. Have you seen him before, however briefly? Please think.'

She took the photograph back and held it by the very edge, as if she didn't want her hands to come into contact with the dead image. 'There is something familiar about him but I don't . . . No, I'm sure I've never seen him.'

Wesley took the photograph from her as Gerry Heffernan waded in. 'We'll have to examine your husband's car, love. We've arranged for it to be done before lunch. Okay?'

Martha Willerby looked at him with distaste. 'I don't suppose I've got much choice in the matter,' she said with a first, tentative show of defiance.

'Could you tell me if you've had a garden fire recently?' asked Wesley politely, trying to make up for his boss's lack of finesse.

'We have an incinerator at the end of the garden. I think Brian burned some garden rubbish in it on Wednesday . . . or it might have been Thursday, I'm not sure.'

'Thank you, Mrs Willerby. You've been very helpful.' He stood up.

Martha looked worried, as if she'd given too much away. But she made the best of it and saw them off the premises with confident civility. For a woman described by her own brother as a nonentity, she wasn't doing too badly.

The forensic team were just arriving to examine Willerby's car as they left. Heffernan strolled over to have a word with them.

'What do you think?' Wesley asked Rachel as they stood watching the team go about their business.

'That photograph meant something to her, I'm sure it did.'

'Yes, I'm sure she knows more than she's letting on.'

Gerry Heffernan returned, having issued loud orders to the forensic team to examine the contents of the incinerator in the back garden while they were about it. Rachel and Wesley looked at each other: there were times when Gerry Heffernan pushed his luck. They just hoped Martha Willerby wasn't well up on the ins and outs of search warrants.

'Me belly thinks me mouth's gone on strike. Anyone fancy coming to the King's Head for a butty?' called Heffernan loudly, approaching with a wide grin on his face.

Following the maxim that silence gives consent, Wesley and Rachel fell in behind their boss without a word and walked the fifty yards to the ancient hostelry that stood, white-painted and creeper-clad, at the centre of Earlsacre village.

This time the lounge door was locked and they had to enter through the public bar. Some men standing at the bar, ostentatiously local, stopped their conversation in mid-sentence when Wesley walked in and stared at him for a few moments before turning away and taking up where they'd left off. Gerry Heffernan returned their stare boldly, then marched through into the lounge, a place more suitable for strangers and those wearing suits.

'Don't you lot ever do any work?' he said loudly as he spotted Neil hunched in a corner of the lounge with Matt, Jane, Jake and Charles Pitaway. 'Every time I see you you're always swelling the profits of some brewery or other.'

Neil looked up from his pint with calm amusement. 'I could say exactly the same about the police force.' He beckoned to Wesley. 'Come and sit down, Wes. I've got something to show you.'

Charles Pitaway stood up and greeted Rachel with a smile, which she returned shyly.

'Don't mind us – that's the best offer you're going to have all day,' said Heffernan. 'Go on, Wes. If it's anything to do with our murders you'll let us know, won't you?' He handed round the drinks and sandwiches and retired to a window seat with Rachel, leaving Wesley to join the group in the corner. Pitaway's eyes followed Rachel. Wesley noticed. If it weren't for Gerry Heffernan, Charles would have been over there trying his luck. And from the signals Rachel was giving out, he might not have been wasting his time.

Wesley turned back to Neil. 'So what do you want to show me?'

Neil extracted a crumpled piece of paper from the pocket of his jeans. 'This is just a photocopy. Claire found the original among a load of old papers to do with Earlsacre Hall. The papers are all mixed up in an old trunk so it's possible there could be more letters still waiting to be discovered. They've been given by the Wilton family, who lived at Earlsacre from the late 1940s to the early 1960s, but they're just dumped in the trunk; not sorted or anything. Claire's not rushing it: she's cataloguing them one by one.' He handed Wesley the paper as Matt, Jane and Jake took their leave, anxious to return to their excavations.

Charles Pitaway left with them. Rachel watched him go, and Wesley saw him give her a smile on his way out. He turned his attention resolutely to the letter. When he'd read it he let out a low whistle. 'This is amazing. So this John Lantrist was Richard's father and he's writing to his elder son to ask him to persuade the younger brother, Richard, not to go off and join the Duke of Monmouth's rebels?'

'That's about it. We just need to find some more correspondence now to fill in the gaps. We've got Richard Lantrist as a hot-headed, idealistic young rebel in 1685, then when we meet him again eighteen years later in Jacob Finsbury's account of his stay at Earlsacre he's turned into a grumpy old fart, to put it bluntly. I'd just like to know what happened to him in between. And what turned him into a murderer. It must have had something to do with his experiences when he was transported to the West Indies as a slave. That'd be enough to change anyone, I suppose.'

Wesley looked down at his glass. 'Too right. Man's inhumanity to man, eh?' He was silent for a few moments.

Neil watched him, not knowing quite what to say. 'Yeah, you're right,' he muttered after a while. The conversation was getting a bit deep for him.

'Whereabouts in the West Indies was Richard sent?' asked Wesley quietly, thinking of his family connections.

'Dunno,' Neil replied, glad their talk had returned to bare history, to facts. He was comfortable with facts. 'It just says the West Indies in all the books I've read. Anyway, he got back somehow and claimed the estate after his dad and elder brother died. I wonder how he managed to get back. And how he knew he'd inherited.'

'Things might have eased up for the Monmouth rebels once James II had gone and a new king was on the throne. He might have been able to persuade some sympathetic sea captain to give him a passage back. If so, he was luckier than most,' Wesley added softly, a hint of bitterness in his voice.

'If Claire finds more letters we might get to know. It'd be brilliant if we could learn the whole story and find out what turned an idealistic young lad into a double murderer.'

'And find out who the skeletons were. Perhaps they were people who betrayed him to the king's army during the rebellion,' Wesley speculated.

'One of them was only a young girl who probably wasn't even born in 1685. Try again, Acting Detective Inspector.'

Wesley picked up his glass and drank. Neil was right. 'Did I tell you my mother's maiden name was Lantrist?' he said suddenly.

Neil looked at him, surprised. 'No. Maybe you're related. Do you know of anyone English in the family?'

'We've all sorts in our family: African, Spanish, Venezuelan, bit of Indian. Trinidad's one of the most cosmopolitan places in the world, so there's a good chance there's some English in there somewhere.'

'Funny if you turn out to be related to these particular Lantrists.' Neil looked Wesley in the eye. 'How would you feel about having an ancestor who's a double murderer?' he asked bluntly.

Wesley took another pull at his drink. It was something he hadn't considered before and he didn't want to think about it now. He saw again in his mind's eye the delicate bones on the mortuary trolley, and imagined once more her slow agonising death; her battle to move and breathe beneath the weight of the earth. There was no way he could be linked by blood and genes to the creature who would do that to another human being. It was unthinkable. He needed to change the subject. 'How's Claire?'

'Okay,' answered Neil non-committally. He studied his soil-stained hands. He had known Wesley a long time; he knew he could trust him. But he also knew that, as a police officer, Wesley would consider it his duty to investigate anything he was told that might have a bearing on Brian Willerby's death. Claire was innocent, he told himself firmly. There was no need to bother Wesley with the fact that Brian Willerby's name had been scored angrily out of her address book ... no need at all. There would be some simple explanation.

'I'd better go,' said Wesley, taking the last bite of his sandwich. 'I might come and see you later, introduce myself to Claire.' He hesitated. 'Was that her I saw before the cricket match? She was in the carpark by the stable block talking to someone,' he said, feeling as low as a dung-beetle for uttering such a blatant lie.

'Could have been.' Neil shrugged. 'She disappeared off somewhere. Don't know what she was doing.'

Wesley forced himself to sound cheerful. 'When Pam's settled down again at work you'll both have to come round for a meal.'

Neil attempted a smile which turned out to be more of a weak snarl. He hoped Wesley hadn't noticed.

Gerry Heffernan looked around the incident room for Wesley, but he was nowhere to be seen. Steve Carstairs was sitting near by, his eyes glued to a computer screen but his mind elsewhere.

'Fancy a bit of fresh air, Steve?' the inspector called over. 'Come on, tear yourself away from that thing and we'll take a stroll around the grounds. There's someone I want to see.'

Steve rose without a word and followed his boss out into the daylight, his hands firmly in the pockets of his designer jeans.

'How are you getting on with our Acting Inspector Peterson these days?' Heffernan asked as they walked towards the hall.

'Okay,' Steve replied sulkily.

Heffernan turned to the younger man, his eyes narrowed. 'I've heard tales that you've been mouthing off in the canteen . . . saying he's only got promotion because he's black. What was the phrase you used? Political correctness gone mad?'

Steve flushed. 'Well, I . . . well, he hasn't been here five minutes.'

'So the fact that he's a bloody good officer and deserves the promotion has never crossed your tiny mind? Do I look like the politically correct type, Stephen? Have I been making nice cups of tea for female officers? Have I started a refuge for one-legged gay foxes? Would you associate me with political correctness in any way, shape or form?'

Steve was forced to answer in the negative.

Heffernan's expression became serious, all trace of humour gone. 'I'll just say this once,' he hissed, putting his face close to Steve's. 'If I hear that anything else like that has been coming out of your thick, ignorant gob, I'll make bloody sure you're not only chucked out of CID but out of the job too. Do I make myself absolutely clear?'

Steve backed away slightly, swallowed hard and nodded.

'And I think Inspector Peterson's shown a remarkable degree of tolerance – something you're sadly lacking. You should be grateful to him. Think about that, will you?'

'Yes, sir,' Steve almost whispered, stunned.

Gerry Heffernan held his gaze for a few moments, just to make certain that he had got the message across. 'Anything else bothering you?' he asked, a little more gently.

'No, sir,' Steve said, trying to sound confident. Then he hesitated, wondering if he should mention the money that he had lent the old man while under the influence of the fair Jackie. He had waited for the post each morning since, but the promised cheque had so far failed to arrive. But, on reflection, he decided to say nothing.

'Right, then,' said the chief inspector. 'I've said me piece so let's get on. Do you think we'll need hard hats to go into that hall? Looks a bit precarious with all that scaffolding.'

'Dunno, sir.'

'Well, go and ask one of those workmen over there and find out. And while you're about it ask where Martin Samuels is. Say we want a word with him.'

Steve scuttled off obediently and returned, much to Heffernan's surprise, with Samuels himself. Maybe things had begun to improve already.

'Ah, Chief Inspector Heffernan. Any news about our statues?' Samuels asked anxiously as he approached. 'I really did think they'd be safe in the pavilion.'

'Some people'd pinch anything that's not screwed down,' observed Heffernan, his mind on other matters. 'We've been having a word with your guests.'

'Guests?' Samuels repeated, puzzled.

'The guests who ate at your house last Tuesday night.'

'Oh yes?'

Heffernan had to admire the masterful way in which Samuels was hiding his irritation. 'They mentioned that you left your house at approximately half past eleven saying you were coming here to pick up some important papers that you needed for a meeting the next day. When they left at midnight you hadn't returned.'

'Well, a round trip between here and the far side of Morbay does take longer than half an hour, Inspector,' Samuels replied with a smug smile. 'It's quite true that I slipped out. I'd only just remembered that the papers were still here and our guests were about to leave anyway. I needed the documents urgently for a meeting in London the next morning.'

'What were the documents?'

'Mainly financial. Balance sheets, projections – you know the sort of thing.'

Heffernan nodded solemnly, trying to look as though he was well up on accountancy matters. 'Why did you forget to bring them home in the first place if they were so important?'

'I thought I had them until I checked everything for the following day. It was a simple mistake. I forgot them.'

'And what time did you find they were missing?'

'About eight o'clock. I couldn't go for them then because our guests were due to arrive for a meal. I got away at the first opportunity. Why are you asking all these questions? Brian died on Saturday, so why . . .?'

'Why didn't you mention this nocturnal paper-chase when you were questioned before?' Heffernan looked Samuels in the eye.

'I didn't think it was relevant,' Samuels replied smoothly. 'In fact, I never thought about it. It was just a minor irritation, nothing important.'

Heffernan produced a photograph of the dead John Jones. 'Do you recognise this man?'

'No,' Samuels said, affronted. 'Of course I don't. Why?'

'Are you sure? Take a good look.'

Samuels took the photograph from Heffernan and studied it. He shook his head. 'Sorry. I've never seen him before. I'm afraid I can't help you.'

'Right, sir. I think that's all for now. Thank you for your time,' Heffernan said, using his favourite thick-plod persona.

'Any time. Always happy to help the police. Pity you didn't bring your other sidekick with you. That rather cultured black chap. Nice bloke. Did you know he has a first in archaeology?'

Heffernan turned to look at the expression on Steve's face, but Steve was wise enough to let nothing show.

'Is that what he's got? Well I never. No doubt he's about somewhere digging something up for us, then. I'll be off now, Mr Samuels. Crime calls. If we hear anything about your statues we'll let you know.'

As Gerry Heffernan strolled slowly back towards the stable block with Steve skulking in his wake, he spotted Wesley in the distance and his footsteps quickened.

'Good lunch, Wes?'

'Mmm. But Neil's not his usual self. It really must be love. I've never known anyone to change overnight like that before.'

'Given up illegal weeds and starting taking baths, has he?'

141

Wesley laughed. 'This Claire must be quite something. I never thought I'd see Neil in this state.'

'Let's hope it continues. And talking of love, how's your randy mother-in-law and her supermarket bargain?'

Wesley raised his eyes heavenward. Della was one person he would rather forget. 'Don't ask. We're just waiting for the next midnight phone call.' He paused. 'Actually I've been feeling a bit uneasy about this new bloke of hers. He's talked her into investing some of her money.'

'Oh aye. Looked him up on our wonderful computer, have you?'

'Yes, but there was nothing on him. He calls himself a financial adviser . . .'

Heffernan nodded knowingly. He'd heard stories like this too many times before to show any surprise. 'And you think he advises wealthy widows to offload their cash into his wallet, do you?'

Wesley smiled. 'Perhaps I'm getting too suspicious.'

'This job makes you like that, Wes. Just tell her to be careful, eh.'

'I doubt if she'd take any notice,' Wesley said. But Della was a grown woman: what she did was up to her. And he had work to do. He sat himself down by a computer and punched a few buttons.

'What are you doing?' asked Heffernan, looking over his shoulder.

'I sent an e-mail to the Gloucestershire force earlier asking for a better picture and more details about their missing postgraduate student from Chipping Campden. I'm just seeing if they've replied.'

'Well, well. In my day it was posting it in the letterbox and hoping for the best.'

'They call that snail mail nowadays,' said Wesley with a grin. 'You should learn more about computers, you know.' He looked round and saw that his boss seemed unconvinced. 'Don't forget that it was new technology that caught Dr Crippen.'

'Contrary to popular rumour, he wasn't one of my collars . . . before my time. Hey, that's a good picture,' he said as a well-defined colour photograph appeared on the screen. 'What does it say underneath?'

Wesley stared at the picture; a graduation photograph, complete with cap, gown and diploma, the subject beaming proudly at the camera. Heffernan leaned over Wesley's shoulder to read the text underneath. Michael Patrick Thoresby, aged twenty-four. He read on: address; occupation; last seen; height; blood group.

'It's not him,' Wesley stated softly. On closer inspection the image looked nothing like John Jones. And Colin Bowman's report had said that the dead man was two inches taller; and he was blood group O whereas Thoresby was group A. Wesley sighed. Back to square one.

'Any other likely missing persons?' asked Heffernan in quiet desperation.

Wesley shook his head. 'Nobody who matches the description. But our mystery man's picture has been sent out to all forces, so we're bound to get some feedback sooner or later. He can't have just landed here from Mars; someone must know him. As John Donne said, no man is an island.'

'Who?'

'John Donne, the poet.'

The chief inspector chuckled. 'I thought you were talking about John Dun, who I put away for five years for armed robbery . . . hardly one to come over all poetic. And talking of poetry, I was thinking that it might be worth having a word with that Jacintha woman, the poet in residence. She seems to float around Earlsacre, and it's always possible she's picked up some interesting snippets of information on her travels. And I reckon she was the long-haired woman Willerby was talking to before the cricket match.'

'It's possible. She seems to get everywhere. And I suspect that everyone thinks she's a bit batty so they might be off their guard when she's around.'

'And is she batty?'

'I really couldn't say. But apart from the poetry – which Neil tells me is pretty dire – it seems that her favourite hobby is chasing the male of the species. Charles Pitaway was trying to avoid her at the cricket match. And she seems to have Jake in her clutches.'

'What a woman. Why don't I meet anyone like that?'

'It looks like she goes for younger men,' said Wesley with a grin.

'Can't win 'em all. Fancy a trip into Tradmouth?'

'What for?'

'Remember I saw Brian Willerby going into that house opposite the church when I was on my way back from choir practice on Friday night?'

Wesley nodded.

'I think it might be worth paying whoever lives there a visit, don't you?'

Wesley couldn't argue with that. In fact the thought had been at the

143

back of his own mind, but he had been too preoccupied to do anything about it.

It took them twenty minutes to drive down the narrow winding lanes that led to the main road into Tradmouth. The ancient port hadn't been developed with the car in mind, so Wesley parked in the police station carpark and they walked past the memorial park, through the shop-lined streets and up a steep, cobbled alleyway to the medieval church of St Margaret. The exercise, Wesley thought, would do them both good.

When they reached Church View, Gerry Heffernan didn't hesitate. He marched up to the glossy black front door of number seven, raised the polished brass lion's-head in the centre of the door and brought it down with a crash three times. 'That should wake 'em,' he mumbled.

They could hear shuffling from within, then bolts being drawn back. Whoever lived at number seven had either been reading the constabulary's home security leaflets or had something to keep from the outside world.

For some reason Wesley had been expecting the door to be opened by a nervous old-age pensioner, so he and Heffernan were quite unprepared for the reality. A beautiful young woman of slightly oriental appearance stood before them in a red silk kimono, her slender arms holding the edges of the embroidered garment together for decency's sake.

She was the lucky owner of creamy skin and hair like black spun satin. Somehow her exotic loveliness seemed out of place in Church View, Tradmouth. The two policemen stood on the pavement for a few seconds gawping. Until Wesley realised that it was up to him to do the talking: he produced his warrant card and took a deep breath.

'Sorry to bother you, madam, but I wonder if you know a Brian Willerby. He is . . . was a solicitor with an office in the High Street. He was seen calling at this address last Friday evening.'

The young woman looked them up and down for a few seconds, then gave Wesley a shy smile. 'You'd better come inside,' she said with a soft, accentless voice, stepping aside to let them in. 'Wait in there, please,' she said, indicating a door to the left. 'I'll get Carlotta.'

She disappeared, and Wesley opened the door. The room was small but sumptuous with a profusion of red velvet and gold sofas, like quicksand, and a scarlet-draped divan in the corner, tented with rich fabrics like something out of a sultan's harem.

'Pam would say this looks like a tart's boudoir,' said Wesley, looking round, wrinkling his nose in distaste.

'Then she'd be remarkably accurate, Wes, because that's exactly what it is.' Heffernan paused to watch Wesley's reaction. 'I haven't come across old Carlotta for a few years,' he continued. 'And she's kept very quiet about this place. Talk about discreet – even our lot haven't had wind of it. I reckon this must be an upmarket offshoot of her place in Morbay.'

'You mean she's a madam and that girl's one of her . . .'

'That's right, Wes. The oldest profession. Don't look so surprised. Sex isn't confined to Greater London, you know.'

'I never thought it was.' Wesley grinned. 'So Brian Willerby paid for his pleasures?'

'Paid through the nose, I should think. Girls like that one don't come cheap . . . so I've heard.'

The door opened and a tall, elegant woman entered. Wesley guessed that she must be nearing sixty. She had an immaculate blue-rinsed coiffure and wore a businesslike blue suit of the type worn by Margaret Thatcher in her days of power. She would have looked comfortable serving on the committee of any Conservative club in the land. Respectability oozed from every pore. Wesley wondered what she was doing in such an establishment. Selling raffle tickets for party funds perhaps?

'Hello, Carlotta. Still up to your old tricks?'

'Gerry Heffernan. Long time no see. How are you keeping? And who's your friend?' she asked, looking at Wesley speculatively.

'This is Acting Inspector Peterson. I'm taking him on a tour of the local attractions, so I thought I'd call in here and show him the sights. Nice place you've got here.'

'For the more discerning client. I'll give you one of our cards, Gerry. Never know when it might come in useful.' She gave Wesley a most un-Thatcherlike wink.

'I couldn't afford it, love. Not on a policeman's salary. We've come about one of your, er . . . clients. At least, I presume he was a client: I saw him coming in here last Friday evening. Name of Brian Willerby.'

'I never discuss clients. Confidentiality is most important in my business.'

'It's always possible that one or all of your establishments might be closed down if there were complaints from . . .'

'Oh, come on, Gerry. What's wrong with allowing some respectable young ladies to meet gentleman friends in a house which I happen to own? The police didn't even know about this place, so that's how much of an outrage to public decency it is. Besides, I number some very important local figures among our, er ... gentleman friends here. I think your Chief Superintendent would be rather upset to know that you've been harassing me.'

Heffernan refused to be intimidated. 'I'll tell him you refused to co-operate in a murder inquiry, then, shall I?' He looked her directly in the eye, challenging.

It was Carlotta who backed down. 'All right. Brian Willerby was a client of ours. He visited us around once a week in general.'

'Did he, er, visit any young lady in particular? Or wasn't he particular?' Heffernan asked cheekily.

Wesley stared, still stunned by the reference to the Chief Super.

'He rather liked Lilly; that's the girl who opened the door. He liked young, dark, pretty girls rather than the more, er . . . obvious type.'

'Can we have a word with the lovely Lilly, then?'

Carlotta gave him a cool look. 'I'll get her.'

She left the room and Wesley tapped Heffernan on the arm. 'Do you think the Chief Super actually . . .'

'Who can tell? It'll have to be one of life's little mysteries.'

Carlotta returned with Lilly, who sat down in a red plush armchair opposite and pulled her kimono across her body again in a gesture of modesty.

'What can you tell us about Brian Willerby?' Wesley began.

Lilly glanced nervously at Carlotta before answering.

'He visited me around once a week. Usually on a Friday night. He wasn't much trouble.' She shrugged as if Brian Willerby was of no interest to her.

'You know he's dead? Possibly murdered?' said Heffernan, looking her in the eye.

'I don't know anything about that.' She looked down and fidgeted with the cheap silver ring she wore on the middle finger of her left hand.

'What were you doing on Saturday afternoon?'

She looked up at Heffernan as though he were stupid. 'Working, of course. Weekends are my busiest time.'

'Do you live here?' asked Wesley.

'I've got a flat in Morbay. I'm at university there but I work here at weekends and whenever I'm free.' She looked across at Wesley and saw he was staring at her. 'Well, I've got to live somehow,' she pronounced defensively. 'What with tuition fees and student debts I can't manage otherwise. I don't have rich parents who can bale me out and I'd rather do this than slave away in some bar every night.'

'Is there anything else you can tell us about Willerby? Anything at all?' Wesley asked more gently.

Lilly shook her head, her expression hidden behind a fine curtain of silken hair. 'No. Nothing.'

Heffernan gave Wesley a nudge and they both stood up.

'Thanks, love. If you remember anything else, give us a call, will you?'

Wesley handed Lilly one of his cards. 'Sorry to have bothered you,' he said softly, his eyes meeting hers. She gave a weak smile.

' 'Bye, then, Carlotta,' shouted Heffernan as they left. 'I'll give your love to the Chief Super, shall I?'

'Do as you please, Gerry. I don't suppose I'll see you again . . . not professionally at least,' she added with a knowing smirk.

'How long have you known Carlotta?' asked Wesley, burning with curiosity, as they walked back to the station.

'We go back years. I booked her for soliciting when I was a young and innocent constable. She's come up in the world since then, as you can see.'

'And that Lilly . . .'

'Student, eh? That's market forces for you: if you've got it, sell it . . . and she's got it all right.' He shook his head. 'These student fees are a bugger. Costs me a ruddy fortune to keep my two at university, I can tell you. When she was talking I kept thinking about how I'd feel if it was my Rosie doing something like that . . . satisfying the lusts of the Brian Willerbys of this world.' Wesley saw him shudder. 'Not a nice thought.'

'No. It's not,' Wesley said with some feeling.

Neil Watson scraped away at the foundations of the shell grotto with his trowel. Shells. They were everywhere, no doubt tumbled from the grotto when it had been demolished in the nineteenth century. He placed each one in the large plastic box at his side and scraped on, hoping for something more interesting.

At first he thought it was just another shell lying there, white and chalky against the soil. But as he dug, he realised that it was bigger than a shell, much bigger, and longer. Torn between excitement and dread, he dug faster. If it was what he feared, it would mean more delays, more fuss.

He called Jane over, trying his best to sound calm. 'Is that what I think it is?' he asked as she bent over for a better look.

She said nothing but began to use her trowel to loosen the earth around the top of the object. 'Oh yes,' she said, sitting back on her heels. 'That's a bone all right. Looks human. Right cemetery this is turning out to be. If Wesley's around, I'd call him over if I were you.'

Neil nodded, resigned. Another human burial. Just what he needed.

Chapter 10

12 June 1685
My dear brother
I write this from the Red Lion in the town of Taunton where I
wait upon events. I can say naught of what is expected because
the King has spies in all places and I have no wish for you to be
known as a friend of rebels – our family's fortunes are perilous
enough. You still have a place to keep in society, whereas I, as a
younger son, may follow my heart and my conscience.

You may be gratified to know that I am joined in this enterprise
by Joseph Marling, son of our gardener at Earlsacre. I fear my
talk of the rebellion and the wrongdoings of this government did
persuade him to our cause. Pray that he and I come through this
safe and that we return to Earlsacre, having ensured the freedom
of our faith.

Be assured that you and our father are ever in my prayers.
Your loving brother
Richard Lantrist

Wesley stood at the edge of the trench, looking down at the bones,
now almost completely uncovered. He still hadn't shaken off the
memory of the first skeleton – the young girl who had struggled
against the choking soil. He hoped this one had met a kinder end.

'Well, there's no chance that these are recent if they're beneath the
foundations of an early eighteenth-century building,' he said, turning
his thoughts to practical matters. 'Is there any chance they could have
been buried here once the grotto had been demolished?'

Neil shook his head. 'I don't think so. The bones were buried then
the grotto was built on top of them, isn't that right?' He looked to his

colleagues for confirmation and Jane, Matt and Jake nodded earnestly in agreement.

Wesley sighed. 'We'll still have to go through the motions, I suppose.' He thought for a moment. 'Are we sure this garden wasn't some sort of family burial ground?'

'There's no record of it. The family vault's in the village church,' said Claire, who was hovering at the edge of the group. Wesley looked round at her and smiled. This was his first encounter with her face to face. She returned the smile nervously.

'So what date are we looking at for this building?' Wesley asked nobody in particular.

'According to the garden accounts the shell grotto was built in May 1702,' said Claire. 'I've just been looking it up for Neil,' she added by way of explanation, giving Neil a shy glance.

'So that's the probable date of the burial? May 1702? The body was buried and then the grotto built on top of it?'

'More evidence against the wicked Sir Richard,' said Neil. 'He's the only one who had the opportunity to bury all three without anyone asking too many questions.'

'Or someone like a head gardener,' suggested Claire. 'That's always a possibility.'

Neil looked sceptical. 'I've read that book you lent me about Jacob Finsbury's visit. From Finsbury's comments I'd say this Sir Richard sounded very iffy indeed. In those days if you had enough money and power you could get away with murder.'

But Neil's musings on the abuses of privilege were interrupted by Gerry Heffernan, picking his way clumsily over the spoil heaps and trenches. 'I've heard there's another body.' He sounded worried, fearing an increase in his workload. 'Is Colin Bowman on his way?'

'It looks like another old one,' said Wesley calmly. 'No need to panic. It's nothing for us to worry about.'

'Be that as it may, it still takes up our valuable time.' He looked at Wesley in mock despair. 'Then I find my sergeant – sorry, acting inspector – lurking around trenches dying to get his mitts on a trowel to dig something up. Don't think I don't know, Wesley, I can read you like a book.'

He drew Wesley to one side, away from the trench. 'Tell you what,' he said in a loud whisper. 'You hang round here and wait for Colin and I might go and see that poet woman, Jacintha Hervey.'

Wesley glanced at Claire. 'Jacintha's not the only long-haired woman around here.'

'I know, Wes. Maybe you can have a tactful word with Neil's young lady when you get the chance, but I think it's about time we had a word with Jacintha anyway.' He leaned towards Wesley confidentially. 'Let's hope I escape with my virtue intact, eh?'

'If I hear a scream I'll come and rescue you,' answered Wesley, straight-faced.

As Heffernan picked his way back across the rough terrain towards the gatehouse, there was a mumble of cautious excitement from Jake, who was down in the trench scraping away at the bare, mushroom-coloured bones. Wesley scampered back to the side of the trench and looked down. There in the earth lay the unmistakable glint of gold.

'Coins. Gold sovereigns,' announced an excited Jake. 'Just by the waist. It looks as if he was carrying a purse or pouch of some kind at his belt. And there's a piece of rusted metal here; could be a belt buckle.'

Neil stepped carefully into the trench and squatted beside him. He brushed the last residues of clinging soil off the mystery object. 'It looks like a buckle all right.' He began to scrape away at the skeleton's chest, where the ribs lay like tramlines, half exposed against the soil.

As he dispersed the veil of earth, he noticed that something round and metallic, something just a little larger than an egg, was wedged between two of the ribs on the left-hand side, just above where the heart would have beaten in life. Wesley watched from the top of the trench, breath held, wishing he was down there digging.

Neil brushed the soil from the object and, once it was free, lifted it out with careful fingers. Claire, Matt and Jane, watching with Wesley, stood quite still, and Jake stopped work and stared.

'It's a pocket watch,' said Neil, awed. 'Might be silver.' The watch was attached to a chain. Neil lifted up the blackened object and held it cradled in his palm for everyone to see. The glass had cracked long ago and the white enamelled face was filthy and discoloured. The hands were most likely still resting somewhere in the earth.

'Is there any inscription?' asked Claire.

Neil, who hadn't had inscriptions on his mind, examined the watch gently and found what looked like an engraved pattern on the back. He shook his head.

'Sometimes they opened up,' suggested Wesley. 'Is there a catch?'

151

Neil searched the object and found a tiny catch at the side. He pressed it tentatively, fearful of damaging the delicate mechanism. To his relief the back opened stiffly. He stared down at the inside of the back of the case. 'There seems to be some sort of inscription but I can't make it out.'

Wesley produced a clean white handkerchief from his pocket. 'Here, clean it up a bit.'

Neil began to rub gently at the tarnished metal and soon the lettering grew just clear enough to read. He squinted down, trying to angle it towards the light, and began to read slowly. ' "Presented to Captain Jonah Parry by the officers of the *Merry Venture*. June 1701". It looks like he was a seafaring man.'

'Then I wonder how he ended up here,' said Wesley as Colin Bowman appeared at the gatehouse with a cheery wave.

Gerry Heffernan had decided to take Rachel with him to see Jacintha Hervey. What he'd heard about Jacintha made him suspect that he might be in need of a chaperone. She was what Steve Carstairs would have referred to as 'a man-eater' . . . and Heffernan had no desire to be on anyone's menu.

They found her in her lair. The first part of Earlsacre Hall to be made habitable was the wing that had housed the kitchens and the senior servants' rooms. Distant sounds of drilling and hammering held the promise that the rest of the ground floor would soon be in use.

Jacintha had set herself up in what had been the housekeeper's parlour. The once austere room was now decorated with large posters depicting the more romantic excesses of the Pre-Raphaelite painters. Jacintha's desk was heaped with notebooks. The bin was full of scrunched-up paper, rejected poems perhaps.

'What exactly does a poet in residence do?' asked Heffernan naïvely as he sat down in an armchair covered by a bright Indian print throw.

'My brief is to record the awakening of the Earlsacre Hall estate after its long years of sleep and neglect. To chronicle the work in a creative rather than a factual way.'

'Er, yeah,' said Heffernan. He'd stick to facts from now on. Rachel had perched herself on a stool near by and was wearing an expression of puzzled disapproval.

'Had you ever met Brian Willerby, the man who was found dead after the cricket match on Saturday?' he asked, getting straight to the point.

'No, our paths never crossed. In fact I've only just learned that he was Martin Samuels' brother-in-law. Small world, isn't it.' Jacintha sounded as if she were discussing some light-hearted social event.

'Has Mr Samuels ever mentioned Willerby?'

'Not in my hearing. But I do have a friend – or I suppose I should call her an acquaintance – who worked for him. She said he was a strange little man; a bit of a creep really.'

'What's the name of this acquaintance?' asked Heffernan, reaching for his notebook.

'Her name's Imogen. She works as a receptionist in the solicitors' where he worked. We're in the same writers' circle.'

Heffernan put his notebook down on his knee. He remembered Imogen all right: creator of Gothic horror novels and tales of lecherous employers. 'So you never actually met Willerby yourself?'

Jacintha shook her head. 'As I said, I only made his acquaintance once he was well and truly dead.'

'And Jake Weston, your, er . . . friend. Did he know Willerby?'

'I don't think so. We didn't know who it was when we saw the body. We knew he was one of the cricket team because of his clothes but . . .'

'And when you and Jake Weston were, er . . . in the woods, did you hear or see anything strange?'

'I've been asked all this already,' she said, exasperated. 'No, I didn't, and neither did Jake. We had other things on our minds.'

'Where were you during the tea interval, around three o'clock?'

She thought for a while. 'I was here in my office. Then I decided to stroll along to the cricket pitch.' She smiled to herself. 'I wanted to see if there was anyone I knew down there.'

'And you found Jake?'

'That's right. I wanted a word with Charles Pitaway but he was talking to that other detective; the rather dishy young black one; Neil Watson's friend.'

'So you made do with Jake?' Heffernan noticed that Rachel's lips were pressed together disapprovingly.

'You could say that.' Jacintha gave a feline smile. 'I found him more than adequate, I might add.'

'And you went into the woods straight away?' asked Heffernan, eager to get the interview back on track.

'I told the police all this when the body was found. We came back here for a coffee. Then Jake went to do a bit more digging in the water garden. We met up again at about five-thirty and went for a walk in the woods. One thing led to another and . . .'

'I think we get the picture,' Heffernan said quickly before she began to go into detail. 'The pathologist reckons that Willerby probably died during the tea interval, and he's come up with some-thing rather interesting. There's every indication that he died where he was found and that he had had a cricket ball bowled at his head several times. Now if someone was chucking a cricket ball at me I think I'd make a bit of a noise. Please think again. On your travels did you see or hear anything unusual?'

'Sorry, Inspector. I can't help you. I didn't go near the trees during the tea interval.'

'So you're, er . . . friendly with another gentleman who works here.' He looked down at his notebook. 'Charles Pitaway.'

'So?' Rachel thought she could detect a certain pride in her voice. 'I don't believe in commitment, Inspector. *Carpe diem*, that's my motto.'

'Seize the day. Aye.'

'You know Latin, Inspector?'

Heffernan flushed, fearful that he was getting out of his depth. 'No. But I know a man who does,' he replied, giving Rachel a meaningful grin. He turned back to Jacintha, who was watching him like a predatory cat. 'Has Charles Pitaway ever mentioned Brian Willerby?'

'He must have met him because Willerby did some legal work for the estate. Charles was the last owner, you see. But Charles has never mentioned him to me. I shouldn't imagine that such an insignificant little man would be of much interest to him.'

'How do you know he was insignificant if you'd never met him?' asked Rachel quickly.

Jacintha began to scribble in one of her notebooks nervously. 'I'm only repeating what I've heard.'

Heffernan took a photograph from his pocket: the likeness of John Jones, the man found dead and half naked in the caravan. 'Have you seen this man before?'

She studied the photograph carefully then shook her head. 'No. He's not bad,' she grinned. 'Who is he?'

'He was found dead in a rented caravan up near Bloxham last week. We're trying to identify him.'

'Sorry I can't help you. But I would have remembered if I'd seen him,' she added significantly.

As Jacintha handed back the picture, the door to her office burst open to reveal Charles Pitaway standing on the threshold, poised for flight like an athlete on the starting blocks. He seemed relieved when he saw the two police officers installed in the only available seating. He looked at Rachel and blushed visibly, giving her a nervous half-smile which she returned.

'Er, sorry. Jacintha, one of the workmen said you were looking for me. He said it was urgent.' He stepped back into the corridor, waiting for her.

'Just one more thing,' said Gerry Heffernan firmly before Jacintha was distracted. 'Before the cricket match you were seen talking to Brian Willerby outside the stable block. What have you got to say about that?' He sat forward, awaiting an answer. He suspected that, given half a chance, this woman would give him the runaround – and he wasn't going to let her.

Jacintha squirmed in her seat. 'Someone must have made a mistake. I was here in my office before the match. I've never even met Brian Willerby. Someone's made a mistake,' she repeated vehemently.

'Okay, love. That'll be all for now. But we might want another word.'

Jacintha rose, looking relieved at her sudden release. 'If you've finished I just want a word with Mr Pitaway in private.'

'Don't mind us, love,' Heffernan called out to her disappearing back as she left the room and closed the door behind her.

He nodded at Rachel, who understood immediately what was required. She tiptoed over to the door and pressed her ear to the wood. She could make out most of the conversation. Jacintha was asking Charles to meet her that evening. She was suggesting a rendezvous, even hinting at an evening in his flat. But Rachel could sense that he was stalling; the excuses were coming thick and fast: he had the decorators in; he was meeting an old friend. But Jacintha was not a woman to be put off.

Rachel turned to Heffernan. 'It would be an act of kindness to put that poor man out of his misery. She's not taking no for an answer,' she whispered.

Heffernan marched over to the door and flung it open. Jacintha jumped but Charles looked relieved. 'Mr Pitaway. I wonder if we could have a quick word in here.'

'Certainly, Chief Inspector,' he said, smiling openly. 'But I've already told the police everything I know.'

'If we could use your office for a couple of minutes, Ms Hervey?'

Jacintha nodded graciously, grabbed one of her notebooks and made herself scarce.

'You realise you'll probably be responsible for another of her poems,' Charles whispered to Rachel as he sat down.

Their eyes met and she returned his smile. 'I hope not. I shouldn't like that on my conscience.'

'Can you tell us what you know about Brian Willerby?' asked Gerry Heffernan, interrupting the cosy scene.

'Not much,' Charles replied, glancing at Rachel. 'I've met him a few times to sign papers and all that, but we've never had anything to do with each other socially. Not until the cricket match anyway, and I hardly talked to him then. He was late and then he went and disappeared after the first innings, so apart from the odd comment when we were fielding, I hardly said a word to him.'

'But there was a time when you were standing next to him on the boundary. I saw you whispering to each other.'

'I was only relaying the captain's orders: he tells us where he wants us when we're fielding. And I probably commented on the direction of the ball, the batsman's technique, tactics, that sort of thing.'

'Have you played in matches with him before?'

'As a matter of fact, no. He wasn't at the other matches I played in this season. He only turned out when we were a few men short, and I think he was only asked on Saturday as a last resort.'

Gerry Heffernan leaned forward, looking Charles in the eye. 'So you wouldn't say you knew anything about his private life?'

'I knew he was Martin's brother-in-law but nothing else, I'm afraid. Sorry I can't help you.'

'Where were you during the tea interval?'

Pitaway's cheeks reddened. 'Avoiding Jacintha ... and I was talking to your colleague, Wesley, for some of the time. Nice chap.'

Gerry Heffernan drew the photograph of John Jones out of his pocket once more. It was worth another try. 'Have you ever seen this man?'

Charles took the picture and studied it earnestly. 'No. No, I don't think so, sorry. Is this the man who was found in that caravan in Bloxham? I saw it on the local news.'

'Yes, that's right. We're trying to identify him.'

'Best of luck, then.' He handed the photograph back. 'Surely someone must know who he is. It's only a matter of time, I expect.'

'Mmm. I expect it is. Well, we'd better go and let Ms Hervey have her room back.'

'Thanks, Inspector . . . er, DC Tracey.' He gave Rachel a dazzling smile which, Heffernan noticed, she returned with quite unpolice-womanlike enthusiasm.

'He's nice,' commented Rachel as they walked back to the incident room.

Heffernan looked at her and shook his head. What a wonderful thing it was to be young.

Colin Bowman had finished. He had pronounced the life of Captain Jonah Parry well and truly extinct with his usual aplomb, and ordered the bones to be brought to him at the mortuary for examination as soon as the archaeologists had lifted them from the earth.

As soon as Neil Watson had seen the bones safely into the mortuary van, he wandered off towards the stable block. He heard Matt calling after him. 'Come on, Neil. Give us a hand with this trench. Where are you off to?' But Neil didn't answer. He had other things on his mind.

His pace quickened as he approached the room where Claire worked. He opened the door and found her sitting at her desk, poring over what looked like an ancient letter. When she saw him she stood up, smiling shyly.

'I've found a couple more letters,' she said. There was excitement in her voice. 'This one's dated June 1685 and it's actually from Richard Lantrist telling his brother that he's meeting up with the rebels at Taunton. It's fascinating. Richard sounds so nice in this letter, so enthusiastic for his cause. I wonder if he's not the murderer after all. I still think the dodgy head gardener theory needs looking into – he'd have as much opportunity as Sir Richard for burying bodies in the garden. Mind you, if he'd been a slave all those years, that would be enough to change anyone's character. What do you think?' Neil stayed silent. 'You're very quiet. What's the matter?' she asked anxiously.

'Why did you cross Brian Willerby's name out in your address book?' he heard himself saying, not quite believing that he'd summoned up the courage to utter the words.

His answer was silence. Claire stood quite still, staring down at Richard Lantrist's letter. It was a full minute before she looked Neil in the face. 'It's none of your business,' she said with quiet determination.

'But he was murdered. If you knew him don't you think you should tell the police?'

'If he was murdered, he deserved everything he got,' she said with sudden and unexpected brutality. 'I'm not telling the police, and if you mention it to your friend Wesley you can forget anything between us.' She swallowed hard, then began to speak again more softly. 'I promise you that I had nothing to do with his death. I'm just asking you to trust me. It was just something that happened a long time ago and it's got nothing to do with all this. Please.'

Neil saw that her eyes were beginning to glisten with tears. He went to her instinctively and put his arms around her.

'Just trust me,' she whispered.

'Okay,' said Neil gently, kissing the top of her head.

Wesley Peterson looked at his watch and then at his desk. It was 5.30 – time to grab the chance to get home at a reasonable time. But he knew that work would be the place to stay if he wanted peace and quiet: thanks to Pam's return to teaching on Wednesday, home had descended into chaos. The paperwork generated by a class of thirty ten-year-olds, even before term began, almost exceeded that of a murder inquiry, and presently all that paper seemed to be deposited on Wesley's dining-room table.

Pam herself was tense and harassed and Michael, sensitive to his mother's mood over the past few days, had lost his usual easy-going nature and whinged each time she left the room. Things would settle down once term began, Wesley told himself optimistically: he had always been one to look on the bright side. But for the moment he was in no hurry to get home.

It wasn't as if he was short of something to do: there was a mound of paperwork on his desk. But he found himself fighting the temptation to seek Neil out; maybe to indulge in a pint in the King's Head and discuss the skeletons and the strange history of Earlsacre Hall.

The discovery of Captain Jonah Parry's pocket watch had fired his imagination. The skeleton, he assumed, was that of a seafaring man who possessed the watch bearing the date 1701, the same year in which the other two skeletons had probably met their grim deaths. He must have been well liked and respected if his fellow officers had presented him with such a gift. He was a man who would have been missed.

Then, by force of habit, he began to consider other possibilities. The man whose bones lay beneath the shell grotto might have been a common thief who had stolen Captain Parry's watch. But then why was the watch buried with him if not to hide his identity? Such a timepiece would have been of considerable value in those days and, unless the inscription would lead to questions being asked about the captain's whereabouts, the murderer would have had nothing to lose by disposing of it for profit. And what self-respecting thief would bury gold sovereigns with the body of their victim? The skeleton was that of the captain, Wesley was certain.

The desire to share these speculations with Neil eventually triumphed over the prospect of the waiting paperwork. He left the incident room and opened the door to the room the archaeology team were using as their office. He looked round at the tables laden with plastic trays full of finds. A couple of computers sat at the end of the room, their grey screens lifeless. It looked as if everyone had gone home.

As Wesley shut the door behind him he spotted Neil's retreating back. He called after him, but Neil began to walk away faster and disappeared towards the hall at a cracking pace. Wesley looked at his watch again, wondering whether he should take the trouble to follow him. It never occurred to him that Neil was trying to avoid a meeting: they had been friends a long time and old friends didn't avoid each other.

After a few moments Wesley's conscience got the better of him and he made the decision to go home. He knew Pam might need some support, as the next few days were going to be tough. And besides, he was hungry.

At ten past six he opened the front door of his house and found Pam in the hall, sitting on the stairs with the telephone cradled in her lap. She smiled bravely up at him and covered the mouthpiece. 'I'll get supper in a minute. It's my mum,' she said in a loud whisper. 'She's on about Jamie. She wants to bring him round again.'

Wesley pulled a face. Pam was capable of making her own decisions, but he hoped she'd be firm with her wayward mother. He went into the kitchen and began to set the table. As his mother had always had a demanding job as a family doctor, he had been house-trained at an early age, something Pam was eternally grateful for.

After a few minutes Pam walked into the room and looked at him approvingly. 'I had a struggle getting her off the phone. She's coming round again tomorrow night and bringing lover boy. She's bringing a takeaway with her. I insisted on that.'

Wesley felt a wave of anger. It wasn't fair on him during a murder inquiry – and it certainly wasn't fair on Pam. 'But you start back at school the next day. Can't she wait till the weekend?' He mentally added the words 'thoughtless cow'.

'They're going away on Friday. A romantic break in Paris.'

'Very nice,' said Wesley, trying to conceal his envy. 'I'll probably be working again this weekend. An unromantic break with Gerry Heffernan.'

'How's it going?'

He took a deep breath, glad that she was taking an interest in his day. But then it was a reciprocal arrangement: he would be expected to listen sympathetically to her complaints about a teacher's lot when she was back at work.

'We're still no nearer identifying the body in the caravan but there's a possibility that the second victim might have killed the first. And Neil's found another skeleton in the Earlsacre gardens – possibly a sea captain. Some valuable statues have been nicked . . . and we've uncovered a brothel in Tradmouth staffed by students eager to supplement their meagre loans. But apart from that . . .'

'A brothel in Tradmouth?' Pam raised her eyebrows. Wesley's job certainly threw up more interesting things than a day in the classroom. 'You never know what goes on behind closed doors, do you? And students? Makes a change from the holiday job in a supermarket.'

'The Chief Super's name was mentioned too. And the madam was a dead ringer for Maggie Thatcher.'

Pam had been about to inquire about Neil and his budding romance with Claire, but Wesley's last revelations rendered her temporarily speechless; she shook her head, a bemused smile on her lips. Wesley decided to take charge of the food.

'Did your mother have anything else to say for herself?' he asked as the spaghetti slithered from the pan on to the table, narrowly missing the plate.

'Only that she had something important to tell us. Wonder what that means.' She raised her eyebrows questioningly.

'He might have proposed,' replied Wesley, rounding up the rogue strands of spaghetti. If someone wanted to whisk his mother-in-law off into the sunset, who was he to argue?

DC Steve Carstairs got back to his flat in Morbay at seven, having called for a takeaway pizza on his way home. Still smarting slightly from Gerry Heffernan's criticism, he opened the front door and marched into the communal hallway, banging the pizza box down on the side table. The grease seeping through the box's base marked the newspaper below, a crisp, unread *Independent* belonging to the frosty young woman in Flat 4. Steve picked the box up quickly and tried to brush the grease away with his hand. His efforts were useless, but what did it matter? She was a stuck-up bitch anyhow.

He put the pizza box down on the paper again and studied the pigeonholes above the table which held the post for the six flats in the converted Victorian house. He reached up and pulled two letters from his box. His heart thumped as he scanned the envelopes for the telltale Manchester postmark. But the promised cheque hadn't arrived. The old man, so plausible, hadn't kept his word. All he had were a couple of irresistible offers; one for a credit card, the other for free access to the Internet. Disgusted, he threw the envelopes in the bin, where they joined others of their kind.

If Steve had been at all concerned about the environment he would have regretted the unnecessary destruction of the trees that went to make all this unwanted correspondence. But his only worry was how he was going to live it down at the station. The man he wanted to be didn't get taken in by con men – didn't become a victim.

Rachel Tracey had decided to work late, to catch up on the piles of statements and reports that adorned her desk. Dave had asked her to go to the pictures but she had put him off. She was too busy, she had said. The truth was that she had not felt like spending the evening with him. At her mother's insistence, he was now back staying on her family's farm – ostensibly to help out with the holiday flats and then the harvest – and this had made matters worse. There was some truth in the old saying that absence made the heart grow fonder.

She was increasingly sure that her relationship with Dave had run its course. Now it was just a matter of convincing others of the fact. And breaking the news to Dave, who still followed her round like an adoring puppy.

The phone on her desk rang and she picked it up. The voice on the other end was unfamiliar, yet she knew she had heard it recently. Then she realised. It was Charles Pitaway. The man she had rescued from Jacintha Hervey. In spite of her outward calm, her heart began to beat a little faster.

'I hoped you might still be here. I just wanted to thank you for rescuing me earlier. You've not eaten, have you?'

'No, but . . .'

'Good. I'll meet you outside the stable block in half an hour. See you then.'

Rachel smiled to herself. This was an unexpected turn of events. For the next half-hour she paced the empty office, paying frequent visits to the ladies' to check her appearance and make adjustments to her make-up. She wished she could have changed into something a bit more special than her working clothes, but if Charles Pitaway wanted to sweep her off her feet straight from work, he would have to take her as he found her.

The long half-hour's wait was punctuated with stabs of guilt. She was seeing another man while Dave dutifully watched television with her family. But at the end of the half-hour, pulse racing and palms tingling, Rachel Tracey locked the incident room door behind her and walked slowly out of the stable block.

Charles was waiting for her outside as promised. The Earlsacre birds were in good voice, but the only other sound she could hear as she walked towards him was the distant sound of a car engine revving farther up the drive. Charles held out a hand to her. She took it.

'Where are we going?' she asked.

'It's a surprise. Wait and see.'

'I don't like surprises,' she said matter-of-factly.

'I can guarantee you'll like this one.' He held on to her hand and began to lead her away from the house and gardens, down the driveway towards the road. After a while they drew level with the cricket field and he stopped. Rachel shuddered. She had no desire to be romping round a murder scene in her leisure hours, no matter how attractive her new-found companion was.

'Shut your eyes,' he whispered. She hesitated then obeyed.

She was led off to the left, over the smooth grass of the cricket field. 'We're not going to the woods, are we?' she asked, feeling a small twinge of anxiety.

'Of course not. Just close your eyes.'

162

She allowed herself to be led onwards. 'There are three steps here. Be careful,' said Charles, his voice gentle but containing a hint of excitement.

She negotiated her way up three wooden steps. The cricket pavilion. Rachel wondered what the hell she was doing alone near a murder scene with a perfect stranger leading her towards goodness knows what with her eyes closed. But at the same time she felt exhilarated at the thought of things being delightfully beyond her control.

'You can open them now,' Charles said triumphantly.

Rachel opened her eyes and all doubts faded. The cricket pavilion was aglow with candles, their golden light making that most functional of buildings seem like a romantic hideaway. The door was wide open, and in the centre of the bare, utilitarian room was a trestle table laid with white plates, a pair of champagne glasses and an orderly line of foil dishes. A bottle of champagne stood in the centre of the table.

'Like it?'

'I like it. But I thought you were doing something tonight . . . meeting an old friend?'

'What makes you think that?' He smiled as understanding dawned. 'Were you listening at the door?'

She nodded. 'I'm afraid so.'

'Well, I only told Jacintha that to put her off. As you can imagine, she doesn't take no for an answer. And she's hardly my type. Unlike present company.'

Rachel smiled. 'I can't believe you did all this for me.'

'And why shouldn't I do something special for the best-looking policewoman in Devon? And before you start interrogating me, I haven't interfered with a crime scene. I asked one of the uniformed PCs if it was okay to use the pavilion again after the break-in and he said all the fingerprint people had finished.' He shrugged. 'So here we are.'

He began to pour the champagne. Rachel took a sip. The bubbles, and the company, went straight to her head.

'I asked the landlady of the King's Head to make us a takeaway. Is that all right? It's not very exotic, I'm afraid. We've got roast beef, vegetables, new potatoes. You're not a vegetarian, are you?' he asked nervously.

'I was brought up on a farm. Being a vegetarian was never an option.'

'Do you still live on the farm, or do you have a place of your own?'

'I still live on the farm at the moment, but I wouldn't mind a place of my own soon,' she said, toying with the idea of domestic freedom. She picked up her glass and began to wander around the pavilion. 'You've made this place look quite homely,' she said with genuine admiration. 'I don't know how you've done it, but you've even managed to get rid of that awful smell; you know, the one you always get in sports changing rooms. Sweat and testosterone.' She turned to him and smiled. 'You're quite a miracle worker. Tell me about yourself,' she said, before taking another long sip of champagne.

'Where shall I start?'

'At the beginning.'

'My name's Charles Edward Pitaway. I was born in Tradmouth hospital in 1976. I lived here at Earlsacre Hall till I was five, then my parents decided they'd be more comfortable in a smaller place, so we moved to a bungalow on the outskirts of Dukesbridge. My mother died when I was eight and I was sent away to boarding school, so I can't claim to have had an idyllic childhood. I left school at seventeen and did various things, then when my father died I came home, sold the family bungalow and sold Earlsacre to Martin's trust. With the proceeds I set myself up in business as a garden design consultant and bought myself a rather nice flat overlooking Dukesbridge harbour. That's enough about me. What about you?'

Rachel shrugged. 'Not a lot to tell. Brought up on a farm near Tradmouth. Three brothers.'

'Do you like your job?'

'At times.'

'I was talking to your colleague at the cricket match . . . Wesley. He's a very nice chap.'

'Yes.' Rachel looked down into her champagne glass and stared at the escaping bubbles. 'Yes, he's very nice.'

She smiled sadly at Charles, then strolled over to the double row of lockers. 'What do you men keep in these things? I've always wondered.'

Idly she began to open the unlocked metal doors one by one. Most were empty or contained isolated items of grubby equipment. But one locker, at the far end of the row, housed something more interesting. As the door creaked open Rachel saw an unusual object lying in the bottom.

'What's this?' she asked, taking a sip of her champagne.

Charles walked over to join her and stood staring down at the object, a cricket ball stuck on to a sturdy handle. 'It's a knocking-in mallet. When you get a new bat it needs to be knocked in before you play. You bash it for a while with the mallet and that strengthens the bat. If it wasn't prepared properly there's a danger it would split during a match. That answer your question?' She didn't reply. 'Why the sudden interest in cricket equipment? Are you a cricket fan? I didn't see you at the match last Saturday. I would have noticed.' He bent and kissed her neck. She felt a shiver of pleasure but tried hard not to let it distract her.

'This wasn't here when the police searched these lockers,' she stated simply.

'Well, if someone's bought a new bat they probably borrowed it. There's nothing unusual in that.'

Rachel remembered Brian Willerby's injuries and the preposterous theory that a speeding ball was bowled at his head several times. But this object, like a hammer with a cricket ball for a head, would fit the bill perfectly. She was as certain as she could be that she had found what had killed Brian Willerby.

'Here, there's an old bat over there. I'll show you how it works if you're that interested,' said Charles, reaching inside the locker. It was an unusual line in seduction, he thought, but then life was full of surprises.

'No,' she snapped quickly. 'Don't touch it whatever you do. I'll have to contact the station.'

'Surely it can wait.'

'Sorry.' She shook her head apologetically, torn between duty and pleasure.

'Want to borrow my mobile?' asked Charles, taking his phone from his pocket.

'Thanks, but I've got my own,' she said, taking it from her bag and punching in the familiar numbers.

'If you don't mind me asking, why exactly are you ringing the station?'

'That mallet thing . . . I think it's what Brian Willerby was killed with.'

Charles looked shocked. 'Oh dear. I see. I suppose it rather spoils our plans if we're soon going to be joined by a horde of policemen in size-twelve boots, doesn't it?'

'Oh, they won't be here for a while. What about giving this

165

representative of the police force a square meal and some more champagne before they arrive?' she said, feeling strangely unprofessional.

Charles smiled. 'Then after we've eaten and sorted out this business of the mallet, why don't you come back to my flat in Dukesbridge for a drink? I feel I have to make up somehow for bringing you to a place where someone's dumped a murder weapon,' he added disarmingly.

A guilty image of Dave waiting patiently at the farm flashed through her mind. But then Rachel Tracey ran her finger around the top of her champagne glass and smiled.

Chapter 11

August 1685
Dearest good Father
The passage is rough and the conditions on the Merry Venture *are wanting of comfort. Yet your acquaintance with Captain Parry is a blessing. He is a likeable Welshman with a ready wit and much respected by his crew. The good captain is unaccustomed to a human cargo yet he treats the prisoners with as much fairness as conditions allow. He has promised to deliver any letters I write to you into your hands and may the Lord bless him for that. I know not where we are bound except that it be the Indies where we shall be sold to plantation owners. Joseph Marling is with me and begs you to bear his greetings to his father.*

Sir, it grieves me to think that the last time I saw your beloved face was in Dorchester at my trial, the injustice of which together with the evil of Lord Chief Justice Jeffreys shall remain in my thoughts always. I pray that somehow I may endure this enslavement and live to return, but I fear the years to come. I know that our family's fortunes are low at present and that my liberty cannot be bought as others have bought theirs (the corruption of the Lord Chief Justice is known to all). Yet be of good cheer, dear father, and remember me to my good brother, John. Pray for me.

Your loving son, Richard Lantrist

Wesley arrived at Earlsacre at nine the next morning. He had left Pam asleep, reluctant to disturb her on her last morning of freedom before term began.

Rachel was already at her desk, bright and alert. She walked over to him as he was about to sit down. 'Want to hear the latest? The weapon that probably killed Brian Willerby's been found: one of those knocking-in mallets – a sort of cricket ball on a stick. It's used to prepare cricket bats before you use them in a match.'

Wesley raised his eyebrows in surprise. It was quite unlike Rachel to know the ins and outs of cricket equipment, given her hostility to the game. 'I know what it is. It's so obvious now. I don't know why I didn't think of it before. Where was it found?'

'In a locker in the pavilion.'

'The lockers were searched.'

'It must have been put back since.'

'By whoever took the garden statues?'

'It's possible.'

'Who found it?'

Rachel blushed and changed the subject. 'And have you heard the latest about Steve?'

'No. Go on, amaze me,' said Wesley, contemplating his mound of waiting paperwork. But gossip about Steve was far more interesting.

'Last week he found this old bloke who'd had his wallet pinched and he lent him some money.'

'Wonders will never cease. There's hope for him yet.'

'But doesn't that story sound familiar to you?'

The truth suddenly dawned on Wesley. 'The reports of that suspected con man?' Rachel nodded. 'And Steve didn't realise anything was wrong?'

'Reading between the lines I'd say he had a woman with him whom he was trying to impress, so what passes for his brain wasn't firing on all cylinders. He's still saying this man he met was genuine. He said he could tell. He's expecting the cheque in the post, he says. Only it's just not arrived yet. How's that for optimism?'

Wesley looked at Rachel with interest. 'It's easy to be cynical but what would you have done?'

Rachel paused. 'Do you know, I've no idea,' she said thoughtfully. 'What about you?'

Wesley shrugged his shoulders. It was a difficult one. He had always been taught by parents and Church that helping those in need was the thing to do. But as a police officer he was only too aware of the depths of human deceit. 'Did the man's description match the other reports?'

'Afraid so. It looks as though Steve's lost himself eighty quid.'

'Eighty quid!' exclaimed Wesley, astounded at Steve's benevolence.

'For a train ticket to Manchester. If this con man's getting greedy we're bound to catch him sooner or later. We can tell Steve to keep a special lookout.' She grinned wickedly.

Wesley's telephone began to ring and Rachel returned to her own desk with a secret smile. There was something different about her, Wesley thought, a sparkle in her eyes. Perhaps she had had a good night out with Dave.

He picked up the receiver and was surprised to hear a soft female voice on the other end of the line. When he finished the call he wandered out of the office in search of Gerry Heffernan. He needed some advice.

He found Heffernan at the cricket pavilion, contemplating the flaking wooden door. He could see that the pavilion's interior had changed since he had last been there. A trestle table bore the remains of a meal, along with the stumps of burned-down candles. A champagne bottle stood in its centre, indicating that someone had had a good evening.

'Wes. Just the man I wanted to see,' Heffernan shouted as he approached. 'Have you heard about this mallet thing – cricket ball on a stick? Just the job for giving someone a good whack on the head and making it look like they've been hit by a demon bowler. It went off to Forensic last night.'

'So who found it?'

'Charles Pitaway was using the pavilion to entertain a lady friend, hence the burned-down candles and the empty champagne bottle.'

'What lady would this be? Our resident poet?'

'Er, not exactly, Wes. It seems the lady's name was Rachel Tracey.'

'Oh,' said Wesley. 'I see.'

'Now what did you want to see me about?'

Wesley took a deep breath, trying not to think of Rachel alone with Charles Pitaway in the pavilion. 'I just wanted to tell you that I've had a phone call from Lilly. You remember Lilly? At that place in Tradmouth near the church.'

'Carlotta's ever-so-discreet new knocking shop, aye. And what did the lovely Lilly have to say for herself?'

'She says she's got something to tell me but she wouldn't say what it was over the phone. I've arranged to meet her at the Copper Kettle tea room in Tradmouth at ten.'

'Well, go on then, Wes. Don't keep the lady waiting. It is about Brian Willerby, I hope?'

'Do you want to come with me?'

'Oh, I think you're old enough to be let out on your own, Wes – not like some people round here. Have you heard about Steve's little act of charity?'

'Yes, Rachel told me. A good deed in a wicked world. Pity it was probably a con. It won't do wonders for the development of Steve's better nature, will it?'

'Has he got one?' Heffernan replied automatically. Then he thought for a moment. 'Wasn't our Rachel settled with that Australian bloke? What was she doing drinking bubbly with Pitaway?'

Wesley shook his head. This was one bit of station gossip he felt no inclination to share. 'No idea,' he said.

Gerry Heffernan's mobile phone squealed loudly for attention. He took it from his pocket and grunted into it. After a cryptic, one-sided conversation, he turned to Wesley.

'Interesting news, Wes. The statues that were nicked from the pavilion have turned up in an architectural salvage yard. A young PC on a routine visit spotted them, and you'll never guess who the dealer got them from.'

'Who?' asked Wesley impatiently. He had too much on his mind to be playing guessing games.

'They were sold to him by a builder he does a lot of business with . . . a Les Cumbernold.'

'Who had a key to the pavilion and made it look like a break-in.'

'Exactly.'

'So do we pick him up?'

'All in good time, Wes. We'll pop over later for a cup of tea and a chat. Off you go, then. Don't keep the lovely Lilly waiting.'

Wesley paid a quick visit to the gents' to check his appearance before setting off towards his car.

Lilly's slender body was encased in jeans and a checked cotton shirt. As Wesley approached the round oak table where she sat, she looked up and smiled. She was pretty, beautiful even, but she had shed the exotic aura she had exuded when they had first met.

'Thanks for coming,' she said as Wesley arranged himself on a Windsor chair after ordering tea from an elderly waitress. 'I thought it best if we met on neutral ground. I shouldn't like Carlotta to think I'd been talking about a client. You can assure me that my name won't come into this?'

'If that's what you want. What do you want to tell me?' He looked around. Fortunately the Copper Kettle tea room was half empty, the height of the tourist season being over, and the nearby tables were unoccupied. Wesley hoped they stayed that way.

'It's about Brian Willerby. Look, I don't know if this'll have anything to do with his death. I read in the paper that he was found dead under suspicious circumstances at a village cricket match. Is that right?'

Wesley nodded. 'Yes. We're treating it as murder.'

Lilly took a deep breath. 'Well, it's probably unconnected but . . . he liked a record, a photographic record of what we did, if you see what I mean. He'd arrange a camera on the dressing table and set the timer. He described it as a little hobby of his,' she said with some bitterness. 'I didn't like it. I mean, if any of the pictures fell into the wrong hands later on . . . I want to work in television and I couldn't afford . . .'

'Quite,' said Wesley. 'So did you object?'

'I did at first but Carlotta said he was an old and valued client and very discreet and he assured her that the pictures were for his own private use and would never be seen by anyone else. She said I had to go along with it so that was that. I didn't have much choice if I wanted to keep my job.'

'Haven't you considered getting a more, er, conventional job?' he said, realising as soon as he'd spoken that he had probably sounded disapproving. But sometimes being non-judgemental was hard work.

'There's nothing that would pay me so much for working so few hours. I see my friends slogging their guts out in bars and shops and coming to lectures completely knackered. This is easy money and most of the clients are okay. They're all vetted by Carlotta, so you don't get any nutcases or anything too kinky. So why not?' she asked, a challenge in her voice.

'Don't your parents mind?' Wesley heard himself saying, realising with increasing horror that he was sounding like a concerned parent himself. But he couldn't help thinking of what his own parents' reaction would have been if they had caught even a whiff of his sister being involved in anything remotely unsavoury during her long years studying medicine in Oxford.

Fortunately Lilly didn't seem to have taken offence. 'They're divorced,' she said matter-of-factly. 'Dad lives abroad, Mum's got a new boyfriend. Why should they care? I'm my own boss. I don't answer to anyone.'

'When did you last see Willerby?' Wesley asked, relieved to move on to bare facts.

'Friday night. The night before he died.' She shuddered. 'Creepy that, isn't it.'

'Did he mention anything he was worried about?'

'No. He never talked about anything personal. Not like some of them. I didn't even know if he was married. Some of them love to talk. In fact they prefer the talking to the sex, I reckon . . . but not Brian. He seemed a bit uptight on that Friday night but he never said why . . . and it didn't affect his performance.'

She gave Wesley an apologetic smile. He averted his eyes and pretended to study the mouthwatering array of cakes displayed on the counter near by. But somehow he didn't think he could manage to eat one.

'What are you studying at university?' he asked after a few seconds.

'English. Why?'

'My wife read English.' He smiled sadly and sipped his tea. 'Why did you want to tell me about the photographs?'

'Well, I thought if he had pictures of other girls they might have a motive for killing him if he was . . . if he was blackmailing them.'

She paused. It was clear to Wesley that she was putting her own fears into words.

'We've searched his house and his office I can assure you that no photographs were found.'

'Perhaps he kept them somewhere else.'

'If we did find any I can assure you they'd be treated in the strictest confidence,' Wesley said, omitting to mention that they'd probably be leered at by half the police station first. He drained his teacup then looked her in the eye for the first time during their interview. He saw a vulnerability there, a softness that she kept well hidden. 'You will be careful, won't you, Lilly?' he said gently. 'There are some very nasty people about.'

She brushed her dark silken hair back from her face. 'I can take

172

care of myself,' she said with brittle assurance. 'I'll be fine. Don't you worry about me.'

Wesley Peterson left the Copper Kettle tea room feeling mildly depressed.

'So that's what he used that darkroom for. The old goat,' said Gerry Heffernan loudly. 'And the lovely Lilly featured in these pictures, did she? What I want to know is what's happened to them. Has some worried ex-call-girl, now leading a blameless life with her husband and kiddies and or with a respectable career, bumped off the man with the evidence of her colourful past? And where does our dead man in the caravan come into all this? Was he an irate brother trying to get the pictures back for the lady? Maybe he got into an argument with Willerby. He might have had the name of his college or local pub on his T-shirt so he could be easily identified. What do you think, Wes?'

'I think we should go and have another word with Mrs Willerby. See what she knows about all this.'

'Do you think she knows anything?'

'I find it hard to believe that she doesn't. That darkroom had been thoroughly cleared out; everything neat and tidy but no sign of any photographs. Either Brian repented of his wicked ways and cleared it out himself or Martha discovered it and got rid of everything incriminating – maybe with the help of her brother.'

Heffernan nodded in agreement. Martha Willerby was hiding something. 'You could be right, Wes. Let's get over there. We'll walk; get ourselves a bit of exercise.'

They left the stable block in companionable silence, falling into step on the uneven drive that led out of the Earlsacre estate. After a while Heffernan spoke. 'We haven't seen much of your mate Neil lately, have we? All the other times when you two have been working near each other I've got sick of the sight of him. Is it that pretty dark-haired lass he's taken up with or what?'

'I think it's Claire, yes. Normally Neil's love life comes a poor second to his work, so it must be serious.'

'Must be,' said Heffernan, a faraway look in his eyes as he contemplated the joys of love from a safe distance.

They were nearing Brian Willerby's house. As they passed Les Cumbernold's bungalow, they noticed that Les was working in his garden, clipping the front hedge into a neat square shape.

173

Wesley looked at his boss inquiringly but Heffernan gave a barely perceptible shake of the head. 'He'll keep,' he muttered under his breath.

Les spotted the two police officers but he carried on clipping obsessively, making no acknowledgement of their presence.

Martha Willerby must have been watching from her window because she opened the door when they were only half way up the garden path. Wesley noticed that she looked anxious; there were dark rings beneath her eyes as though she hadn't slept for several nights.

'Sorry to bother you again, Mrs Willerby,' he said, unexpectedly feeling sorry for the woman. 'Can we have a word?'

He allowed Martha to lead the way into the drawing room, wondering how to tackle the subject. What was the best way to ask a newly widowed woman whether she knew about her husband's visits to a brothel and his taste for featuring in erotic photographs? There was no best way, he concluded. He'd just have to ask the questions and hope for the best.

But to his surprise Martha Willerby took it all remarkably calmly. She sat in a massive armchair facing them, her legs tucked up beneath her in an almost childlike pose of comfort.

'Of course I knew, Inspector. I'm not stupid, you know. Brian had certain tastes which I didn't share. As for the photographs, I burned them. As soon as I learned he was dead, I cleaned out his darkroom – I never normally went in it, of course, but I knew it was there and what he used it for – and I burned everything in the garden incinerator apart from . . . well, I kept back one photograph of each of the girls.'

'Why did you do that?' asked Wesley.

'I don't know why I did it but I thought that one day . . . I don't know.' She took a tissue from her sleeve and wiped her nose.

'You intended to blackmail the girls?' asked Wesley, mildly surprised.

'I don't know why I kept them really. Insurance? In case I started to remember Brian too fondly and needed to remind myself what he was like? I really don't know. But some instinct made me hold on to them.'

'Can we see these photographs, love?' asked Heffernan, trying to control his impatience.

Martha Willerby said nothing. She stood up and left the room. She must have hidden the pictures well because there had been no sign of them when the house had been searched before. Wesley and Heffernan sat in silence, waiting for her to return.

When she came back she handed the glossy coloured pictures to Heffernan without a word. There were five in all. The girls he had chosen, paid for, were all of the same type: young, very pretty, dark-haired.

Heffernan looked through them but didn't hand them on to Wesley, who noticed that his expression was uncharacteristically solemn.

'Did you ever have any dealings with these girls?' Heffernan asked after a few moments. 'Did any of them ring or call here?'

'No, never. I wouldn't have stood for that. As long as he kept his little tarts well away from his home I found that I could tolerate his infidelities.'

Heffernan handed the pictures back to her. Wesley hardly liked to ask if he could see them, knowing that such a request would earn a witty riposte from his boss. But he felt curious all the same.

'Please keep those pictures safe, just in case we need to see them again,' Heffernan said as he stood up to go.

Martha Willerby looked relieved as she saw them off the premises.

Heffernan waited until they were half way down the front path, well out of Martha's earshot, before he spoke. 'Come on. Let's go next door and bring in Les Cumbernold,' he said with unseemly enthusiasm.

He surged on ahead, Wesley following with more on his mind than a pair of purloined garden statues.

They found Les Cumbernold still tending his garden, his bottle-blonde other half nowhere in sight. He looked up when he saw the two policemen approaching, an expression of resigned dread on his chubby face.

'We've been hearing tales about you,' began Heffernan affably. 'We've heard that you flogged a pair of garden statues to a dealer in architectural antiques over near Neston . . . a pair of garden statues that match the descriptions of the ones nicked from the cricket pavilion at Earlsacre on Sunday night.'

Wesley could almost see Cumbernold's brain working with the effort to come up with some clever excuse. But he just wasn't up to it. 'Prove it,' he challenged.

'We will, Les, we will. Your neighbour Brain Willerby, has he been burning anything in his garden recently?'

175

Les Cumbernold seemed rather startled at the sudden change of subject. 'He's got one of them incinerators; he uses it a lot. He was using it last week.' He looked relieved that the spotlight had moved away from his own misdeeds.

'Was he using it on Wednesday?'

'Yeah. I'm sure it were going on Wednesday ... or was it Thursday? Why?'

'What time was this?'

Cumbernold thought for a moment. 'Early morning. Up at sparrow fart, he was.'

'And this was Wednesday?'

'I said, didn't I?'

'And you'll give a statement to that effect when we get down to the station?'

Cumbernold pulled himself up to his full height. 'I'm saying nothing without my solicitor.'

At a nod from Gerry Heffernan, Wesley pulled out his radio and called for a patrol car to take Les to Tradmouth. The wait would do him good. A bit of stewing would concentrate the mind of Brian Willerby's next-door neighbour wonderfully.

'Why didn't you let me see those photographs at Martha Willerby's?' asked Wesley once Cumbernold was safely installed in the patrol car.

'That sort of thing isn't suitable for you. You're too young and innocent,' answered Heffernan lightly.

'And shouldn't we have taken them as evidence?' He had known Gerry Heffernan long enough to know that he was hiding something. 'I can always go back to Mrs Willerby and ask to have a look.'

Heffernan looked at his companion, wondering how best to tell him. It was a few seconds before he found the right words. 'I recognised one of the girls in those pictures, Wes.'

'Lilly?'

'Not just Lilly, another one. I didn't want to tell you, Wes, I really didn't. But ... Let's just put it this way – your mate Neil's in for one hell of a shock if he ever finds out.'

'Claire?' Somehow Wesley found it hard to believe. It crossed his mind that it might be another of the boss's jokes – but he didn't usually joke about things like this.

'Yeah. Claire. In all her glory with Willerby. Not a pretty sight if she happens to be your best mate's girlfriend. That's why I didn't want you to see it, Wes. I was sparing your feelings. I thought it best if I broke the news gently, like.'

Wesley stopped and thought for a moment, taking in what he'd heard. 'Does Neil have to know?'

'Not necessarily. We can have a discreet chat with the lass and see what she's got to say for herself.' He looked suddenly solemn. 'We've got to face the fact that she's got the means – anyone working here with access to the key to the pavilion could have got at the mallet thing. The motive – she wants her past kept quiet. And the opportunity – she disappeared back to the hall half way through the cricket match leaving Neil behind. She could easily have arranged to meet Brian in the woods and have got there via the gardens. That lad saw him before the match talking to a long-haired woman. For some reason I'd got it into my head that it must have been Jacintha, or even Martha Willerby. But now I'd say this Claire has some explaining to do.'

'What about John Jones? Don't you reckon the same person killed them both?' Wesley knew he was trying to persuade Heffernan – and himself – of Claire's innocence.

'Of course, Willerby might have killed Jones for some reason unknown to us,' mused Heffernan. 'He was seen there on the night Jones died: he was burning things in his garden incinerator the morning after, according to Cumbernold. Or alternatively it might have been someone else entirely; nothing to do with this case.'

'Have we got the forensic report on Willerby's car yet?'

'Not yet. With any luck it'll arrive some time today. And then there's the knocking-in mallet. If traces of blood and hair are found on that then we can be absolutely certain that's what killed Willerby. At the moment there's always the awful possibility that some innocent member of the cricket club might have had it at home lovingly knocking in his new bat and has only just returned it to the pavilion. It belongs to the whole club, apparently; members just borrow it when they need it. So let's just hope it turns out to be our weapon or we're back to square one.'

Wesley's mind drifted back to Claire, and he began to think the unthinkable. Whatever his personal loyalties were, he would have to face the unwelcome possibility that she was involved. 'Of course, this John Jones might have shared Willerby's interest in photography and might have been blackmailing Claire. She might have killed him too and searched the caravan for any photographs. Her picture was in that newspaper cutting too, remember.'

Heffernan nodded earnestly. 'The sooner we have a word with Miss Claire O'Farrell, the better. We'll try not to be too obvious, eh? Don't want Neil asking awkward questions.'

Wesley nodded, trying not to think of Neil and the questions he would be bound to ask eventually if he found out about all this.

But there were other possibilities to be considered, and one of them sprang to mind at that moment. 'Do you think Les Cumbernold could be our murderer? He could have got the knocking-in mallet any time and put it back on Sunday night when he nicked the statues. And he had a motive for getting rid of Willerby. He was going to be sued over those trees. He would have had time to kill him in the tea interval; he was never in the same place long enough to establish a solid alibi. And don't forget that he found the body; or was found near the body by Jake and Jacintha after the match.'

'Aye. They always say that murderers have the urge to return to the scene of the crime – can't resist it, some of 'em. I'd say our Les was another likely candidate. Maybe Willerby found out about his little sideline in nicked architectural antiques. And, as you say, he had plenty of opportunity to replace the mallet when he pinched the statues.'

'What time are we interviewing him?'

'No hurry, Wes. Let him stew till tender, as my cookery book says.'

As they reached the stable block they saw a familiar figure flitting towards the gardens. Claire O'Farrell walked quickly, frowning with scholarly concentration, a large book of considerable age clutched to her chest.

'It's better if I leave you to it,' Heffernan whispered. He moved away nimbly and disappeared into the stable block. Wesley was alone.

Claire looked round and spotted him. She hesitated before hurrying on.

'Claire, can I have a word?'

She swung round and her eyes met Wesley's. He could tell she was nervous. She stood still, poised for flight. 'Please, Claire, I need to talk to you.'

'He told you, didn't he?' she said almost in a whisper.

'Who?'

'Neil.' The way she spoke his name sounded positively murderous.

'I haven't seen him since yesterday. He hasn't told me anything.' He paused, considering the best way to begin. 'Brian Willerby's wife has some photographs.'

Her expression changed to one of horror. The horror of a trapped animal realising that escape wasn't an option. Wesley found himself feeling sorry for her. But he knew that pity was a trap he mustn't fall into.

'I'm going to have to talk to you about it sooner or later, Claire, and now's as good a time as any.'

Claire nodded, resigned to her fate, and Wesley began to walk slowly towards the house. She fell in beside him. 'Where are we going?' she asked.

'I thought we could walk around the edge of the gardens. I assume that you don't want Neil to know anything about this. He's digging away in the walled garden so he won't see us.'

'So you won't tell him about . . .'

'Whatever you tell me will be in the strictest confidence,' he said, knowing that he was sounding like something from a training manual but lost for friendlier, more reassuring words.

They walked in silence for a while then, when they were well away from the house, Claire spoke.

'When I was at university I got into debt. I shared a house with some other girls. They all came from rich families who helped them out with the exorbitant rent, but I soon found I couldn't keep up with the rest of them. I had a job in a bar in the evenings and another in a shop at weekends but it still wasn't enough. I knew a girl – just an acquaintance – who always seemed to have a lot of money to splash about and one day she told me about her job. She said she worked as a hostess at a posh place in Morbay at weekends; said she'd have a word with the manageress and see if there were any vacancies. I was called for an interview just like with an ordinary job. The woman who interviewed me was called Carlotta. I thought she seemed really respectable, strait-laced even.'

Wesley nodded. 'I've met her. Go on.'

'She said her clients liked students. She said they liked someone who could make intelligent conversation. It wasn't until I actually started working there that I realised that the clients usually expected more than a cosy chat. I could have stormed out when I found out what sort of place it was but I was so desperate for the money by then. I'd built up debts of over five grand so I went along with it.'

She swallowed hard. 'The men weren't nasty or perverted or anything like that: they were mostly just sad, a bit pathetic. But sometimes I used to be sick afterwards.' She looked Wesley in the eye challengingly. 'Are you shocked?'

Wesley shook his head sadly. 'Tell me about Brian Willerby.'

She walked on by Wesley's side, her eyes downcast. 'He took a shine to me and he was a bit of nuisance, to be honest. He visited about once a week and after a while he started bringing a camera with him. He said he'd cleared it with Carlotta and she didn't mind. He took photographs, you know. I told Carlotta I didn't like it but she just said it was harmless, that he just wanted a record of what we . . . Anyway, he started suggesting that we meet at other times. One day he took my address book out of my handbag and wrote his address down, pleading with me to ring him, to arrange to meet somewhere other than Carlotta's. I didn't, of course. I just scribbled out his address – I didn't want to be reminded of it. I should have got a new address book but you know how it is, I never got round to it. Anyway, when I left university I never heard from him again, thank God. I'd paid off all my debts, got a job with the Earlsacre Trust and put the past behind me. Then when I started here I found out that Willerby was Martin Samuels' brother-in-law and that he occasionally did some work for the trust. I just prayed that I'd never come across him – and that Martin wouldn't find out.'

'And did Willerby tell Martin?'

'No, I don't think so. In fact I never saw Brian Willerby at Earlsacre until he played in that cricket match. I bumped into him before the match and, er . . . I asked him if he still had the photos. He said yes so I had a go at persuading him to give them back. He said he'd like to see me again. Then he said he'd think about giving the photos back if . . . Well, you can imagine the rest.'

'How long did this conversation last?'

'A couple of minutes. I didn't want to spend a second longer than was necessary in that creep's company.'

'And was the return of the photos conditional upon you agreeing to see him again?'

She looked at Wesley and gave a bitter smile. 'I got that impression, yes. But there was no way . . .'

'And did you see him talking to anyone else before the match?'

She shook her head and sighed. 'It would have been better if I could have got a job far away from here in a different part of the country, but this was such a great opportunity.'

'Where were you during the tea interval?'

'I just locked myself away in my office and did some work. I didn't want to risk bumping into Willerby again. It was hard to concentrate, of course, but . . .'

'Can anybody confirm that?'

She shook her head.

'Did you see Willerby again that afternoon?'

'No. Definitely not.'

'Have you ever been in the cricket pavilion?'

'No. Why?'

Wesley stopped just as they reached the edge of the woodland and produced the photograph of John Jones from his pocket. 'Do you know this man?'

Claire took the photograph in her long slim fingers and studied it. 'No. Sorry.' She looked at the picture again, more intently. 'But there's something vaguely familiar about him. Is this the man who was found dead in that caravan?'

'That's right. We're still trying to identify him.'

But Claire's mind was on other things. 'If you know where the pictures are, is there any chance that they can be destroyed? Please?'

She looked at Wesley appealingly, and he found himself wishing he could lay his hands on the photographs and cast them into some furnace. It was one thing to have made mistakes in the past but quite another for someone else to possess an explicit and embarrassing photographic record of them.

'I'll see what I can do but I can't promise anything.'

'And you won't tell Neil?'

'Don't worry, I won't breathe a word.'

She gave a weak smile. 'Thanks.'

'I'm afraid you'll have to make a statement.'

'I know.' She clutched the old book that she carried closer to her chest. 'I was just going to take this book to Neil. It's a notebook written by Richard Lantrist outlining the work to be done in the gardens. I was going to show Neil the section on the shell grotto.' She smiled again, raising her eyes to his. 'Is it all right if I go back now? I'll come and see you later when I know Neil's out of the way.'

Wesley nodded. 'See you later, then.'

As Claire hurried away, back towards the gardens and the stable block, she almost collided with a couple who were strolling towards the house. Wesley recognised the woman as Rachel. She walked close to Charles Pitaway. Their hands were almost touching, and they seemed to be lost in conversation and each other. Wesley decided to take the long route back to the incident room. He would leave Rachel and her new lover undisturbed.

'I wondered where you'd got to,' said Gerry Heffernan as soon as Wesley reached his desk.

After he had given his boss a quick résumé of Claire's revelations, Heffernan handed him a couple of sheets of paper. 'The police carrier pigeon's found its way here at last with these two forensic reports stuck in its beak. Brian Willerby's car's clean and that knocking-in mallet thing is definitely the murder weapon: they found traces of Willerby's skin tissue and hair in all the relevant crevices, apparently, but it had been wiped clean of fingerprints. So where does that leave us?'

'It's always possible that Willerby didn't murder John Jones; he just visited him for some reason shortly before he died. Young Billy didn't hear raised voices when he saw Willerby leaving but his mother claims she heard them, which makes it possible that Jones had two visitors that night. And I'd say Willerby was murdered by someone who knew about cricket and had access to the pavilion.' As Claire, to his knowledge, wasn't a cricket enthusiast, Wesley found this theory rather comforting. 'Has anyone found out where the mallet was before the murder?'

'It was kept in the pavilion in case anyone needed to use it, often on full display on top of the lockers, so anyone could have known it was there.'

'And who has access to the pavilion?'

'There are several keys. Martin Samuels has one because he was storing those statues in there. Les Cumbernold had one, but with the statues there it was a bit like letting a fox have the key to the chicken coop. The captain and a few other members of the team had keys – and a man from the village who mows the cricket field. And Uncle Tom Cobleigh and all by the sound of it. Martin Samuels leaves his on a hook in the stable block, so anyone who's connected with the restoration project can help themselves. If someone saw that mallet, even by looking through the pavilion window, and fancied it as an unusual murder weapon, it wouldn't be hard to pinch – or put back.'

'Did anyone see it in the pavilion when they were getting ready for the cricket match?'

'Well, did they? Come on, Wes, you were there.'

'It was pretty packed in there. I certainly didn't notice the mallet.'

'So either it had already walked by then or someone managed to pinch it in the general pre-match confusion.'

'Either option's possible.'

'Then we have this statement.' Heffernan removed a document carefully from the file he was holding. 'A certain Mr Jake Weston was having a bit of how's your father in the pavilion last Thursday night with a certain Ms Jacintha Hervey, and in both their statements it says that they heard someone hanging round the pavilion, trying the door. I reckon it was either Les Cumbernold trying his luck or it was someone after the mallet.'

'But was the mallet there then?'

'Neither of them can remember. Shame. I wish people would be more observant; it'd make our lives a lot easier. So what have we got, Wes?'

'Still no firm ID on John Jones. He rang someone on the night before he died, said he wanted to talk and gave directions to the caravan site. His killer stripped him of his T-shirt which had a coat of arms with foreign writing underneath. Could have been Latin . . . a college crest perhaps? And we didn't find any other ID so the killer might have taken that as well. Brian Willerby is the only person to have been seen with him, possibly quarrelling. There's an Earlsacre connection somewhere – Jones asks about it at the caravan site and there's that cutting under his mattress. Then we come to Willerby. His office is broken into and a file on Earlsacre pinched. He has a taste for pretty girls and he doesn't mind paying for their services – he also likes taking photographs of them in compromising situations.'

'That's a very tactful way of putting it, Wes. Carry on.'

'He was killed with a mallet most people around Earlsacre would have had access to. And he was either followed into the wood by his killer or he arranged to meet him or her there during the tea interval. As for motive . . .'

'Claire O'Farrell has a motive. His wife maybe; or her brother. Les Cumbernold, of course. But I can't think of anyone else at the moment.' Heffernan sighed. 'What about the caravan murder? Any thoughts on that?'

'Martin Samuels disappeared from a dinner party on the night Jones died – and he went back to his office just before the tea interval. Let's face it, his alibi for the caravan murder stinks.'

'If he was willing to make the journey to Earlsacre in the middle of the night, why didn't he just wait until his guests had left?'

'Not everyone has your flair for etiquette, sir,' said Wesley with a straight face.

But Heffernan hadn't heard him. He was just warming to his theme. 'If Willerby's not Jones' killer, I'd say Samuels is a good bet.' A grin spread across his face. 'Maybe we should ask Forensic to give Samuels' car a good going-over and all.'

'Willerby's car's as clean as the driven snow. No traces of blood, nothing. And when Forensic looked at the incinerator in his garden they found no traces of clothing; no buttons or buckles, anything like that, which means that bloodstained clothing probably wasn't burned there in spite of what Cumbernold says about early morning bonfires.'

'So what do you think, Wes?'

'I'm sure this whole thing is linked with Earlsacre somehow, but apart from that . . .'

The mobile phone in Wesley's pocket rang. He fumbled for it and put it to his ear. After a brief conversation he turned to Gerry Heffernan. 'That was Colin Bowman. He wants me to pay him a visit at the mortuary.'

'What about?'

'I've no idea. Let's hope he's come up with something new because, let's face it, we're not getting very far, are we?'

'You can say that again,' answered Gerry Heffernan as Wesley picked his car keys up.

Wesley had omitted to mention that Colin Bowman had asked him to bring Neil along with him to the mortuary. He found his friend drawing a section of masonry protruding from the earth of the walled garden. Soon they were driving towards Tradmouth. Claire's secret was at the forefront of Wesley's mind, making him feel awkward in Neil's presence. He remained quiet for most of the journey, fearing that some unguarded word might lead to an indiscretion, to some involuntary mention of Claire's past. But as they turned on to the main road leading to Tradmouth, with its tantalising glimpses of the sea through gaps in the hedgerows, Neil broke the silence.

'You're not saying much, Wes. Anything wrong? Pam okay?'

Wesley felt relieved that the first words had been spoken. He only hoped that he could keep Claire's name out of the conversation. 'Pam's fine. Back at school tomorrow so she's panicking a bit, but apart from that . . .'

'I've not seen much of you at the site. I thought you'd be taking more interest in the dig – especially as your mum's maiden name was Lantrist. There can't be that many Lantrists about, and this one did live in the West Indies.'

'Are you still suggesting that I'm related to a mass murderer, Neil?' said Wesley with a dismissive smile that indicated he didn't want to take the suggestion too seriously.

'Perish the thought. But I've found out a lot about Richard Lantrist from the letters he wrote to his brother and father. There are a load of them among the papers. There are even a few he wrote from the West Indies, but I haven't got around to reading them yet. The letters I've seen are fascinating. He fought for the Duke of Monmouth at Sedgemoor, got himself captured, then he was tried by the evil Judge Jeffreys at Dorchester assizes. No wonder they were known as the Bloody Assizes: two hundred people condemned to be hanged, drawn and quartered, and eight hundred transported to the West Indies to work as slaves on the plantations there. Richard Lantrist wrote to his father from a ship that sailed for the West Indies out of Poole. Apparently he got quite well in with the captain on account of his family connections, so he wasn't treated too badly, and the captain agreed to deliver the letter on his return. And you'll never guess what the captain's name was.'

'Jonah Parry?'

'You knew?'

'It was a lucky guess,' said Wesley as they descended the steep hill into the town, relieved that the subject of Richard Lantrist's fate was keeping the conversation well away from Claire. 'So Captain Parry showed Richard kindness and compassion in what must have been his darkest hour. Then years later he ends up buried under Richard's newly revamped garden. Richard Lantrist must have been an ungrateful bastard. Unless something happened in between that we don't know about yet.'

This speculation kept their minds occupied until they reached the mortuary. Colin Bowman greeted them in his office with his usual bonhomie and offers of tempting refreshments which they managed to resist.

'I've had a look at your latest skeleton,' the pathologist said as he led the way to the room that had housed the other Earlsacre bones. They lay there still on their crisp white sheets, now joined by the earthly remains of Captain Jonah Parry.

Wesley avoided looking at the smallest skeleton, the young girl. Her fate still haunted his thoughts sometimes in the time between sleeping and waking. But Colin Bowman's cheery voice banished all ghosts.

'He's a man in late middle age, I should say. There's some evidence in the bone development of an intermittently poor diet which, if he was a seafaring man, would be explained by the privations of long sea voyages from a fairly early age. He was a big man, well built. And he was probably killed by a blow to the skull,' he added as an afterthought. 'I thought you gentlemen would like to meet the good captain.'

'So he was definitely murdered?'

'I can't say for certain, but probably. That's why I thought Wesley would be interested. An early-eighteenth-century serial killer. Fascinating, don't you think?'

'And the evidence all points to one man – the man who owned Earlsacre Hall, Richard Lantrist,' said Wesley quietly.

'Sounds like you've cracked the case already.' Bowman looked at his watch. 'I must leave you to it, gentlemen. Duty calls. I've got a post-mortem in ten minutes so can you see yourselves out?'

'Where to now?' asked Neil as the double doors of the mortuary swung shut behind them.

'That's a good question,' answered Wesley. 'I've no idea. Those murders back in 1701 have been easier to solve than the ones I'm working on now.'

With a sigh he climbed into the driving seat of his car and started the engine.

Steve Carstairs and PC Wallace were walking past the mortuary on their way back to the police station when Steve spotted Wesley Peterson getting into his car. He had that friend with him, the scruffy archaeologist. Steve hurried on, hoping he hadn't been seen, and Wallace quickened his pace to keep up with him.

'What's the hurry, Steve? Avoiding someone, are you?'

'Something like that.'

'Who is it? A woman?'

'Mind your own bloody business,' Steve snapped, crossing the busy road towards the Memorial Park and narrowly avoiding being hit by a delivery van.

It was a good thing that he didn't see the man until he was safely on the pavement or there might have been a nasty accident. He stopped suddenly and Wallace, following behind, almost cannoned into him.

'See that man?' he whispered to Wallace. 'The old bloke there talking to that woman?'

'Yeah. What about him?' Wallace stared, puzzled, at the respectable elderly gentleman talking to a well-dressed young woman. He seemed a little unsteady on his feet and wore a worried expression, as though he'd lost something. The woman looked concerned, touching his arm comfortingly from time to time. 'He hardly looks like public enemy number one,' said Wallace dismissively. 'Come on, let's get back to the station.'

'Hang on,' snapped Steve. 'I want a word with him.'

He began to march towards the man at a furious pace. The elderly man turned, saw Steve bearing down on him and began to jog away, leaving the woman staring, open-mouthed, after him. The man ran on, no sign of unsteadiness or weakness now, just a calm assessment of the situation he'd found himself in.

'Stop that man,' Steve shouted, enjoying the drama. With true British reserve the strollers in the Memorial Park looked the other way.

Steve pursued his quarry for a while then stopped, breathless, horrified that he was so unfit. It was Wallace who eventually caught up with the man at the bandstand and led him firmly over to where Steve was getting his breath back.

Steve straightened up and looked the man in the eye. 'What was wrong with the trains to Manchester? Leaves on the line, was it? You owe me eighty quid, mate.' He fumbled in his pocket for his warrant card which he flashed at the captive, who seemed to have shed twenty years in the past few minutes. 'You're nicked, sunshine,' he pronounced in the time-honoured fashion of his favourite TV cops.

'What's the charge?' The man had suddenly acquired a northern accent.

Steve thought for a moment. 'Obtaining money by deception,' he decided. 'You were good, I'll give you that. You had me fooled.'

The man smiled and shook his head, then meekly allowed himself to be led to the police station fifty yards up the street. As the trio entered though the swing-doors Sergeant Bob Naseby leaned on the reception desk. 'Afternoon, lads. What have we here, then?'

'We're bringing this suspect in for questioning,' announced Wallace eagerly.

The suspect himself wasn't paying much attention. His eyes were fixed on the station notice-board to the right of the front desk.

Bob nodded sagely. 'Let me guess. Obtaining money by deception?'

'That's the one,' said Steve. 'Is there an interview room free?'

But before Bob could reply the suspect spoke with all the authority of an Old Testament prophet. 'Do you know this man?' he boomed, quoting from the poster pinned in the centre of the notice-board. 'I certainly do. He was kind enough to lend me ten quid for a meal. Nice chap.'

Steve and Bob Naseby looked at each other. 'You mean you actually met the man who was found dead in that caravan? You met John Jones?' said Steve sceptically.

'Was that his name? I don't remember. I meet so many people in, er, my line of work.'

Steve thought for a moment. 'I wrote my name and address down when I lent you, er . . .' He looked at his colleagues, embarrassed, and didn't finish the sentence. 'I don't suppose there's any chance you've got his written down somewhere, is there?'

'It's possible. If you'll allow me back to my hotel room, I'll have a look through my things.'

'You've got a hotel room?' said Steve in disbelief.

'Oh yes. The Majestic in Morbay. I never stay anywhere with less than four stars.' He looked at Steve with calculation in his narrow grey eyes. 'And what do I get in return for all this co-operation?'

'Don't push your luck, mate,' was Steve's automatic reply.

Chapter 12

Barbados, November 1686
Dearest Father
Captain Parry did visit the master today inquiring of me. Master
Jackson did give permission for me to write, yet now as I put pen
to paper I am lost for what to say. I labour in the sugar
plantations, as does Joseph. Hacking the sugar cane is punishing
work in the heat that calls to my mind the fires of hell itself. Of
my fellow labourers, all slaves, many were followers of
Monmouth, a few transported for other misdeeds, and many are
African, innocent of any wrongdoing but snatched from their
homes by wicked men who trade for profit, not in goods but in
lives. It grieves me sorely to see my fellow men in such servitude,
as it must grieve God. I only wish it were within my power to end
this evil trade.

Pray for me, dearest father, that I may have the strength to
endure.

Your most loving son, Richard Lantrist

Wesley and Heffernan, summoned from Earlsacre, sat down opposite
the elderly man in the interview room.

'I've been looking up your record on one of our newfangled
computers, Syd,' said Gerry Heffernan, as though he were discussing
a job applicant's CV. 'I see you've done time for this sort of thing
before: 1984 in the Great Yarmouth area, 1989 in Brighton. Oh, you
branched out a bit in 1991; impersonating a vicar in Blackpool,
where you claimed to be collecting on behalf of the street children of
Calcutta. Then you moved south in more ways than one: in 1995 you
were miraculously transformed into a Catholic priest based in south

189

London, desperate for money to set up a hospital in Africa. Then there was the little incident in Manchester in 1997 when you were collecting for that Romanian orphanage. All good causes, Syd. Pity they never saw any of it.'

'The public can be very generous,' said Syd righteously.

'Soapy Syd Parsons, eh? You're a bit of a legend among the police forces of Great Britain. Who would have thought you'd end up on our patch?'

'A man has to live, Chief Inspector Heffernan, and when I got out of Strangeways I fancied a change of scene. I'd always heard that Devon was a lovely part of the world.'

'You're right there, Syd.' Heffernan leaned forward. 'Now I hear you recognised the face on our poster in reception. It's something that's been puzzling us for some time. A man was found dead in a caravan over the river from here. He was half naked and he had no ID. He'd booked into the caravan site under the name of John Jones, but that might not be his real name. We've made inquiries but nobody seems to know anything about him and he's not on any missing persons lists. If you can help us, Syd, we'd be very grateful.'

'How grateful?'

'Word in your favour to the judge grateful. He co-operated fully with the police, that sort of thing. How about it?'

Wesley, who thought it best to remain silent while the boss did his bit, sat forward, awaiting Soapy Syd's answer.

'I'll tell you what I know. But it's not much.'

'Go on,' encouraged Wesley.

'I was in Bloxham and I saw this young man, the man on the poster. I started my usual act and he came up to me and asked if I was okay. Then I went into my patter . . . how I'd lost my wallet, et cetera, et cetera. Anyway, he gives me ten quid for something to eat, says that's all he can spare 'cause he's a bit short himself. I went through the usual spiel about taking his address but he said he didn't have one. He told me he'd been living abroad for a couple of years and that he'd only come back because he had to see someone; something about some property. He said there was a solicitor he had to see in Tradmouth who could tell him what was going on. He seemed a bit worried about whatever it was, but he was quite chatty. He said he'd just arrived off the ferry. He'd got the bus from Plymouth and he was looking for somewhere to stay. He told me he wanted to rent a caravan or something while he got things sorted out. He seemed a nice lad.'

'Did he tell you his name?'

Syd wrinkled his brow in an effort of concentration. 'He gave me the tenner and told me not to worry about it. I must have asked his name but I can't for the life of me remember what it was. They all blend into one after a while, you see.'

'Of course,' said Wesley with what sounded like sympathy. 'If it comes back to you, you will let us know, won't you?'

'You can rely on me,' came the reply, offered with touching sincerity.

'If only that were true,' muttered Gerry Heffernan as they left Soapy Syd Parsons alone to contemplate his wrongdoings.

At Gerry Heffernan's suggestion, Wesley returned home at a reasonable time. They had had a word with Les Cumbernold, who had decided to come clean about the theft of the statues and had asked for several other similar offences to be taken into consideration. He still denied any involvement in Willerby's death, and this time Gerry Heffernan was inclined to believe him.

Heffernan decreed that the team would meet up at Earlsacre first thing the next day for a review of the case. He and Wesley hardly allowed themselves to hope that Soapy Syd would remember anything more about the dead man within the next few hours. And even if he did remember, there was no guarantee that it would help them very much.

However, they now knew a little more about John Jones. He had been working abroad for the past two years but hadn't specified where. Wesley remembered the foreign writing that had been seen on Jones' T-shirt: had this held a clue to where he had been? And who he was? Syd had said that Jones returned to England because he had something to sort out. Was it something to do with the newspaper cutting found under his mattress? Something to do with Earlsacre? The solicitor he wanted to see was surely Brian Willerby. And the Earlsacre file had been stolen from Willerby's office. Had Willerby wanted to discuss whatever it was with Wesley? Is that why he had arranged to speak to him? Had Willerby himself been involved in some sort of fraud or wrongdoing, and had he killed Jones in the caravan to silence him? The possibilities whirled around Wesley's brain as he walked back up the steep streets to his house at the top of the town.

By the time he placed his key in his front-door lock, he had forgotten all about the imminent domestic crises that awaited him. But as soon as Pam greeted him, he knew that he wasn't in for a tranquil evening. He fought a fleeting temptation to use a fictitious surge in criminal activity as an excuse to return to the office for some peace.

'They'll be here in an hour and I'm shattered already,' Pam said weakly as he stepped into the hall. 'I'm going to need an early night if I'm going to be in any fit state for work tomorrow. I've been preparing lessons all day and I've got one hell of a headache.'

Wesley shut the front door behind him and took his wife in his arms. 'Come and sit down. I'm going to ring your mother and tell her you're not feeling up to it.'

'She's going into Plymouth this afternoon. She said they're coming straight here. There's no way of getting in touch.'

'Well, school probably won't be too bad tomorrow,' he assured her – like an executioner assuring a condemned man that he would only be a little bit dead.

Pam nodded, unconvinced. 'I've given Michael his tea already. I'll get him off to bed in half an hour. Why has my mother got to be such a selfish, thoughtless cow?' she asked rhetorically before storming up the stairs, leaving Wesley in the hallway staring after her helplessly.

As Pam reached the landing the telephone began to ring. Wesley picked up the receiver hoping it was Della, and that he could tell her not to come in no uncertain terms. But he heard his own mother's warm Caribbean accent on the other end of the line. He took a deep breath and sat down on the bottom stair, preparing for a lengthy conversation.

'I've just called to wish Pamela good luck for tomorrow,' Dr Peterson began cheerfully. 'I hope you're helping. It won't be easy for her, you know.'

Wesley, feeling a little guilty, was anxious to assure his mother that he was being the model husband. 'I'm doing my best. How are you, anyway? How's Dad?'

She gave a tinkling laugh and Wesley wondered, not for the first time, how she managed to stay so bubbly after a day tending the sick. 'Working hard as usual – there are some strange viruses about at the moment, sore throats and headaches, so the waiting room's been full. You know how it is, son – no rest for the wicked. Your father's got a conference next week in Switzerland. All right for these consultants, isn't it, not like us humble GPs. How are you anyway, Wesley? How's life as acting inspector?'

'So far so good. Did I tell you I played in a cricket match at the weekend?'

'That's great. Your Great-Uncle Garfield would have been so pleased. Remember that time he took you to the Queen's Park Oval when you were small?'

Wesley knew he had to interrupt before the conversation became dominated by his mother's favourite sport. 'Mum, how much do you know about your family? About the Lantrists?'

There were a few moments of silence while she thought. 'I can go back to your great-grandparents on my mother's side – your great grandmother was from Surinam and your great-grandfather from Venezuela. I don't really know much about my father's family except that I'm sure my grandfather came from Barbados. I remember my Grandmother Lantrist telling me about it but I guess I was far too young to be interested in family history at the time. Why do you ask?'

'It's just that I've come across someone called Lantrist who was transported to the West Indies in 1685, possibly Barbados. Probably no relation,' he added hopefully.

'That's interesting,' said his mother, innocent of the facts. 'I wish I could remember what my grandmother said about the Barbados connection. She certainly said something, but I don't suppose I was paying much attention. I was a young girl then with other things on my mind.'

'It doesn't matter.' Wesley heard Pam's footsteps on the stairs. 'Here's Pam now. I'll let you speak to her.'

Pam took the telephone and sat herself down on the stair Wesley had just vacated. She looked a little better now and was soon chatting volubly to her mother-in-law, visibly more relaxed. 'Why can't my mother be more like yours?' she muttered bitterly as she put the phone down.

A loud ring on the doorbell saved Wesley from having to think up a tactful answer. Della swept in like a pink-clad tidal wave, followed by Jamie, who was bearing a paper carrier bag which Wesley recognised as being from the Golden Dragon. In the other hand he carried a bottle of champagne – Bollinger. Wesley and Pam exchanged glances and he noticed that Pam looked tired again.

'We're celebrating,' gushed Della as she sat down on the sofa.

'How much do we owe you for the takeaway?' asked Wesley, wanting to call the tune in his own home.

'We wouldn't hear of it,' said Jamie smoothly. 'As Della said, we're celebrating – or rather she is.' He lowered his eyes modestly. 'The shares I advised her to buy last week have trebled in value.'

'You're so clever.' Della reached out her hand and pulled Jamie down beside her.

'Not really clever, darling. It is my job. One builds up expertise over the years, you know.' He turned to Wesley. 'I did my time in the Stock Exchange before I set up on my own in Leeds.'

'And luck doesn't come into it?' Wesley asked.

'Luck comes into every job – even yours, I should think. Only we become luckier with practice, don't we?'

Wesley nodded. He had a strong urge to say something clever or witty that would wipe the smug smile off Jamie's face. But his mind was blank after a day of mental exertion, so he stayed silent.

Pam called through wearily from the kitchen. The plates were out and they were to come through and help themselves. As Jamie popped open the champagne, Wesley went through to the kitchen, feeling he ought to lend a hand.

As he sat down at the table, he felt a sudden wave of tiredness engulf him. He looked across at Jamie, who was raising his glass in a toast to his successful investment. It seemed that Della's new man was on the level after all.

Wesley picked up his glass and drank. He had misjudged the man. Perhaps he was losing his touch . . . or his luck.

Neil Watson knew that the light would soon begin to fade. He stood up and looked about him, surveying the excavations. The archaeological work would soon be finished. The trenches in the walled garden would be back-filled and the garden experts would move in to recreate the paths and parterres. Then they would fill the beds with a riot of flowers, carefully researched and in keeping with the age of the garden.

The shell grotto would be impossible to rebuild in time for the opening, so the garden experts were going for a summerhouse set against the wall instead. The plinth would be replaced in the centre of the garden and a new sundial was being made by local craftsmen to form the centrepiece of the whole thing. The garden would be, as far as was possible, a replica of the one Richard Lantrist would have known – without the bones.

Neil's task was almost done. He and his colleagues had discovered what lay beneath the overgrown remnants of the Renaissance gardens of Earlsacre. It only remained to process the finds, and then it would be Jake's responsibility to record the lot for future reference. The more exciting finds would be used in the exhibition planned for the restored main house. This would tell the story of Earlsacre Hall, skeletons and all.

Neil started to head for the stable block where he knew Claire was still working. Her job of discovering all she could about the family that created the house and gardens would last a good deal longer than his own, and her knowledge would be needed to create the exhibition.

He was surprised to see her running towards him, her dark hair falling about her bare shoulders. Neil hastily ran his fingers through his hair in a feeble effort to tidy himself up.

She waved and called to him. 'Neil. Come and look at this. See if you agree with me. Come on.' She turned and ran back into the building like a ghost.

He had no option but to follow her into the gloom of the stables. He walked into the office, where she was already sitting, hunched over a pile of old documents, and stood behind her, bending to kiss her hair, which smelled of herbs and wood smoke. She didn't look round but placed an ancient letter and an equally ancient notebook neatly on the desk in front of her. 'Tell me what you see,' she ordered, obviously excited.

'An old letter – one of the ones Richard Lantrist wrote to his dad – and the notebook he used to record what he was doing in the garden. Why?'

'Have a closer look. Go on.'

Claire's excitement was infectious. Neil bent over the documents. He didn't see it at first but then the truth dawned. 'Bloody hell,' was all he could say.

Claire looked up and grinned, her eyes shining with the excitement of the chase. 'Just wait till I tell Martin.' She skidded her typing chair over to her waiting computer. She hit a button and the flashing screensaver disappeared.

'What are you doing?' asked Neil.

'I'm sending some e-mails to museums and historical societies in the West Indies, starting with Barbados where Lantrist landed up.

According to Richard's letters home, he was sold to a plantation owner there called Jackson.'

'He managed to get letters home?'

'Occasionally, but only when Captain Parry's ship docked there. It seems that Parry took quite an interest in Richard and got permission from Jackson to take letters back to England. Anyway, I plan to ask all the museums and societies in the area if they have any records relating to anyone called Lantrist. I'll send out the e-mails now. There's no time like the present.'

She began to type. Neil watched her closely. 'What happens if our suspicions are correct?' he asked.

'I'd say there are going to be some fireworks around here if we can prove it,' Claire answered as she pressed the key that would send her questions half way round the globe.

Soapy Syd Parsons took the tray from the young police constable and thanked him politely. Just because he was incarcerated in a small bare cell in the bowels of Tradmouth police station with nothing but a stainless-steel toilet and a thin, plastic-covered mattress for company, that was no reason for him to forget his manners.

'What's your name?' he asked the constable.

The young officer blushed. 'PC Jarvis. Why?' he asked nervously, hoping he hadn't given any cause for complaint.

'What's your first name?'

The officer blushed again. 'Charlie. My mum's a great fan of the royal family,' he answered, swallowing nervously. He hoped the prisoner wasn't trying to distract him before overpowering him and making a bid for freedom. The custody sergeant had told him to watch out for all the tricks.

But the elderly man made no move. He sat on the blue mattress beside the tray bearing his evening meal with a faraway smile on his face.

As PC Jarvis turned to go, Syd called to him. 'Tell that Chief Inspector Heffernan I want to speak to him, will you, Charlie? Tell him I've got something to tell him.'

'I'll see what I can do,' replied Jarvis as he left the cell, locking the door carefully behind him.

'What do you think of him?' said Pam as she slipped her nightdress over her head.

'Who?'

'Jamie. What do you think?'

Wesley looked up from the book he was reading, a new and much-hyped biography of Judge Jeffreys, and thought for a second. 'I must say he surprised me tonight. I really had him down as a con man, but the shares he bought for your mother actually came up trumps, so it looks like he's above board after all. But I still can't say I like the man. As Gerry Heffernan would say, he's as smooth as an eel's armpits.'

Pam smiled at this Heffernanism, as she called the chief inspector's more colourful sayings.

'I suppose you're right.' She picked up her book then put it down again. The subject wasn't closed yet: it was still in her mind and she would worry at it like a terrier until she had unloaded all her fears. 'It makes me sick the way they're all over each other.' She wrinkled her nose in disgust. 'I still reckon there's something iffy about him.'

'Your mother's grown up.'

'I sometimes wonder. She's just the kind of woman a con man would target: widowed, looking for affection and comfortably off. There must be something we can do.'

'Sorry. James Delmann's got no police record, so if there's anything to be found out about him, Della'll have to find it out for herself. But so far it sounds as if he's genuine. He's made her four thousand quid already.'

'There's still something about him I don't trust.'

'Perhaps you're just comparing him with your father.'

'Oh, don't get all Freudian on me, Wesley. I can't take it at this time of night. And I'd better get some sleep if I'm going to be up for work in the morning. Unless . . .' She took the book gently from his hands and kissed his ear. Judge Jeffreys would have to wait.

Then the telephone rang.

Wesley sighed and picked up the receiver. Gerry Heffernan's voice on the other end of the line was so loud that Pam, lying a couple of feet away, could hear every word he said.

'Hey, Wes, you'll never guess what Soapy Syd's come up with. Only another name for our mystery caravaner. Want to know what it is?'

Wesley, tired, frustrated and in no mood for guessing games, answered in the affirmative.

Chapter 13

Barbados, October 1697
My dearest Father
The news of my brother's death grieves me greatly. The swiftness
of his sickness reminds us that we must all be prepared to meet
our Maker at any time He so chooses. In answer to your inquiry
concerning Joseph Marling, I can assure his father that he is in
good health and doth now work in Master Jackson's gardens. I
myself am well and, as my sentence is served and through your
entreaties conveyed by the good Captain Parry, I no longer work
in the plantation but am given employment in the household as a
clerk, for which I am truly grateful. Joseph and I have better
fortune than the Africans who work the plantations in conditions
of great hardship, even though Master Jackson is considered a
kinder master than most. It is an unhappy and wicked trade and
all Christian men should do all in their power to end it. It is
surely against the will of the Almighty that man should treat his
fellow man thus for greed and gain.

It is well that your fortunes have increased and that you offer
to bring me home. I am resolved not to return as yet but I must
beg a favour of you. There is a young African woman, born of
slaves here on the island and daughter of the overseer on the
plantation. She is a household slave, greatly favoured by Mistress
Jackson, and works as that lady's maidservant. In secret I have
taught her to read and write our language and she has proved an
able pupil. Her name is Rebecca and she is the sweetest and
loveliest of women. I beg you, dear father, to offer Master
Jackson whatever sum he names to buy her freedom, for she has
become most dear to me.

I give this letter into Captain Parry's hands before he sets sail and be assured that my prayers are with you. Please oblige me in these humble requests and God will bless you for it.
I remain your most loving and obedient son

Richard Lantrist

Rachel Tracey lay asleep, her hair spread out against the dark blue pillow. Charles Pitaway propped himself up on his elbow, watching her. He touched her hair gently and she stirred.

'Haven't you got to be at work?' he whispered.

'Mmm,' she murmured sleepily, opening her eyes. 'I'd rather stay here.'

'Now where would the law-abiding citizens of Devon be if all the police decided to stay in bed, Detective Constable Tracey,' he teased, pulling the sheets down to expose her naked body. She squealed and grabbed at the sheets as Charles rolled on top of her and began to kiss her, stifling her laughter. Then the urgent sound of the doorbell made them freeze, statue still.

Charles jumped off the bed as the bell rang a second time. 'I'd better get that,' he said. 'Might be the post . . . something urgent. Don't go away,' he added as he planted a kiss on her forehead.

Rachel lay still and listened. Whoever was at the front door of Charles' modern flat overlooking Dukesbridge harbour, it wasn't an employee of the Royal Mail. They had come into the flat and they were talking. Rachel froze with horror as she recognised the voices. Then she scrambled out of bed and pulled on her clothes, her heart beating fast. This was a punishment, she told herself; a punishment for telling lies to her mother – and to Dave; for saying that she was spending the night with a broken-hearted WPC Trish Walton, who had just broken up with a fictitious boyfriend. Her mother had always told her that her sins would find her out. With Gerry Heffernan and Wesley Peterson standing on the other side of the thin bedroom door, she was convinced for the first time in her life that her mother was absolutely right.

She pressed her ear to the door and listened, hoping desperately that Charles wouldn't give her presence away . . . and that Wesley and the boss wouldn't take it into their heads to search the place for some reason.

She heard Gerry Heffernan's loud voice asking the questions. 'A witness has come forward who says he met a man called Charles

Pitaway a week last Monday. This Charles Pitaway had just arrived in the country from abroad where he'd been working in a vineyard for two years.'

She could just make out Charles' reply. 'Well, I had a job in a vineyard near Bordeaux for a while. I make no secret of it. I was working there when a letter came from our solicitors to say that my father had died and that I'd inherited the estate. I don't know if someone's been impersonating me or what . . .'

'Your family solicitor – that would be Brian Willerby?'

'Yes, that's right. But I never had any contact with Willerby myself before he wrote to me on behalf of Martin Samuels to offer to buy the estate. I never met him until I came to Tradmouth, and then it was only to sign some papers,' said Charles, spelling out the facts patiently.

'And would it surprise you to know that our witness identified the Charles Pitaway he met as the unidentified man found dead in a caravan near Bloxham?'

Rachel's mouth went dry. She held her breath and listened to Charles' reply.

'I'm as puzzled as you are, Chief Inspector. I really don't know what to say. I can only guess that someone's been using my name in some sort of fraud attempt. Or, of course, there's a chance that his real name was Charles Pitaway and it's just a coincidence. May I have a look at the photograph of the dead man if you've got it with you?'

There was silence for a few seconds. Rachel breathed again. Charles was telling the truth. As he said, someone might have been using his name, or it was coincidence. There would be a simple explanation.

When Charles broke the silence, Rachel nearly jumped. 'He does look a bit familiar. There were so many people who just worked at the vineyard for a few weeks – students, itinerant workers, drifters. One of them could easily have picked up on my name and decided to use it for reasons of his own. I can assure you, gentlemen, I'm as puzzled as you are.'

Rachel could almost see him giving her two colleagues his most charming smile. One thing that Charles wasn't short of was charm. She heard him say, 'Sorry I couldn't be more help. I'll look forward to meeting you on the cricket field again next year, Wesley. Are you getting much practice in the nets now the season's over?'

Rachel crept away from the door and picked up her handbag from the floor. It opened and her purse fell out, spilling coins underneath the bed. She swore under her breath and fell to her knees. Then she lifted up the valance and peered under the bed. As she gathered up the stray coins her hand came into contact with cardboard. Absent-mindedly she pulled it out and looked at it. It was a file, thick with documents. She could see a name scrawled on the front in black felt-tip pen – Earlsacre. She opened it. The file was crammed with long-winded legal documents, letters and copies of letters sent. She flicked through the papers, then began to read one of the letters. It was dated eighteen months ago and was written from an address near Bordeaux. It was handwritten, not too easy to decipher. She peered down at it, trying to make sense of what she was reading.

As she hadn't heard Heffernan and Wesley leave, she hadn't expected the door to open at that moment. She jumped, pushed the file underneath the bed, and looked up at Charles guiltily.

'They've gone,' he said quietly. 'I'll make us a coffee.'

Claire O'Farrell had got up early, telling Neil that she was going to Earlsacre to check if there were any replies to her e-mails. Neil, not wanting to miss out, hauled himself out of bed and woke himself up under the shower. If there was any news about Richard Lantrist, he wanted to be the first to know.

When they reached the stable block they passed the open door of the police incident room. He could see a handful of officers working purposefully, typing into computers or speaking on the telephone; he was mildly irritated not to see Wesley anywhere about.

The computer awaited them in Claire's office, its blank, dark grey screen inscrutable. Claire booted it up and waited. It was a couple of very long minutes before she discovered that one of her e-mails had been answered.

A Winston Paul, curator of a small museum on the island of Barbados, was delighted to convey the news that he was in possession of some early-eighteenth-century letters concerning a man called Richard Lantrist, donated to the museum by one of his descendants many years ago. He said he would search his records to see if there was any more material hidden in the archives. Mr Paul's enthusiasm positively bubbled from the screen. He was excited to hear about the Earlsacre project and asked to be sent all the archaeological reports when they were completed. There was an old plantation house and gardens that a local history society in Barbados was longing to excavate; but their task wouldn't be easy as the site was overgrown by thick jungle. Neil, glad that his digs weren't quite so harrowing, was only too pleased to oblige; he felt it was the least he could do for the distant and helpful Mr Paul.

The text of the letters appeared below Winston Paul's words. Mercifully, they weren't long. The first was apparently from Richard to Rebecca, the young African woman mentioned in his letters to his father. They both worked on the Jackson estate; Richard as clerk and Rebecca now as lady's maid. Presumably John Lantrist had bought Rebecca's freedom as the pair seemed now to be married with a child. Neil found himself liking old John Lantrist – and the Richard of the letters. He couldn't quite match the taciturn Richard Lantrist of Jacob Finsbury's gossipy accounts with the Richard who emerged from his correspondence with his father and now with his wife as a likeable, compassionate man: a man of firm faith and principles; a man who felt strongly about the evils of the slave trade and who treated Rebecca, an African woman, with love and respect. But people change. He read on.

As I write this we sail towards England and I am in good spirits although the voyage has taken a full three months. It is excellent that you continue as maidservant to the mistress: it would grieve me sorely to think of you alone and unprotected in my absence. But, dearest one, I will send for you and our son as soon as this business is done. Though I am perplexed as to why my father's lawyers did not write to inform me of his death.

If it were not for Captain Parry's chance meeting while he was ashore in Tradmouth with the Vicar of Earlsacre, I should not know to this day that I am come into my inheritance. I know not why I was never told that my father had died. For two long years I have wondered why he never responded to my letters. I had thought him sick perhaps. I have another sad task to perform when I reach Devon. I must break the news to Joseph Marling's father that he disappeared from the island two years since, that most like he had met with some accident or ill fortune. Pray, dearest one, that he is yet found safe for his father's sake, who was ever a loyal servant to our family.

There were fond endearments and promises that they would soon be reunited. Claire scrolled down to the second letter. This bore the

202

words, printed at the top in a neat, almost childlike hand, 'his last letter'. Neil was filled with a sense of foreboding.

I write this from the Castle Inn at Tradmouth and I shall entrust my letters to Captain Parry as his ship leaves for the Indies on the morrow. I have not yet journeyed to Earlsacre as I hear strange stories of the place that I can scarce believe. Sweet one, I fear there is villainy of some kind afoot. I did visit with my father's lawyer who swore that I was an impostor and should be thrown into prison. I thought it prudent to leave his chambers before he called the constable. There is a misconception somewhere that I must resolve before I send for you, my love. But fear not. I will visit Earlsacre on the morrow and all will be well. My prayers are with you.

'When's that one dated?' asked Neil, peering over Claire's shoulder.

'July second, 1701, would you believe,' said Claire quietly. She thought for a moment. 'But Richard Lantrist was . . . The plinth was put down in the walled garden on the fourth of July. This means that the Richard who built the gardens wasn't the Richard who was transported. We saw that the handwriting in the letters and the handwriting in the garden notebook were completely different. There's the nice Richard, the real heir to Earlsacre, who married Rebecca in Barbados and was a great mate of Captain Parry, and there was nasty Richard, who Jacob Finsbury stayed with and wrote about in 1703. There were two of them.'

'I'd just about worked that out for myself.'

'And if nice Richard, the real Richard, planned to visit Earlsacre to see what was going on the third of July, that means . . .'

'That he was murdered by nasty Richard as soon as he showed his face and buried in the middle of the walled garden. It's beginning to fit together nicely. A serving girl went missing about that time . . . Jinny something. I bet that's the girl who was buried alive. She witnessed something she shouldn't and nasty Richard got rid of her. He probably drugged her or knocked her out then he buried her with nice Richard and plonked the plinth on top of them both – only she was still alive.'

'And then later on Captain Parry came along looking for the Richard he'd befriended: he found that the man who called himself Richard Lantrist was an impostor and was killed to keep him quiet.'

'But who was the nasty Richard?'

'Haven't you worked that out yet, Neil?' said Claire, shaking her head.

'The gardener's son, Joseph Marling; the one who disappeared from Barbados two years previously around the time the real Richard's father died?'

Claire nodded smugly. 'It's my guess that Joseph was a slippery character. Maybe he was in the habit of reading Richard's letters if he got the chance. I think he intercepted the letter to Richard saying that his father was dead and had an idea. If he could get back home to Devon he could take Richard's identity. They had known each other since childhood, and Joseph must have been as well acquainted with the estate as Richard. If they looked a bit alike he could probably have got away with impersonating him; after all, fourteen years had passed. The real Richard, settled in Barbados with his wife and child, might never have been any the wiser. Joseph hadn't bargained for the real Richard being so pally with Captain Parry, of course.'

'Is there another letter?' asked Neil.

Claire pressed a key and the screen revealed the third letter in the possession of the little museum in that far-off island.

'It's from Captain Parry to Rebecca,' said Neil, awed, leaning over her shoulder but rendered oblivious to her proximity by the unfolding story on the computer screen. 'It's dated February 1702, Bridgetown, Barbados.'

He read: ' "Your letter awaited me at the inn upon my arrival in Bridgetown. I share your concerns regarding your husband. You say you have not had word from him since July of last year and that in his last letter he wrote of villainy and strange tales concerning his inheritance at Earlsacre. Trust me, madam, that I will visit Earlsacre on my return to England and seek out the truth of the matter. I send this with a servant now but I will call upon you before I sail. I know my dear friend Richard would be concerned for your welfare and that of his son. I remain, madam, your servant, Jonah Parry." '

He looked up at Claire. 'So Captain Parry was going to visit Earlsacre when he got back to England. The voyage took about three months in those days, so that'd be around May, wouldn't it? It fits. He goes to Earlsacre and finds that the man who's claiming to be Richard is an impostor, so he's murdered and buried under the shell grotto. I can't wait to tell Wesley all this.'

Claire looked uneasy at the mention of Wesley's name. 'He'll be busy. He won't have time.'

'Nonsense. He'll want to know. I'm going to see if he's about.'

'No, Neil, please . . .'

But Neil wasn't listening. He rushed out of the room in search of his quarry.

'Where the hell is Rachel?' Gerry Heffernan paced to and fro across the floor of the incident room. 'Ring the farm, will you, Wes. Tell her to get herself down here now.'

Wesley looked uneasy. 'Surely if she wasn't well she would have let us know.' The Rachel he knew was hardly the unreliable type.

'Yeah. This isn't like her at all.'

Heffernan was right. It wasn't like Rachel not to turn up without an explanation. They both sensed that something was amiss but neither man wanted to put his fears into words. The fact that Rachel was clearly involved with Charles Pitaway didn't make them feel any easier. But they had no evidence against Pitaway. None at all apart from the word of a con man who could convince even the most level-headed that for a small fee he could introduce them to mermaids selling their favours in the River Trad at high tide. Pitaway might be as innocent as the average newborn babe for all they knew . . . probably was.

Wesley rang the farm and spoke to one of Rachel's brothers. She had stayed the night with Trish Walton, he was told; some sort of emotional crisis on Trish's part. Wesley looked up and saw that Trish was at her desk sorting through witness statements, seemingly untouched by the storms of emotion. He went over and spoke to her. Trish was puzzled. Rachel hadn't stayed with her and, she added, blushing, she was fine: she had no emotional problems. Whatever had given him that idea?

Wesley, feeling a little foolish, broke the news to Heffernan.

'Have you tried her mobile?' Heffernan asked anxiously.

'Yes, several times. But there's no answer. I'll keep trying.'

'Try Charles Pitaway's flat and all. There's always a chance she might have called in there.'

Wesley obliged, waiting a full minute while the phone rang out at the other end. 'Nobody's there,' he said, replacing the receiver.

'Right, tell all patrols to keep a look out for Pitaway's car.'

'Aren't we overreacting?'

'I don't know but I'm not taking any chances.'

Neil hovered by the door of the incident room, peering in, looking for Wesley. Gerry Heffernan spotted him, but instead of his customary wisecrack he greeted him with the wave of a worried hand and beckoned him to come in.

Neil spotted Wesley in the corner of the room, a telephone held to his ear. He marched over to him.

'What's up with everyone, Wes? Looks like a wake when the drink's run out.'

'Rachel's not come in and we're worried. She hasn't been home all night and the person she told her mum she was staying with hasn't seen her. It's not like her at all.'

'She's a big girl. Probably having a bit of . . . Charles Pitaway was sniffing around, you know.'

'We've checked him, went there first thing. There was no sign of her. He's not answering his phone now, so I assume he's gone out.'

'He's down here most days,' said Neil, losing interest in Charles and Rachel. 'You'll never guess what we've found.'

'What?' said Wesley impatiently. He was in no mood for guessing games.

'Only the solution to the puzzle of the skeletons in the walled garden. Claire got an e-mail from Barbados. They've got some old letters in a museum there. Two from Richard Lantrist to his wife, Rebecca, in Barbados, and one to Rebecca from Captain Jonah Parry. I reckon I've pieced together the whole story,' he concluded with pride 'I'll be after your job next.'

'But Lantrist already had a wife. Didn't he marry a local heiress?'

'That wasn't the real Richard Lantrist. That was an impostor. The gardener's son who got transported with him pinched the letter which told Richard his dad had died and he'd inherited the estate. Then Joseph Marling came back pretending to be Richard and when the real Richard twigged what had happened and came back, Marling murdered him.'

Wesley began to take notice. 'So the girl's skeleton was the real Richard's wife?'

'No. I think she was just some maidservant who saw something she shouldn't: a maid called Jinny Cartwright did go missing around that time. There was a lot of talk about it in the village, according to Jacob Finsbury's journal. And when Captain Parry came to see what had happened to Richard, he got bumped off too.'

'And the real Richard's wife? What happened to her?'

'Last I heard she was still in Barbados with their son. There's nothing more about her in the correspondence. It all stops when Parry was killed.'

'Have you any proof of all this?'

Neil shrugged. 'Come and have a look through all the documents yourself and see if you don't come up with the same story. It took a while to put together – like a jigsaw with half the bits missing – but once I thought about it and all the dates, it's the only explanation.'

Wesley plonked himself down on a nearby office chair, deep in thought. After a while he looked up at Neil, who was still grinning triumphantly at the thought of his detective prowess.

'I've just had an idea.' Wesley stood up so quickly that the office chair skidded away on its castors. 'I've got to see the boss.'

Neil watched open-mouthed as Wesley rushed across the room, a man in a hurry.

Charles Pitaway took the file out from under the bed and placed it carefully on top of the duvet. He sat down on the bed and flicked through it. It was a detail he hadn't thought of, and details couldn't be ignored. He should have been more careful. He sat staring at the two handwritten letters in the file; letters saying that Charles Pitaway would be interested in selling the Earlsacre estate should it be his to sell one day in the future. Martin Samuels had never been one for holding back tactfully where his obsession with Earlsacre was concerned. Charles sat for a few moments comparing these letters with his signature on the later legal documents and cursing his own incompetence.

He tucked the file underneath his arm. He would get rid of it on the ferry crossing, throw it into the sea and let the salt water destroy the evidence. He had already disposed of the real Charles Pitaway's T-shirt and his own bloodstained clothing in this way, flinging them off a high cliff at Little Tradmouth Head into the swirling sea below.

Through the open bedroom door he could see Rachel. She looked peaceful, like a child fast asleep. It was a pity, he thought. But he knew that he had been sailing close to the wind conducting a relationship with a policewoman. Perhaps he had been attracted by the risk. Perhaps he had just liked Rachel. But it was too late for those thoughts now.

He walked over to where Rachel lay on the brightly coloured rug beside the black leather sofa. He looked at the coffee cup on the glass table. She had drunk the lot. That was good. Then he knelt beside her and touched her fair hair with gentle fingers that crept down towards her throat.

Chapter 14

e-mail from Winston Paul, Bridgetown Museum, Barbados:
Dear Claire
I've turned up one more document. Another letter from Captain
Parry to Rebecca Lantrist . . . dramatic stuff. Hope it's helpful to
you. Winston.

I feel I must write to inform you that I have made investigations
into the whereabouts of your husband and I fear some villainy is
afoot. Upon my arrival at Tradmouth I travelled to Earlsacre and
I did stay at the inn there where I heard disturbing tales. The
Richard Lantrist who dwells at Earlsacre Hall is, I fear, not your
husband, whom I knew as a good and upright man. I saw this
Sir Richard riding through the village and it was not your
husband but another that I recognised . . . one Joseph Marling
who, I confess, did bear a passing resemblance to Richard.
*   I fear, madam, that an impostor dwells on your husband's*
estate, but I must have proof if I am to bring this before the
authorities. I stay at the inn tonight and I shall visit Earlsacre on
the morrow. The landlord here has promised to place this letter
in the hands of a captain of my acquaintance in Tradmouth who
sails for Barbados in the next week.
*   I remain, madam, your servant, Jonah Parry*

Wesley Peterson kept his eyes on the winding road. When the
carriageway straightened as it ran into Dukesbridge, he began to
speak. 'This is sheer speculation, but stop me if you think I'm going
wrong.'

Heffernan nodded. 'Don't I always? Carry on.'

'I think Charles Pitaway, the real Charles Pitaway, was probably a bit of a free spirit. He most likely backpacked around Europe and Asia – hence his penchant for travelling light, as witnessed by Dilys at the caravan park – and then he got a job in a French vineyard for a while. While he was there a letter arrived for him saying his father had died and that he had inherited the lot, including the Earlsacre estate. But he never got the letter. It was opened by one of the other workers on the estate, an Englishman who had befriended him, someone who perhaps shared accommodation with him. This man probably looked a bit like him and could get away with using his passport – the photos are never good anyway. Then somehow the impostor pinched Charles' ID papers; and remember the real Charles had no idea that his father was dead. All he knew was that his papers were missing and that the other bloke had gone. Eventually the impostor presented himself at the family's solicitors; at the offices of Blake, Willerby and Johns, where Brian Willerby was dealing with the late Mr Pitaway's estate, and also with the proposed purchase of Earlsacre by Martin Samuels' trust. A lot of money would be coming Charles Pitaway's way, certainly enough to kill for. The real Pitaway would have been oblivious to all this going on until some expat working on the vineyard for the summer showed him an English newspaper with the piece about Earlsacre and the photograph of his fellow vineyard worker, who had mysteriously disappeared at the same time as the real Charles' ID papers and passport. He came straight over to Devon, of course, and contacted Brian Willerby, who visited him in the caravan where he was staying. The killer took his victim's T-shirt off – I strongly suspect that the coat of arms and foreign writing on it had something to do with the vineyard where they'd both worked. Any sort of French connection – if you'll pardon the expression – might have put us on the right track. Are you with me so far?'

Gerry Heffernan nodded. 'I'm with you. Sounds a bit risky.'

'Where's the risk? He's got all the ID and seems to know what he's talking about. You've met him. He's plausible. And he's well spoken, with that public school confidence that people don't question. If the real Charles turned up, he'd just turn the tables on him and say that he was the impostor. By all accounts the real Charles was far less impressive, so who are people going to believe?'

'So why did he call himself John Jones? Why not use his real name?'

210

'Perhaps he didn't want to take the risk of the bogus Charles finding out he was here; after all, he might have come across someone with connections with Earlsacre and word would have got back. It was safer to be John Jones until he'd convinced Willerby and notified the authorities.'

'Surely there would have been someone who knew the real Charles. What about his family?'

'He had no family. His parents were dead. No relatives. And I bet the real Charles talked a lot about his background when he was with this bloke in France, so he'd know all the details. A good con man can convince anyone – look at Soapy Syd and Steve. But I imagine there would have been correspondence from the real Charles in the file stolen from Willerby's office . . . different handwriting.'

'So he broke in there as well?'

Wesley nodded. 'It fits, doesn't it?'

'Perhaps someone should get on to the police in Bordeaux – see if they know anything about any shenanigans involving a Charles Pitaway. Might be worth a try.'

'I've been in touch with them already. They're calling back if they've got anything.'

Heffernan looked impressed. 'So you reckon this false Charles Pitaway killed Brian Willerby too?'

'I think Brian had found out the truth from the real Charles when he visited him at the caravan site on Tuesday night; that's when young Billy saw him. Then Charles had another visitor about an hour later . . . the man who killed him. I think that was why Willerby was so anxious to talk to me: he probably still wasn't sure who to believe and he didn't really know what to do. Of course, the impostor felt he had to shut Willerby up too before he had a chance to speak to the police and cause awkward questions to be asked. He was cool, I'll give him that. He must have killed Willerby just before he came into the pavilion and started chatting to me.'

'Bloody cheek,' said Heffernan under his breath.

'He seemed a bit breathless, come to think of it.'

They turned into the road that led to the harbour. To their right was a block of brand-new apartments, its frontage dotted with tasteful black iron balconies, giving it the look of a converted warehouse.

Wesley jumped from the car and pressed the bell of Pitaway's apartment. He kept on pressing it as if he believed his persistence would be rewarded.

'He's not here,' said Heffernan, defeated.

'Let's have a word with the neighbours.' Wesley began to press each bell in turn. Only one bore fruit. A bored-looking blonde emerged from the front door in a pristine tight white T-shirt and jeans and regarded Wesley suspiciously.

She had seen Charles Pitaway about half an hour ago in the underground carpark, she said, in a bored drawl. She knew Charlie, she added significantly. Wesley suspected that there was some attraction there, on her side at least. He had had a couple of large suitcases with him, and she had asked him where he was off to. He said he was going away for a few days and asked her to water his plants. He had been carrying a rug out to the car – said he was taking it to be cleaned, and that he'd been having a bit of a clear-out. He had seemed perfectly normal and he hadn't had anybody with him.

Wesley didn't know whether to be relieved or apprehensive about this last piece of news. Then he thought of Rachel and experienced a gnawing fear in the pit of his stomach. If she wasn't with Charles Pitaway, where was she?

Gerry Heffernan used his dubious charms to persuade the blonde that it was imperative they examined Pitaway's apartment as soon as possible. She looked defensive at first, as though she were about to refuse. But when he told her it might be a matter of life and death, she handed over Pitaway's spare keys without a word.

They found the flat bare, abandoned. The occupant hadn't intended to go away for a few days: he had gone for good. There were still some clothes in the wardrobes and drawers; he had left the things he knew he wouldn't use, wouldn't need. They continued the search. No passport, no credit cards or driving licence. It looked as if Charles Pitaway had flown his stylish nest.

'He's taken his passport, Wes. Where do you think he'll go? Where would you go if you were him?'

Wesley thought for a while, opening doors and drawers absentmindedly. Then he turned to his boss. 'I'd probably head for France. It's somewhere he knows, somewhere he can get lost. I reckon he'll head for the South, ditch the car if necessary, revert to his own identity, whatever that is.'

'What time's the next ferry from Plymouth?'

'He might not go from Plymouth.'

'It's nearest. Presumably he's guessed that we're on to him so he'll want to get out of the country quick before all hell breaks loose.'

Wesley made a quick call on his mobile. 'There's a ferry sailing from Plymouth at twelve-thirty.'

'Get on to the local police there – tell them to keep an eye out for him. Let's get down there quick.'

'What about Rachel?'

'Well, she's not here. And according to Miss Tight T-shirt he didn't have anyone with him when he set off in his car, so your guess is as good as mine.'

'Have her family been told?'

'If we haven't found her in a couple of hours I'll send someone up to the farm, but there's no point in worrying them before we have to. She might turn up safe and sound,' Heffernan added optimistically.

When they left the apartment, Wesley handed Heffernan his mobile phone. 'Keep trying Rachel's mobile number, will you?'

Heffernan nodded, stabbing at the buttons while Wesley took the turning on to the Plymouth road and put his foot down to the floor.

The red Toyota rolled forward slowly, taking its place in the line of cars waiting for the 12.30 ferry. The driver fumbled for his ticket and passport and placed them neatly on the passenger seat beside him. It was all there. There would be no problem.

A tap on the driver's window made him look up with a start. A fresh-faced young police constable was staring in earnestly. The driver pressed the button that sent the electric window gliding downwards.

'Excuse me, sir, would you mind getting out of the car?'

'Certainly, Officer.' He climbed out. If he kept calm, kept cool, all would be well. It always had been.

'May I see your passport, sir?'

The driver got back into the car and leaned across to retrieve the passport from the passenger seat. He gave it to the constable, who studied it for a few seconds before returning it to its owner.

'Sorry to have bothered you, sir,' said the constable officially. 'That's all in order.'

The driver nodded and looked ahead. The first vehicle in the queue was crawling up the ramp into the bowels of the huge ferry.

Wesley's mobile began to ring just as they turned into the ferry terminal. Gerry Heffernan, slumped beside him in the passenger seat, picked it up and answered it.

'The incident room's just heard from the French police,' he announced to Wesley after a lengthy conversation. 'They have a record of a Charles Pitaway, a British national doing casual work in a place called the Château des Arbres – a vineyard. Castle of the trees – sounds nice, doesn't it?'

'What about him?' asked Wesley impatiently.

'He had his passport and all his other ID and money nicked . . . reported it to the local gendarmes. He'd passed out in his room and when he was found he had to be taken to the local hospital to have his stomach pumped out 'cause they reckoned he'd been drugged . . . barbiturates. Apparently they might have killed him if he hadn't been found in time. The hospital put it down as an attempted suicide but the patient denied it. Anyway, when he got back to the château the bloke he'd been sharing a room with had buggered off, and so had his passport: apparently the two men were a similar height and colouring. Pitaway reported the theft and claimed that he'd been doped. But the missing room-mate was never found. The gendarmes reckoned he was long gone, so the whole incident remained on the file as just another unsolved theft. This was in late August last year.'

'And what was the other man's name? The one who disappeared at the same time as the passport?'

'Mark Helston. They've looked up his record and he's been a bad lad. Con man with lots of charm and a vicious streak. Clever bastard too, by all accounts.'

Wesley said nothing as he brought the car to a halt outside the ferry terminal in a space reserved for staff. He didn't put his fears into words: they would become more real once they were spoken. He could see the line of cars, some bearing GB plates and others, returning holidaymakers, bearing the letters of other European countries. He scanned the queue for the red Toyota but he couldn't spot it. Perhaps he'd been wrong. He climbed out of the car and began to walk over to the line, which was moving slowly as the cars disappeared one by one into the monstrous belly of the ship like little fish being fed to a whale.

A young constable was standing near the ferry talking on his radio. Wesley rushed up to him, his warrant card held in front of him to announce his identity. Gerry Heffernan lumbered behind, trying to keep up.

Fortunately the young constable seemed to be in the know. 'He's just this minute driven on board, sir,' he said to Wesley earnestly. 'It

214

was his car, all right; I checked the registration number. And he's still using the name Pitaway; had a passport and everything. All looked kosher to me. I didn't know whether I should stop him or . . .'

'That's okay. You did fine. He's just gone on, you say?'

'About a minute ago.'

'Then with any luck we'll catch him as he parks up.'

'The cavalry's arrived,' announced Gerry Heffernan as Steve Carstairs brought his Escort XR3i to a screaming halt diagonally across the concrete. Steve climbed out and slammed the door, donning a pair of dark glasses. A shaken PC Wallace climbed unsteadily out of the passenger door. They both stood there for a moment like a pair of indecisive sheep.

'Well, come on – what are you waiting for? Christmas?' shouted Gerry Heffernan.

Without a word Wesley made for the car ferry's vast jaws, followed by his three colleagues from Tradmouth and half a dozen local uniformed officers. The local police had stopped any more vehicles going aboard but, walking up the ramps, he still felt unsafe. The huge space where the cars spent their journey was dimly lit and stank of petrol and exhaust fumes. But as the bowels of the ship were still half empty, it wasn't difficult to spot the red Toyota, its paintwork gleaming under the bulkhead lights, in a row next to the metal door that led to the ferry's passenger quarters.

'Give it a good going-over,' Heffernan said to the local officers quietly. 'Steve, Wallace, you get up them stairs. We've got to find him.' He turned to Wesley. 'Wes, you keep trying her mobile.'

The dark-haired young man leaned on the ship's rail and stared down into the murky water. He looked at his watch – a Rolex: he liked the best – and saw that it was almost time for the ferry to depart. He would soon be back in France, and this time his visit would be more comfortable, more enjoyable than the last. He smiled to himself. The last time he had made the journey across the Channel he had left behind one dingy room in a London council flat; penniless, unemployed. He had always fancied France, and the prospect of working in a vineyard for a while had seemed exotic, attractive. He loved cultivating plants, watching them grow: he had enjoyed designing the prison garden during his last stretch inside. So why not give vines a try?

But it had been hard work. And he had had to share a room;

accommodation for the seasonal workers. He hadn't liked that. He needed his privacy. And his room-mate had got on his nerves with his public school ways and casual boasts of his expected inheritance.

Always a good mimic, he had learned to imitate Charles, copy his mannerisms. His drama sessions in the young offenders' institution hadn't been completely wasted. This trick had caused a lot of hilarity among his motley crowd of fellow workers from all over Europe. He and Charles had even looked alike and were sometimes mistaken for each other by the boss, Monsieur Petit. *Les jumeaux terribles*, they were called: the terrible twins. Until one day he got sick of Charles – sick of his talk of his cosy, privileged childhood in the large Dukesbridge bungalow; his expensive education in some posh boarding school; and his financial expectations, which even included a manor house that his family hadn't lived in for years. He felt no sympathy for the fact that Charles had no family apart from an invalid father, that his mother had died when he was small; that he had no family or friends with which he had kept in touch in England. He made the alarming discovery that he could feel no sympathy for anyone but himself – in fact, he could feel nothing. No pity, no guilt – nothing.

And when an official-looking letter had arrived for Charles, Mark – feeling instinctively that it might be to his advantage – had pocketed it secretly and opened it when he was alone. It said that Charles' father had died. Mark had hidden the letter, keeping the knowledge to himself. Why shouldn't he? It was time life dealt him some good cards for a change. He had thought the sleeping pills he had given Charles in France would finish him off; that his death would be taken for suicide so there would be no awkward loose ends.

So it had been a shock when Brian Willerby cornered him in Earlsacre village, just outside the King's Head, and asked if he could have one of his 'discreet words'. He had said that a man claiming to be the real Charles Pitaway had rung him from a caravan park in Bloxham; that he had compared Charles' handwriting with his own in his office file and had found a discrepancy; he was worried and was contemplating mentioning it to a policeman he knew . . . discreetly, of course. Poor Brian – he really hadn't been very good at that sort of thing. What a mistake it had been for the solicitor to tell him everything he knew, and exactly where the real Charles was staying. He had had no choice: he had had to eliminate Charles, the threat to all

216

he had acquired, and he had had to silence that pathetic little man Brian Willerby at the first opportunity.

Now he was on his way back to France with the prospect of a new future. And the police had no solid evidence against him. He wasn't a fool; he had covered his tracks well. He had the file containing his correspondence with Brian Willerby – and the letters in the handwriting of the real Charles – with him in his briefcase: it would go straight into the English Channel once they had set sail. And as for Rachel – well, the police already knew that they were seeing each other, so that would explain away any forensic evidence of her presence in his flat. Pity about Rachel. But when you've killed twice, murder – the disposal of a human obstacle – is easy. And she'd never be found – he had seen to that.

He smiled to himself as he turned away from the rail, intending to head for the bar. He needed a drink.

'Where is she?' The voice made him jump. He saw a figure emerging on to the deck. 'Where is she?' Wesley repeated, walking forward slowly, his hands clenched by his side.

Mark Helston, otherwise known as Charles Pitaway, drew himself up to his full height and smiled. 'I've really no idea who you're talking about,' he replied, kicking his briefcase over the side of the ship.

Wesley came out of the interview room on the ground floor of Tradmouth police station. He needed a break; needed to get out before he was tempted to punch Helston in his smug, inscrutable face, to take him by the scruff of his neck and strangle him till he told the truth. Wesley Peterson would never have considered himself a violent man. His God-fearing parents had always taught him that violence solved nothing – that it was the peacemakers who were blessed, not those who resorted to using their fists. It had never occurred to him to disagree with this point of view – until now. Now he found himself wanting to smash Helston's face to pulp each time he shrugged those elegantly clad shoulders when he was asked what had happened to Rachel Tracey.

Gerry Heffernan joined him outside in the corridor and put a fatherly hand on his shoulder. 'Don't let him get to you, Wes.'

'He knows where she is.'

'We don't know that. He said she left first thing this morning before we arrived to question him. At the moment we can't prove otherwise. Forensic are going over his car and his apartment, but by the look of it the car's been scrubbed clean recently. He's had lots of time to get rid of any evidence.'

Heffernan was making a great effort to sound professional, detached – but he wasn't making a very good job of it. The expression on his face betrayed every emotion, every fear and doubt.

They heard the sound of rapid footsteps and WPC Trish Walton appeared round the corner, hurrying towards them, her face set in an earnest, worried frown. 'I've just heard from the mobile phone company, sir. They say her mobile's somewhere in Dukesbridge. They can't be more accurate than that, I'm afraid. And the briefcase has been retrieved from the water. Forensic have got it now.'

'Thanks, Trish,' said Wesley quietly.

'Dukesbridge, eh?' mused Heffernan as Trish headed back to the CID office.

Wesley closed his eyes, trying to focus on the evidence. They had to start thinking clearly, for Rachel's sake.

'The neighbour said he'd been having a clear-out and had a rug with him. He told the neighbour he was taking it to be cleaned.'

'Strange thing to do, unless he was getting rid of the evidence. Bloodstains,' Heffernan added, almost in a whisper.

'It wasn't in his car so he must have got rid on it *en route*. Which road would you take from Dukesbridge to Plymouth?'

'The A379, I suppose. That's the obvious route. The most direct.'

Wesley thought for a few moments. He felt helpless: he had to take some action, however futile it might turn out to be. 'I think we should go to Dukesbridge; drive along the route he must have taken. He must have left that rug somewhere. Has someone rung all the cleaners in the area?'

Heffernan nodded earnestly. Then a thought came to him. 'We've been assuming that he was ditching the rug to get rid of evidence. But what if Rachel was rolled up in it, Cleopatra-style?'

That same thought had already occurred to Wesley.

Heffernan looked at him, more resolute now. 'Come on, Wes, let's get out of here. Then at least we can feel we're doing something instead of hanging around contemplating our belly buttons and thinking the worst.'

Wesley led the way, pushing open the swing-doors with uncharacteristic violence. Without a word he drove out of the police station carpark and on to the main road. Even Gerry Heffernan spent the journey in silence, racking his brains for the tiniest clue that might betray Rachel's whereabouts.

When they reached the outskirts of Dukesbridge, Wesley pulled the car up on to a grass verge and stopped. 'Let's try and follow his route from his flat to the ferry. We know her mobile's somewhere in Dukesbridge, within a mile or so's radius of the town centre. There are all sorts of possibilities. The mobile might not be with her for some reason. He might have taken a detour off the route. But let's not think about that now. Let's assume that he made straight for Plymouth and that she still has the mobile with her. Okay?'

Heffernan nodded, fearing that the alternative scenarios Wesley mentioned were only too possible. But he didn't put his misgivings into words. Now wasn't the time for negative thought.

Like Tradmouth, Dukesbridge was perched on a river estuary, although the Duke's was less impressive as estuaries go, and at low tide the river was an expanse of mud punctuated by hungry wading birds. It had been low tide when they had first arrived that morning, but now the tide was rising as Wesley drove to Pitaway's waterfront apartment and parked outside. He looked up at the balcony of the empty flat and stared at the gleaming, lifeless glass of the French window. Heffernan stared too. Neither man uttered a word. After a few minutes Wesley thrust the gear lever into first and set off. He negotiated his way along Dukesbridge's narrow main shopping street, making for the main road out to Plymouth. Old properties gave way to Victorian, then to houses built in the twenties and thirties. As they reached the outskirts of the small town, newer estates sprawled out, nibbling at the countryside.

On the very edge of town they passed a colourful notice announcing that Southair Homes were in the process of building forty executive three- and four-bedroomed detached houses. Suddenly Wesley braked, causing the car behind to sound its horn aggressively.

'What have you stopped for?' Gerry Heffernan sounded mildly annoyed. 'Now's hardly the time for house-hunting.'

Wesley turned to him, impatient. 'Helston was involved in garden design. He told me at the cricket match that he'd designed gardens for some new showhouses on the outskirts of Dukesbridge.'

Heffernan wasn't given time to take this in. Wesley jumped from the car and ran over to the building site. Heffernan followed, but slowly at a distance: he really wasn't up to all this leaping about at his age. He puffed behind as Wesley ran past the showhouse set in its small, newly landscaped front garden – probably Helston's handiwork – towards the back of the site, where construction was still going on. A few hard-hatted men seemed hard at work on the new dwellings that the powers that be considered necessary to house Devon's swelling population in the twenty-first century. A huge yellow digger squatted by a ditch filled with concrete drainage pipes.

Wesley stopped. To his right a burly labourer was standing with tattooed arms folded challengingly, staring at him. 'No unauthorised persons,' he said with barely disguised hostility. 'And where's your 'at. Health and safety,' he added righteously.

Wesley rooted in his inside pocket for his warrant card. 'Police. I'm Acting Detective Inspector Peterson.'

The man shifted from foot to foot uneasily. 'I'll get the foreman,' he grunted, edging away across the furrowed ground.

'What time did work start here this morning?'

The man looked Wesley up and down suspiciously. 'What do you want to know for?' he asked cautiously.

'Just answer the question,' Wesley barked. This was no time to worry about police–public relations.

'We were late this morning, started work about ten 'cause we knew some materials we needed wouldn't arrive till then. We'll work late tonight, mind. Why?'

'So at around nine this morning this site was deserted?'

The man nodded.

'Were those sewer pipes there this morning?' he asked, looking at the trench where the concrete tubes lay waiting to be covered. A small crane stood by with another pipe dangling from its chains, ready to extend the line towards where the new houses would be built.

'Aye. Why do you want to know?' The man's aggression had now given way to curiosity.

The digger's engine had started up and it was edging forward, ready to fill the trench with the soil heaped at its edge. It was getting nearer, moving forward relentlessly on its caterpillar tracks like some giant crocodile slithering towards the water. Wesley shouted, but his voice could hardly be heard over the throbbing engine.

It was Gerry Heffernan who acted. He stumbled over to the digger and stood a few yards in front of it waving his arms like a brave revolutionary confronting a dictator's tank. The machine halted; fortunately the driver's shower of colourful expletives was lost under the continuing noise of the engine. Eventually, when he realised the large, scruffy man in front of him wasn't going to budge, the driver turned the key in the ignition.

'I want a look inside these pipes,' said Wesley, making for the end of the row, his clean and unsuitable shoes slipping on the hillocks of discarded soil. He half jumped, half fell into the trench, past caring about the state of his suit. Gerry Heffernan trotted after him, followed by the labourer and the driver. A few other workmen had begun to gather to see the entertainment that would distract them from the dull routine of house construction.

Wesley could just make out a shape: something was lying about ten feet inside the sewer pipe. It was too far in to be easily detectable when the next pipe was added to the row. In fact, once the pipes were covered it was unlikely to be detected at all, unless it caused a blockage. It looked like a rug or a roll of carpet, tied at both ends and lying at the bottom of the concrete tube. If they had been half an hour later it would have been buried unseen along with the sewer pipes.

'I'm going in,' said Wesley. 'There's something in there.' He refrained from saying 'someone'.

But the labourer pushed him out of the way. 'Quicker if I do it,' he said impatiently, and he fell to his knees and began to crawl into the pipe.

His voice echoed around the ring of concrete as he uttered an oath of amazement. 'Fuckin' hell. It feels like there's something inside here.' The man sounded shaken by his discovery. 'I'll pull it out.'

'Can you manage?' asked Wesley anxiously.

He couldn't make out the reply, but the man emerged, bottom first, dragging the now filthy roll of rug behind him. It was secured at either end with string, like a Christmas cracker. The man drew a penknife from the pocket of his soil-covered jeans and looked at Wesley inquiringly. Wesley nodded.

The string cut, the rug remained tightly rolled around the shape in its centre. Wesley stared at it as though paralysed, not daring to touch it, fearing what he might find. But Gerry Heffernan pushed him out of the way. 'Let the dog see the rabbit, eh?' He bent and picked up an edge of the rug. 'Well, we've all seen the film, haven't we?' He yanked at the edge and the rug began to unroll. An arm flopped out.

Wesley, shaken from his torpor, knelt down in the grey mud at the base of the trench and gave the rug another heave. Rachel lay there absolutely still on the brightly coloured pile. Her plain grey sleeveless dress had ridden up, revealing a long expanse of thigh. She wore a matching grey jacket, strangely formal in the circumstances, and her black leather shoulder bag was slung around her neck. She had been about to leave for work when it had happened. Her flesh was pale but apparently unmarked by violence. As Gerry Heffernan shouted for someone to call an ambulance, Wesley grasped Rachel's icy hand and held it to his cheek.

It was seven o'clock when Wesley Peterson reached home that evening. He called out as he opened the front door but there was no answer. The house was silent. The phrase 'silent as the grave' flashed through Wesley's mind, and he shuddered. The grave wouldn't be silent if you were buried alive: it would be filled with your own desperate cries, hopeless, unheard screams for help choking in your throat and fading with your strength. What a way to die.

He pushed open the living-room door. Pam lay on the sofa, eyes closed. Michael lay curled up beside her. They were fast asleep. He had no need to ask how she felt after her first day back at school. He stood watching his wife and son, listening to their even breathing as he had stood listening to Rachel's in the hospital before she had finally come round after the drugs had been pumped from her stomach. He closed his eyes and realised that he was exhausted himself. Exhausted and relieved.

He crept out of the room and into the kitchen, searching for something to eat. He hadn't had anything since twelve, when Trish Walton had brought him and Heffernan a sandwich as they took a break from questioning the man they now knew as Mark Helston. Pam had left a frozen lasagne standing inside the microwave. He pressed a button and after a few minutes it emerged piping hot.

He sat alone at the kitchen table to eat it. Solitary eating was not an experience he enjoyed, and he ate rapidly, refuelling rather than relishing. He wished Pam would wake up. He wanted to talk to her: he felt he had to tell someone about the day's events. A near-tragedy shared was a near-tragedy halved.

The doorbell rang, breaking the silence. Wesley rushed into the hall, eager for human contact. He just hoped it wasn't a salesman . . . he was in no mood to listen to the virtues of replacement windows.

But when he opened the door he saw that Neil was standing there, his face solemn. Wesley was glad to see him, glad of the company, and he stood aside to let him in, warning him that Pam was asleep. They made for the kitchen, sat themselves down at the table and poured themselves a beer, pushing the dirty dishes to one side, just as they had done in the flat they had shared in their student days.

'Rachel nearly died today,' Wesley began quietly.

Neil's mouth fell open. 'What happened? Is she okay?'

Wesley told him, a swift, succinct narrative of the facts. 'They say she'll be okay,' he added with relief. 'But if we hadn't arrived when we did she would have been buried alive in that sewer pipe. He'd drugged her coffee then dumped her on the building site before setting off for France.'

It had been a perfect opportunity, Helston had boasted during his long interrogation. He had worked on a building site once so he knew how things were done. When he had checked the showhouse garden yesterday, he had seen that the sewer pipes were almost laid and that a digger was standing by to bury the last ones . . . and Rachel. He hadn't noticed that she'd left her mobile on in her handbag. He hadn't thought to check, he had added regretfully.

Mark Helston had no other regrets, other than the fact that he had been caught. But Wesley tried not to think of the man; every time he did so he experienced a heart-wrenching wave of anger.

Emboldened by a rapidly consumed pint of Boddington's bitter, Neil claimed he had never liked the look of the man he had known as Charles Pitaway. His eyes were too close together, he pronounced sagely. Hindsight was a wonderful thing, Wesley thought sadly, knowing that Neil had been taken in just like everyone else.

Neil raised the empty beer can. 'Got any more of this? I'm drowning my sorrows.'

'Why? What's the matter?' Wesley asked, opening another can and handing it to his friend, glad to change the subject.

'It's Claire. She's going up to Manchester to work at the university.' He took a long swig of beer. 'I asked her why and she just said she wanted a change. You don't think it could be this business with the murders, do you?'

'I shouldn't think so.'

'I never told you this, Wes, but I found Brian Willerby's name scribbled out in her address book. I didn't know whether to say anything at the time but . . .'

'Don't worry. She didn't have anything to do with his death,' Wesley said quickly. 'It was probably something to do with work.' He hoped he sounded convincing.

'Mmm,' said Neil, half listening. 'It was all very sudden, this Manchester job. She said she'd only just applied. I can't think why she should want to get away from here. We were getting on so well and . . .'

'She probably had an offer she couldn't refuse,' Wesley said with finality. He had no intention of betraying Claire's confidence.

'Ah well,' sighed Neil, taking another drink. 'Plenty more finds in the trench, as we say in archaeological circles.'

Neil drained the can and grinned bravely. He had never been one for displaying his emotions. Wesley could only guess what was really going through his mind.

'You could try and persuade her not to go,' he suggested.

Neil shook his head. 'It's almost as if there's something here she wants to get away from. But I can't think what.'

Wesley thought of Carlotta and said nothing. 'As I said, she's probably had a better offer. I can't see the Earlsacre Project paying very well, can you?'

'Money's not important,' said Neil virtuously.

'It might be to Claire. It is to some people. There are those who will do anything for money, and I should know – I've seen it all in my job.'

'Money is the root of all evil,' said a quiet female voice. Pam had woken up and was standing in the kitchen doorway. Wesley wondered how much she had overheard.

He went over and kissed her lightly, putting a supportive arm around her shoulder. 'How was school?'

'I'm shattered. But I dare say I'll get used to it. Michael's exhausted too after his day at the childminder's. He fell fast asleep as soon as he got home.' She yawned. 'Haven't you poured me a drink?' She lumbered over to the kitchen table and sat in the seat her husband had vacated.

Wesley poured Pam a glass of red wine from an already opened bottle. Then he leaned against the fridge, thinking of Mark Helston and the lengths he'd gone to to acquire and keep the proceeds from the Earlsacre estate. And three centuries before, Joseph Marling had similarly killed and betrayed for the love of money and power.

He handed Pam the glass. 'And by the way,' he said, 'according to St Paul, it's not money that's the root of all evil, but the love of it.'

'Too right,' said Neil as Pam raised her glass and drank deeply.

Epilogue

Six Weeks Later

The living statues shivered in the weak October sunshine. Two men and two women, painted a tasteful green and dressed in skimpy draperies of an identical colour, made a brave attempt to stand still and ignore the goose bumps on their bare limbs. They stood, one at each corner of the great rectangular plinth in the middle of the walled garden, as though guarding the newly restored sundial at its centre.

The garden still had a bare look. The soil in the parterres was fine and weed-free – mostly flower-free as well, as the garden wouldn't blossom into life until the spring. The archaeologists who had revealed the ancient garden's layout had long finished their work, and after their departure the gardening experts had moved in like an occupying army to recreate the historic garden. The Lantrists, they claimed, would have recognised their handiwork; the perfect recreation of a seventeenth-century ornamental garden. And hopefully a real draw to tourists and garden enthusiasts alike.

Now archaeologists and gardeners sat together on the terrace to witness the rebirth of the house and gardens, although the two groups tended not to fraternise. Neil sat beside Matt, Jane and Jake. Wesley Peterson, sitting with his police colleagues on the other side of the terrace, noted Claire's absence. She would be up in Manchester by now. Neil, he thought, was looking remarkably cheerful. But then, in all the time he'd known him, Neil had never dwelt on the past – unless it was in the course of his work.

Wesley, seated in front of the newly restored west wing of Earlsacre Hall, which had shed its scaffolding specially for the occasion, nudged Gerry Heffernan. 'She's on next,' he whispered, glancing down into the garden where Pam was standing in front of a group of eleven-year-olds. He studied the children, his wife's class. Some of the girls, he noticed, towered above the boys already, having acquired the form and maturity of young women. The boys, standing puny beside them, looked as if they longed to be somewhere else. One boy, Wesley noticed, was leaning on a garden statue; one of the pair filched by Les Cumbernold and now restored to its rightful place in the garden.

Rachel Tracey sat on Wesley's left, staring down at the scene below.

'You didn't have to come,' Wesley whispered to her.

'I'm fine,' she answered. 'Don't fuss. As if it isn't bad enough at home I've got to put up with it at work too.'

'Sorry.' He pretended to study the glossy programme on his knee.

'And before anyone asks, Dave's decided to continue his travels. He's gone off to Europe,' she said bluntly.

Wesley was hardly surprised. 'I'm sorry,' he said again, lost for words.

He was trying to think of something else to say, something comforting, something appropriate, when Gerry Heffernan nudged his elbow. 'She's on,' he said, pointing to the programme.

Pam's class didn't disgrace themselves. In fact their rendition of three traditional songs which, Pam had judged, had been top of the pops when the gardens were first created seemed to go down well with the audience of locals, project workers and assorted dignitaries. The main platform on the terrace had been reserved for an assortment of local mayors, councillors and MPs, a delegation from the American foundation that had so keenly supported the project, and the Chief Constable and his wife. Gerry Heffernan straightened his tie and kept glancing at the latter, on his best behaviour for once.

Martin Samuels' speech followed, a well-judged address which emphasised the work that had gone into the restoration of the gardens without touching upon the unhappy events of the recent months.

But Jacintha Hervey was unable to resist adding a touch of drama. Wearing flowing pink, she launched into her latest poem, a composition of epic proportions. She had decided to dwell upon the darker side of Earlsacre's history. The tale of Richard Lantrist, the murderous Joseph Marling, Captain Parry and the unfortunate interred maidservant was told in colourful and bloodthirsty blank verse. Wesley glanced at the Chief Constable, who was looking a

227

little concerned for his crime figures. He prayed that Jacintha would bring the story to a close before she reached the present day. There was no way he wanted Rachel reminded of Mark Helston, who was now awaiting trial. Some things were best forgotten.

When the music began, played by an earnest-looking string quartet, the living statues began to move gracefully around the garden, and the guests began to mingle. Gerry Heffernan grabbed Wesley's arm. 'Let's get out of here before we're cornered by the Chief Constable. I'd rather be downing a pint at the King's Head than having to mind my p's and q's over some silly little bits of fancy food that wouldn't fill the belly of a ruddy canary. Hurry up.'

'I'll have to say hello to Pam.'

'Do that on your way out. She's got to keep an eye on them kids anyway, and make sure they don't nick anything. Hurry up,' he repeated impatiently, a weather eye on the Chief Constable's whereabouts.

Wesley allowed himself to be led off in the direction of the gatehouse. But Neil had been on the lookout and caught up with them in the centre of the walled garden. He had a booklet in his hand which he waved under Wesley's nose. 'Seen this?' he asked without ceremony.

'What is it?'

'Never mind that,' said Heffernan. 'We're making our escape to the King's Head.'

'What about the free grub?' asked Neil greedily.

Wesley shrugged. He wasn't hungry anyway. And standing there, on the stone plinth under which Richard Lantrist had been buried and the young woman, the innocent maidservant, had met her horrifying end, wasn't doing wonders for his appetite. 'What's the book?'

'Claire and Martin Samuels were working on it. It's the history of Earlsacre, and it covers the Lantrist case. It's going to be sold in the souvenir shop.' He looked at his watch. 'Did I tell you the vicar here's agreed to rebury the skeletons we dug up?'

Wesley shook his head. Although maybe Neil had told him and he had forgotten – he had had a lot on his mind over the past few weeks.

'Jinny and the captain are going in the churchyard and he's giving the real Richard Lantrist a place in the family vault, which I thought was very decent of him. Don't know if he's chucking the impostor out, though.'

'He should do. He's got no right to be there,' said Wesley vehemently, surprised by the strength of his own feelings.

Neil looked at him curiously. 'Yeah ... right,' was all he could think of to say.

'When are they being buried?'

'Half three. That's why I'm keeping an eye on the time. We thought we ought to be there, the archaeological team.'

'I'd like to be there too,' said Wesley quietly. He turned to Heffernan. 'Feel like coming to a funeral, Gerry?'

'So long as there's a good wake afterwards,' Heffernan mumbled in reply. 'But I mustn't have too much to drink. I'm meeting Susan this evening.'

There was a loud crunching sound that was getting nearer. Wesley looked round and saw that Rachel was approaching, her feet crunching loudly on the new gravel of the path. Crime prevention officers recommended gravel to deter burglars. They clearly had a point.

'I hear you're going to the reburial of the murder victims,' said Rachel, slightly breathless. 'Can I come with you? I'd like to come.'

Neil nodded. 'Don't see why not. More the merrier.'

'Are you sure?' asked Wesley.

'Yes, I'm sure,' she replied with certainty.

Wesley didn't argue. Perhaps there would be something cathartic about the reburial for Rachel. The case would be closed – on the present as well as the past.

Neil raised his hand as though he had just remembered something important. 'Hey, Wes, didn't you say your mum's maiden name was Lantrist?'

'That's right.'

'And did any of her family come from Barbados?'

'I believe her grandfather did.'

'You don't think . . .?' He didn't finish the sentence.

'I don't know what to think.' Wesley paused. 'But I can think of worse ancestors to have than Richard Lantrist; the real one, that is.'

'Yeah,' said Neil, a faraway look in his eyes. 'Richard was one of the good guys.'

Wesley turned and noticed that Heffernan was staring into the distance like a hunted animal sniffing the air for the scent of his pursuer.

'Come on, Wes,' he said, putting a firm hand on Wesley's shoulder. 'Get a move on. He's seen me. He's on his way over.'

But before they could escape the Chief Constable bore down on them, smart in his uniform, eyes gleaming like those of a hawk. Rachel stepped back, her own eyes lowered as if she had no wish to be noticed.

'Congratulations on your promotion, Chief Inspector Heffernan,' the Chief Constable began jovially. 'We were sad to see Stan Jenkins retire through ill health, of course, but I've no doubt the reorganisation will work well at Tradmouth. We have a fine team there, a very fine team.' Then he turned to Wesley and shook his hand firmly, beaming like one who has been presented with a much-coveted trophy. 'And this must be our new inspector. Delighted to meet you. Treating you all right at Tradmouth, are they?' he asked anxiously, glancing over at Gerry Heffernan, who was standing there with a fixed grin on his chubby face. 'Hope they're making you feel at home round here.'

'Oh yes, sir. I think I can safely say I feel at home,' Wesley replied.

'Are you, er . . . joining us up at the house? They've put on a bit of a spread,' the Chief Constable said with the awkward jollity of those who are trying to be matey with their social inferiors.

'No, ta, sir. We've, er . . .' For once in his life Gerry Heffernan's mind went blank.

'We have to attend a funeral, sir,' said Wesley.

'Oh, I'm sorry.' The Chief Constable rearranged his expression into one of appropriate seriousness. 'A relative, is it?'

'Do you know, sir, I rather hope it is.'

The Chief Constable looked puzzled but didn't inquire further. He walked away, visibly relieved to return to his fellow VIPs and their drinks and canapés. Wesley noticed Pam shepherding her charges into the marquee where the humbler guests would receive humbler refreshments. She turned and waved to him. He waved back.

The others were already strolling towards the gatehouse. He walked quickly to catch up with them and fell in beside Neil.

'I'm glad Richard's going into the family vault where he belongs,' he said as they walked side by side down the drive past the cricket ground. 'You've done a good job at Earlsacre – a very good job.'

Neil smiled, but his thoughts were far away as the little band of mourners walked in silence towards the village church.

Historical Note

James Scott, Duke of Monmouth and Buccleuch, was born in 1649, the illegitimate son of Charles II. When Charles died in 1685, his brother, the Roman Catholic Duke of York, was proclaimed King James II.

Monmouth, expecting support in the West Country for his claim to the throne, landed at Lyme Regis, Dorset, on 11 June 1685: many flocked to his cause (730 from Devon alone) as he marched inland, and he was proclaimed King at Taunton. His followers were mostly, like Richard Lantrist, idealistic dissenters who feared that James II would not be sympathetic to their faith and would not allow them freedom of worship. John Whiting, the Quaker, said that there would have been no rebellion 'if liberty of conscience had been granted'.

On 6 July the rebels met the King's army (which was under the leadership of John Churchill, later Duke of Marlborough and an ancestor of Sir Winston Churchill) at Sedgemoor in Somerset and, in what was to be known as the last English battle fought with pitchforks, the rebels were soundly defeated. Monmouth himself was beheaded for treason, but many of his supporters met a more terrible end.

James II sent Lord Chief Justice George Jeffreys to punish the rebels, and this led to one of the darkest hours in West Country history. In the 'Bloody Assizes' at Dorchester nearly 200 were condemned to death and nearly 800 transported as slaves to the West Indies. As well as being cruel, Jeffreys was also corrupt, taking bribes and extorting money from defendants. These events left a fearful impression on the region, and houses where the Lord Chief Justice stayed are still known as 'Jeffreys Houses'.

Most of those sent to the West Indies lived lives of great hardship

231

and degradation. An eye-witness said, 'I have seen such cruelty there done to servants as I do not think one Christian could have done to another.' Those executed met the deaths of traitors and were hanged, drawn and quartered. Tradition still points to where the rebels' dismembered bodies were publicly displayed. Surgeon Yonge of Plymouth wrote of encountering severed heads and quarters 'at all the little towns and bridges and crossways'.

In 1688, three years after the Monmouth Rebellion, James II fled the country and William III landed at Brixham, Devon, and made a triumphant entry into Exeter. Judge George Jeffreys was arrested and imprisoned in the Tower of London, where he later died, the horrors that he unleashed, etched, to this day, on the folk memory of the south-west of England.

FICTION   Ellis, Kate,
Ellis   1953-

        The bone garden.

$23.95

DATE			